T

BLOOD
KING

MICHAEL
ALEXANDER
MCCARTHY

Rogue Maille
Publishing

This is a work of historical fiction. Any references to real people, events, organizations and places are intended only to give the fiction a sense of reality and authenticity. All names, characters, places and events are either the product of the author's imagination or are used fictitiously.

Copyright © Michael Alexander McCarthy 2020

Michael Alexander McCarthy fully asserts the legal and moral right to be identified as the sole author of this work.

First published in 2020

Rogue Maille Publishing 2020

Also by Michael Alexander McCarthy

Death's Head – Hitler's Wolf Pack

The First War of Scottish Independence Series

KingMaker – Army of God

KingMaker – Traitor

KingMaker – Bannockburn

KingMaker – Death of Kings

Dedication

To Marlee and Mable. The best girls in all the world.

Place Names

Arder Fort	Ogle Hill, Auchterarder
Black Fort	Moncreiffe Hillfort, Perth
Bodor's River	River Forth
Brude's Rock	Dunadd Hillfort, Argyll
Bull Fort	Burghead, Moray
Crag Fort	Dunollie Hillfort, Oban
Din Eidyn	Edinburgh
Ern Fort	Dundurn, St Fillans
Fort of the Fisherfolk	Dunaverty, Kintyre
Fort of the Heights	Dumbarton Rock
Giudi	Stirling
Great Fort	Dumyat Hillfort, Stirling
High Fort	Craig Phadrig, Inverness
Keld	Dunkeld, Perthshire
Mother's Seat	Bennachie, Inverurie
Oval Fort	Dun Skeig, Clachan
Pert	Perth
River Clut	River Clyde
Sea Fort	Dunstaffnage, Dunbeg
Sken	Scone, Perthshire
Stone Fort	Dun Creagach, Connel
The Tae	River Tay

SCOTLAND
410 A.D.

Drui

Phocali

Caereni

Smertae

Cornavii

The Dead Grey Sea

Decantae

Carnonacae

Vacomagi

Caledones

Creones

Venicones

Dal Riata

Epidii

Manau

Maeatae

Antonine Wall

Din Eidyn

Alt Clut

Voladini

Hadrian's Wall

Ulaid

Brigantes

Anglii

The Groans of the Britons (446 AD)

'To Agitius, thrice consul: the groans of the Britons. The barbarians drive us to the sea, the sea drives us to the barbarians; between these two means of death, we are either killed or drowned.'

This was the final, desperate appeal made by the Britons to the Roman military for assistance against the Picts and the Scots. The collapsing Western Roman Empire had few military resources to spare and so left the Britons to their fate.

The Pictish King List

'412 AD – Drest, son of Erp, ruled a hundred years and fought a hundred battles.'

From the Pictish Chronicle.

Wolf-Torn

It was Talorc who spotted the tracks and gestured at his friend to halt. Drest, the taller of the two although they had both seen eleven winters, hesitated and glanced at the backs of the men as they advanced deeper into the forest. His father had been clear that he would be beaten if he did not stay with the hunting party at all times. The prospect of tracking and killing a wolf was exciting enough to overcome his fear of Erp's hard fists and harsh discipline. He gripped the shaft of his spear tightly and nodded his agreement. Talorc grinned happily in response and let Drest take the lead in the hunt, not out of respect for his status as the son of the Mormaer, but because he was stronger, faster and more accomplished in using his spear.

The boys followed the tracks just as they had been taught to do. They kept their eyes fixed on the soft earth of the forest floor and pursued the wolf stride by stride as the trees thinned and the ground beneath their feet became harder and more strewn with rocks. Drest came to a stop at the entrance to a wide gulley and carefully surveyed the ground before them, just as he had seen his father and uncles do as they closed in on their quarry. He held his hands out in front of him and pushed his fingertips together to show that their prey was now trapped in the rocky gorge. Talorc nodded his understanding, his eyes dancing with a mixture of fear and excitement. Drest hefted his spear in readiness and pointed to indicate that he would follow the right wall whilst his friend was to advance on the left.

Drest felt his heart begin to pound in his chest as he edged forward. He knew he would be punished for disobeying his father but was certain the Mormaer would be filled with pride as much as with anger when he dropped the wolf's carcass at his feet. A smile crossed his lips as he imagined how his father would sit at the feasting table and boast about the bravery of a son who had slain a wolf when he was still young and beardless. The smile froze in place and his heart seemed to stop when a low growl filled the gulley. He caught sight of the beast only when it pulled back its black, slavering lips to reveal its great, yellow fangs. Its dark grey fur had rendered it almost invisible amongst the gulley's rocks and the boys had come within striking range without realising it was there. The wolf's haunches tensed before it launched itself at the wide-eyed Talorc. Drest opened his mouth to call out a warning but it was already too late. Talorc did not even have time to lift his spear before the animal was on him and closing its jaws around his skull.

Drest found himself rooted to the spot by the horror of what was unfolding before his very eyes. It did not seem possible that the wolf had his friend in its jaws and was shaking him so violently it seemed likely his head would be ripped from his body. Talorc's high-pitched screaming tore him from his paralysis. He ran at the beast and rammed his spear into its side with all of the strength he could muster. The beast roared in fury, tossed Talorc aside and threw itself at its attacker in a frenzy. Its weight alone was enough to smash Drest to the ground and drive all of the air from his lungs. His vision was filled with fangs and drool as he gasped for breath and reached up for the wolf's throat in the vain hope of holding it at bay. The beast thrashed wildly, snapping at his face and scrabbling so hard at his body with its claws that his clothes were reduced to rags and his flesh torn down to the bone. The boy's eyes filled with blood when one yellow incisor ripped down his face from hairline to eyebrow. Drest knew he was about to die but still gripped the wolf's throat and squeezed so hard the pain in his arm muscles eclipsed that from his wounds.

He said a silent prayer to Epona as his strength began to wane and asked her to carry both him and Talorc safely to the Underworld. He was conscious of the distant sounds of feet scrabbling over rocks and of men calling out but they were too far away from his struggle with the beast to trouble him. He prepared himself for death.

Mormaer Erp and his placeman, Thane Cinloch of the Arder, were the first to reach the gulley's edge. The older man hissed at the scene of carnage below them and they both scrambled down as quickly as they could. Erp retrieved his spear from the gulley's bottom and advanced towards the wolf. Cinloch reached out and grasped his arm to stop him from killing the beast.

'You should leave it, Mormaer.' Cinloch suggested, retaining his grip even when Erp of the Epidii tried to wrench his arm away.

'Have you lost your mind?' Erp spat back angrily. 'I'll not leave my son to die!'

'Look!' Cinloch insisted. 'The wolf is old, mortally wounded and close to death. Would it not be better to let the boy finish the task? What man can boast of killing such a beast with his bare hands when he was little more than a boy? Think of his reputation! Think of what this will add to his name!'

Erp nodded reluctantly. He could see the wolf's eyes bulging from their sockets and its movements growing weaker. He kept the point of his spear aimed at the wolf's chest and watched on until Drest had choked the life from it and pulled himself out from under its carcass.

'I thought I told you not to wander away from the hunt.' He growled.

He then wiped his hand across his son's blood-soaked face to make sure he had suffered no serious wounds. When he was satisfied the injuries were nothing worse than tears and scratches, he cracked his knuckles hard against the back of the boy's skull.

'If you just did what you were told then you wouldn't have these scars to carry for the rest of your life and the herder's son wouldn't be lying here with his head torn open!'

'Talorc!' Drest called out in panic as he tried to push himself to his feet on legs too weak to support his weight.

Cinloch heard the boy's cry and left the men gathered in a circle around the prone herder's son. His expression was grim and his brow furrowed when he rejoined the Mormaer and his son beside the wolf's lifeless corpse.

'Will he live?' Erp demanded, his tone betraying that he held out little hope of receiving a positive response. 'Or must I trek to his father's roundhouse and tell him he has lost a son because of my boy's stupidity?'

'He still breaths, Mormaer.' Cinloch replied with a shake of his head. 'But I doubt he will survive for long. The wolf's fangs have broken his skull, torn away half of his face and ruined his left eye. It would be a mercy if he did not live. It would be better for us to leave him here and let Epona carry him away. He would not survive a night out in the open.'

Erp nodded slowly, his mind already considering the words he would use when delivering the sad news to the boy's father.

'Let us leave him to the Goddess then. If his skull has been crushed, he would likely be a great burden to his family.'

'No!' Drest protested as he pushed himself unsteadily to his feet. 'We will not leave him to die! We must carry him to Uurad. The Brude will be able to heal him!'

Cinloch placed his hand on the boy's shoulder to console him. 'I doubt that even Brude Uurad

5

has the powers necessary to save him, Drest. It would be kinder to let him go. Even if he did live, he has suffered such injury to his skull I fear he would be left much changed.'

'Damn you, boy!' Erp snapped in irritation. 'Has your disobedience not caused us enough trouble already? This decision is not yours to make. Do as you are bidden or, so help me, I'll do you more harm than this wolf has already done!'

Drest's eyes shone with defiance in a face still dark with his own blood. Cinloch groaned inwardly at the prospect of another monumental battle of wills between father and son. He wished the boy was less headstrong but could not help but admire his courage in standing up to a man so imposing that few others had ever dared to challenge him.

'Did you not teach me that a man must face up to the consequences of his own actions?' Drest demanded of his father. 'Did you not also tell me that our family has a duty to protect the people of our tribe? Talorc's injuries were suffered as a consequence of my actions. Does it not follow that I should now take responsibility for him? Is it not my duty, as the son of the Mormaer, to protect him in his weakened condition?'

Cinloch saw Erp's fists clench tightly in fury at his son's continued insubordination. He tensed in anticipation of him unleashing his temper but the older man hesitated and narrowed his eyes as he considered his response to having his own words thrown back at him.

'I suppose I should be pleased you have finally heeded one of my lessons.' He snarled at Drest. 'Very well. Have it your way! But you and you alone will bear the burden. No man here will lift a finger to help you. Carry him to Brude Uurad on your back and see if he can save him. But, if he is left damaged by this, it will be you who feeds and cleans him and wipes the drool from his mouth. I will not have his family suffer because of your foolishness.'

Cinloch stayed with Drest as he stumbled along and fell further and further behind his father's hunting party. He watched with growing admiration as the boy toiled on through the forest, across the valley of the Tae and then up the steep slope beneath the Black Fort. He fell to his knees several times but immediately pushed himself back to his feet and continued on with grim determination. It pleased the Thane of Arder that he never once asked for help in spite of his exhaustion, even when they were far beyond his father's sight.

1

The Beltain summer festival was in full swing in the meadow beneath the Black Fort. The animals corralled there for the winter had been driven out to their summer pastures and all the people of the Epidii had gathered amongst the fire pits dug for the roasting of cattle, pigs and sheep. Columns of smoke rose into the still, clear air all across the valley of the shimmering Tae as the farmers set about burning the old grass off to make way for the new. Brude Uurad bustled around irritably as he prepared for the evening's rituals. He inspected the animals chosen as offerings to the gods and supervised the building of the bonfire that would be lit before the feasting began in earnest. The finest of the Epidii warriors strutted and stretched in nervous anticipation of the tournament that would decide which of them would be crowned the Beltain King and Queen and have the honour of lighting the great bonfire.

Cinloch handed Mormaer Erp of the Epidii a horn of myrtle ale and watched as he leaned against the fort's rampart and savoured his first mouthful of the bitter-sweet brew. He saw that the grey in his beard that had first begun to show when Drest was a boy had spread slowly and surely until only a few lonely, isolated, dark hairs were left. The creases at the corners of his eyes had deepened into furrows that put Cinloch in mind of the bark on an ancient tree. He averted his gaze when the Mormaer turned to him with a quizzical expression on his face.

'How did we grow so old, my friend? It seems like only a few months since we charged up these slopes under a blizzard of Manau spears.' The old man rubbed at his shoulder subconsciously, his fingers digging into the hollow of the wound left there by the sword of Flegid, the Manau Usurper. 'Do you think of it, Cinloch? Do you think of what we endured that day?'

'I dream of it each night, Mormaer.' Cinloch replied with a sigh. 'I relive the horror of how we suffered and pray to Epona to spare us from ever having to experience it again.'

'Was the price too high, Cinloch? That is the question that keeps me from sleep in the dark hours of the night. So many good warriors lost. Was it worth it for all of this?' Erp waved his arm out across the Tae valley and the lands he had won that day.

'What choice did we have?' Cinloch replied gravely. 'The Dal Riata slaughterers had forced us from our lands and left us wandering in the wilderness with no place to call our own. When Red Cloak, the Manau King, promised us this valley in return for defeating his traitorous brother, how could we refuse? Look at what you have achieved in the years since then. We are rich in cattle, horses and grain and can raise near eight hundred warriors. The walls of this fort are thicker and far higher than they were when we took it. The improvements you have made to its walls and ditch defences have rendered it damn near impregnable. Only a fool would lead his men up these slopes now!'

Erp drank deeply of his ale before replying. 'I know you speak true, my friend, but I cannot wash the bitter taste from my mouth. Red Cloak removed two threats to his throne in that single day. His brother was defeated and the great losses we suffered weakened us so much I was forced to renounce my Epidii kingship. I became a mere Manau mormaer and now must kneel to that snivelling bastard every time he comes to strip my stores and claim his tribute.'

Cinloch knew he could say nothing to divert the Mormaer from his dark mood and so stayed silent and busied himself with his ale. The older man continued to frown and glare out across the sunlit valley.

'When I dream of that day, I always think of Ugrint the Giant.' Erp sighed after a long and uncomfortable pause. 'He was as tall as Uurad the Brude but was easily three times the width. A bull of a man. He had three Manau spears in him when he hoisted me up onto the ramparts and still he fought on. He must have slaughtered a hundred men that day.'

'They will sing of him and his courage around the bonfire tonight, Mormaer.' Cinloch replied breezily in the hope of lifting Erp's mood.

'Will they sing of his screams when his wounds turned bad and he started to rot? Will they sing of how he cried out for his mother and of how

I crept to him in the night and put him out of his misery? No! They won't sing about any of that!'

Cinloch let the silence drag on and pretended a fascination with the building of the bonfire on the pasture below them. It seemed an age before the Mormaer snapped out of his low spirits.

'I remember another man that day.' He declared with the ghost of a smile on his lips. 'You were too young to fight and were only supposed to carry my spears. I can distinctly recall telling you to stay close but forbidding you from entering the fray. I would have died if you had not been at my side when Flegid the Usurper drove his sword into me. I can still remember how my jaw dropped open in surprise when I saw it was you who had ripped his throat with a sword taken from a dead man's hand. Such courage and loyalty in one with only soft down on his chin. It is one of the few memories from that day that makes me smile. I can still picture you soaked in blood as we hacked our way across that damned courtyard!'

Cinloch shuffled awkwardly and his cheeks reddened in the face of such praise. He had heard the story a thousand times over the years but it still filled him with pride to hear the words spoken by the Mormaer of the Epidii.

'You rewarded me well, Mormaer. Never in my wildest dreams did I dare to believe I would be a thane with five petts of land to call my own. I can never thank you enough for your kindness and generosity.'

'Say not a single word more, Cinloch! The lands of the Arder were the least you deserved. I would have given you so much more if only it was within my gift. On Epona's name, I would have endowed you with a strip of land that stretched from the Short Sea to the mountains of the Stallion's back.' The old man then paused and let his head drop as if he contemplated what he and his people had once possessed and what was now lost to them.

Cinloch called out to a servant to bring more ale and turned his gaze back to the pasture below them. The crowds no longer milled aimlessly around the firepits but had coalesced into a single mass around the horseshoe-shaped tournament ring. They broke into cheers when the first of the warriors made their way to its centre and prepared to test themselves against their peers. The Thane of Arder felt his heart begin to pump with excitement and, for one instant, he considered marching down to show the young pups how it was done. A sharp twinge from his left knee brought him back to the stark realisation that his tournament days had long since passed. He watched on as the Mormaer's son strode into the ring full of swagger and bravado. The people hailed their champion and favourite and Cinloch smiled to see it was the young girls who cheered him the loudest, followed closely by their mothers and grandmothers.

He could not deny that Drest was every inch a warrior. He stood at least half a head taller than his opponents, his shoulders were broad, his arms sinewy and well-muscled and his dark tattoos stood out clearly on the pale skin of his taut torso.

His skill and strength were such he bested one opponent after another. His good nature was so powerful that each vanquished foe was quick to embrace him, even those who had been bloodied or whose heads had been cracked.

'Mormaer!' Cinloch cried out in excitement. 'Look at your son! Has he not been blessed by the war god Camulos? Not one challenger has been able to lay a single finger upon him! Such a warrior could conquer the world!'

'Or destroy it!' Erp snapped back sourly. 'The boy is impetuous and his skill and strength make him arrogant and incautious. Look! His shadow dogs him even as he fights.'

Cinloch grimaced as he too caught sight of Talorc, his scarred face and dead, white eye clearly visible despite the distance between them. He felt himself shiver involuntarily. He could not help but think it would have been better if they had left the boy to die in the forest all those years ago.

'My first mistake was to allow Drest to carry him home after the wolf had savaged him.' The Mormaer declared, surprising Cinloch with his ability to read his thoughts. 'My second was to give him to Uurad to be trained as a brude. I did it out of pity and thought it might be a suitable calling for one too injured and deformed to either fight or take a wife. I even thought his vile countenance might be an asset to one whose trade is ritual, magic and premonition.'

'It does give him a certain presence, Mormaer.' The Thane replied. 'A brude commands more respect from the common folk if he can instil some fear in them.'

'Ha! I cannot speak for the common folk, Cinloch, but he scares the shit out of me. Do you hear what honeyed words he whispers into my son's ear? He tells him he will be King and Drest drinks it up like a dog who has run all day without water. Such reckless foolishness could spell the end of us when we are like an island in a sea of enemies. Even the suspicion that we intend to reclaim the kingship of the Epidii would be enough to bring the armies of Dal Riata swarming in from the west, those of Alt Clut from the south, Manau warriors from the east and Caledone hordes from the north. Even these high walls could not save us from annihilation. The herder's son's dangerous delusions and my own son's soft-headedness could bring an end to us all!'

'His dead, white eye makes my skin crawl, Mormaer.' Cinloch replied as he rubbed at his beard in agitation. 'He claims to have the ability to gaze into the Underworld and see the fate of men but Brude Uurad dismisses it as nonsense. The boy boasts that he dreamed of an island divided by two long walls and describes the lands to the south of those walls as being empty and barren. He claims this is a vision of the future and foretells of the day when the Roman armies will pack up and leave. He says they will abandon their allies in the lands of the Brigantes, the Alt Clut, the Manau and the Votadini. It is nonsense, Mormaer, nothing more than the ravings of a lunatic.'

14

'I care nothing for his dreams.' Erp snapped back. 'It is his words that vex me. It is his idiocy that could lead us to ruin.'

Cinloch nodded his agreement. 'But no-one will believe him. The royal line of the Epidii comes from your mother. Your brother Elpin will inherit your titles and lands. Drest would have no valid claim.'

'That is true.' Erp retorted through lips pursed in distaste. 'But a king must be worthy of the name. You know my brother to be a weak man who is drunk more often than he is sober. I am certain Talorc reminds Drest of it each and every day. I am also sure he reminds him that his mother was a princess of the Phocali and that her royal blood pumps in his veins. I have seen thrones won and lost for much less than this. I must end this whispering before it is too late.'

'Talorc is as obstinate as Drest, Mormaer. It will not be easy to persuade him to abandon his dangerous fantasies.'

'I will not even attempt to reason with him, Cinloch.' Erp replied with a resolute shake of his head. 'I will separate them. I will send Drest to train with his uncle at the Ern Fort. A little time in Elpin's company should be enough to reveal our essential weakness to him. It may be enough to temper his ambition and bring him to caution.'

'Then Talorc will follow him there, I am certain of it. It is not so easy to shake off a shadow.'

'That is not his fate. I will send him north with my youngest brother, the Thane of Keld.' Erp paused and reached out to pull Cinloch closer so he could speak more quietly. 'Talorc will not be returning with him.'

'You mean to have him killed?' Cinloch gasped, his eyes wide with shock. 'Such a murder would bring great misfortune to our door. The gods would punish us! It is forbidden to harm a brude!'

'Talorc is no brude!' Erp hissed as he squeezed Cinloch's shoulder. 'You said so yourself. Do not fret, I have Uurad's blessing in this. Now, let's speak of it no more. Let's walk down to watch my son lighting the Beltain fire before we join the feast and listen as Brude Uurad recites the tale of the Epidii. Come! You always enjoy it. The Brude is a better bard than he is a sorcerer or a reader of the fates.'

2

Mormaer Erp's assessment of Brude Uurad's abilities was free of both flattery and undue criticism. He himself would readily admit he had few gifts when it came to magic and foresight but would rightly assert his superiority when it came to teaching, healing, astrology, rituals and his knowledge of the secrets of the gods. In his youth, the Epidii court boasted thirteen brudes, each with his own special talents. It was there he had been instructed in the arts of the bard and, despite the great catastrophe that had seen his tribe decimated and its rulers cast out, he had forgotten none of the lessons of storytelling. He stood at the centre of the ring with his back to the bonfire so the bright, orange glow of the flickering ash seemed to turn his white hair, beard and robes to the colour of flame. He knew well that his face would be in shadow and that its effect would be to lend him an added air of mystery that would improve the telling of the tale.

Cinloch sat at the Mormaer's left side, the position of honour he had held since standing with him during the taking of the Black Fort. He was glad of the chair the servants brought for him as he knew his joints would have ached for days if he had been forced to sit on the cold earth like the common folk. He glanced around and saw no sign of discomfort on their faces. Every face was rapt and their eyes were locked on the Brude as he began the epic tale that was part legend, part poem, part history, part song and part royal propaganda. He found himself wondering about Uurad's age as he sang about Epona and how she had transformed the foam-capped waves into the horses of the Epidii so Eochaid and his people could travel the land and work the fields. Even in his boyhood, Uurad had seemed ancient. He was unnaturally tall and painfully thin and both his beard and his hair were as white as snow and so long they reached past his waist. Cinloch must have heard the tale a thousand times but it never failed to excite and entertain him. Uurad used his hands to bring his words to life and the Thane of Arder found himself smiling when he waved them around wildly to show how Epona had turned the Great Stallion into stone so the Epidii would have a mountain range to defend them from the raiders to the east.

The old man leapt forward with unexpected agility as he told of how the mighty Romans had come to take their land. The suddenness of his lunge caused all of the children to scream out in surprise and half of the adults to jerk back in fear. Cinloch laughed at his antics and supped on his ale. Uurad soon had both adults and children cheering with joy when he described how the invincible Romans had known no peace in the lands of the Picts. He told of how they had retreated in the face of their repeated attacks and built the Wall of Shame to protect them from the

18

enemy they could not conquer. They clapped and held their sides in laughter as the Bard crouched down and bent his knees to show how the cowardly, short and bow-legged Romans had scuttled away in fear.

The loudest cheers and most frantic clapping came when the bonfire had turned to grey, smoking ash and the Bard's voice had grown hoarse from bellowing for so long. His face was grave as he told how the Romans had sent the evil general Stilicho to slaughter all the tribes of the north. He screwed his eyes up and twisted his mouth so no one would doubt he was the most vicious and merciless of beasts. He then paused and let the silence grow until every man, woman and child was leaning forward in eager, breathless anticipation of what was to come next.

The words then exploded from him as he roared about how the great legions of Stilicho had been forced to retreat and how Erp, Prince of the Epidii, had ridden out of the mist and fallen upon the last of these legions, setting it to flight and capturing its eagle standard. As he shouted this out, Talorc stepped out from the back of the crowd and rammed the standard into the earth at Erp's side. The Mormaer accepted the adulation of his people with quiet dignity, a tight smile and a nod of thanks. Cinloch could not stop himself from grinning as he gazed up at the battered and tarnished symbol of Roman humiliation. He had not yet been born when Erp pulled it from the hands of some dying legionary and had been brought up on the glorious tale of how it had been won. He reached out and clapped Erp's shoulder in congratulation, his face flushed with pride at having the honour of sitting at the Epidii leader's side. The old man leaned towards his most trusted thane and smiled weakly in return.

'It is quite a story, is it not?' He asked, furrowing his brow as he spoke. 'It is such a pity the Brude must continue with the telling. The next part fills me with sorrow and I don't much like the tale's ending.'

Cinloch could appreciate that Uurad had strained every sinew and employed all of his considerable skills in attempting to make the tribe's recent history more palatable, but even the most powerful of wizards could not disguise the tribe's decline from glory to abject defeat. The Brude raged hard about the cruelty and deceit of the slaughterers from across the water. He hurled curses and threats at the treacherous Dal Riata for accepting Epidii hospitality when they were cast out from their own lands, only to turn on their hosts and drive them out and make them dispossessed. The people hissed and booed, just as they were meant to, but the sound was filled more with melancholy than it was with fury. The Brude barely remarked upon the great defeats suffered by King Uradech of the Epidii or how Erp had carried his father's body away from the battlefield at Maben's Rock to deny the Irish dogs the opportunity to mock and mutilate the High King's corpse. Neither did he dwell on the long years of wandering and humiliation, which was wise as the

Mormaer's face was rendered dark and downcast by the mere mention of it.

Uurad performed admirably in using the telling of the taking of the Black Fort to raise the crowd's spirits again and to bring the day's proceedings to a suitably triumphal climax. He danced around the ring and used his staff as a spear and then as a sword as he played out the different phases of the battle. Cinloch's chest puffed out with pride when his own part in the battle was praised but saw that Erp remained impassive in the face of all of the many compliments the Brude showered upon him. The people were immune to their leader's miserable disposition. They cheered until they were hoarse when Uurad told the tale of the heroics of Ugrint the Giant and of how he had fought on though a hundred Manau spears had pierced his flesh. They then joined with the Brude in singing brave Ugrint's praises but made no mention of how he had screamed like a pig when his wounds turned to rot.

'It took longer for him to tell the tale of the battle than it took us to fight it.' Erp observed sourly as he took his leave. 'Is it not strange to celebrate such a victory when it won us only crumbs from the Manau King's table?'

Cinloch shook his head as he watched him go. He then called for more ale and sat back in his chair to watch the dancing. He would not brood on the past when the young Epidii women were naked and leaping over the Beltain fire to ensure their fertility over the coming year.

3

Brude Uurad pulled his cloak tightly around his shoulders in a vain attempt to protect his aching joints from the ravages of the frigid winter air. He flexed his toes inside his frozen boots but they remained stubbornly numb.

'The frost will have carried me off by the time you reach me.' He grumbled to himself as he watched the small group of horsemen cross the Tae at the old ford and begin the long climb to the hilltop where he awaited them on his own horse.

He recognised their leader in spite of his failing eyesight and the distance still left between them. It was not just his great height and his broad shoulders that marked Drest out from the other men. He held himself with great confidence and arrogance and seemed to swagger even when standing perfectly still or sitting on horseback.

Uurad inclined his head in deference and called out a greeting when they finally reached him.

'I hardly recognise you, Drest. It would seem your uncle has treated you well. The waters of the Ern must have agreed with you.'

Drest returned Uurad's smile with genuine warmth. He had always liked the old man and it gave him pleasure to know he had noticed the changes in him. Long days of hunting and of training with both spear and sword had built muscle and his shoulders were even broader than they had been when he left the Black Fort in the spring. Skirmishes with cattle raiders from Dal Riata had enabled him to prove himself and the dark tattoos on his face stood in testament to his manhood.

'Aye, Brude Uurad. I have grown much since last I saw you.' He traced his finger over the crescent moon that had been marked around his left eye after he made his first kill.

'The Thane of Ern is not with you?' Uurad enquired with concern. 'Your father requested his presence. Red Cloak of the Manau will come to take his tribute on the morrow and the Mormaer wanted all warriors there in a show of strength. Is he unwell?'

Drest curled his lip and snorted. 'You know my uncle, Brude. He drinks so much ale he is often drunk and whenever he is sober he suffers such headaches he finds he can do nothing but start drinking again.'

'No matter.' The Brude replied, though his tone made it clear the news was unwelcome and that he did not relish telling his master his brother would not be joining him. 'You should not speak ill of your uncle.' He chided the boy without enthusiasm. 'Do not forget that he will inherit your father's lands and titles should he die.'

'Come, Brude Uurad!' Drest instructed him cheerfully without responding to his half-hearted scolding. 'Ride at my side. Tell me all I have missed while I was away. Has my father built more ditches around the Black Fort? Has he spent more silver on stone so we may raise the walls still higher?'

Uurad chuckled at Drest's gentle teasing and happily told him of all that had passed in his absence. He spoke of the great harvest they had gathered, of the calves, lambs and foals they had delivered and of the births, deaths and couplings they had celebrated or mourned. He spoke quickly without pausing for breath until his flow was cut off by the one question he had hoped to avoid.

'And where is your apprentice?' Drest enquired lightly. 'I was sure Talorc would come out to greet me. Have you set him to his chores and his studies so hard he has no time for his oldest friend?'

The colour seemed to drain from the old man's face and his lips moved soundlessly as if he was struggling to select the most appropriate words with which to begin his response. He looked downwards to avoid Drest's gaze and, for the first time in his life, felt fear in the presence of the Mormaer's son.

'Out with it, Brude!' The young horse warrior commanded him. 'I see a nervousness in you that makes me think you have ill tidings for me.'

Uurad slowly raised his eyes and flinched involuntarily at the harshness of Drest's glare.

'Talorc is lost.' He stuttered in response. 'He went north with the Thane of Keld and his men to trade with the Caledones and was separated from them in a mountain fog. They searched for him for two days but could find neither him nor his corpse.'

Uurad cringed inwardly through the long silence that followed his words. He winced when he saw Drest's knuckles turn white from gripping his reins so tightly.

'He showed great promise.' Uurad offered when he could bear the tension no more. 'He would have made a great brude. He was quick to learn the rituals and the secrets of healing.'

Drest nodded to acknowledge the kindness the Brude had intended but kept his jaw clenched as though he could not trust himself to speak without showing weakness.

The scouts came in a little after dawn to announce that Red Cloak of the Manau and his retinue had crossed Bodor's river and were advancing quickly over the hard ground. Warriors galloped in at regular intervals to report on their progress and estimated that they would reach the slopes below the Black Fort before the sun had reached its highest point.

Mormaer Erp paced nervously in the newly brushed courtyard and barked out questions to ensure all of his orders had been followed. His apprehension was infectious and his thanes, placemen and attendants all found that they too were shuffling their feet and rubbing at their beards. Drest leaned towards his father and spoke in a low voice so he would not be overheard.

'Stop fretting, Faither. We are well prepared. All of the weeds have been pulled, every shield has been repainted and every spearpoint and sword blade has been ground and polished until they shine like silver. Half of the cattle, sheep and horses have been driven into the forest and the grain cellar door has been sealed and buried in earth. Red Cloak will see just what we want him to see and can only demand his share of what is visible to him. Your best warriors fill the walls of this fort and their presence will dissuade him from demanding anything more.'

'Tis not that, Drest.' Erp replied mournfully. 'It is the thought of kneeling before him and calling him king. It sticks in my throat more now than it did when he first demanded it of me. I do it only to preserve my people but the shame of it hangs heavily on me.'

'It will not always be this way. Think of that and steel yourself to swallow all these indignities.'

'I grow old, my son, and I fear I will end my life on my knees having spent most of it bowing and smiling while that smirking weasel takes what is ours. I cannot see us ever being strong enough to cast off our chains when Red Cloak can run to his Roman masters and beg them to send their legions over the walls to slaughter us.'

Cinloch joined them to announce that the Manau banners had been seen fording the Tae.

'We should prepare ourselves!' He declared needlessly, betraying his own nerves.

Drest watched from his father's side as the Manau King and his retinue rode in through the gate. He thought that Red Cloak looked more like a rat than a weasel. He was so painfully thin he seemed incapable of bearing the weight of the faded, crimson cloak hanging from his rounded shoulders. The cloth was worn and ragged and should have been cast aside long ago but Red Cloak refused to relinquish it. It had been presented to him in Rome by the Emperor Theodosius himself and he wore it as a symbol of the authority the Romans had vested in him in the lands to the north of their wall. There was so little meat on his face the contours of his skull were plainly visible. His smile was broad and filled with yellow teeth but it lacked real warmth or humour and failed to mask his arrogance and disdain for the men before him.

His son, Edern, was mounted to his left. Drest recognised him from the puckered scarring on the left side of his face but any man could have identified him as the King's son as they shared the same narrow skull and rodent-like facial features. The only difference between them was their age and the fact that Edern's contempt shone out from a frown rather than from a smile. Red Cloak's grandson, Cunedda, flanked him on the other side. Drest thought that Cunedda's mother must have spread her legs for a man other than Edern for he was handsome and well-built and had inherited none of his father's or his grandfather's ugliness.

Drest helped his father stiffly to his feet when the Manau King was satisfied they had spent long enough in the dirt to serve his royal dignity and gestured at them to rise.

Erp began to welcome his superior to the Black Fort but was interrupted before he had finished describing the great feast he had laid on in honour of the King and his men.

'You must have spent a great deal of silver on raising the walls of this fort so high.' Red Cloak observed dryly as he examined the interior of the stronghold with great care. 'I do hope you have not left yourself short, Mormaer. You are aware, are you not, that I require tribute equal to that paid last year and a tenth more besides?'

'Your stewards were most clear on the amounts required, my King.' Erp replied with a bow of his head. 'I have the silver ready for you to carry away.'

'And what of your livestock, Mormaer?' He demanded without acknowledging Erp's words. 'Your herds are thinner than I expected. I do hope your men have not disobeyed you by driving beasts into the forest in the hope of denying me what is due. Shall I have my stewards consult with the Thane of Arder to resolve any unfortunate discrepancies that may have arisen?' The King's smile did not dim as he spoke but his gaze grew colder and more intense. 'I will have what is mine, one way or the other.'

Erp began to protest but was cut off by the King as he dismounted.

'I must have what I am due, Erp. The Romans have troubles of their own on the continent, so I am receiving less silver from south of the wall. I am sure the situation will resolve itself soon enough but, until then, I cannot rule my kingdom without adequate resources. I am confident you will find ways to tighten your belts. After all, you and your people would have nothing if it was not for my generosity.'

Cinloch was visibly weary and red-faced by the time he took his place beside Drest at the feasting table.

'How went it?' He asked as the older man drank deeply from a horn of ale.

'Not well.' He replied as he wiped the white foam from his beard. 'These bastards would happily see us starve. It seems that they sent men to count our cattle in the summer and now demand one-third of what they saw. They will make no allowance for any that died or were lost or for those we slaughtered in the autumn. Our people will have empty bellies before spring comes around again.'

'That is not the worst of it.' Drest informed him, careful to keep his voice low. 'Red Cloak's son suggested to me that my father should give his Roman eagle standard to the King as a token of his esteem.'

'What? Edern?' Cinloch spluttered in surprise. 'Impudent dog! What did you say to him?'

'I told him that no king worthy of the name would bear such a banner when he had not won it in battle. I also informed him that it was not my father's to give as he has promised it to me.'

Cinloch's cheeks reddened further and he grasped Drest's wrist in his hand. 'You must not insult them, Drest. Our situation here is too precarious.'

'Do not concern yourself.' Drest replied with a grin. 'I resolved the matter satisfactorily. I offered to fight Edern with the standard as the prize. He is such a coward he let the matter drop.'

Cinloch's colour transformed from red to pale in an instant and he swayed in his chair as if he was close to fainting.

'Tell me you did not threaten Red Cloak's son!' He demanded weakly. 'Tell me you would not be so rash.'

'I did not threaten the son alone.' Drest replied with a glint in his eye. 'When the grandson said he would have to kill me if I slew his father, I told him it would be a pity if that happened for then the Manau King would be left with no heirs at all.'

'By the gods!' Cinloch hissed. 'You have threatened the lives of both Edern and Cunedda! You will be the death of us!'

'I will be the death of someone.' Drest retorted happily. 'But not you, Cinloch! Never you!'

The Thane of Arder called for his horn to be refilled though he knew its contents would bring him no comfort that night.

4

Cinloch knew it was both foolhardy and dangerous to push on in the darkness but he was determined to avoid spending another night in the open or huddled in some draughty, stinking peasant's hovel. The ride from the Arder Fort to the Tae would have taken less than a day in the summer months but the blizzards and deep snow had made the going so difficult he had already spent four gruelling days in the saddle. The cruel winds had chilled him to the bone and the knee injured on the slopes below the Black Fort all those years ago now seemed to ache worse than it had when the Manau spear pierced it.

The winter had been the longest and hardest he could remember and the more it dragged on the more his people had suffered. The tribute exacted by the Manau King had depleted their food stores and the hunting had become so poor he had been forced to strictly limit the amounts of grain distributed to each household. He had watched the faces of his warriors grow thin and gaunt and had found he had so little energy he had taken to staying beneath his blankets for much of each day. He thought the situation was even worse than that they had endured while they wandered the land without a home to call their own after the great defeat at the hands of the Dal Riata. He had answered the Mormaer's summons as soon as the messengers brought it to him but he had done so reluctantly and with ill grace. The long and irksome journey did nothing to improve his mood.

He cursed at the guards when they did not open the gates of the Black Fort quickly enough and left him waiting in the howling wind and heavy snow. He made no apology when he was finally admitted even though he knew full well his beard and hair were so thick with snow his own mother would not have recognised him. He winced in pain as he dismounted and tossed his reins to the waiting groom without bothering to thank him. He limped towards the hall in search of a fire and hot food to warm and revive him.

The Mormaer looked, if anything, far worse than he did. He too was painfully thin and his cheekbones jutted out sharply against his grey and lifeless skin. His brothers' condition was little better. Curetan, the Thane of Keld, was slumped in a chair before the fire and looked ten years older than he had just a few months before. Elpin, the Thane of Ern, was still plump in comparison to all of the other men gathered in the hall but his jowls and belly were so diminished he seemed to be a shadow of what he had been before. Brude Uurad had always been tall and emaciated but his back was now bowed as though he no longer had sufficient strength to bear the weight of his own head. Only Drest seemed unchanged, though there was a tightness to his face even his youth could not hide.

'By Epona's eyes!' Cinloch exclaimed with a weary laugh. 'I thought I was bad until I caught sight of all of you! I have seen corpses raised onto their funeral pyres that looked healthier and less downhearted than you. What misery has caused you to bring us together? I can tell from your faces it is something grave.'

Erp pushed himself stiffly to his feet and came to embrace him and to wave him to a chair by the fire.

'You must warm yourself by the fire, my friend.' He fussed. 'Your fingers are blue with the cold. I will have broth brought for you and some heather ale to quench your thirst. We will talk of the business at hand once you have refreshed yourself and have something hot in your belly.'

'There is no need for more talk!' Drest spat in irritation. 'The matter is simple enough. Maeatae raiding parties have attacked our lands to the east. They have driven off thirty head of cattle and killed two of our warriors! We must raise a war band and take our revenge. If we do not, they will think us weak and will be encouraged to send more raiders to pillage our lands.'

Erp waved his hand to silence his son. 'We have known Mormaer Manath for longer than you have been on this earth. I cannot believe he would sanction such an attack against us. Like me, he was forced to renounce his kingship under threat of slaughter from the Manau King. Like us, he is forced to kneel before him and offer thanks when he deprives his people of the grain they have grown and the livestock they have raised. I count

33

him as kindred and will not make war against him. What say you, Thane Cinloch?'

Cinloch paused for a moment and looked from one man to the next in order to read their expressions. He saw that Erp's brothers shared the Mormaer's reluctance to take up arms against their neighbour while Drest was filled with rage and was eager to seek vengeance for the slight against his father's authority. He tipped the bowl of steaming broth to his lips and drank of the fatty liquid as he considered his response.

'You are both right.' He finally proclaimed as he swallowed. 'We must hear what Mormaer Manath has to say. The long friendship between us demands no less.'

'Ha!' Drest interrupted furiously. 'You will let him offer his excuses while our cattle roast over his fires! It is punishment that is needed here, not more of your words. Give me leave to unleash our warriors and I will bring you ten cattle for every one they stole from us and cut down ten Maeatae warriors for each of those we lost! They will think long and hard before they assault us again.'

Cinloch met Drest's angry graze and nodded, a faint smile playing on his lips in response to his youthful hot-headedness and his burning desire for revenge. He could recall a similar argument between Erp and his father, King Uradech, back in the days before the Dal Riata slaughterers had crossed the Short Sea and laid waste to the kingdom of the Epidii. It seemed strange to find himself now on the side of the old men calling for caution in the face of the vigorous impetuosity of youth.

'There may well be a need for vengeance, Drest.' He began in a tone intended to placate and persuade. 'So, we will ride for the Great Fort in strength and hear what the Maeatae Mormaer has to say. If his words do not satisfy us, then we will turn you and your warriors loose to exact punishment for what we have suffered.' He held his hand out before him to keep Drest from objecting. 'Young men are deaf to caution but you must heed us in this. Red Cloak of the Manau would like nothing better than to see the Epidii and the Maeatae tear each other to ribbons. If we weaken one another, then we serve only to make him stronger. He would use that strength to demand even greater tribute from us. Would you see more of our people starve to avenge an insult without first hearing what Manath has to say?'

'Very well!' Drest conceded with both reluctance and no small trace of petulance. 'But I will send for our warriors and ready them to ride out on the morrow.'

His sour mood was not improved when his father and uncles began to debate the wisdom of setting out for the Maeatae stronghold when the weather was so bad. He snorted in derision as each objection was laid out and rolled his eyes at Cinloch when the Thane of Ern argued that the heights of the Wolf's Crag on which the Great Fort stood would be impassable when so much snow had fallen.

'Then you should stay here by the fire.' He berated them. 'Neither snow nor flood will keep me here. I will go without you!'

The bickering continued unabated and unresolved long into the night. Cinloch struggled to keep his eyes open as the bitter exchanges ran in circles and covered the same old ground over and over again. It all proved to be just so much wasted breath as, shortly after dawn, Erp's scouts saw the banners of the one-time king of the Maeatae riding for the Black Fort.

'It is Manath!' Drest reported from his position above the gate. 'I can see the three spears on his banners.' He then rushed off to prepare his men and order them to the wall.

Cinloch strained his eyes as tightly as he could and examined the approaching horsemen.

'There are too few of them to attack us.' Erp opined, his voice tinged with both tension and relief. 'He must have come to talk.'

The Thane of Arder nodded without shifting his gaze. 'Aye! He comes with only his house warriors and they hold their spears pointed at the ground. If the gods will it, this will all be resolved this day and your impulsive son can sheath his sword once more.'

The gates were opened and Manath of the Maeatae was admitted to the courtyard. Cinloch was taken aback by how much the Mormaer had changed. He had been a fearsome warrior in his youth, broad of shoulder, well-muscled and known for his ferocity with the great, long-handed hammer he wielded in battle to deadly effect. He, like all Maeatae warriors, wore his hair pulled back in a braid that hung down his back. Once a dark brown, it was now fully grey. Though he was still a big man, his frame seemed shrunken and his muscles had wasted away. His house warriors looked similarly unhealthy, their faces lean and pinched and their eyes sunken and sickly. Only the female warrior at his side boasted any sign of vitality. Cinloch's eyes widened in shock when he realised it was Manath's daughter, Mael. She had been a scrawny girl when he last laid eyes upon her but she was now a strong and beautiful woman and he had to force himself to avert his gaze. He saw immediately that Drest was similarly enchanted but noted with a smile that he did not seem able to stop himself from staring.

'It seems that my son has been distracted, Cinloch.' Erp observed wryly. 'It is now a very different sword he would like to unsheathe.'

'I cannot blame him, Mormaer. Not when he is presented with such a pretty scabbard.'

Erp was unable to reply as Manath had dismounted and now approached them, his expression bleak and sorrowful.

'Hail, good Mormaer!' Erp greeted him. 'What brings you to my gate in such foul and inclement weather? It would have been a hard ride from the heights of the Wolf's Crag to the banks of the Tae.'

Manath grimaced and placed his hands at the small of his back to relieve the stiffness there.

'You speak true, Mormaer Erp. It is no time for old men to be in the saddle and sleeping in the open. I would not have ventured so far from my fireside if the matter had not been so grave. I have no doubt you already know what brings me here.'

Erp nodded sadly. 'Aye! Thirty head of cattle taken and two good men cut down. Twas a bad business right enough. I take it you knew nothing of it?'

The old warrior shook his head and seemed unable to meet Erp's eyes.

'Red Cloak demanded so much of our cattle and stores we have been left with too little to see us through these hard winter months. It is not easy to watch on as your people starve.' He held up his hand to forestall any objection though none had been made. 'I know it is no excuse. My foolish nephew, Taran, rode out with his men and took your cattle.'

He jabbed his thumb over his shoulder in the direction of a shame-faced and forlorn young man who sat upon his horse without a spear in his hand or a sword at his waist.

'I have come to make amends. I am responsible for my people and will pay what is appropriate. It is for you to name the punishment.'

'We have been friends for too long for me to make demands of you.' Erp began. 'I would not so disrespect you. I can see that you and yours have endured even greater hardship than my own people have suffered. What would you offer to make things right?'

38

'I have so few cattle left I can only replace those that were taken and promise the same number again in the spring when the calving is done. As for the blood that was spilled, I will subject my nephew and his attendants to your justice. Blood must be paid for in blood, much though it would vex me.'

Everyone gathered in the courtyard scarcely dared to draw breath while Erp ran his fingers over his beard and considered what had been proposed. Cinloch felt his heart begin to pound when Erp shook his head.

'No!' He exclaimed. 'That will not do! That will not do at all. Red Cloak might take food from the mouths of your people and leave them hungry, but I will not. I will not weaken my ally when we both suffer at the hands of the same enemy.'

Manath blinked in astonishment. 'What then, good Mormaer? What would you propose?'

'I will give you thirty cattle to add to those already taken. They should carry you through to the spring when you will pay me back in full. I will not take the heads of your kinsmen but will take them into my household until the debt has been repaid. They will be fed and quartered but they will work hard for their keep.'

Cinloch turned his eyes towards Drest as the Mormaer spoke. There was none of the outrage he had expected from him at the leniency of the terms. In fact, the young warrior seemed oblivious for he only had eyes for the fiercely beautiful Mael. He simply gazed up at her and was deaf and blind to all else.

'And what will you ask in return for this generosity?' The Mormaer of the Maeatae asked hesitantly. 'I have no silver to give.'

'I ask only that we bind ourselves together in friendship and loyalty so we are better able to resist the greed of the Manau King. I ask for your oath to lead your warriors here to me if I call for it so that our men and women can fight side-by-side to protect both of our peoples.'

Manath snorted and screwed his face up in distaste. 'You would have me kneel to you and to Red Cloak?'

'No, Manath.' Erp replied gently. 'I do not seek to make you subject, I seek to make you family. Let us join our people together. Let your daughter take my son as her husband. When we are dead, they will rule a greater tribe and grow it back to strength. What say you?'

Manath turned to his daughter and raised his eyebrows to indicate that she should give her response to the proposal. Mael tilted her head to one side and squinted as she slowly examined Drest from head to foot. Her careful scrutiny put Cinloch in mind of a warrior looking over a horse before deciding whether or not to part with good silver for it.

'Aye!' She declared when she has done. 'I'll take him for a year and a day to see if he can put a child in my belly.'

The feast was not as lavish as it would have been in better times but there was ale enough to slake thirsts long into the night. Brude Uurad officiated as effectively as he always did. A scrawny goat was sacrificed to the Maiden, the Mother and the Crone and the union was duly blessed.

'You dealt with the matter most wisely today.' Cinloch told Erp when he found him alone by the fire. 'You avoided bloodshed and have bound us to Manath and his people. Red Cloak will be less bold now that we stand together. He will have to look elsewhere to replace the silver that no longer flows to him from beyond the wall.'

'Thank you, my friend.' Erp chuckled happily, his eyes bleary and bloodshot and his voice made thick and slurred from a long day of drinking. 'You might say that I have brought down two birds with a single stone. I think we will now expend far less time and energy on reining in the worst impulses of my difficult and rebellious son. I have no doubt that the Maeatae princess will be more than a match for him. If the gods smile down on us, she'll so occupy him he will trouble us little.'

5

There was still snow on the distant mountain tops and a chill in the air when the Imbolc spring festival came around again. Brude Uurad seemed determined to banish the suffering of winter by staging a celebration large enough and grand enough to jolt the gods into bringing on a long and early summer. All men women and children were forced into his service and spent long days dragging wood from the forest and adding it to the great pile in the centre of the meadow. Uurad told anyone who would listen that this year's bonfire would dwarf even those that had burned at the royal Crag Fort in the days of King Uradech. He proudly proclaimed that it would blaze so brightly it would be seen by the gods.

He demanded so many cattle, sheep and goats as sacrifices the thanes and their placemen lined up to complain to Mormaer Erp that he asked for too much.

'I would give him what he asks.' Erp told them all. 'We should not stint when we are in such dire need of a fruitful summer. We require the gods' favour more than we ever have before. Think of this too.' He added with more than a little mischief in his eyes. 'If you refuse to bring him beasts, he will likely decide he must sacrifice people instead.

42

As we have no prisoners, you would have to choose from amongst your own placemen.'

'What about the Maeatae murderers and cattle-raiders?' The Thane of Ern demanded sourly. 'I would rather have them slaughtered than any of the few cattle I have left.'

'You should see my son about that.' Erp laughed in response. 'He spends his days hunting and training with Taran, Manath of the Maeatae's nephew, and his nights tupping his daughter, Mael. He might not take kindly to the idea of sacrificing Taran and his men. I would take your sword with you if you intend to put the suggestion to him.'

Elpin went off muttering under his breath but Erp was confident he would provide what the Brude had requested.

'Might we persuade Uurad to do less?' Cinloch enquired when the thane had left the hall. 'It is not as if we have beasts to spare.'

'He tells me we should not scrimp.' Erp replied. 'I can see the sense in it. We will need the blessings of all the gods if we are to recover and prepare for next winter. We must sacrifice to the Maiden, the Mother and the Crone if our beasts, women and fields are to be fertile, to Maben if we are to be healthy and ward off the plague and to Lug if the harvest is to be good. But we must not forget Camulos, the god of war, if we want peace and Tal, the god of the night, and Len, the moon goddess, must not be angered if we are to avoid storms and floods. Then there is the river goddess Tae, the giver of life. I will not choose one god over another just to save a few cattle or sheep. Tis not worth the risk.'

Cinloch nodded his agreement. It would be a foolish man who refused the gods when their need was so great.

Any lingering animosity the thanes felt towards Brude Uurad melted away as the festival unfolded. Even Elpin would grudgingly agree he had seen nothing like it since his boyhood in the ancestral lands of the Epidii. The firepits burned from dawn until dusk and, though there was less meat and more bread than in previous years, there was no belly that was not filled to bursting by day's end. The games were fiercely contested and what little silver the people still had was wagered on the outcomes of the various events. The loudest cheers were for Drest and Mael, though Taran of the Maeatae did his utmost to deny them a clean sweep of the prizes. Drest brought his horse home first in the long race across the Tae but Mael and Taran reached the marker stone so close together that no-one could decide which of them had taken second place. The three of them lost out to a stout woman from the Arder Fort when she threw her spear further than all of them. Cinloch congratulated her and enjoyed Drest's reaction as he shrugged his shoulders in bemusement.

'She must have caught a gust of wind.' Drest offered by way of explanation.

'The only wind I've felt today is that coming from the flapping of your lips!' Erp retorted tartly.

The melee was, as always, the highlight of the games. A hundred warriors entered the ring in search of glory but Cinloch only had eyes for Mael. She was strong and quick and there was a gracefulness to her movements that contrasted with the brute force employed by her husband to force one opponent after another to submit and leave the ring.

'She is a beauty, is she not?' Erp asked from his side, breaking into his thoughts. 'She reminds me of my own wife when she first came down from the Dark Isles.'

'I see it.' Cinloch agreed, though he thought Mael was far more beautiful.

'I often wonder if she would have taken me if she had known how things would turn out. She came thinking she would be the Queen of the Epidii one day, not the wife of a mere mormaer.'

'She came, did she not?' Cinloch replied in an effort to divert his leader from another fit of melancholy. 'She could have gone if she had wanted to. She chose to stay with you.'

The discussion was cut mercifully short when a great groan went up from the crowd. The champion of the Thane of Keld had rammed his shield hard into Mael so its rim caught her nose and caused it to bleed profusely. She bowed her head to her opponent and left the ring as she was required to do now that she was blooded. The fight wound on until only Drest and Taran were left standing. Both men were soaked in sweat and were so exhausted they could scarcely hold their shields. They circled one another wearily in search of any opening that could bring them victory. First one and then the other would step forward and batter his sword vainly at his opponent's shield before stepping back again.

'Uurad will surely call a draw.' Erp declared when the stalemate had drawn on for quite some time. 'Otherwise, the bonfire will not be lit before the dawn and he'll still be reciting the history of the Epidii at this time tomorrow.'

Cinloch opened his mouth to reply but shut it again when Drest suddenly dropped his sword, grasped his shield with both hands and launched himself at Taran. The Maeatae warrior was taken by surprise and was forced back by the weight of the attack. He crashed to the ground when his foot struck a discarded spear and he did not have time to raise his sword before Drest rammed the rim of his shield into his throat. The people roared in approval when Taran slapped his hands against the ground to show that he submitted. Drest basked in his people's adoration but was gracious enough to pull Taran to his feet and to hold his hand aloft so the crowd could applaud his skill and bravery.

Even Erp appeared satisfied with how the day had unfolded. Cinloch was happy to see him fill his belly with ale and enjoy the bonfire and Brude Uurad's lengthy and animated telling of the great tale of the Epidii. He even stayed in his chair to watch the young men and women discard their clothes and jump over the glowing ashes so the Mother would bless them with children. It was then that Uurad came to them with the pedlar.

Cinloch examined the man as Uurad introduced him as Uhtric of the Brigantes and explained that he had come in the hope of selling silver plate, brooches, combs and mirrors to the Mormaer and his thanes. The Thane of Arder thought he looked strange. His face was unmarked by symbols of manhood and both his hair and his beard were unnaturally neat. The clothes he wore were of finer cloth than even those of the Mormaer. He could not help but wonder how a pedlar could afford such things. When the man spoke, his voice was soft and high-pitched and his words flowed without inflection, making it impossible to tell where one word ended and the next began. He also grinned like an idiot and kept nodding at each of the men seated before him. Cinloch decided he neither liked nor trusted him.

'Uhtric would like to show you his wares, Mormaer.' Brude Uurad announced after listening to the man babble away. 'He says he has news from the south and he would like to share it with us while we examine his goods.'

The pedlar signalled to the two boys who accompanied him to step forward and unfold the heavy blankets they carried on their backs. He kneeled down and laid out his treasures for his audience to examine. A small crowd gathered around with wide eyes and clucked and cooed at the sight of so much silver. Cinloch glanced down and saw there were goblets and plates, brooches and bracelets and rings of finer quality and more intricate design than anything he possessed.

'We should tell this man nothing.' He barked at the Brude. 'I fear he has been sent to spy on us. We should cut his throat and keep his silver.'

'Oh, Thane Cinloch!' The Brude protested. 'We cannot do that! I have given him welcome. We will anger the gods if we slaughter him now we have offered him our hospitality!'

'We know nothing about him.' Cinloch countered. 'How do we know he was not sent by Red Cloak? How do we know he will not report back to him on what we have bought and how much we paid for it?'

Brude Uurad glanced nervously at the pedlar but the fool had not understood a word of their conversation. He still grinned inanely and held out a bracelet for the crowd to inspect.

'I have not met him before but his father and grandfather used to come to the Crag Fort to sell their silver to King Uradech. It was there that I learned their strange tongue.'

Cinloch had no reply to this and had to satisfy himself with grumbling sullenly under his breath while the Mormaer and his thanes emptied their purses and purchased his baubles. Drest spent all he had on a polished silver mirror, a comb and a brooch depicting an eagle for his new wife. Cinloch thought the brooch more closely resembled a crow, or a raven at best, but Mael was impressed and practically danced with delight. Even the Thane of Ern overcame his reluctance to part with his silver and bargained for a necklace of thick, silver chain to hang from his neck. The pedlar spoke all the while and Cinloch was roused from his ill-humour as Uurad translated his words and whipped all there into a frenzy of celebration.

'The Romans have gone!' The old man gasped in disbelief. 'Every last one of them has been called back to Rome! The tribes south of the wall have been told they must fend for themselves.'

Servants were sent to find more ale so toasts could be drunk to these momentous tidings. The shadow of the might of the Roman legions had hung heavily over the land for long as any man could remember. It seemed beyond belief to learn that the threat had been removed and that their placemen could no longer call on them for support in suppressing their neighbouring tribes.

'Ha!' Cinloch exclaimed in delight. 'I doubt that Red Cloak will be sleeping soundly in his bed now that his masters have abandoned him. He made a lot of enemies when he thought he could count on their strength. Now he will have to watch his back!'

'We will all have to watch our backs.' Erp retorted with a sigh, spreading gloom as he so often did. 'The Roman exodus will cause great instability and instability is bad when, like us, you are surrounded by enemies. The absence of the legions will encourage the Dal Riata to expand their territory eastwards and we are squarely in their path. In the south, the Manau, the Votadini and the Alt Clut will be starved of Roman silver and will look northwards for opportunities to grow. Their gaze will fall upon us and then upon the tribes to our north. The Romans may have gone but they have left their dogs behind. I fear it will not be long before they come sniffing around.'

6

The dogs of the Romans came sniffing before the summer was out and they came in great numbers. Drest and Cinloch watched from the forest's edge as the long column forded the Arder

'It is the Alt Clut, just as the Mormaer feared.' Cinloch declared darkly. 'See the black axe on their banners?'

Drest nodded, his expression tight. 'Aye! I see a hundred horse warriors and four hundred on foot. They come for a fight!'

Cinloch shook his head as he peered at the tail of the column. 'See how many carts they have brought with them? They come to empty our stores and drive off our cattle. The warriors are here to intimidate us and to dissuade us from resisting them.'

'Then they will soon come to regret it.' Drest growled fiercely. 'Let them throw themselves at the walls of the Black Fort. We will slaughter them there and fill the Tae with their corpses!'

'Tis a nice thought.' Cinloch sighed unhappily. 'But there are too many of them for us. King Ceretic of the Heights can call upon an army five times greater than this. What you see below us is merely a fraction of his strength. If we refuse his demands, he will bring all of his forces to the

Black Fort and trap us there until we either surrender or die.'

'We shall see about that!' Drest snapped belligerently as he turned his horse for the north. 'I will not stand meekly by while those bastards take the food from the mouths of my people!'

The Thane of Arder watched the Alt Clut advance for a few minutes longer before turning his own horse and following the Mormaer's son on the long ride for the Black Fort.

The blood drained from Mormaer Erp's face as his son reported what they had seen and his whole frame seemed to sag as he sank back into his chair. His head dropped into his hands as Drest ranted and raged and urged him to prepare to give battle.

'Enough!' He cried weakly in the face of his son's increasingly fervent exhortations. 'We must comply with whatever demands the Alt Clut King makes. There are too few of us to defeat them.'

'Then we must make them pay a heavy price for their thievery!' Drest protested. 'Surely it is better to die than to lay down like lambs.'

The Mormaer now lifted his head and his eyes glinted with a steely determination as he glared at his son.

'You think I will throw the lives of our people away on a gesture? Is that why I have suffered such humiliations all these long years? Just to sacrifice all on the altar of your pride and your temper? Foolish, intemperate boy! Ride out and die on their spears if you must! We will make ready to receive King Ceretic while the crows peck at your eyes.' The Mormaer then turned to the Thane of Arder. 'Send out riders to summon all of our warriors here. I want every wall and ditch filled with spears by the time the Alt Clut reach the Tae. We must make a show of strength to mask our weakness. They must be led to believe that they would waste all of their armies if they sent them up these slopes.'

The Alt Clut came at dawn. Their column advanced slowly through the morning mist so Cinloch's first sight of them was of grey, ghostly shapes at the foot of the long hill. He called out the order to stand ready and felt some of his nervousness seep away at the great crash of spear-butts being thumped into the earth. What little comfort he took from this proved to be fleeting as the Alt Clut halted and began to beat at their shields as their foot soldiers spread out across the slope and aligned themselves in their battle formations. They did not point their spears at the earth to show that they came in peace as the Maeatae warriors had but brandished them at the Black Fort so that their shield wall bristled menacingly. Cinloch moved aside as Drest helped his father up the steep steps to stand at the centre of the ramparts above the gate. He felt a pang of guilt for noticing his leader's frailty and turned his gaze back to the Alt Clut. A small group of riders now advanced towards them and Cinloch recognised King Ceretic at their centre and assumed that the two boys who followed him were his sons. The young King had matured in the long years since he had last set his eyes upon him but he had lost none of his youthful arrogance. He swayed in his saddle and looked about him as if he passed through nothing more threatening than a tranquil glen and appeared oblivious to the ranks of spearmen glaring down at him.

'Look at these dogs!' Erp exclaimed, his voice strong and edged with malice. 'They are like children wearing their father's clothes. See how they try to dress like their Roman masters! The Romans wore helmets of bronze but these pups lack the craftsmanship required to make them. They seek to emulate those who ruled them and so make them in leather instead. Pathetic!'

Cinloch nodded and grunted his agreement though he did not think they looked pathetic at all. The shield wall now stretched out on both sides of the fort and was undeniably formidable. The great, rectangular Alt Clut shields would protect their warriors from Epidii spears and even the best of their warhorses would baulk at charging into such a solid obstacle. The household warriors escorting King Ceretic to the gates of the fort were armed with spears and had both swords and axes hanging from the belts at their waists. The layers of scars on their forearms marked them out as hardened warriors and their determined expressions left him in no doubt that they would leave the fort with whatever they chose to take.

The horsemen drew to a halt below them but King Ceretic did not speak. He continued to conduct a leisurely examination of the ditches and walls of the Black Fort's defences as if he had not a care in the world. When he frowned, his eyes almost seemed to disappear beneath the great, bushy brows that stretched unbroken from one side of his face to the other. Cinloch wondered why he did not have his servants trim them just as he had them neaten his beard and hair.

'Look there, Cluim!' The King of the Heights instructed the black-toothed and sullen warrior on his right as he pointed up at the wall. 'See how they have blackened the timbers. They think that scorching the wood will prevent it from rotting and will make it impervious to fire.'

'Aye, my King.' He replied. 'Tis just like that Novantae fort on the coast. The scorched timbers there were hard to light at first but, in the end, they burned fiercely enough.'

'Well-observed, Mormaer.' Ceretic replied with a smile. 'Do you also see how they seek to exaggerate their strength by sending their women to the walls to shake their spears at us?'

'Our women will more than match your men, King Ceretic!' Erp growled down at them. 'They are not on my walls for decoration.'

'Ah! Mormaer Erp!' Ceretic cried out as if he had been unaware of the men above the gate. 'I did not see you there. I must apologise for my remark about your women. I often forget that civilisation has not yet reached these parts and that the tribes here still send the bearers of their children into battle. You must forgive me! Now, have your men open this gate so I may enter.'

'I see you have learned no humility since last we met. You ask me to forgive your words when you have brought an army to my door.' Erp replied archly. 'Then you demand that I open my gates and let armed men into my stronghold. Do you think me a fool?'

Ceretic smiled in amusement and shook his head. 'If you are afraid, I will come with only my sons to accompany me.'

Erp glared down at Ceretic for long moments but the Alt Clut King returned his gaze steadily with a pleasant smile that was intended to irritate and infuriate.

'Open the gates!' Erp gave the order clearly before lowering his voice. 'But do it slowly enough to give Drest the time to help me down the steps. I will not have this bastard witness my infirmity. It will only encourage him to make greater demands.'

'Is that a Roman standard?' Ceretic gasped in genuine awe when he entered the hall and caught sight of the eagle on its pole behind the Mormaer's chair. 'How did you come by it?'

'Some tribes never kneeled before the legions of Rome, King Ceretic.' Erp replied, his tone dripping with spite. 'I tore the standard from the hands of a dying legionary as we drove the slaughterer Stilicho from our lands.'

Ceretic's smile did not falter in the face of this insult and he turned to grin good-naturedly at one of his sons and then to wink at the other before he responded.

'I remember it now. I was just a boy when my father took me to see the ragged remnants of that ill-fated force as they crossed the Clut. It was a pitiful sight and my father used it to teach me that a good general must avoid defeat. But I did not know you had taken their standard. What an amazing feat! I am impressed, Erp! Very impressed indeed.' He then paused and held the Mormaer's gaze. 'Such glory! Such honour! Such a pity then, that you could not hold those lands against the invaders from the other side of the Short Sea.' He shook his head in a parody of regret. 'I cannot imagine the shame you must have felt at losing your lands to the Dal Riata after defending them against all the might of Rome. To lose a kingdom and be reduced to this!' Ceretic waved his hand dismissively around the interior of the hall. 'I would rather face death than endure such a humiliation.'

Cinloch placed his hand on Drest's wrist to still him for he was grinding his teeth together with such force that both of the King's sons were staring at him in fear.

'What do you want?' Erp demanded abruptly, the redness of his cheeks clearly showing that the insult had struck home and wounded him deeply.

'It is not what I want.' Ceretic replied, the smile now absent from his lips. 'It is what I am due. You will pay me tribute.'

'I owe no tribute to you!' Erp responded. 'I am sworn to Red Cloak of the Manau. It was he who granted me these lands and made me Mormaer. It is to him that I must pay tribute.'

'But why.' The King of the Heights of Clut began. 'Would you kneel to a king who is too weak to protect you? I see no sense in that.'

'Then you will protect us when Red Cloak comes demanding what little is left in our fields and our stores?' Cinloch demanded.

'That is no concern of mine. Your arrangement with the Manau King is not my business. I will leave forty wagons here and you will fill them with oats, grain and barley. You will drive three hundred head of cattle onto the meadow below the fort and my men will return to collect them all once I have dealt with King Manath of the Maeatae. I am certain you will not disappoint me.'

Ceretic then leaned to his left so his younger son could whisper into his ear. He favoured him with a smile and a pat on the shoulder before turning to face Erp once again.

'And you will give me your Roman standard as a token of your appreciation. My son thinks it would be more appropriate for a Roman eagle to stand at the side of my throne. It does not belong in a hovel like this.'

'The standard is not my father's to give!' Drest interjected angrily. 'He has promised it to me and I will not give up an honour won in battle unless it is taken from me in combat.'

Ceretic was unmoved by Drest's aggression and met his eyes with an infuriating air of indifference. He casually examined him from head to foot and then sighed as if what he had seen had left him unimpressed.

'Your son is old enough to know better, Erp. I am a king and my sons are princes. None of us would sully ourselves by brawling with the son of a lowly and impoverished mormaer. I will leave you carts to fill with grain, a meadow to fill with cattle and sacks to fill with silver. Have them all ready for me to collect three days from now and I will send my steward for the standard.'

They watched in sullen silence until King Ceretic and his sons cleared the gate. Brude Uurad spat on the ground and called on Camulos to curse them with all manner of foul afflictions but they all knew it was a futile and empty gesture.

Drest paced furiously back and forth across the courtyard, his fists and his jaw clenched tightly in anger and frustration.

'We will ambush them on their return and slaughter every last one of them!' He raged wildly. 'Impudent, thieving dogs! Did you see the sons as their father humiliated us? They could scarcely keep themselves from laughing. I will cut them open and see how they laugh when their guts are spread across the ground! Miserable bastards! Cowards! Thieves! We must send riders to King Manath and demand that he joins his warriors with ours. Together, we would smash those dogs and leave not a single one alive!'

'Shut your mouth!' Mormaer Erp ordered him harshly. 'We do not have the time for your childish ranting. Our situation is far too grave for us to indulge you in your fantasies. We must take action or we will lose everything. When Ceretic has emptied our stores, Red Cloak will come to take what is left. We must be ready for him.'

'You will defy the Manau King?' Drest exclaimed in shock. 'You will actually stand up to him after all these years of crawling on your belly at his feet?'

'He is now the lesser of our enemies. We must fight him or starve but we cannot do it alone. Even if King Manath answers my call, we will still be greatly outnumbered.'

'But if we take him by surprise.' Drest began enthusiastically.

'Be quiet, Drest!' Erp ordered him, though he spoke more gently than before. 'This is no game. While I buy time by paying tribute to the Alt Clut and begin preparing the Black Fort for a Manau siege, you and Cinloch here will ride north to the King of the Caledones. We will need strong allies if we are to prevail. Your mother will accompany you. She will persuade her sister to whisper sweet words into the ear of her husband, King Onnus. We are finished if he will not send men to our aid. Promise him whatever you need to. You go with my full authority.'

They left the Black Fort at dawn the following day with ten pack horses and fifty horse warriors to escort them. Few words were exchanged as they made their way north and Cinloch found he was weighed down by a deep sense of foreboding. The Mormaer had embraced him tightly when he wished him farewell. He now wondered if his old friend had sent them away to put them out of harm's way rather than because he really believed King Onnus and Queen Ness would support them.

7

The long ride north did little to ease Cinloch's nerves. They entered the lands of the Venicones on the second day and were soon overcome by a feeling of being constantly watched from the forest's edge, though they did not catch sight of a single person. The nights were worse than the days as the men were on edge and jumped at the creaking of every branch and at the scurrying of every small animal in the thick undergrowth. Only Brin, the Mormaer's wife, was unperturbed by it all.

'Sit at peace!' She ordered her son as he fidgeted around the fire. 'The Deer People offer no threat. They will watch and track us but do us no harm.'

'Their creeping around makes my skin crawl.' Drest protested petulantly. 'I would rather they came out and attacked us.'

Cinloch marvelled at how Drest turned into a little boy when he was in her presence. A single word of rebuke from her lips was enough to silence him while he would defy and rail against all the rage his father could muster. The Thane of Arder smiled as he recalled the day Erp brought her back from the Dark Isles as his bride. The people of the Epidii had cheered their future king and his Phocali Princess and Cinloch had thought her to be the most beautiful creature he had ever seen. He wondered if she would have smiled so brightly if she had known that the kingdom would be lost and that neither she nor her husband would ever sit upon a throne. He sighed deeply and gazed into the burning embers with a longing for those distant days.

'Do not fret so, dear Cinloch.' Brin cajoled him gently. 'The situation is grave but I am certain my sister and brother-in-law will help us. Did Brude Uurad not say that the gods go with us?'

Cinloch smiled in spite of himself. He was no more able to resist her than her son was. She was an old woman now but her beauty still shone through and lightened his heart.

'I remember King Onnus well. He is a good man but is both stubborn and cautious. That may well be a bad combination for our cause. He holds tight to his throne and will do nothing that risks loosening his grip. Why would he involve himself in our fight when we have so little to offer him?'

'The situation must be even more grave than I thought if even you have lost faith in me. Do you doubt my ability to charm that oaf into giving us warriors enough to throw Red Cloak back into the sea? Do you think he has the strength to resist two Phocali Princesses?'

'I do not believe that any mere man could resist such an assault.' He conceded happily.

He took great comfort from her fortitude and slept soundly that night and every other night they spent in the lands of the Venicones. His optimism only began to fade once again when they entered

61

Caledone territory. The temperature dropped as they advanced and riders were seen to their east. They were soon joined by horsemen tracking them to the west and another group to their rear.

'What are they doing?' Drest demanded as he snapped his head from one side to the other to keep them in sight. 'They should approach us or attack! Why do they track us at a distance like cowards?'

'They do not track us.' Cinloch informed him. 'They are escorting us to the High Fort. They drive us like sheep so we will not wander into places where our presence is unwanted.'

Cinloch's guts clenched when they came in sight of the Caledone King's stronghold. It seemed to rise out of the forest and was perched on a hill at least twice as high as the one the Black Fort sat upon. The summit had been cleared of trees and bushes so the sheer scale of the fortifications could be seen from a great distance. The mere sight of the long climb, the ditches and the three ring walls would be enough to intimidate any enemy force and send them scuttling away. They were too far from the fort to see individual warriors upon the walls but their presence was given away by the sunlight glinting off the hundreds of polished spearheads awaiting them there.

'It is not the welcome I had expected.' Drest complained as they began to ascend the long slope. 'Why has he not sent someone to meet us? Why have us ride in with spearmen glaring down at us?'

'King Onnus likes to display his power, my dear.' Brin replied despairingly. 'He thinks we will speak of it wherever we go and so strike fear into the hearts of anyone who might gaze towards his possessions with jealous eyes. I do not doubt that every travelling peddler is treated to the same spectacle. Just grin and bear it and let the Thane of Arder and I do the talking.'

Drest grumbled sourly when they were ordered to dismount at the gate and protested more when he was ordered to surrender his weapons. Cinloch was no happier to comply but did so silently and gestured at the Mormaer's son to do as he was bid. They then exchanged a glance and arched their eyebrows in surprise when Brin extracted a slim and wickedly-pointed Phocali dagger from her sleeve.

'They are less likely to search me now.' She confided to Cinloch in a whisper as they were escorted into the hall. 'So, they will not find the others.'

King Onnus and Queen Ness of the Caledones awaited them standing before their thrones on a low wooden platform at the far end of the chamber. Cinloch took the opportunity to study them as they approached. He saw that Onnus, though younger than him, had not aged well. His nose and cheeks bore a redness that spoke of too much time spent drinking and his loose robes disguised, but did not hide, a belly that had grown large and distended. Ness still retained some of the beauty she shared with her sister but her face now bore such wrinkles that a stranger would think she was the older of the two. He assumed that the man who stood with them was Donal, their son and heir to the throne.

Cinloch dropped to both knees before them, as befitted his station as the man of the lowest rank there, while Brin inclined her head and Drest laid one knee on the floor. For a moment, he feared that the coldness and formality of their reception did not auger well but breathed a sigh of relief when Ness stepped down to embrace her sister and the pair squealed in delight like young girls.

'It is good to see you again, Thane Cinloch!' King Onnus declared without warmth. 'What calamity brings you to my door? I know you have not come for the joy of my company.'

Cinloch hesitated but decided there was no advantage to be had in delaying the request he had been sent there to make. Onnus was even more dour than he remembered and he doubted that there would be a time when he would find him in lighter spirits. Even his beloved strong ale made him more maudlin and rigid rather than more frivolous and full of joy.

Apart from an occasional nod and a grunt, Onnus listened impassively as Cinloch told his tale of woe and asked for Caledone warriors to reinforce the Black Fort. The King's eyes wandered as he spoke and he spent long minutes examining Drest.

'So, old Erp has sent his most trusted and eloquent advisor to make his case, my nephew to pull on my heart-strings and his wife to charm her sister so that she, in turn, will gnaw at my ear until I give him what he wants. Is that how it is?'

Cinloch inclined his head and made no response as his instinct told him that one was neither expected nor wanted. He decided it was better to let the King speak and hear his decision.

'Do not mistake me.' Onnus continued. 'I would like nothing better than to ride to my brother-in-law's aid. I mean, he is an honourable man and has suffered so much in his life. I cannot begin to imagine what it was like to lose a whole kingdom.' Onnus paused and seemed to shiver at the thought of such a dire fate. 'But I cannot allow myself to be ruled by mere sentiment. I have troubles enough of my own here. The Smertae and their dark allies nip constantly at my northern border and the Vacomagi grow stronger to the east. It would be foolhardy to meddle in the affairs of the southern tribes. Why would I risk conflict on a border that has been secure for so long?'

'Will you offer us no help at all, Onnus?' Brin demanded. 'Would you see us driven from our lands?'

'Your husband has already lost a whole kingdom. It cannot be harder for him to walk away from what little he now holds in the valley of the Tae.'

'We will be slaughtered if you forsake us!' Brin insisted, her eyes flashing with anger. 'The Manau and the Alt Clut will slaughter our warriors and enslave our children.'

'I would not forsake you. You are kin to me!' King Onnus responded, his voice tight and high-pitched as if he was gravely offended by the suggestion. 'I will bring Erp here and grant him mountain lands far greater than those he now holds. You will have my protection. I can do no more than that.'

Brin snorted and shook her head. 'You know full well that my husband will not abandon his people and I know that you would not welcome so many warriors into your lands. Can you not spare us a few hundred warriors when more than a thousand stand on the walls of this fort alone? I ask for only a small fraction of those you can call upon!'

'And I wish I could spare them.' Onnus sighed wearily. 'If my own enemies were subdued, I would gladly put men and horses at your disposal. I cannot weaken myself while they pose such a threat to me.'

'Then I must go north and sail to the Black Isles to beg my brother for help.' Brin replied, her face set hard in determination.

Onnus exchanged a glance with his wife and shook his head. 'That would be foolish, Brin. It is unlikely you could even reach the coast. The northern tribes are dangerous and would not let you pass. They worship only the dark gods and anyone unfortunate enough to fall into their hands would suffer the worst of deaths. Even if you were to reach your brother, I doubt if you could persuade him to lift a finger in your defence. He has allied himself with these vile and wicked peoples. He may be kin but he is no friend to any of us.'

'What choice do I have?' Brin retorted angrily. 'The Black Fort will soon be under siege. I will not abandon hope and leave my husband to his fate. I will crawl at my brother's feet and make any promise he demands of me in return for the service of his warriors.'

'Onnus!' Queen Ness implored her husband. 'They are family. There must be something we can do.'

The King grimaced in response to his wife's plea and held his hand up to silence her. He then paced the floor, his fists clenching and unclenching at his sides.

'Very well!' He declared at last. 'I will give you fifty men to escort you to the coast. I cannot spare them but will do so to discharge my obligations to you as my wife has bid me to do. I can do no more than this.'

If the situation had not been so grave, Cinloch would have laughed when he first saw the Caledone men sent to escort them north. A few of them might have been warriors at some time in the past but their best years were far behind them. The rest were so scrawny and poorly formed he suspected they were peasants who had never wielded the warped and ancient spears and the rusted swords they now carried.

'He thinks these poor specimens can take us safely to the coast?' Drest asked in disbelief.

'No!' Cinloch replied. 'He has sent us only men and arms that have no value for him. He does not expect us to reach the coast. He expects us to die. These poor fools are to be sacrificed so his wife can convince herself that they did not abandon us.'

8

Cinloch pulled his cloak tighter around his frozen body and urged his horse on through the snow and ice. The cruel wind cut through the thick fabric and chilled him to the bone.

'I feel eyes upon us.' Drest called out from his right. 'Just as I did when we were in the Venicone lands.'

Cinloch clamped his jaw shut and tried to contain his irritation. The boy seemed impervious to the cold and would not stop his chattering.

'How would anyone stalk us here?' He snapped back at him. 'Where are they concealing themselves on this barren mountainside? There is nothing but snow and boulders and we have seen no tracks since you insisted on scaling this blasted peak instead of riding around it as any sane person would do. Is it not bad enough that my blood is freezing in my veins without you subjecting me to your endless prattling?'

Drest nodded as if the Thane of Arder had agreed with him. 'I know. It's as if I can feel their eyes boring into the back of my head. We should double the guard when we make camp tonight.'

'Aye!' Cinloch retorted with undisguised sarcasm. 'When your uncle's miserable peasants catch us up, you should make them stand sentry.

They will keep us safe from your imaginary watchers.'

Drest nodded absent-mindedly. 'Let's push on for the plain below us. It will be a hard slog if we are to reach it before it grows dark but it will be worth the effort. It is so wide and flat any attackers will come in sight of our sentries long before they reach us.'

Cinloch cursed under his breath and gritted his teeth. He was already sore and stiff from a long day in the saddle and the great distance between them and the plain made him pray for the cold to carry him off rather than let him suffer on for so much longer. The gods ignored his plea and he had lost all feeling in his extremities by the time he reached the camp. He was grateful to the young Epidii warriors who had galloped on ahead to set a fire but the wind was so fierce and frigid the flames offered him little warmth even though he leaned close enough to them to singe his beard.

'Be careful, good Thane!' Brin warned him. 'You will set yourself alight!'

'It would be an improvement on my present condition.' He moaned. 'I fear that my toes have frozen and turned black in my boots.'

'Take some broth, Cinloch. Warm yourself from the inside out.'

He took the bowl from her hands and sipped at the hot liquid. He gazed forlornly into the fire as the warriors around him slurped at their broth and stretched their frozen limbs. He did not look up when Drest thumped himself down at his side. He did not regret speaking sharply to him earlier in the day but did not want to repeat the offence in his mother's presence. He bristled internally as the young man exchanged barbs and stupid insults with the other young warriors and bit his tongue when he chewed with his mouth open like a cow chomping at grass. He told himself that it was normal for men to become irritable when they were forced to spend too long in each other's company.

'For the sake of the Mother, Thane Cinloch!' Drest cried out suddenly. 'Your guts are rotten!'

Cinloch felt his temper spike in fury at being so insulted. Drest had clasped his nose in his hand and his fellow warriors quickly followed his example. They rolled around in the snow holding their nostrils shut, some laughing and others shaking their heads in disgust. He opened his mouth to protest but then gagged when the stench hit his nostrils.

'It wasn't me!' He protested indignantly, his words serving only to heighten the amusement of Drest and his fellows. He was about to deliver a stinging rebuke when Brin grasped his wrist and squeezed it tightly.

'Do you see them?' She demanded breathlessly as she stared out into the night. 'They have surrounded us!'

He followed her gaze but saw nothing in the impenetrable gloom. He was about to tell her so when the darkness itself seemed to ripple and shift as if it had come to life.

'Smertae!' Brin hissed in fear and disgust. 'I should have known it from their foul stench. They carry the bones of their dead with them so their spirits can join them in battle. They let the flesh rot on their bones and the stink of corruption hangs around them in a cloud.'

Cinloch caught sight of them as his vision adjusted to the blackness. They advanced slowly, their footsteps so careful they made no sound as they crossed the frozen ground even though there were thousands of them. Cinloch thought them to be small, heavyset and humpbacked but quickly saw that they were hunched over under the weight of the huge bags strapped to their shoulders. The hairs on the back of his neck stood on end when it struck him that those bags were filled with the bones of their fallen comrades. All of the warriors were dressed in ragged, dark robes, they carried no shields and were all armed with sickles rather than spears or swords. Drest and his foolish companions still laughed and joked in blissful ignorance of the mortal threat that was about to engulf them. Their laughter died on their lips as the air was filled with a hideous, high-pitched and mournful keening that put Cinloch in mind of the pathetic squealing of a dying animal.

'What the hell is that?' Drest demanded as he leapt to his feet, his eyes wide and full of fear.

'Tis the death song of the Smertae.' His mother replied, the slight tremor in her voice betraying her dread. 'Make ready! They will attack the moment it is finished!'

'Where are my sentries?' Drest asked in desperation. 'Why did they not call out a warning?'

'I would not worry about them.' Brin replied without taking her eyes off the swaying Smertae warriors. 'They are beyond harm now. Circle the men around the fire! All that is left for us now is to despatch as many of these foul creatures to the Underworld as we are able before we are cut down!'

'Will they carry our bones away?' Cinloch asked as he unsheathed his sword, the thought of it causing his flesh to crawl like a living thing.

Brin shook her head and drew her Phocali dagger with a defiant flourish. 'No, Thane Cinloch. They will bathe in our blood and leave our corpses to rot as an offering to their twisted night god. I would say your prayers now. I have heard that they do not sing for long.'

The Thane of Arder gasped when the Smertae stopped their swaying and their frightful noise. The plain fell to a silence that was heavy and full of foreboding. Cinloch raised his sword, just as he had been commanded to do, although he already knew it was hopeless. When the Smertae launched themselves forward, they would cut through the Epidii warriors with ease. The tension grew as long minutes crawled by without any movement.

'What are they waiting for?' Drest cried out in fear and frustration. 'Come now! My blade is ready for you!'

'Wheesht!' His mother ordered him. 'Listen! Do you hear that?'

The crunch of boots on frozen snow came closer and the Smertae line parted to let two columns of men pass by. Cinloch saw that they were unnaturally tall and dressed in dark, hooded cloaks so voluminous that none of their flesh was visible. The black cloaks seemed to shimmer in the light of the moon. Both columns carried stout poles on their shoulders with a sling strung between them. They came to a halt ten paces away from the Epidii party and lowered the sling to the ground.

'By the gods!' Brin exclaimed. 'They are Drui from the Island of the Priests. The brudes told tales of them when I was a girl. It was said that they devote themselves to the dark magic and never cross the sea to the lands of men. See their cloaks? I heard that they learned to weave moonlight into their cloth. See how their cloaks seem to shine. What would they want with the Smertae?'

The closest of the Drui leaned down to the bundled sling and extended his arm towards it. A gnarled and twisted hand reached out from the heap of cloth and grasped it. The Drui pulled gently and lifted a bent and broken creature from the blankets. Cinloch did not think it was human at first because it was so hunched and crooked it appeared to walk on all fours. It was only when it approached them that he saw it was a woman of greater age than any he had seen before. Her face was so mottled and wrinkled she looked more like a dried-out corpse than a living being. Her fingers were knotted and twisted like claws and her eyes were milky and red-rimmed.

The Drui and the hag ignored Brin and Cinloch and came to a halt before Drest. The crone barked out a question in a strange tongue reminiscent of a man clearing phlegm from his throat. Her voice was dry and brittle like desiccated leaves being crushed. The Drui answered her from the depths of his hood and she nodded her approval. She pushed Drest's sword aside with her fingertips and stretched her hand up to his face. Cinloch did not know how he could bear her touch without flinching. Her fingernails were black and torn and her hands were stained with dried blood. Cinloch could hardly keep himself from gagging at her stench but Drest stood still while she caressed his face and ran her thumb up and down the scar a wolf had torn into his flesh when he was still a boy.

'She eyes him like she is starving and he is a cut of beef.' Brin muttered under her breath. 'Look! She has entranced him. I should plunge my dagger into her back and be done with it.'

The nearest Drui slowly turned towards her and shook his head. His movements were slight but carried enough menace to silence her.

The crone then dropped her hands to her side, threw her head back and let out a shriek that sent shivers down Cinloch's spine. The Smertae warriors answered her call with a great screeching of their own. They then lifted their sickles high above their heads and advanced across the frozen ground towards the firelight. The Thane of Arder raised his sword and tensed in readiness for their attack. His heart thudded in his chest as the light from the fire illuminated the beasts and exposed the fullness of their obscenity. Their faces were smeared red with blood and several of them carried staffs topped with skulls that still bore scraps of flesh upon them. He felt hot bile rise in his throat when he realised they were the skulls of the poor, pathetic warriors provided to them by King Onnus of the Caledones.

They halted three sword-lengths from the fire and crowded in to listen to the crone as she limped around the circle, her screeching and squawking causing them to cheer and shout in a growing frenzy.

'Tis like a ritual.' Cinloch muttered through gritted teeth. 'Just like Brude Uurad before he slaughters a bull. I fear that the old bitch means to take our souls and give them to whatever foul god they worship.'

The Drui made no sound, but the shaking of his shoulders told Cinloch he was laughing at him. The Thane of Arder decided that he would be the first to feel his blade when the final moment came. The crone came to a halt at Cinloch's side and favoured him with a grin as she waited for her people to come to silence. He shuddered at the sight of it for her mouth was filled, not with teeth, but with stumps, rot and blackened gums. The hag then turned to Drest and met his gaze.

'Hail Drest, son of Erp!' She began, her voice loud and clear in spite of the hoarseness brought on by her shouting. 'Behold! The Wolf-Torn King of prophecy has been brought to us! Praise Tal! The night god has delivered us. Drest, Blood King of the Epidii, King of kings, great slaughterer and ruler of all the lands from the Dead Grey Sea to the Wall of Shame! All hail, King Drest, who will lead us all to glory! All hail, King Drest, who will lead the northern tribes and soak the earth in blood from sea to sea and beyond great Caesar's walls! All hail the Wolf-Torn King, who will lead the Smertae, the Caereni, the Cornavi, the Drui, the Vacomagi and the flame-haired Caledones south to reclaim the lands bequeathed to them by Tal. Rejoice! The Wolf-Torn King has come and Tal will drink his fill of blood!'

The Smertae cheered and drummed their feet against the earth as the hag sagged to the ground and began to spasm wildly. Drest watched as she foamed at the mouth and thrashed her limbs so hard he thought she would surely shatter her old bones.

'Aren't you going to help her?' He asked the Drui. 'I fear she will injure herself.'

'She will come to no harm.' The Drui replied casually. 'In any case, she has already served her purpose. My only concern now is you, my friend.'

Drest's eyes shot open in surprise. 'You!' He exclaimed in disbelief. 'It cannot be! I was told you were dead.'

'I was!' The Drui replied. 'Now, come! We have much to speak of.'

9

'It is good to see you, brother!' Drest exclaimed joyfully as he went to embrace the Drui. 'I have mourned you all these long years. Now, let me see your face so I will know it is really you!'

The Drui bent his head and pulled the hood back to reveal himself. Cinloch gasped at the sight. There could be no doubt. The scars were less angry than they had been when he was a boy but the dead, white eye at their centre was unchanged and no less horrific than it had been when the wolf released his skull from its jaws.

'Talorc!' He exclaimed in shock and disbelief. 'But we were told you were dead!'

'I was, Thane Cinloch.' Talorc replied, his deformed lips curled into a hideous grin. 'But the gods were not yet done with me. Come! Join me at the fire. My men will bring meat and bread for us to eat while I tell the tale.'

Cinloch and Brin exchanged rueful glances as they sat, both of them aware they were now in the power of a man their master had sent to his death. They listened as Talorc spoke but could not bring themselves to join their companions in the feast provided by the Smertae. The roasted meat looked and smelled like venison but neither of them was willing to eat any flesh that came from Smertae hands.

'It was as we were passing through these mountains that I overheard your uncle's men whispering amongst themselves. Their voices grew louder as they argued about who should commit the murder. It was only when one man said he would be cursed by the gods if he laid his hand upon a brude that I realised they were plotting to put an end to me.'

'My uncle will answer for this treachery!' Drest growled, his face twisted in fury. 'I will put my sword through his guts, I swear this to you!'

'Hush, brother!' Talorc replied as he patted Drest's shoulder. 'You must listen now! All that went before is of no importance now. I hold no grudge against your uncle for his attempt or even your father for commanding it. All that has happened has brought us here and that is just as the gods intended it. You must let it go just as I have. Now, let me tell my tale. Our time is short.'

Drest nodded his reluctant agreement though Cinloch could tell from his knitted brow that the unwelcome revelations were far from being forgotten.

'I decided to slip away when our progress was slowed by a terrible blizzard. I quickly became disorientated and lost my footing. I fell so far in the swirling snow it seemed that I would never hit the ground. I remember nothing after that until I awakened by the fire in Mamm Ru's hovel.' He pointed his thumb over his shoulder towards the place where the old crone had fallen and now slept deeply and snored loudly. 'She told me that a Smertae hunting party found my corpse at the foot of the mountain and carried me to her hovel so she might use my cadaver in her rituals. She would have cut me open and used my innards in her spells if it had not been for this!'

Talorc paused and pointed his finger at his ruined eye. Cinloch followed the gesture and saw that Talorc's fingernails had been painted black and their ends sharpened into points. He shivered at the sight of it for he believed it signalled that Talorc now worshipped the dark gods.

'She called it my 'moon-eye' and saw it as a sign that I had been savaged by Bladd, the wolf god, himself and that I had been granted insight into the Underworld. She summoned the Drui and the brudes of all the northern tribes and called on them to employ all of their powers to bring me back from the Underworld so that Tal's will might be known on earth. I was told that the rituals and the sacrifices lasted for thirteen days and thirteen nights before I was drawn back to the realm of the living.'

'Perhaps you were not dead at all.' Cinloch interrupted him. 'I have seen it before when a warrior takes a blow to the head. There was a girl at the Arder Fort who suffered just such an injury. She lay as if dead for a week. Her funeral pyre had already been built when her eyes fluttered open and she asked for water to moisten her throat. She lives still but claims no mystical powers. The last time I saw her, she had a child at her breast and was berating her husband for his idleness.'

Cinloch ignored Drest glaring at him angrily and held Talorc's gaze. He searched his eyes, both the whole one and the dead one, for any sign of doubt or deceit. Talorc smiled back at him with no sign of annoyance at the interruption.

'You may well be right, Thane Cinloch, but it matters not. I have not yet reached the point of my story. I'll get there soon enough, if only you'll let me.'

'Aye!' Drest retorted. 'Let the man speak! I will hear what he has to say.'

'Do not chastise him, brother. He is not the first to raise such objections. The King of the Caereni went further than he. He denounced me as a fraud and an imposter and demanded that I foretell the future so he could expose my deceit. His people shouted and jeered at me and said I should be burned for my trickery. I told them that their king had so displeased the gods they would not suffer him to live beyond the next full moon. They found him cold and dead in his bed not one week later and his ashes were strewn before the moon was full. The brudes of the Caereni now kneel to me and beg me to counsel their boy-king.'

'When I first went to the Fort of the Cornavi, their queen refused to have me inside her walls. Her brudes were suspicious and jealous and poisoned my name with their whispering. I slept out in the open for three nights before she came to me weeping and wailing because her young son was sickening. I sent her away and told her to command her brudes to whisper him back to health. I ignored her pleas for three days more until she kneeled at my feet, clutched my robes in her hands and gave an oath that she would pledge herself to me as her master if only I would save the boy. I did no more than lay my hand upon him before the colour came back to his cheeks. He is hale and hearty now and will make a fine king one day. The Cornavi have no brudes now and they kneel at my feet whenever I command it.'

'The Drui were the hardest of all to convince. When men have devoted their whole lives to the rituals, they are stubborn and reluctant to acknowledge another's superiority. They took me to the Island of the Priests with promises of instruction in the secrets of magic, healing, ritual, foresight and the ways of the gods. They lied and instead subjected me to torments intended to test me, break me and bring me to death. They starved me, but I did not die. They drowned me, but I did not die. They buried me in a stone chamber in the ground but I still lived when they returned to retrieve my corpse. They forced me to climb Tal's Staff, the great sea stack on the west of the isle, and told me they would kill me if I climbed down. With neither food nor water and no shelter from the cruel winds that swept in from the Dead Grey Sea, they left me for more than a month. I can still remember the horror on their faces when they came to collect my bones and found me still living and with enough vigour to curse them all.'

'I was half-mad when they carried me down. I thought that the gods had spoken to me and told me the secrets of the Drui. I knew I was sane when my ramblings caused each one of them to turn deathly pale. Their leader fell to his knees when I pointed at him and denounced him for killing his own brother so that he might take his place on the island. He confessed right there and then and it is his fleshless bones that are now blasted by the winds at the top of the stack. The Drui now have a new leader and will follow wherever I command.'

'It means nothing!' Cinloch interjected. 'Kings die when they are poisoned. Boys sicken if they are given certain roots or berries and recover if a potion is administered. A man might survive beneath the ground if he has stomach enough to eat worms and insects and birds nest and lay eggs on even the highest and most rocky of crags.'

'It is good to see that you have not changed, Thane Cinloch.' Talorc replied, still smiling, though perhaps less happily than before. 'I still recall how much the Mormaer relied on you for your wise counsel. I am just as keen to hear your thoughts but would ask that you allow me to finish first. You have again interrupted me before I could reach the most crucial part of my tale. I would be grateful if you could keep your objections to yourself until I am done.'

Cinloch shrugged his shoulders and gestured at him to continue. Drest shook his head in disapproval and stared at him with daggers in his eyes.

'You have prospered here!' The Mormaer son's exclaimed in admiration. 'It is to your credit that you have achieved so much when you have suffered so much hardship.'

'All of that is nothing compared to what has followed it.' Talorc replied. 'I tremble at the thought of relating it to you, my brother. I have never forgotten how you saved me when the wolf crushed my skull between its jaws. You threw yourself at the beast so I might live. I never dreamed that I would ever be able to repay my debt and I can scarcely believe that the hour is now upon us.'

'Tell me, Talorc.' Drest urged him. 'I can barely contain myself. All of this does not feel real to me. It is like a dream to have you at my side once again. Your tale so far borders on the fantastical and now you say there is more to tell. Speak now!'

'Very well!' Talorc paused to take a breath and shake himself before continuing. 'I must tell you of the prophecy that has spread through these northern lands like a summer fire. Tal himself came to Mamm Ru in a dream when she was but a little girl. He told her that a king would come to join all the tribes as one. He said she would live to see a wolf-torn king rise from nothing to rule all the Picts from sea to sea. He told her he would send a one-eyed priest to show him the way.'

'It is you who will guide me?' Drest laughed in delight. 'Did you not always tell me I would be king? Now you will lead me to my throne.'

Cinloch locked eyes with Brin and grimaced. He had thought the boy to be dangerous when Mormaer Erp sent him away but he now knew it to be true. He silently cursed the Thane of Keld for failing to put an end to him.

'When did the crone have this prophetic dream?' He asked. 'If it was when she was young, why has it taken so long for it to set the heather alight in these parts?'

'She conversed with the god long before you were born, Cinloch. It was too much for a young girl to bear. She put it out of her mind and only recalled it in more recent years.'

'Don't tell me!' The Thane retorted. 'Did it only come back to her after you came into her life?'

Talorc smirked and winked at him. 'It did, good Thane. Tis a curious and fortunate thing, is it not?'

'Tis fortunate indeed, my friend.' Drest agreed with great enthusiasm. 'The gods must have brought us here, for I am sore in need of warriors and it seems you have many to call upon. I must ask you to raise them now. My father's lands are under threat and we must ride to his aid. Let me tell you what has unfolded these past months, so we may make our plans. There is no time to lose! The Black Fort may already be under siege.'

Talorc waved his hand dismissively. 'We have time yet, good Drest.' He reassured his friend. 'I know all that has passed between your people and the Alt Clut and the Manau. I can also tell you that the Black Fort is still at peace and that the Mormaer works from dawn to dusk to strengthen his defences.'

'How can you know this?' Brin demanded. 'The Black Fort is far from here, too far for word to have reached you ahead of us. The Manau may already be at its gates.'

'The Drui tell me that Red Cloak has yet to gather his warriors at Giudi. He awaits the first frosts of winter so the roads will be hard enough to bear his carts when they are filled with grain from the Black Fort's cellars.'

'We cannot wager the fate of the Mormaer and our people on your conjecture!' Cinloch retorted in exasperation. 'All will be lost if you are wrong!'

'It is no conjecture, Cinloch. The Drui send their crows south to fly above the Epidii, the Manau and the Alt Clut. They see all and fly home to tell their masters all. You must take my word that all is well and that we have time enough to do all that must be done.'

'And what must be done, Talorc?' The Thane demanded. 'You have warriors and we are in need of them. The matter is simple enough. Let us march south at dawn!'

'Tis more complicated than that.' Talorc insisted. 'Even if I call for all the warriors of the Caereni, the Cornavi, the Smertae and the Drui to march with us, the armies of the Alt Clut alone will still far outnumber us. There is more that needs to be done to address that imbalance. We need to persuade the Phocali and the Caledones to join with us.'

'Then I will go to my brother.' Brin declared with determination. 'I will not leave until he agrees!'

'Good!' Talorc replied. 'Offer him his weight in silver as his reward. King Forcus is much heavier than he was when last you saw him and his greed for silver surpasses even his appetites for food and ale.'

'And how are we to convince King Onnus of the Caledones to make common cause with us?' Cinloch demanded. 'He is so afeart of his enemies he is loath to release a single warrior.'

'Then we must leave him with no enemies to frighten him, good Thane. We will bring him the northern tribes as his allies and together we will vanquish the Vacomagi so he faces no menace from the east.'

'You make it sound so simple, Talorc.' Cinloch retorted with a laugh. 'The Bull People will not be defeated so easily and we do not have the time for a drawn-out war!'

'Then we must finish them quickly!' Drest declared grimly. 'King Onnus will be unable to refuse us once his kingdom is secured.'

10

The Caledone King's rage was quite something to behold. His muscles might have turned to fat with the passing of the years but it was clear he had lost nothing of his strength or his temper. Cinloch stepped back quickly to protect his shins as Onnus crashed a heavy chair against the floor and reduced it to splinters.

'You have brought those foul creatures into the very heart of my kingdom when I ordered you to destroy them!' He bellowed, his face red and the veins at his temples bulging so alarmingly Cinloch thought they would surely burst. 'Do you know how many of my people I have lost to the dark magic of the Smertae and the Drui?'

Drest stood defiantly before him and held his ground in spite of his fury. 'You ordered me to tame them but offered only fifty of your men to devote to that task. Against all the odds, I have returned here with five hundred men under my command and Talorc and my mother will soon follow on behind with the same number of warriors from the northern tribes. I have done exactly what you demanded of me and your lands are no longer threatened from the north and west. These warriors are now your allies and will fight alongside your men to vanquish the Vacomagi and so secure your kingdom! You must honour your oath and furnish me with the warriors you promised!'

'Foolish, impetuous boy!' King Onnus seethed. 'You think I will throw my kingdom away as easily as your father and your grandfather did? I would no more trust a venomous serpent than I would those hateful, malevolent beasts. In any case, I promised you nothing until the Vacomagi are defeated. Go! Throw your dark hordes at the walls of the Fort of the Bulls! If you survive it and bring me the head of their king, I will give you men enough to vanquish all of your father's foes!'

'Then I will hold you to your word, King Onnus.' Drest replied. 'Ready your men! I will march them south the moment I return.'

'I do not doubt it.' Onnus drawled, his eyes twinkling with amusement. 'I will send out the summons immediately!'

Cinloch bowed his head to the King and watched him stride from the chamber, the sound of his laughter echoing around the ceiling as he went.

'He has no intention of summoning his warriors!' He informed the younger man. 'He hopes to see you suffer the same fate at the Bull Fort as your father did when Red Cloak sent him up the slopes beneath the Black Fort. He anticipates a prolonged siege that will tie up his enemies for long months to come. He cares not who emerges victorious so long as both the northern tribes and the Vacomagi sacrifice thousands of warriors in the struggle. He will then take advantage of their weakened state to extend his own dominion.'

'Then we must prevail and do so quickly.' Drest countered doggedly. 'We can countenance neither delay nor defeat!'

Three more nights spent sleeping on the cold, hard ground did little to raise Cinloch's spirits. His limbs were stiff and sore and the Smertae stench hung around their makeshift camp like a fog.

'I swear I can taste it!' He complained to Drest as they drank beside the fire. 'And those Drui priests make my skin crawl. I see them floating around in their robes and watching me with their faces buried deep in their hoods.' He shivered and drained the last of the ale from his horn.

'Are you afraid they will steal your soul and carry your bones around in their bags?' Drest teased him.

'Mock me if it amuses you but I swear I would have nothing to do with them if our situation was not so desperate. I fear there will be a heavy price to be paid for their service and I am certain we will not find it to be palatable.'

'You worry too much, Thane Cinloch. Have some more ale. You will feel better when Talorc and my mother arrive with more warriors to add to our numbers.'

'Perhaps.' He conceded without conviction. 'But will there be enough of them to defeat the Vacomagi and to do it quickly enough to enable us to march south before the Black Fort falls?'

His doubts receded and his confidence grew when scouts rode in at dawn to report that the northern tribes had been seen entering Caledone territory. His mood positively soared when he joined Drest on the hillside to watch as they all marched in. The Caereni came first with Talorc at their head, their spearheads glinting in the morning sunlight and their shields marked with their ram's head insignia swaying in time with their steps. The fearsome Cornavi followed in their wake, their shields and banners marked with the Horned God's five-pointed star and their helmets adorned with curled goat horns so huge it was a wonder they could bear their weight.

'Look!' Cinloch exclaimed in delight. ''Tis the Phocali with their walrus banners. Your mother has done well. There must be four hundred of them!'

'I think I might be about to meet my uncle!' Drest replied happily. 'See, at the centre! That must be their king.'

Cinloch strained his eyes for several moments before the figure came into focus. 'You are correct. That is King Forcus himself. I last saw him at your father's wedding. Can you see the staff he carries? It is the Phocali Standard. It was torn from the mouth of a sea monster by Narwa, the Father of the Phocali. Your mother has worked wonders in persuading him away from the Dark Isle to collect his silver for himself.'

'She is not the only one who has shown her powers of persuasion, Thane Cinloch. It seems that Talorc has spread his net wide. Look to the west! What tribe is this with a coiled serpent on their banners?'

'By the gods, it is the Carnonacae!' Cinloch exclaimed in surprise. 'Your father used to talk of them and their great war trumpets. He said their sound was enough to stop Roman legions in their tracks.'

'King Onnus will shit himself when he sees what an army we have gathered here.' Drest laughed as the warriors filed into the glen and began to make their camp.

'He will not be pleased.' Cinloch chuckled. 'There won't be a bird or a beast left for him to hunt by the time these warriors have scoured his forests and filled their bellies.'

Cinloch's good spirits did not survive the day. The tribal leaders had hardly touched their welcome feast before the bickering began. King Forcus was the first to claim superiority and demand that he be recognised as sole and supreme commander. The Carnonacae King took great offence to this. He argued that the command was his by right given that his royal line stretched back a thousand years and had been established when the other tribes had been nothing more than savages. Talorc succeeded in uniting these two rivals in their rage by pointing out that he had brought more warriors than both of them combined and that he would only agree to surrender his command to Drest.

'Only a king can command an army!' Forcus spluttered furiously. 'My nephew might have royal blood running in his veins but he is only the son of a mere mormaer.'

'What experience have you of battle?' King Birst of the Carnonacae demanded of Drest. 'I have received no word of battles fought by the remnants of the Epidii. I heard that Erp still cowers behind his walls and meekly offers tribute to the Manau King. What victories can you boast of to persuade us to subject our men to your command?'

'I daresay he has fought no more and no fewer battles than you, King Birst.' Cinloch snapped back, his anger roused by the attack on the Mormaer's reputation. 'I heard no reports of your military prowess while we cowered behind our walls. I heard only that you had retreated to your mountain fastness and let King Onnus expand his territory at your expense. I would wager that Drest is the finest warrior upon this field and would follow him just as I followed his father and his grandfather before him!'

He regretted his outburst immediately. Erp had sent him north to employ all of his skills of diplomacy to bring allies to their side. He had instead indulged his temper and endangered whatever fragile unity might have existed. He racked his brain to find any words that might placate the glowering and furious Carnonacae King but could find none that were likely to heal the wound. It was Brin who came to his rescue as he gaped helplessly at Birst in mute horror.

'Let us not bicker, gentlemen.' She chided them all. 'There is both glory enough and silver enough for all of us. Will our warriors not fight better when they follow the leaders they are sworn to? Why waste time arguing over who is paramount when we have not yet taken a single step into the lands of our enemy? My father always said that leaders are forged only in the heat of battle. Let us make battle so the gods of war can reveal who amongst us is paramount. They will make the determination regardless of what we mere mortals decide here.'

Cinloch could not help but admire her skill and further regret his own impetuous rage. She had outflanked them all by calling for a delay in resolving the matter. Birst, Forcus, Drest and Talorc all agreed to it immediately, each of them content that their own claim had not been rejected outright.

'I must offer you my apologies.' He grovelled when the feast was over and he found her alone. 'I should have bitten my tongue.'

'Indeed, you should have.' She scolded him. 'Tis a delicate enough balance without you picking fights with our skittish new friends.' She then paused and let her scowl soften. 'Though I cannot deny I was glad you did not let the insult pass. Erp is worth ten of him, even on his worst day.'

'Do you think we will be able to hold this alliance together long enough for us to reach the Black Fort?' He asked, his tone revealing that he harboured grave doubts.

'That will depend on what we find when we reach the coast, Cinloch. It will not take much for the Carnonacae King to lose faith and even my own brother will not stay long if the prospect is too daunting. We will need the gods to smile down on us if we are to prevail.' She then sighed and shook her head. 'I'll tell you one thing! My son had better live up to all of his promise when battle is joined. If he does not, we will find ourselves at the command of one of those fools and I could not suffer that!'

Cinloch cursed as he crested the hill and the coast came into view. The Bull Fort was directly ahead of him and the sight of it caused his guts to clench. He now fully understood why King Onnus had laughed so merrily when he took his leave of them. Even at such a distance and despite the pouring rain, he saw immediately just how formidable the defences were. The fort sat on a rocky promontory surrounded by the sea on three sides. The landward side was a thin neck of land defended by a high stone wall behind three imposing earth ramparts and three massive ditches. The wooden causeway that had allowed men and carts to cross those defences was in the process of being broken up and burned by the men who scurried around it like busy ants. Both the scale and the layout of the fort caused him to groan. The citadel stood on his left and was heavily fortified. A larger enclosure stood to the right and was filled with enough cattle to keep the garrison fed for months, if not years, to come.

'It seems that we were expected.' Talorc announced cheerfully as he and Drest reined in at the Thane's side. 'At least one of their scouts was quick enough to evade the Smertae. I have never known that to happen before!'

'Tis more likely that the Caledone King sent word to them.' Cinloch replied gruffly. 'It would be to his advantage to have all of his enemies tied up in one place.'

'Must you always be so full of gloom?' Talorc chastised him. 'It matters not what Onnus intended. Think only of the warriors he will provide when yonder fort is turned to ash.'

'Can't you see what is before you?' Cinloch spat furiously. 'That fort is damned near impregnable! They have driven all of their livestock within its walls and we can only stand by and watch as their ships sail in to bring them all the men and supplies they could wish for. We can either waste all of our people on their walls or sit in impotence until we starve. We will win nothing here. We should abandon this ill-fated enterprise and march swiftly south with only the warriors you have brought to us.'

'Hush, good Thane. Do not give in to melancholy.' Talorc replied in a tone that was as irritating as it was reasonable. 'We might well defeat Red Cloak with the support of the northern tribes but we would then be swept away by the full strength of the Alt Clut. We must persevere and so bind the Caledone King to our cause. In any case, no stronghold is impregnable. The Bull Fort is merely a puzzle to be solved.'

'We will not solve it from up here.' Drest interrupted them. 'Let us march our army to their door so we might assess their strengths and weaknesses at closer quarters.'

11

'How went the council?' Brin asked as Cinloch ducked through the door of the dilapidated hovel requisitioned for her use.

'I doubt if it could have gone worse!' The Thane of Arder replied with a sigh as he shook the water from his cloak. 'We have examined the stronghold from every side and can find no weakness for us to exploit. Your son argued most passionately for a full-frontal assault but neither of the two kings showed any enthusiasm for the plan. King Birst has threatened to take his men away and Forcus complains that the rain has fallen so heavily his camp has turned into a bog. He moans that the Vacomagi ditches are now so full of water they are almost impassable.'

'What of Talorc?' Brin enquired. 'What says he to all of this?'

'He remains stubbornly cheerful and tells us all that Tal will deliver us. He has set the Drui to their rituals and they pace and chant from one dawn to the next to no good effect. I fear that he now has Drest fully in his thrall. Your son is oblivious to our plight though our boots rot upon our feet and the Vacomagi warriors mock us from their walls as we crawl impotently in the mud below them. Still, I cannot fault him for his effort. He has gained the respect of the two kings by besting their foremost warriors in single combat but these tournaments will not be enough to keep them here. Our alliance hangs by a thread and the slightest of setbacks may cause it to fully unravel.'

'We cannot allow that to happen!' Brin declared, her mouth pursed in determination. 'If the Vacomagi see half of our strength march away after so few days, it will harden their resolve and we will never shift them. If the promise of plunder is not enough for my brother and the inconstant Birst, then we must fill their purses with silver to keep them here. I will ride south to my husband and convince him to empty his treasury.'

'It would be better to use it to purchase temporary friendships here than to leave it where it might fall into Manau or Alt Clut hands.' Cinloch agreed. 'You might also use your powers to persuade the Mormaer to lead his warriors here. He will be safer with us and we will need every man we can get if we are to assault those walls.'

'I will try my best, dear Cinloch.' Brin replied as she laid her hand tenderly upon his arm. 'I too would rather have him here with this great army to protect him but you know him as well as I. He will not abandon the Black Fort willingly.'

Cinloch took his leave of her and stepped back out into the deluge to trudge through the thick mud in search of her son. He had no difficulty finding him. A crowd had formed around the Mormaer's son and they pressed in close to him to better hear the speech he was delivering from the back of his horse.

'I will ride to the gates of the Bull Fort and give challenge to the Vacomagi King!' He roared to the delight of the gathered warriors. 'I will offer him the chance to settle this man-to-man so we might spare the lives of our warriors.'

'It is impossible!' A Phocali warrior cried out. 'The ramparts are too high and the ditches too deep and filled with water for any man to cross!'

Drest threw his head back and laughed. 'But I am no ordinary man! I am a horse-warrior of the Epidii and I will ride wherever it pleases me!'

Cinloch groaned as he turned his horse and set it galloping towards the Vacomagi defences. He knew immediately that he intended to display his skill and courage to instil confidence in their allies. He also knew that a single slip would be enough to have the opposite effect. He held his breath as Drest tore up the first earthen rampart and cantered along its top before digging his heels in sharply so the beast launched itself across the first of the ditches. Cinloch exhaled sharply as the horse landed on the soft, wet earth and thrashed its hooves in a desperate bid to find some purchase. Just when he thought it must surely slide backwards into the ditch, the stallion found enough grip to propel itself to the rampart's top. Drest raised his arm in triumph and set the warriors to cheering again.

Cinloch watched with bated breath as he repeated the process until his horse stood on the ground before the Bull Fort's gates. He shook his head in admiration of Drest's skill and in disapproval of his foolishness. His path across the defences was marked by churned mud and Cinloch was sure he would have failed if a few more hours of rainfall had preceded his attempt.

The drumming of the rain upon the ground and the distance between the outer defences and the gate prevented Cinloch from hearing anything of the exchange that took place between Drest and the Vacomagi King. He could only watch on as Drest rode his horse up and down and made it rear up on its hind legs in a show of skill. He breathed a sigh of relief when the young warrior wheeled around and galloped back towards them. His heart still thumped in his chest as he was only too aware that a single, well-aimed Vacomagi spear would be enough to bring all of their hopes and efforts to naught. He sent a silent prayer of thanks to Maben as Drest crossed each obstacle.

Drest bowed his head in false humility as he dismounted amongst the cheering warriors.

'Their wretched king is a snivelling coward!' He bellowed as he thumped at his chest with his fist. 'He was too afeart to accept my challenge and still hides behind his walls! How can they stand against us when their leader is so weak?'

'What really happened?' Cinloch demanded when he was finally able to usher Drest away from the crowd.

'He mocked me!' The young warrior admitted with a candour that impressed his counsellor. 'He said that a king could not lower himself to fight with a turd that has fallen from a miserable mormaer's arse. He said he will content himself with watching from his walls as the winter brings us to starvation and then, when we are sorely weakened, he will ride out and slaughter us.'

'Then it sounds as if his plan is much better than our own.' Thane Cinloch replied with bitter sarcasm.

'Far better!' Drest conceded with a wry grin. 'Although you will admit that I did succeed in impressing the Carnonacae and Phocali warriors. Word of it will reach the ears of our inconstant kings and may keep them here for a few days longer. I will have to think of something else after that.'

'It was a risk.' Cinloch acknowledged with a grimace. 'But it paid off, though I was certain you would drown in one of their ditches. You did well and we were in sore need of something to cheer us. Let us go to your mother so we can drink to your success before we send her on her way.'

A Drui priest intercepted them before they were halfway to Brin's quarters.

'A great army approaches from the south, sire!' He informed them in a voice that was croaky and buried deep in the folds of his hood.

'What army?' Drest demanded. 'Does my father come?'

'Tis the Venicones.' The Drui replied with a slow shake of his head. 'The Vacomagi King must have sent for them to join him here. They are his vassals.'

'Maben's breath!' Cinloch cursed. 'You are certain?'

'Aye, sire. I have seen them for myself. My crows fly over them now. Eight hundred warriors march with King Uuid at their head. They bear the stag's head emblem on their shields and he wears the Antler Crown.'

'Then we are finished!' Drest raged. 'Forcus and Birst will not fight them with the Vacomagi garrison at our back!'

'Talorc instructed me to tell you not to lose faith.' The Drui informed them. 'Great Tal will deliver us.'

'So far, he has delivered us nothing but enemies and reluctant allies.' Cinloch seethed. 'Where is Talorc? Let him come to me with his assurances himself. I will punch him in the mouth if he again dares to tell me to keep faith.'

'It would be unwise to lay your hands upon him, sire!' The Drui hissed with barely disguised menace. 'Not when he has ridden out to tame your enemies.'

'Talorc has ridden out against the People of the Deer?' Drest spluttered in surprise. 'How many men did he take? I gave him no permission.'

'He requires no authority but his own, sire.' The Drui drawled. 'He rode out alone. He has power enough to stop them in their tracks.'

The tension in the camp grew palpably as day turned into night with no word of Talorc. The twinkle of hundreds of distant campfires in the darkness added to the sense of unease and it was further heightened by the flaming torches the Vacomagi had placed along their ramparts to guide their allies to them.

The small hours of the morning found Cinloch pacing through the sprawling camp with his mind racing too hard for him to sleep. The long hours spent trying to persuade the northern kings to hold their ground had been wasted. Both Forcus and Birst would withdraw if the Venicones took to the field against them. He clenched his fists tight in frustration at the prospect of losing all when the possibility of victory had been dangled so tantalisingly before them. He came to a halt at the sight of Mamm Ru, the Smertae crone, hunched before a fire feeding oats and milk into her mouth with her fingers.

'Your boy has ridden out to bring all the might of the Venicones to a halt!' He sneered at her. 'He may already lie cold upon the ground.'

The crone made no response to his provocation but continued to stare into the fire, her eyes milky and sightless. She sucked greedily at her fingers with her foul, toothless mouth, the slurping and smacking sounds so disgusting they caused the Thane to grimace and his stomach to churn. He crouched down towards her and waved his hand before her face but she gave no sign of seeing it.

'Tis just as I suspected.' He began, talking to himself rather than to the mute, unhearing hag. 'He has used an old and decrepit creature to give life to his lies and now has my master's son completely in his power. We were right to send him to his death all those years ago and now I can only pray for the Venicones to succeed where the Thane of Keld failed so miserably. Talorc will surely lead us all to destruction if he lives.'

104

'Talorc!' The crone croaked as she swallowed the little oats and milk that had not run down her chin. 'He will be our king!'

'Aye.' Cinloch responded with cruel sarcasm. 'Did he tell you that as well, you disgusting old bitch?'

'Not he!' She cackled, her eyes wide and no longer blank and unseeing. ''Twas Tal himself that foretold it. The one-eyed priest will slay three kings and then perch upon a throne of his own. It will happen whether you will it or not. Watch him well, my brave and bonnie boy, for you shall be witness to it all.'

The crone's words caused a chill to run up Cinloch's spine. The endearment she used was the one his own mother had whispered into his ear when she embraced him as a little boy. Mamm Ru's voice seemed to lose its ancient rasp when she spoke the words and her timbre and pitch so closely matched that of his mother, it caused him to gasp at the sound of it. He shook his head in an attempt to dispel the thought.

'Talorc means to take the throne for himself?' He demanded of her. 'But you told Drest he would prevail! Which is it? Does Talorc mean to betray us?'

'Talorc!' The old crone repeated but her eyes were blank and empty once again and her ears deaf to the Thane of Arder's questions.

Cinloch had barely closed his eyes when the Epidii scout came to rouse him.

'This had better be good!' He warned the earnest young warrior as he rubbed at his face in order to bring himself fully awake. 'I am tired and stiff and in no mood for trivialities.'

'The Venicones have gone!' He gushed excitedly. 'They broke camp before dawn and now march to the south-east.'

'You are certain?' Cinloch asked, scarcely daring to believe it was true.

'Aye, sire.' The lad replied with a grin. 'Now, you must come! Talorc is close by and the whole army awaits him.'

Cinloch could not deny that Talorc knew how to put on a show. He rode out of the morning mist just as it was lifting so he and his black stallion seemed to appear suddenly and magically before the awaiting warriors. Seven Venicone horsemen followed behind him, their helmets bearing antlers that gave the impression of great height and strength. Little attention was given to the cart rattling along in their wake or to the crippled boy who lay inside it. Talorc unsheathed his sword and brandished it above his head as he kicked into his horse's sides to make it rear up.

'Behold!' He bellowed. 'Tal has delivered us! The Venicones no longer threaten our army! They have turned on their Vacomagi masters and now march to besiege their fort on the Mother's Seat! Our enemy will have no further help from the south. Prepare yourselves, my good and faithful warriors! We will assault the walls of the Bull Fort on the night of the dark moon! Praise Tal!'

Cinloch noticed with distaste that most of the warriors joined in with this chant before crowding around the Drui to receive his blessing. He did his best to hide his irritation but could not bring himself to embrace him as warmly as Drest did. The Smertae crone's words still haunted him and it stung him to know he had badly underestimated the priest.

'Come, Talorc!' Drest commanded him. 'I will hear of your triumph. Leave nothing out!'

Talorc shrugged his shoulders as if there was little to tell. 'Twas nothing, brother. I merely told King Uuid he could either choose to continue to bow before his Vacomagi masters or to seize the opportunity to rise up and cast his chains aside.'

'And that's all there was to it?' Cinloch barked in challenge, his tone harsher than he had intended it to be.

'There were some minor conditions, but nothing we need be concerned about.'

'What conditions?' Drest enquired. 'I must know what has been promised.'

'I gave my oath that we would break the Vacomagi here so the Venicones can retake all the territory they have lost to them. I also said I would make his son whole again. That was the greater part of the bargain.'

'The cripple in the cart?' Cinloch spluttered. 'That is the Prince of the Venicones? I have seen his legs and they are so twisted I doubt the Mother herself could straighten them. How long have you been given to perform this miracle and what is the consequence for us if you fail?'

'I have two full cycles of the moon to make him walk again. If I fail, only I will suffer the consequences. See the fine Venicone warriors who now shadow me? They will strike me down and carry their prince away if I do not keep my vow!'

Drest started to laugh and clapped the Drui's shoulder. 'Clever, clever Talorc! I was right to put my faith in you. You have bought us time when we were in such sore need of it and you know full well the Smertae will never allow the Venicones to lay a single finger upon your person. Now, tell me about this battle plan. I am intrigued to know what you have committed us to.'

Talorc talked them through what he intended and even Cinloch had to grudgingly concede that it had no small merit.

'What about the ditches?' He asked after several moments of consideration. 'They are now so full of water they will greatly slow our assault. The Vacomagi spearmen will pick our warriors off at their leisure. Surely we cannot absorb such heavy losses?'

'The Drui have been hard at their rituals for several days.' Talorc responded, raising his hand to forestall the Thane of Arder's objections. 'Tal will deliver us! Can't you feel it in the air?'

'It has grown colder.' Cinloch began, his face creased in confusion. 'You cannot mean?'

'I do.' The priest interrupted him. 'The temperature will drop further until, by the time of the dark moon, it renders the earth as hard as rock and the water in those ditches so frozen that our warriors will simply run across it.'

12

Brin's joy at finding the plain beneath the Black Fort mercifully empty and free of Manau warriors was tempered by her first sight of her husband. Erp smiled as he limped out into the courtyard to greet her but his smile was weary and the weight of his age seemed to bear down on him so much his back bent and his shoulders stooped.

'Praise the gods!' He wheezed as he helped her from her horse. 'My prayers for your safe return have been answered. I hope you come bearing glad tidings, for the situation here has worsened since last I saw you.'

'How so, my love?' Brin asked as she embraced him. 'What has happened?'

'Just what we feared.' He replied as he guided her into the hall. 'Red Cloak sent his pup to demand his tribute from us. I told him I could spare nothing after King Ceretic of the Alt Clut emptied our fields and our cellars but he dismissed it as no concern of his. Brude Uurad tried to reason with him and argued that he could not leave our people to starve now winter is upon us. He cared not. He promised to return with his carts and an army and vowed to slaughter every last one of us if I refuse him. His father is determined to have what is his by right, one way or the other.'

'And what answer did you give him, my love?' Brin enquired gently.

'What answer could I give him when he insulted me in my own hall and ordered me to condemn my people to death?' The old man snorted. 'I told him he must do his worst but should not expect us to stand by meekly while he pillages our stores. I counselled him to think carefully about how many of his warriors would perish if he were to throw them against our walls.'

'Will it deter him, do you think? The prospect of so many casualties?'

'Edern is headstrong and has inherited his father's greed.' Erp retorted dejectedly. 'He will march his army here just as quickly as he is able and then will do just what he has promised to do. I have called all of our warriors here to make ready for the siege.'

'Our son has raised an army in the north but must vanquish the Vacomagi before King Onnus will send Caledone warriors to aid our cause. He already besieges the Bull Fort but it will not fall easily. I doubt he will reach us before Edern and his Manau warriors cross the Tae.' Brin reached out and grasped Erp's hands in hers. 'We must flee, my love!' She urged him. 'We must flee north and join with Drest. We will be safe there and can return to retake the Black Fort with an army at our back!'

'I will not run! I refuse to abandon the Black Fort and leave it to those savages.'

'Then we will die, husband!' Brin insisted. 'We can fill our ditches with Manau dead but they

111

will still come on at us. They will wear away at our warriors until our walls are overwhelmed. You know this to be inevitable!'

'Then we will die!' Erp declared defiantly. 'But we will die here in our own fort and on our own lands. Do you not remember the years of wandering when our people starved? I would rather die than lead them there again!'

'Very well.' Brin agreed with a sigh of resignation. 'Then, for good or ill, we shall make our stand. Let the gods decide how the pieces fall!'

Vacomagi warriors bowed their heads and moved aside as the Bull King strode onto the rampart above the gates. None of them dared to meet his eye as his heavy frown warned them that his temper was stretched to breaking point. He wore no cloak to protect him from the icy air and seemed oblivious to the temperature. His brother, smaller and less muscular than him, followed on behind wrapped up tightly in his furs.

King Garthnac banged a meaty fist against the stonework in frustration. The height and solidity of his walls still gave him confidence but this had waned somewhat in the days following the withdrawal of the Venicones. He had sworn bloody vengeance against them when word reached him of their siege of his cousin's fort to the south and had raged in impotence when the sea remained stubbornly empty of ships bringing supplies northwards.

'How has this upstart brought all the warriors of the north to my door?' He seethed. 'How has he turned my own vassals against me?'

'They are no threat to us, brother.' Guram declared in a bid to comfort him. 'Look! They have built a great pyre outside our defences and their one-eyed wizard dances before the flames and screeches like a bird. What use are his distant flames against solid oak and thick stone walls? Their warriors have spent a week felling trees to feed their fire. They achieve nothing and sap their strength while we sit happily inside our stronghold. Leave them to starve as winter bites and then we will rush out and cut them down when they are at their weakest.'

'Something about this discomfits me.' Garthnac muttered to himself rather than to his brother. 'Why would they expend such efforts on building a fire that cannot harm us? Why do they mass their warriors behind it? There is something dark afoot and it troubles me greatly.'

'Perhaps they mean to attack and have the fire light their way.'

'What kind of fool assaults a wall when the light is fading?' The Bull King snapped in irritation.

His brother opened his mouth to reply but gasped instead when robed priests began to douse the bonfire with buckets of water and throw sodden hay and green branches onto the smoking, hissing embers. The thick white smoke billowed lazily into the air before a great cloud of it was carried towards the fort on the light evening breeze.

Cinloch was quickly left behind as the warriors of the northern tribes surged forward across the frozen Vacomagi defences. Their young legs carried them on at greater speed in spite of the weight of their rectangular shields and the long, half-shorn tree trunks they carried between them. He heard the sound of wood striking the stone of the ramparts above him but could see nothing in the smoke of the warriors who now sent spears thundering down at them. Men screamed as they were struck down and others shouted out in defiance as the weapons thumped into their shields and knocked them backwards as they attempted to climb the trunks to the top of the wall. It was clear that a stalemate had been reached by the time he arrived at the gate puffing and wheezing from his exertions and the effect of the smoke on his lungs. The men holding the tree trunks in place now cowered beneath their shields and grimaced as spears and rocks battered down upon them. Some instinct caused Cinloch to step aside just in time to avoid being hit by a falling Carnonacae warrior. He winced at the sight. He thought she must have reached the rampart only to be struck by a Vacomagi axe. The blow had reduced her skull to a bloody pulp.

Spears thudded into the frozen earth around him and he thanked the gods for the smoke that prevented the defending spearmen from throwing more accurately. He thought he heard Drest cry out above him and he began to pull himself upwards to join the fray. His feet had hardly left the ground when he was knocked backwards by a man slipping and slithering down the tree trunk that now ran red with blood. The warrior's shield was broken and splintered and he threw it to the ground in disgust.

'I am sorry to have kept you from the fight, Thane Cinloch.' The warrior gasped breathlessly as he turned to face him.

'Talorc!' Cinloch blurted out in surprise. 'The fight goes badly for us! It rains corpses!'

'Never fear, good Thane.' Talorc shot back with a grin. 'Tis about to turn in our favour.'

Cinloch felt his guts clench in sudden fear. Talorc had drenched his face in blood and his eyes burned with madness as they shone out from that frightful and gory mask.

'Can you not feel it all around us?' The priest demanded with manic intensity. 'The Night God is with us! Great Tal has answered our call! Praise to him! He will bring us victory!'

'You will lead us to our destruction!' Cinloch shot back as he tightened his grip on his sword. 'You must persuade Drest to abandon this attempt! Can you not see that we are being slaughtered?'

'Listen!' Talorc hissed at him, cocking his head to one side. 'The battle already turns in our favour! Can you not hear it?'

All the Thane could hear were the sounds of battle, the grunting of men as they struggled for their lives and the screaming and moaning of those who had been grievously wounded. He drew breath to rage at the madman but stopped short when a distant crackling reached his ears.

'What is that?' He demanded, straining to identify the sound.

'That!' Talorc leered insanely. 'Is deliverance! The Vacomagi fleet now burns at its moorings! Hark! Their warriors falter now that they are attacked from their rear!'

Cinloch snapped his head upwards to where the wall was enveloped in smoke. He could see nothing more than shadows and vague shapes above him but his ears detected a subtle change in the tone of the battle.

'But how?' He demanded in confusion and disbelief.

'I sent Acotti warriors out into the sea in their little coracles!' Talorc crowed happily. 'Now the pride of the Vacomagi is aflame!' Talorc waved Cinloch towards him and smirked as if he had a confidence to share. 'But that was nothing. Behold Tal's power! Behold the ruin of the Vacomagi!'

The Drui then threw back his head and roared so loudly and for so long the sound of it caused Cinloch to grimace in discomfort. There was a brief silence before his call was answered by an unspeakable, animal shrieking. The Smertae horde came streaming out of the gloom like the legions of the Underworld. The sight of their charge chilled Cinloch to the bone. Their faces were painted red with blood, they held their sickles high above their heads and were so

116

burdened by the bags of bones on their backs they almost seemed to run on all fours. They did not slow as they reached the walls of the Bull Fort but ran up the tree trunks without pausing like some swarm of hellish insects. The night was filled with a terrible screaming before the last of them disappeared from sight.

Cinloch pulled himself stiffly up after them, the sharp pain in his knees causing him to hiss and clench his teeth as he climbed. His breathing was laboured by the time he reached the rampart but he found no warriors there to oppose him. He pulled himself over the wall and gazed down into the courtyard where the battle boiled and raged furiously. The flickering torches provided enough light to illuminate the slaughter. The Smertae sickles rose and fell with such sickening speed the defenders were unable to fill the holes torn in their shield wall. He watched as they broke under the relentless assault. More than one man slipped in the blood that ran in rivers across the stone flags and they screamed as the Smertae hacked down at them.

Vacomagi warriors now streamed from their places on the wall and ran for the citadel, not yet aware their path was already blocked by the sickles and the piled corpses of their comrades. Cinloch turned at the sound of men roaring in triumph and saw Phocali, Cornavi, Caereni and Carnonacae warriors spilling over the ramparts and running in pursuit of those who had repulsed them and slaughtered their fellows only moments before.

The Thane of Arder descended into the courtyard taking care with his footing on the slick and slippery stone steps. He called warriors to him and ordered them to throw the gates open so those still massed below the walls would be spared the exertion of scaling the heights. He picked his way through the tangle of corpses and wounded warriors, shaking his head in bewilderment at how many of them had been decapitated. Hot bile burned at the back of his throat when he realised the Smertae had taken the heads with them even as they advanced and threw the defenders back.

The Vacomagi collapse had occurred with such suddenness the gates of the citadel had not been closed before the Smertae reached them. Cinloch followed the trail of dead and the din of the battle raging within the confines of its walls. What the Vacomagi had intended to be their final sanctuary had become a place of slaughter. Groups of them turned and fought with great fury now that they were trapped but warriors of the northern tribes lined up behind the Smertae in their eagerness to wet their blades.

Cinloch looked for the Epidii and found them fighting alongside the Smertae with Drest in their midst. The best of the Vacomagi warriors had formed up around their king and they fought with a ferocity born of desperation. It was clear that the weight of warriors pressed against their shield wall could not be held for long. Cinloch pushed his way in beside his own house warriors and added his weight to theirs. He heaved at the shield in front of him and thrust his sword hard into the space that opened up between his shield and the one next to it. He felt the blade rip through leather and on into muscle and flesh and was rewarded with a roar of agony and a teetering of the wall before him. Half the length of his sword was coated in blood when he drew it back and he attempted to make the most of his advantage by gripping the wavering shield with his left hand and pulling at it in a bid to breach the wall. He jerked his head back instinctively and grunted in pain as a Vacomagi spear darted out and tore his cheek open just below his eye. All advantage was lost in that instant and he returned to heaving at the Vacomagi line until his legs ached with the effort of it.

It was as he rubbed the blood and sweat from his face that he saw Talorc striding towards the centre of the line with six Drui following behind him. He drew his hood up over his head as he advanced and then held his hand out for a sickle carried by the nearest of the priests. Cinloch found himself transfixed. He could not avert his gaze even though the Vacomagi were pushing hard at his back and one of them was furiously attempting to skewer him with his blade. He gasped as the Smertae line opened up before the priest even though he had given no order and not one of them had turned their heads to see that he approached. His mouth fell open in astonishment when the Vacomagi warriors also parted to let him pass. The battle raged on around him but no warrior seemed to see him and no blade or spearpoint was thrust in his direction.

Cinloch pushed himself to his full height to enable him to see over the heads of the mass of brawling combatants. He shook his head in wonder when the circle of Vacomagi warriors around King Garthnac meekly moved aside at Talorc's approach. They seemed blind to his presence and to that of the Drui priests. They continued to call out orders to their men and to snarl and growl at their attackers. The Vacomagi King himself did not seem to set his eyes upon the priest until he lowered his hood and spoke some words to him. Garthnac's head then snapped up in surprise and his expression turned to one of fear just as Talorc brought his sickle down with vicious force.

No man among the royal party or the King's bodyguard so much as blinked when Garthnac crashed to the ground, his legs twitching and jerking so that his boots drummed against the stone. Talorc then reached out with his left hand and jabbed his sharpened fingernail into the throat of the smaller man who had stood at the King's side. He flinched at the priest's touch and his eyes widened in fright as Talorc lowered his head and spoke into his ear. He then nodded and called out to the men around him. Cinloch did not hear what he said but saw his warriors turn in confusion before he repeated it. Some men dropped their weapons immediately while others argued before throwing theirs to the ground in anger.

Cinloch cursed and shook his head in disbelief when the pressure at his back suddenly eased and the Vacomagi shield warriors stepped back and let their weapons fall from their hands. Some men fought on before realising that the air was no longer filled with the din of battle. An eerie and unnatural silence fell over the fort and was only broken by the pitiful moans of the dying and the crackling of the oak ships as they burned at the quayside.

The suddenness and manner of the collapse created a moment of indecision as warriors gaped at both friend and foe in confusion and uncertainty. Cinloch recalled a similar hesitation when the Black Fort had finally fallen and men seemed unable to grasp that the long battle was won. Erp had acted quickly to seize the moment by climbing to the top of the wall to claim his victory and so strengthen his name as the leader of the Epidii. Cinloch had not forgotten the lesson and moved swiftly to ensure that the void created by the Vacomagi defeat was not filled by the Phocali or Carnonacae Kings. He ordered two of his warriors to hoist him up so every man and woman in the citadel would see him.

'All hail, Drest!' He roared. 'All hail, the conqueror of the Vacomagi!'

The call was taken up and the citadel resounded with cheering as Drest climbed the steps and raised his bloody sword above his head to acknowledge the adulation.

'Nicely done, Cinloch!' Talorc exclaimed from behind him, the bloody sickle still in his hand. 'I half feared he would fail to grasp the moment.'

'You killed the King!' Cinloch replied, his tone revealing that he still scarcely believed what he had witnessed with his own eyes.

'The first of many, my friend.' Talorc smirked. 'The first of many!'

13

Drest moved to consolidate his position with a speed that impressed Cinloch. The young warrior also showed a willingness to heed his counsel that both relieved and delighted him. He ordered the Smertae to stand guard over the Vacomagi prisoners. Less than five hundred of the garrison's two thousand warriors had survived the onslaught and his order was as much intended to protect them from slaughter as it was to prevent them from attacking their conquerors. His own Epidii bodyguard was sent to secure King Garthnac's hall and all of the treasures stored within it. Talorc commanded the Drui to empty the fort's cellars of ale and mead and distribute it amongst the thirsty and weary warriors. Caereni and Cornavi slaves were tasked with slaughtering fifty of the best Vacomagi cattle and roasting them over the kitchen fires and the new firepits hastily dug in the fort's enclosure. The air was already filled with drunken singing and the aroma of roasting beef by the time the Phocali and Carnonacae Kings came to the citadel to make their demands.

'I see that you have seized the Vacomagi treasury.' King Birst snapped from under his great, furrowed brows. 'Can I assume that you do not intend to keep all of King Garthnac's treasure for yourself?'

'You could legitimately claim half of it as it was you who initiated and led the assault.' King Forcus argued sourly. 'But you should not deny us our share. As kings, we could not settle for less than a quarter each. It would be an insult if you were to lay claim to more.'

'I make no claim.' Drest shot back from his seat on King Garthnac's throne. 'You were both reluctant to commit your forces and were not convinced it was worth risking your warriors against these walls. Despite your reservations, you sent your men and women to fight alongside my warriors. Hundreds of them now lie dead and the rest celebrate our victory. I will not insult you or refuse to reward you for your faith. The treasury here is filled to bursting and you will both leave with a full third of Garthnac's silver in your possession.'

'A third?' Forcus exclaimed, his face lighting up in delight. 'You will not take the king's share for yourself?'

'I am no king and will take nothing for myself. Every warrior who fought here will receive a fist of silver from my own hand. The fifty most courageous warriors will receive five fists of silver and those who turned the battle will have ten fists apiece. That includes the Smertae, who swept everything from their path, and those who sailed out into the night and set the Vacomagi fleet alight to distract those who stood atop the wall.' Drest then paused and leaned towards Talorc. 'Who was it you sent out in their coracles?'

'Twas the Acotti from the Isle of Birds.' Talorc replied. 'Shall I bring them here?'

Drest gave a curt nod before turning back to face his uncle and the Carnonacae King. Cinloch stood at his side and suppressed a smile. The two kings were so blinded by the thought of the riches they were about to receive, they seemed oblivious to the fact that all of their warriors were about to benefit from Drest's generosity. Such an act would be long-remembered and the personal loyalty it would buy would far exceed the value of the gifted silver.

'I know you are eager to ride south to come to the aid of your father and my sister.' Forcus began, his expression sly in spite of the forced lightness of his tone. 'You should go now and leave us here to attend to matters in your stead. We will follow on behind once we have razed the fort and executed the Vacomagi prisoners.'

'You can ride with me as soon as the silver has been distributed and our warriors have slept off the ale and beef that now fills their bellies. The fort is now commanded by my liegeman and he will lead his warriors south along with the rest of us.'

'Your liegeman?' Birst spluttered, his face creased in confusion. 'I do not know of whom you speak.'

'Aye!' Drest retorted cheerfully, showing no sign he had seen the look of disappointment the two kings had exchanged. 'Garthnac's brother is to take his throne. He has sworn himself to me and will lead the Bull People under my command. I will need every warrior I can muster in the days ahead and he can lead five hundred now and raise another five hundred before the spring.'

'You cannot put your trust in him.' Forcus insisted as he pointed across the courtyard to where Guram stood with his eyes set upon the ground like a whipped dog. 'You are a fool if you think he will be loyal to you just because you have set him upon his dead brother's throne! He will turn on you the moment he is able. It would be better to finish them here while we have the chance. Why risk having treachery fester in our midst?'

'Guram has sworn an oath to me and will repeat it publicly before the sun sets this day. His wife and three sons are to be taken into my household and will have my protection for as long as his loyalty endures. My protection also extends to him and he will have a bodyguard of thirteen Smertae warriors who will watch over him from one dawn to the next. They will cut down anyone who dares to threaten him and will open his throat if he causes them to suspect that he means to break his vow of fidelity.'

'I do not like it.' King Forcus grumbled with a petulance that came from knowing the argument was already lost.

Drest did not respond to the Phocali King's complaint but gazed towards the citadel's gate and the small group of warriors who followed Talorc through it. Cinloch thought they were dressed in tattered, black rags before they drew closer and he saw they had crow feathers sewn onto their cloaks and tunics and bore the insignia of a crow in flight on their chests. He inhaled deeply at the sight of the warrior who walked at Talorc's side. Her hair was as black as the deepest night and her flawless skin was so pale it was almost white. She returned his gaze with eyes so blue and piercing he could not bring himself to look away even as his cheeks reddened under her intense scrutiny. He did not think he had seen anything as beautiful as her in all his days. He finally forced himself to turn his head when she came to a halt before him. He saw immediately that Drest was just as entranced as he had been. The two young warriors gazed at one another in silence for longer than was comfortable before breaking into smiles of such warmth that Cinloch groaned aloud. All of his instincts told him that this Acotti beauty would bring trouble down upon their heads and he knew there was nothing he could do to prevent it.

'This is Stroma, the last Princess of the Acotti.' Talorc announced as his eyes flicked between the two in amusement. 'It was she who led her warriors out into the darkness to burn the Vacomagi fleet.'

Drest inclined his head and took her hand before pressing it to his lips. 'I owe you a debt of gratitude, Princess Stroma.' He drawled, not yet releasing her fingers from his grasp. 'The courage of your warriors turned the battle in our favour. You will have a hundred fists of silver to share among you as a token of my thanks. Much more will follow if you join with me as I go south.'

'We will come, sire.' She purred, her voice low and clear with a little hoarseness at its edge that was so appealing it caused the hairs to stand up on the back of Cinloch's neck. 'But not for silver. We will come for the joy of it, for the glory and thrill of battle.'

The two were so engrossed in one another that Cinloch decided to take his leave. There was much to be organised before they rode for the Black Fort and it now seemed likely he would be left to bear the greater part of that burden. He called his vassals to him and set them to work on loading packhorses and carts with supplies and with the grain, oats, household goods, silver and weapons looted from the Bull Fort. The Caereni had offered to drive the Vacomagi cattle south along with their own flocks of sheep but the value of the herd was so great he was reluctant to fully trust them with it. Refusing the offer would risk insulting them, so he graciously accepted it whilst insisting that twenty Epidii warriors be sent to assist and support them. He took his leading men aside and impressed upon them the necessity of keeping a count of the number of cattle to ensure none were lost along the way.

Several hours were wasted in reaching an agreement on the order of the march. The Kings of the Phocali and the Carnonacae were both adamant that their royal status gave them the right to lead the army. Cinloch seethed with frustration as he scuttled back and forth between them in an effort to find an accommodation they could agree upon. In the end, it was Talorc who broke the impasse with a sleight of hand and a gentle diplomacy that earned him the gratitude and grudging admiration of the older man.

'Of course, the Kings must lead.' He argued when Cinloch had managed to bring them all together in the fort's great hall. 'All the tribes must be represented. King Forcus and King Birst will ride alongside Drest, the Acotti Princess and the boy-king of the Caereni. I will take the place of Mamm Ru of the Smertae as she prefers to be carried by her warriors. I think I have covered everyone. Wait now! I almost forgot King Guram of the Vacomagi! He must have his place now he has sworn himself to us.'

Forcus and Birst took the bait just as Talorc had intended. Their opposition to the inclusion of Guram united them in common cause. Talorc was skilful in his manipulation and argued with them so vehemently even Cinloch found himself drawn into the debate to refute some of the points he so passionately contended. When he finally relented, the two kings were so taken with their victory they seemed to forget their previous insistence on sole supremacy.

'Very well.' The Drui conceded with feigned reluctance. 'King Guram and his warriors will make up the rearguard along with the Smertae. I doubt Drest will be happy but I will find a way to persuade him of the merits of the decision.'

'That was done well, Talorc.' Cinloch admitted as they watched the kings leave the hall still deep in conversation. 'I feared that their petty bickering would keep us rooted here for days. It is just as well, as I have received word that King Onnus of the Caledones has kept his promise. He has sent five hundred warriors and, although it is the minimum we expected, they should arrive here before dark. We will march south at dawn in greater strength than any of us dared to hope.'

'It is good that we will march without delay.' Talorc replied. 'The Black Fort is already under siege. The slopes around it now crawl with Manau like maggots on a rotting carcass.'

'The Drui crows have told you this?' Cinloch demanded in derision, though his every instinct told him it was true.

The near three thousand warriors of the army of the northern tribes turned for the south just after dawn. The column stretched out over such a great distance that the horse-warriors at the front could not be seen by the Smertae in the rearguard or by the drovers and carters who followed on behind. The speed of their advance exceeded all hopes and expectations. The ground was frozen as hard as iron and no time was lost in wading through mud or in freeing carts from earth churned up by the passing of so many men and horses. There were no complaints as Drest urged them onwards. The exertion of marching so quickly protected the warriors from the frost by causing their blood to pump to their extremities and keep them warm. The Epidii scouts rode in on the morning of the third day to breathlessly report that a great army now blocked their path.

'It must be the Venicones!' Cinloch announced as they crested a hill and caught sight of the ranks of warriors ranged across the floor of the glen beneath them.

'I will not be delayed!' Drest snapped. 'I will sweep the People of the Deer from my path if I must!'

'They outnumber us!' Cinloch protested. 'It will cost us both time and men we can ill afford.' He then turned towards Talorc with a sneer. 'It seems they have lost faith in the bargain you struck with them. Perhaps we were too hasty in praising you for your diplomacy!'

'You fret too much, good Thane.' Talorc countered dismissively. 'They merely seek to renegotiate now that the Vacomagi present no threat to them. King Uuid has no more desire to engage in battle than we do. He will attempt to secure improved terms and then lead his men back to besiege the Vacomagi garrison trapped in the Fort of the Mother. Watch! I will send him scuttling away with his tail between his legs.'

'You better be right!' Drest growled. 'Ride to them with me and do your work quickly! I will not be halted here. If they will not step aside, they will suffer the same fate as their Vacomagi masters!'

Cinloch rode forward with Drest and Talorc and examined the Venicone ranks as he went. The front rank was made up of warriors bearing shields and spears but the ranks behind were less well-equipped. They carried neither shields nor swords and were more plainly dressed than those they stood behind. He concluded that Talorc might well be correct in assuming this was a show of strength intended to wring further concessions from them.

'We should offer them silver.' He suggested. 'It would be better to buy safe passage than to risk a battle.'

'Hush now, Thane Cinloch!' Talorc instructed him gently. 'They will make way for us before our column reaches them. Have faith in Tal and he shall deliver us!'

Cinloch bristled at the mockery in his tone but shut his mouth as a party of twenty horse-warriors had left the Venicone line and started towards them.

'King Uuid!' Talorc called out cheerfully. 'What a pleasant surprise! I did not expect to see you again quite as soon as this. Allow me to introduce my companions. This is Drest of the Epidii, son of Mormaer Erp, conqueror of the Vacomagi and commander of the army of the northern tribes.' He paused and leaned towards Cinloch. 'And this is Thane Cinloch of the Arder.'

King Uuid of the Venicones gave a curt nod of acknowledgement but continued to stare at Talorc with open hostility.

'My wife is unhappy that I chose to place our son in the care of a one-eyed priest.' He growled. 'I assume he is safe.'

'Aye!' Talorc replied, his smile unfaltering in spite of the intensity of Uuid's gaze. 'He follows on behind in his little cart. I will happily return him to you, if you so wish, but that does not negate our agreement. I remain willing to honour my word and make him whole again and I expect you to keep to yours.'

'Tis not a matter of keeping my word.' King Uuid grunted with a shake of his head that caused the great antlers on his helmet to rattle against the metal. 'Tis a question of trust. Should I trust you to make good your word?'

'You have little choice!' Talorc shot back at him. 'Would you have your son walk again? Would you have him stand tall amongst his people or leave him to crawl on the ground like a broken cur? Would you have him named Uurd the Great or condemn him to be known as Uurd the Unsteady, the crippled king? Look to the mormaers and thanes who now stand at your side! The moment you are dead, they will rush to pull your broken son from his throne and take it for themselves! You know this to be the truth. You must decide whether or not to put your trust in a one-eyed priest. It matters little to me.'

Cinloch knew Talorc had hit the mark when Uuid cast his eyes around at the warriors of his bodyguard. These men might be loyal to him but their allegiance would not extend to an heir whose legs were too weak and twisted to hold him upright.

'I will let you pass!' He hissed between gritted teeth. 'But mark this! I will gut you from crotch to throat if my son is not returned to me in the condition you have promised. I give you my word on this and you can rely on me to keep it!'

'And I will let you do it!' Drest interjected with a scowl. 'You have my word on that! Now,

133

withdraw your warriors! I will not have my army impeded here!'

King Uuid nodded and turned his horse. The Venicone ranks broke up before him and ran for the forest. Their whole army had melted away before the tribes of the north reached the valley bottom and those at the rear of the column were unaware that any obstacle had ever stood in their path.

14

The Manau messenger groaned as he reached the Tae and saw two horsemen spurring their steeds down the slope below the Black Fort and across the frozen fields towards him. Red Cloak of the Manau had been clear in his instructions and he knew that neither Prince Edern nor his son, Cunedda, would take it well. Edern was sour and ill-tempered at the best of times and the cold and weary warrior steeled himself against the unpleasantness to come.

'Well?' Edern demanded before he had even brought his horse to a halt. The messenger bowed his head and kept his eyes on the ground in order to avoid having to meet the glowering Prince's fearsome glare. 'What says my father?'

'The King has commanded me to tell you that you are to hold the siege.' The messenger croaked nervously, not daring to lift his head and be confronted by Edern's cruel eyes and ugly, scarred cheek. 'He forbids any attempt to assault the fort and risk the lives of any of the five hundred warriors he has entrusted to your command.' The messenger paused as his guts twisted painfully at the prospect of delivering the next part of the message. 'He said that you must withdraw and pass command to your son if you have neither the strength nor the wit to do as you are bid.'

'Does the old fool expect me to freeze on this windswept hill and let Epidii warriors mock us from their walls while he sits warm at his fireside?' Edern exploded in fury. 'He might have lost his courage as the flesh has withered on his bones but it is intolerable that he expects me to follow suit and sit here like a coward and wait for starvation to bring Erp and his miserable people to surrender. I have the heart and men enough to storm those walls and bring slaughter to those traitorous dogs!'

Prince Edern was so absorbed in his rage he was oblivious to the change in the messenger. He no longer stood with his head bowed in fear but now gazed past Edern and Cunedda with his mouth hanging open in disbelief. Cunedda turned his head to see what so engrossed the staring warrior and his own jaw dropped in horror.

'Father!' He called out, his voice catching in his throat from fright.

Edern turned to snap at him but his fury died the instant he saw what had captured the attention of his son and the hapless messenger. The Manau warriors on the slope above them continued to go about their business just as they had for the past eight days. Those not watching and guarding the encircled Epidii stronghold were engaged in the mundane routines required for the smooth running of a military camp. Bakers baked bread, slaves carried wood for the kitchen fires, smiths repaired and sharpened weapons and herders attended to the cattle, sheep and goats seized from those Epidii farmers who were caught before they reached the safety of the Black Fort's walls.

Not one of them looked to the west and called out a warning as a great mass of horsemen charged out of the forest and raced across the valley floor. Edern kicked his horse into a gallop and rode desperately, screaming as he went. He had covered less than half the distance to the fort when cries of alarm reached his ears and his warriors began to run for their weapons and to form the shield wall. The thunder of hooves told him that it was already too late and he roared in frustration as the attackers accelerated up the slope and tore through the Manau warriors while they were still in disarray. Warriors turned and ran for their lives only to be cut down by spears and swords or trampled underfoot by the charging horses. Tears filled his eyes at the sight of his army being annihilated while he watched on helplessly.

He hauled on his reins with a savageness born of frustration and grief and ordered his son and the messenger to do the same.

'Tis that bastard, Drest!' Cunedda snarled as he pointed up the hill. 'See! It was he who led the charge and now he rides our men down from behind. We must go after him and make him pay for this outrage!'

'No!' The messenger exclaimed as he reached out and took hold of Cunedda's reins to keep him from the attack. 'There are too many of them! Look at their banners! The Epidii have brought

Caledone and Caereni horse warriors here! We must ride for Giudi and join with the King!'

'Father!' The young man pleaded. 'Let us ride him down and salvage something from this disaster!'

'Tis too late!' Edern proclaimed miserably. 'We must flee! Our army is routed!'

Cinloch was left dizzy by the joy of it all. Drest had not hesitated when he saw the Black Fort surrounded by the Manau force but had called for all horse warriors to follow him. No warrior refused to obey his command and they joined him in the charge without waiting for the permission of their chieftains or kings. They streamed after him as he tore across the open ground and cheered him as he battered and cut his way through the half-formed Manau lines. They now clapped him and drummed their spear butts against the ground as he rode in triumph through the Black Fort's gates. The walls were filled with Epidii warriors and their volleys of cheers were loud enough to deafen him. King Forcus and King Birst rode at his side, their pristine tunics and unsheathed swords standing in contrast to Drest's torn and tattered cloak and his blood-splattered face and arms. Cinloch could tell from their glum faces that they knew no one cheered for them, not even their own people.

The Thane of Arder smiled as he passed through the gates and saw Mormaer Erp and Brin waiting in the courtyard to greet them. Erp looked as if the strain of defending the fort had aged him by ten years or more. He was paler and more stooped than before but Cinloch did not dwell on this as his old friend was beaming with happiness and his chest was puffed out in pride at his son's achievements. The Mormaer and his wife greeted the various kings and chieftains and ushered them into the hall to partake in a feast before turning to embrace their son. Erp clasped Drest's shoulders at arm's length and held him in his gaze.

'I watched from the walls as you led the charge, my son.' He croaked, his throat choked with emotion and his eyes filled with tears. 'I thought my heart would burst from the pride that welled up in my breast. I prayed to the gods to return you to me unharmed and they sent me a great warrior instead. I wish my own father could have been here to see this day. I do not doubt he would have wept at the glory of it.'

Drest fell to his knees and took his father's hand. 'I would have crawled through all the fires of the Underworld to deliver you from these dogs. Now we will ride out together and put an end to Red Cloak and all of his kin. I swear that they will pay for every humiliation and insult you have suffered at their hands.'

Erp pulled Drest to his feet and embraced him once again. 'There will be time enough for that but now we must go and celebrate and give thanks to our allies. I set the servants to preparing a feast the moment I had sight of you. Come! Let us eat, drink and give thanks! Brude Uurad will sacrifice a stallion from my own stable.'

'There are important matters to discuss before we join the feast!' Talorc interjected from Cinloch's side as he pulled his hood back to reveal his torn face and dead, white eye. 'It would be better to address them before we step inside.'

Erp nodded and held his hand out for the Drui to kiss. 'Brin has told me of all you have done for us, Talorc. I must give thanks to you for your support and for laying aside all that has passed between us. I thought I acted in the best interests of my house but now know I was wrong. I swear that I will make it up to you when our troubles are behind us.'

'Now is not the moment to address these things.' Talorc insisted with a coldness that seemed to pass the Mormaer by but did not escape Cinloch's notice. 'We cannot deal with our allies on equal terms while we have no king to represent us. Forcus and Birst already bicker over who has precedence and only our victories have stopped them from pressing their claims more urgently. The Epidii throne has remained empty for too long! Now is the time for us to fill it!'

Drest nodded his agreement and turned to face the Epidii warriors who looked down at them from the walls.

'We were forced to leave our lands by the treachery of the slaughterers of Dal Riata!' He bellowed with such force his words echoed back at him. 'We then wandered like vagabonds with no place to call our own. We won the Black Fort through force of arms and spilled our warriors' blood only to cower upon our knees, deny our kingship and pay tribute to our enemies. Now we must stand upon our feet and cower no longer! It is time for us to defy those who would be our masters and take back our rightful place in the world! It is time for us to name our king so he may walk tall and no longer be forced to deny our heritage! It is time for us to name Erp, son of Uradech, as King of the Epidii!'

The warriors on the walls now cheered more loudly and with more vigour than they had when their conquering hero made his entrance. They made such a din that all those already gathered in the hall spilled out to find out what had caused such a commotion. Cinloch added his voice to theirs out of happiness for his old friend but, even as he roared himself hoarse, he saw that the proclamation had rendered two of his companions dumb with shock. Mormaer Erp was pale and wide-eyed with disbelief, an understandable condition given that all he had been forced to deny himself for the majority of his life had now been unexpectedly thrust upon him. Talorc's reaction was harder to read but it was not a happy one. Cinloch suspected him of hoping that Drest, still drunk on the victories he had won, would take the throne for himself. He allowed himself a brief moment to enjoy the Drui's disappointment before making his way to the Mormaer's side to offer his congratulations.

'I have dreamed of this day for as long as I can remember.' He told Erp as he accepted his embrace. 'I would part with every scrap of silver in my possession just to be in the courts of Red Cloak and the Alt Clut when they hear of it!'

'I just hope that Brude Uurad can remember the rituals.' Erp cackled merrily. 'He was little more than a boy when my father was raised up.'

Morbeth, Queen of the Manau, reached out in the darkness and shook her husband's shoulder.

'What is?' He murmured groggily as her insistent shaking ripped him from his sleep.

'You were groaning and thrashing as you slept.' She replied soothingly, her hand stroking his arm in a bid to comfort him. 'Was it the same dream as before?'

'Aye!' He croaked. 'The same as these last few nights. The one-eyed priest appears beside my bed and tells me he is coming to take my head. It is so real I can feel his breath upon my face.'

'Tis just a dream, Padarn.' She reassured him as she threw the covers off and went to rake the fire back into life. She then brought him the mead that would make him drowsy and allow him to sleep through until the dawn. 'Tis natural for you to fret when your son and grandsons have ridden out to quash the rebellious Epidii and bring them back to heel.'

'Is it any wonder I am worried?' The Manau King retorted. 'Edern lost five hundred men at the Black Fort because Erp betrayed us and brought Caereni and Caledone warriors to stand against us. I will have no rest until they have been defeated and Erp's head sits on a spike above my gates.'

'And you will have it!' Morbeth crooned softy in an attempt to pacify him. 'Edern leads three thousand Manau warriors north and Cunedda will soon join him with the five hundred he has raised in the south. They will trample the Epidii underfoot and send the northern mercenaries scurrying back to their holes. You are only unsettled because you are too unwell to command our army yourself. You know we are too strong for them and have yourself said it is time for Edern to prove himself to be worthy of succeeding you as king. All will be well, Padarn! I have warmed your mead over the flames. Come! Drink it!'

'You are right, of course!' Red Cloak replied with a smile as he took the horn from his wife's hands. 'All will be well. It is just the waiting that makes me plague myself with doubts.'

Morbeth returned his smile and reached out to stroke his cheek. 'What is this? You have cut yourself.'

The Manau King turned deathly pale and wiped at his skin before shuddering at the smear of blood upon his fingertips.

'Twas there that the one-eyed priest touched me.' He whimpered fearfully. 'His fingernails were black and sharpened to a point!'

The colour drained from Morbeth's face and she found she could speak no words that would lull her husband back to sleep.

15

'Is it set?' King Erp of the Epidii demanded as Cinloch reined in beside him.

'Aye, my King!' The Thane of Arder replied, unable to keep the smile from his lips at being able to give his lord the title denied to him for so long. 'The trap is set and our scouts report that Prince Edern's arrogance and haste for vengeance speed him and his army towards the springing of it! They will reach the slope below us within the hour. By the time they have sight of our horse warriors, the Caereni and Carnonacae will have concealed themselves in the forest to our east. The Vacomagi and the Maeatae will be in place below the banks of the Tae to our west and the Smertae, if Talorc is to be believed, will have looped around behind them!'

'I never thought to see a day such as this.' Erp chuckled wryly. 'I have long dreamed of facing Red Cloak in battle but always thought he would so outnumber us we would have to rely on our guile and ferocity to bring him to defeat. Now we command the greater force and our strength and cunning will lead to the slaughter of the Manau. If it was not for the pain and stiffness in my joints, I would think I was in a dream.'

'I just thank the gods we have been able to hold our unsteady alliance together long enough to reach this place.' Cinloch sighed as he nodded towards the summit of the hill where King Birst of the Carnonacae, King Forcus of the Phocali, Mormaer Manath of the Maeatae, Prince Donal of the Caledones, Princess Stroma of the Acotti, Mamm Ru of the Smertae and the boy king of the Caereni had gathered to watch the battle unfold.

'I just pray that we will win silver enough to bind them to us until the Alt Clut have been defeated.' Erp retorted wearily. 'They bicker like children and throw tantrums at every imagined slight and insult.'

'Not every insult is imagined, my King. Some are real and could easily have been avoided.'

'You are right, Cinloch.' The old king replied with a roll of his eyes. 'It is indeed unfortunate that my son has been so bewitched by the Princess Stroma, beautiful though she is. Mormaer Manath is quietly furious that his daughter has been discarded with such unseemly haste. Mael herself is less restrained and urges her father to break faith with us in vengeance for being cast aside. We will have to work long and hard to heal this wound.'

'I doubt we will be able.' Cinloch snorted. 'Mael is fearsome and headstrong and has her father's ear. I fear they will turn against us no matter what trifles we offer him.'

'Then I will offer him something so substantial he will be unable to refuse. I know how painful it is to be forced to deny your heritage.'

'You will let him reclaim his kingship?' Cinloch asked, his mind racing at the unexpected prospect. 'That will go a long way towards placating him. But what of Mael? She thought she was married to a man who would one day carry the title of mormaer. What salve can be applied to soothe her injury?'

'I must offer her a match of equal stature, Cinloch. Nothing less will suffice.'

'But who? You have made your brothers mormaers but both have wives already. Elpin's wife is sickly but she has been so for as long as I can remember and still she clings stubbornly onto life.'

Erp's eyes twinkled with mischief as he turned to Cinloch. 'You have been true and loyal to me all these long and empty years. I would be a poor king indeed if you were not rewarded for it.'

'No!' Cinloch protested, his guts clenching as he realised what Erp intended. 'She is like a wild-cat. She will eat me alive!'

'Tis already done, Cinloch! I will name you as Mormaer of Arder and grant you all the lands from there to Giudi when this battle is won. You will grow fat and rich with a young wife to warm your bed. Tis a small price to pay for so great a reward, is it not?'

'Was this your son's suggestion?' Cinloch demanded sourly. 'Would he have me clear up his mess so he might pleasure himself between Stroma's milky thighs? Has he learned nothing of responsibility after all we have been through together?'

'No!' Erp replied absently as he peered down the slope. 'It was Talorc who first proposed it and my wife agreed. She thinks you have been without a wife for far too long.' The old man then pointed into the distance. 'Look! We must put it aside for now. Here come the Manau dogs! Let us prepare ourselves!'

Prince Edern brought the Manau column to a halt and ordered his mormaers and thanes to array their warriors across the valley floor in fours ranks stretching from the scrubland on their left to the banks of the Tae on their right. The men were well-drilled and moved quickly to erect a shield wall that bristled with spears and sharpened wooden stakes.

'They have so many horses!' His young son exclaimed in awe. 'Surely we should advance to meet them and so prevent them from charging our line. They will gather such speed galloping down yonder slope, they will surely crash through our shields.'

'Do not fret, my boy.' Edern replied with evident fondness for his beardless and innocent son. 'These savages mean to win by force alone and are too stupid to recognise our superiority. Tis true that their horses will shake the earth as they thunder down at us but they will not breach our wall. See there! I have drawn our men up twenty paces behind yonder small stream. It will be obstacle enough to disrupt their advance and slow them. Our warriors are already busy driving iron spikes into the ground on this side of the stream. They plant them so thickly that few beasts will be spared the agony of having their hooves pierced and ripped. I doubt if more than half of them will even reach our line. Even then, the Caledone horses will baulk at the sight of a solid wall. They will turn into the path of those who follow on behind and reduce their charge to chaos and carnage. The Epidii have trained their horses to leap over barriers but any that do will be impaled on our ranks of spears. Then you will have the chance to wet your blade as we charge out to finish them. It is just as the Romans taught us. Civilised men will always triumph over base animals such as these.'

Typaun nodded at his father's words and smiled to show him he had been reassured. He was both nervous and excited at the prospect of being blooded and could not keep himself from touching the pommel of his sword.

'Stay close!' Edern commanded him. 'Men will sing of this day and record how we stood side by side as the last flame of the Epidii was extinguished. I will ensure that you do not disgrace yourself. Thrones are won and lost on reputation and you will need to show courage if you are to succeed me when my last day comes.'

'They come!' Typaun cried out, his eyes fixed upon the summit of the hill.

Edern saw that his son was right. The Epidii and Caledone banners were being waved and the mass of horsemen was moving slowly off.

'Come at us!' Edern bellowed to hearten his warriors. 'Come and die on our spears!'

The warriors took up his cry and roared at their enemies to hurry to their deaths. A sudden horn blast brought them to silence and men on the far side of the field began to call out in alarm. Edern turned his horse and rode towards them, his eyes searching for the cause of their disquiet. He could see nothing in the forest's shadowy depths at first but then detected movement in the gloom. He cursed when the first of the warriors emerged from the dark interior and cursed again when he saw there were hundreds of them. He barked orders at his thanes and they hurried to form a shield wall from the warriors in their rearmost rank.

'What banners are they?' He demanded of the head of his bodyguard.

'I see the ram's head of the Caereni, the serpent of the Carnonacae, the Phocali walrus and the Acotti crow.' Banna replied, his pock-marked face screwed up from the effort of peering into the darkness of the forest's edge.

'Ye gods!' The Prince exclaimed. 'How has the old bastard brought all these northern tribes against us? We scarcely left him with enough silver to buy the services of the Caledones, never mind all of these.'

'It matters not, sire.' Banna replied with a calmness born of the experience of a dozen battles and a dozen victories. 'Our shield wall is already set. These indisciplined curs will throw themselves against it in a frenzy and will be slaughtered without causing us to retreat a single step.'

Edern was buoyed by the confidence of the battle-scarred, old warrior and by the efficiency and speed of his men as they formed up and over-

149

lapped their shields to make an impenetrable obstacle. This momentary peace was shattered by a horn blast from the far side of the field. He spurred his horse into a gallop and clenched his teeth in fury as the third rank of the wall broke up and its warriors ran towards the Tae. He called for men to hold their positions as he passed them, causing some to return to their places and others to halt in confusion and indecision.

'Hold! Hold!' He cried. 'We'll need three ranks to stop the charge!'

His blood seemed to freeze in his veins when he caught sight of a mass of warriors clambering over the riverbank. He saw the bull's head banner of the Vacomagi and the three-spear insignia of the Maeatae. The first flames of panic began to flicker in his chest when he realised that Mormaer Manath had betrayed him.

'Form up! Form up!' He shrieked at the warriors who stood looking to him for direction. 'Get into line if you do not want my sword in your guts!'

He turned to look for his son and froze as he caught a glimpse of a shadow crossing the plain to his rear.

'No!' He whimpered as his guts clenched painfully. He knew well that even an army of civilised men will not stand when it is assailed from all sides.

The dark creatures raced across the grass in a swarm under their black, sickle banners. A light gust of wind carried a high-pitched squealing to his ears and a foul stench of corruption to his nostrils. He remained paralysed in fear and was oblivious to the thunder of hooves on frozen earth and to the sound of men crying out in fear as the Manau lines began to break.

'Typaun! Typaun to me!' He roared out in dismay. 'We must flee! We must flee!'

'How much further?' Cunedda demanded of the scout.

'Not far.' He replied, his face now barely visible in the fading light. 'Tis just this side of the Tae. See! You can see the moon reflected in her waters just ahead.'

The deepening dusk did little to conceal the horrors spread across the shadowy field. Broken spears littered the ground around the heaped carcasses and the air was so thick with the stench of blood and voided bowels it could almost be tasted. Cunedda bent to lift a Manau shield but it was so splintered it fell into pieces at his touch. Its surface had been hacked with such ferocity it was impossible to make out the Manau eagle painted on it. The trail of dead told the story of the battle. The piled corpses marked the ground where men had stood and fought in shield walls at the forest's edge, across the valley floor and on the bank of the river. The hundreds of bodies strewn and scattered across the ground spoke of men fleeing in panic and disorder.

'They ran?' He asked, though it was a statement more than it was a question.

'They did, my lord.' The scout replied. 'Though none escaped.'

'What happened to their heads?' He enquired as he fought to stop his voice from breaking.

'They cut them off, my lord.' The scout responded. 'They have spiked them on the branches of the trees at the forest's edge. Look! You can just make them out.'

Cunedda did not turn as he had already witnessed more butchery than he could stomach.

'What of my brother and my father? Did they fall in the battle?'

'No, my lord. They were carried from the field, though I could not tell if they were alive or dead.'

'I pray that they were dead.' Cunedda moaned miserably. 'Who carried them away? Did you see that at least?'

'Aye, my lord. They marched under the banners of the sickle and the crow.'

'Smertae!' Cunedda snorted, his lip curling in distaste. 'Even the Romans feared those foul beasts and their twisted, dark gods. How did Erp bind them to his cause? And the crow? That is the banner of the Acotti. It was said that they all died of plague on the island they fled to in order to escape the Emperor's wrath. How did it come to this? What possessed the northern tribes to stop fighting amongst themselves and come together with the decaying remnants of the Epidii?' Cunedda shook his head as if he no longer wished to dwell on it. 'They marched on Giudi then?'

'Aye, my lord. There was a great horde of them. They marched the moment they had looted the dead of weapons and valuables.'

'Then my grandfather is also lost. Giudi is lost. Come! Let us away! It seems that we must seek new lands for those of us who are left. We must go south and away from these Pictish savages.'

Red Cloak of the Manau reached out and laid the back of his trembling fingers against his son's cold, dead cheek. His warriors had washed him before laying him out on the hall's feasting table but the torn and tattered flesh was rendered no less horrific by the absence of blood and dirt. No square of flesh had been spared. His fingers and toes had been removed, his guts torn open and his manhood hacked away from his body. Morbeth sobbed at her husband's side but could not bring herself to touch Edern's mutilated remains.

'Why did they let you bring him to me?' He asked his grandson in a whisper. 'I know it was not a kindness. What message have you brought from them?'

Typaun recoiled at the venom in his grandfather's tone. They had left him whole but his face was so bruised and battered that only one eye remained open. His cheek had been cut open and the salt in his tears caused the wound to sting.

'King Erp commanded me to come to you to persuade you to surrender.'

'King Erp?' Red Cloak spat in fury, his face twisted in rage. 'He is no king! He is a beggar who turned on the one who fed him and his miserable people when I should have let them starve. I will never surrender to one as low as he!'

'Then he will assault the heights of Giudi and bring an end to our line.'

'No sane man would assault these cliffs. Go and tell him to do his worst. Greater men than him have made the attempt and each of them limped away from here having crippled their armies against my walls. Go now and tell him that!'

'We have fewer than one hundred warriors here, my love.' Morbeth reminded him gently. 'Go and look from our walls. You will see what a host Erp has brought to us. There are so many of them their camp stretches all the way to the crag. I doubt that our men could hold them off for more than a single day.'

'You ask too much of me!' He shot back. 'The Emperor himself fastened this cloak around my shoulders when I stood with him in Rome. Have you forgotten the honours he bestowed upon me? You must have if you now ask me to go and kneel before that ragged, Epidii horse trader! I will not do it! I would rather die on my own walls with my sword still in my hand!'

'They will not allow it.' Typaun replied grimly. 'A Drui priest promised Erp he would murder you in your bed if you were to refuse him. He said he would take your head and damn your soul to the Underworld.'

'What priest?' The old man hissed, the redness in his cheeks draining away to leave him deathly pale. 'What did he look like, this Drui?'

'His face is scarred, like it was torn by some wild beast. One eye is white and lifeless while the other is untouched.'

154

The old man slumped into a chair as if his legs no longer had the strength to support his frail and emaciated body. Morbeth let out a whimper and went to his side.

'Then the dreams were true!' The Manau King exclaimed breathlessly. 'I am finished. All is lost!'

'Not all.' Typaun countered. 'Your heirs could still occupy your throne if you were to spare Erp the cost of assaulting your walls.'

The old man held his grandson's gaze and laughed. 'I see now! He will make you his puppet and sit you upon my throne so he can turn to face the Alt Clut without suffering any loss of strength here. You, in turn, will use your royal heritage to demand loyalty from those few warriors left to us and command them to join with the Epidii and their northern allies. Old Erp is more cunning than I gave him credit for.' Red Cloak then paused and rubbed at his unkempt beard in the way he did subconsciously when there was plotting to be done. 'Very well! I will spare Erp from having to attack my fort but I will not debase myself before him. I will ride out from these gates along with any warrior who will follow me and we will charge at my enemies. That way, I will die a king with my head held high, I will escape the priest who has haunted my dreams and I will honour your filthy bargain with the Horse King.'

Typaun and his grandmother watched from the high wall as Red Cloak rode out towards the enemy encampment. They said nothing when they saw that he went alone and tried not to dwell on how disappointed he must have been when none of his house warriors had elected to sacrifice themselves at his side. They saw the horsemen trot out to meet him and held one another when the sun reflected off the old king's blade as he kicked his horse into the gallop. It was a mercy that they did not see the expression of horror on his face as he closed on the enemy and caught sight of the smiling figure bearing down on him from their centre. It was also better that they were too far away to see how his head rolled and bounced on the hard earth after Talorc's sickle had sliced through flesh, bone and sinew and separated it from his body.

16

The boy shivered involuntarily and drew back into
the corner of his bed as Talorc approached him.
The torchlight in the damp Giudi cellar flickered,
causing shadows to dance across the priest's
ravaged and disfigured face. The boy trembled
under the gaze of the Drui's dead, white eye and
fought to keep himself from crying.

'You are right to be afraid, Uurd, Prince of the
Venicones.' Talorc informed him. 'I promised
your father I would heal you and I will keep my
oath. It is a pity that the keeping of it will cost you
so dear.'

'I am not afraid!' The boy retorted defiantly,
though the tears running down his cheeks
betrayed his lie.

'That is good, Uurd. I am encouraged by your
fortitude. You will need all of your strength of
mind and heart if you are to endure. Now, tell me
what you would be willing to bear to have those
weak and twisted limbs grow strong enough to
support you in the battle line? What price would
you be willing to pay to walk tall and have men
fear you, rather than pity and despise you?'

'I would give anything.' Uurd replied, though
he could not stop himself from glancing over to
where four Drui priests were laying out hammers,

pincers and strange iron mechanisms that could only be instruments of torture.

'Good! Good! Then I will tell you the price you must pay. To make you whole, I must give you such pain you will beg for death. I will inflict such agony upon you that you will plead with me to stop and send you back to your father in your little cripple's cart. You must embrace your torment. The more you can suffer it, the stronger you will become. Tis the hottest furnace that forges the strongest blade! You must try to think of this in the days and weeks ahead.'

Cinloch groaned and clasped his throbbing head in his hands. Hot bile burned in his throat and his chamber seemed to spin whenever he dared to open his eyes. He grimaced in pain when the high-pitched screaming assaulted his ears once again. It was as if a knife was piercing his brain. He reached for the goblet at the side of his bed but the merest whiff of the stale brew caused his stomach to roll over and he had to take deep breaths to stop himself from vomiting.

The celebrations in Giudi's great hall had gone on long into the dark hours. The sun was already lighting the horizon by the time Cinloch finally fell into unconsciousness. The defeat of the Manau was cause enough for great rejoicing but even that had paled into insignificance when Red Cloak's cellars were breached. The riches found there had exceeded even their wildest imaginings. It seemed that the old fool had hoarded every treasure and chest of coins received from his

Roman masters. He had stored it away along with all of the cut silver he had extorted and plundered from his own tenants and those neighbouring tribes too weak to resist him. Erp had bound his allies more firmly to him by showering them in so much silver that even the greed of the Phocali and Carnonacae Kings was satisfied. While their eyes still glistened in an ecstasy of avarice, he had called for Brude Uurad and the Drui to perform the rites of kingship to set Manath of the Maeatae and Typaun of the Manau upon their respective thrones. Cinloch smiled at the memory of the satisfaction on Erp's face when the two new-made kings fell to their knees before him and pledged subservience and loyalty to the Epidii King.

He smiled brighter still as he recalled how Drest had conducted himself with a grace and maturity he had feared was beyond him. When Erp declared that he would name his son as Mormaer of the Black Fort as reward for his courage and leadership in the battles against the Vacomagi and the Manau, Drest had refused. When the gathered kings, mormaers and thanes protested, he stood firm and insisted that it was reward enough to be able to serve his father, the King of the Epidii. This proclamation was met with much cheering and a stamping of feet. Cinloch had become badly intoxicated at this point and remembered little else of what had transpired.

The Mormaer of Arder's reverie was brought to a sudden and unwelcome end by a horrible shrieking that seemed to bore into his skull and cause waves of nausea to wash over him.

'In the name of the Mother!' He cursed angrily as he forced himself to his feet and went in search of the source of the pitiful yowling.

The frightful noise was worse in the fort's stone corridors and he winced in discomfort as it echoed around him from below. The cellar steps were worn and uneven and he had to tread carefully as he descended because his dizziness seemed to increase the more he exerted himself. The screams of agony had thankfully reduced to a dull moaning by the time he entered the dark interior and found Talorc wiping sweat from his brow at the side of a makeshift bed.

'Maben's breath!' He exclaimed in shock. 'What have you done to the boy?'

Talorc looked down at Uurd and shrugged his shoulders. He appeared to be wholly unconcerned by the vivid purple bruising and the blood that covered the boy's legs. He reached down and tugged gently at the iron frame that seemed to pierce his young flesh and nodded with satisfaction when the slight movement caused Uurd to writhe and moan in his sleep.

'Some things must be broken before they can be repaired.' He announced in a flat monotone. 'It is the way of things.'

'His legs will rot now you have opened them up.' Cinloch protested. 'His father will come for you when he sickens and dies.'

'I doubt he will come when all the tribes of the north stand in his way. They would not let him lay

160

a hand upon my person.' The priest retorted nonchalantly. 'In any case, his legs will not rot. The Drui will pray over him while he sleeps and will apply potions to keep the bad spirits away.'

'You think the tribes will oppose the Venicone King on your behalf?' Cinloch snorted. 'King Erp will order them to stand aside and let you face the consequences of failing to live up to your word. Why would he risk all we have achieved just to save you?'

'Then it is well that my fate does not lie in the hands of good King Erp, is it not? Do you forget it was I who brought the greater part of the army now arrayed below this fort? The rest came only to take a share of the glory and riches won by the Smertae, the Caereni, the Cornavi and the Drui. If it were not for me, your master would still be mouldering behind the walls of the Black Fort!'

'I see now that you have come here with no good intent!' The Mormaer snapped, though the effort of doing so caused his head to pulse painfully. 'When King Erp offered you the hand of friendship, you refused to take it. Others might have been persuaded by your weasel words but I saw the truth of it. You did not offer forgiveness but said only that now was not the time to deal with the wrongs done to you. Be warned! If you are foolish enough to attempt to take revenge, you will find me in your path! No sickle or black-robed priest will keep me from you!'

'Calm yourself, good Mormaer!' Talorc implored him in a placid and even tone that stood in stark contrast to Cinloch's anger. 'I bear no ill-will towards you or your master. I am here only for my brother. Do you forget how Drest risked all to save me from the jaws of the slavering wolf? I owe him a debt I can never repay in full. I come only to repay what I am able.'

'Do not deny your ambition!' Cinloch raged as he pointed a finger at Talorc in accusation. 'The Smertae crone told me all as we wallowed in the mud before the walls of the Bull Fort. She said that you will kill three kings before taking a throne for yourself. I have seen you cut down two already and cannot help but wonder who will be the third.'

'There are so many deserving candidates. It will be hard for me to choose.' Talorc countered with a smile of amusement on his lips. 'In any case, Mamm Ru sees so many things it is hard for ordinary men to discern when she speaks the truth and when she babbles away in her decrepitude. I can only give you my word I will never lay a finger on the person of the Epidii King. Do not let your distrust distract you from what really threatens your master. If you do not deal with it quickly, you will live to see him torn from the throne that was denied to him for so long.'

'What threat?' The Mormaer demanded, his curiosity piqued even though he suspected he was being skilfully manipulated.

'It is good that King Erp washes his allies down in Roman coins and silver plate. It gladdens my heart to see them applaud him and bathe him in warm compliments. I do not doubt they will continue to sing his praises as they drive their laden wagons north to see the winter out.' The priest held Cinloch's gaze as he paused and tapped his index finger against his chin. 'I just wonder how he will induce them to return in the spring if he has already emptied his treasury to fill their coffers. Some might decide that they prefer to enjoy their new-found wealth instead of marching their warriors south to face the might and the fury of the Alt Clut King.'

'They will come to share in the treasures of the Alt Clut.' Cinloch insisted, though his mind was now clouded by doubt.

'Perhaps they will. I am sure you are right. I just feared they might conclude that Alt Clut silver will be harder won than the riches King Erp now pours into their purses. Weaker men might think it is better to enjoy what is already in their possession than to take the gamble of fighting an enemy far more formidable than any they have faced before. Tis just a thought. I would not relish the prospect of facing King Ceretic's hordes without our allies at our side.'

'No.' Cinloch replied absently, his mind already racing. 'That would not do. It would be better to hold back enough coin to speed their return once their crops are planted and their calves and lambs safely delivered.'

Talorc smiled as the Mormaer shuffled away. It amused him greatly to think of how hard Cinloch would have to work to divert Erp from the joy of buying the adulation he felt was due to him.

'Greed, pride and lust.' He told Uurd as he whimpered in his delirium. 'These are the chains that weigh down all men regardless of their rank.

The trick of it is knowing which one to yank if you want to see them dance.'

It was hard to tell if the boy appreciated these words of wisdom for he did nothing other than mumble incoherently and strain feebly against the bonds that bound him where he lay.

17

Erp came slowly back to consciousness. His forehead was hot and slick with sweat from the fever he had been plagued with from the moment he arrived back at the Black Fort from Giudi. None of Brude Uurad's potions or poultices had helped, even though he had spent the long winter months at his cauldron working on little else. Erp's throat was dry and sore from coughing.

'Brin!' He wheezed. 'I would have some water.'

'She is asleep, poor thing.' A voice informed him from the darkness of the chamber. 'She is exhausted from all those days and nights of sitting at your bedside and praying for your recovery.'

'You!' Erp hissed weakly. 'What are you doing here? Cinloch gave instructions that you were not to be admitted to my presence! Guard! Guard!' He called out in alarm, before being overcome by a fit of coughing.

'He will not come.' Talorc informed him. 'And even if he did, he would find nothing but a sleeping wife and an old man crying out in his delirium.'

'He will come and cut you down at my command.' King Erp retorted, though his red-rimmed eyes were now wide in fear. 'You must leave my chamber!'

'I cannot leave for I am not here! As we two speak, I sit in Giudi before twenty witnesses who watch me in a trance surrounded by my Drui.'

'So, you come to murder me with your dark sorcery. You swore to Cinloch that you would not take revenge for the wrong you suffered at my hand. You will be damned if you break your oath!'

'I made no such promise.' Talorc retorted. 'I only told Cinloch I would not lay a finger upon your person and I will not so much as touch you. If he read some other meaning into my words, I cannot be held responsible for his stupidity.'

The old man began to call out and thrash feebly beneath his blankets but his efforts brought no reward other than a severe coughing fit that seemed likely to tear his frail and failing lungs. When had expended what little energy was left to him, the chamber door remained unopened and his loving wife still snored on gently in the chair beside his bed.

'It would be better for you if you did not resist.' Talorc murmured in a bid to calm him. 'I come only to speed the inevitable. It would be better for you to die here and now and not when you have hauled yourself into the saddle to lead your armies south. Your warriors would see your passing as an ill omen and nothing must distract us from our task.'

Erp's emaciated face fell and he sagged back against his pillow. 'Please, good Talorc! I would live long enough to see the Alt Clut King humbled for all the humiliation he has heaped upon me. Then I could go happily to my pyre.'

'I cannot allow it.' The priest replied without any trace of compassion. 'You sent me northwards to my death because you believed I endangered your son by whispering in his ear of the greatness within him. I whisper no longer but speak openly and he now achieves all that I predicted. He will rule this land from sea to sea and it is my destiny to clear every obstacle and difficulty from his path. You are merely one such impediment. Do not think of me as an assassin. Think of me as a simple farmer who must burn away the old grass so the new can flourish when the old and brittle stalks have been turned to ash.'

'You will lead him to ruin!' Erp raged, his eyes flashing with anger. 'There was always something rotten in you. I saw it in you, even as a boy. Drest will rue the day he fell in with you and will curse you before he dies!'

'Perhaps so!' The Drui replied. 'That will be for the gods to decide. But from this day to that, what a swathe we will burn! What glory we will win! We will leave such a mark they will sing of us for centuries to come!'

Talorc then lifted his hands and held his palms open before him. He closed his eyes before clenching his fists so tightly his knuckles turned white from the strain of it. Erp clutched desperately at his throat as if he choked and drummed his feet hard against his mattress.

Cinloch paused at the chamber's entrance and addressed King Erp's bodyguard in a hushed tone.

'Who has crossed this threshold since I left for my chamber?'

'No one, Mormaer. I secured the door when you left and have not opened it since. Queen Brin remained at her husband's side and did not leave.'

'What of the priest and his damned Smertae crone?'

The guard shook his head emphatically. 'I have seen nothing of either of them and have heard nothing from the men in our pay at Giudi. They would have ridden here with word if either of them had left the heights.'

Cinloch nodded his thanks and took a breath to steel himself before entering the room. Brin came to embrace him, her face pale and her cheeks wet with tears. The serving girls had finished washing Erp's body but the air was still heavy with the stench of urine and excrement. Brude Uurad stood on the far side of the bed waving bunches of smoking herbs over the body while his lips moved silently in the saying of the rituals.

'He looks so small and old.' Brin wept as they both turned to look at the corpse. 'When did he shrivel away to skin and bone? I did not see it while he lived.'

'He died as a king.' Cinloch declared in a bid to comfort both the widow and himself. 'We have that at least. It heartens me to know he had that satisfaction before he passed. I know how much it grieved him that he was unable to make you his queen after the great disaster befell us. He always said he was both surprised and delighted that you did not abandon him for failing to give you what was promised on your wedding day.'

'I loved him, Cinloch.' She replied with a weak and miserable smile. 'And I know he had great love for you. It comforts me to know he had a friend as loyal and true as you to stand with him during the days of darkness and to share his triumph when, at last, it came to him. We two should have no regrets, though his absence pains us so.'

Cinloch thanked her for her sentiments and turned towards the bed to gaze down at his king's remains. The sight of so great a man in such a pitiable and diminished condition caused his eyes to fill with tears. The scratches on his neck and the grimace still etched upon his face spoke of a death filled with pain and fear. He kneeled down at the bedside and took Erp's stiff, cold hand in his and told him that his last wishes would be respected.

'I will go to the pyre to prepare for the rituals.' Brude Uurad informed him solemnly when he had raised himself back onto his feet. 'I still have the relics we used when we sent his father to the gods.'

Cinloch nodded. 'Good! I have roused every warrior to cut wood for the pyre and have sent riders to call every mormaer and thane here to witness it. We will raise King Erp to the gods before the sun sets on the morrow.'

'The northern kings and their men are due here three days from now. Should we wait for their arrival before we commit his ashes to the Tae?'

Cinloch hesitated before answering. 'No, good Brude. Let us do it as soon as they have cooled. It would be better for them to witness the raising of a new king rather than the burning and scattering of the old. We will put Drest on the Epidii throne before he leads them against the Alt Clut. They will see it as a good omen and will march all the more enthusiastically for it. The gods know I will need their strength for I promised King Erp I would cast a portion of his ashes into the sea in sight of the Fort of the Crag so he might join his ancestors there.'

The Brude raised an eyebrow in enquiry. 'The Crag Fort of the Epidii? You would need to unseat the King of Dal Riata in order to keep your word. Have we not enemies enough already?'

'All will be well, good Uurad.' The Mormaer reassured him. 'A man never has too many enemies so long as he faces them one by one.'

Drest turned his horse on the summit of the Romans' upper wall and watched the long column march in from the far horizon. The spring had been so dry and warm their passing threw up a cloud of dust that hung above the marching warriors.

'Did you ever think you would see such a sight, my King?' Mormaer Cinloch asked from a little further down the slope. 'I counted four thousand of them on the plain below the Black Fort when the sun rose yesterday morning and hundreds more still flocked in as we began to march.'

'I am glad you counselled my father to hold some silver back. These warriors return to have their purses filled again and others have joined with them in the hope of winning a share of our glory and our loot. I thank the gods that we now have strength enough to bring the Alt Clut King to defeat. I swore I would have him kneel to me and that I would strike his head from his shoulders to repay him for so humiliating my father. I have vowed to spike his miserable head above my gate and to return my father's eagle standard to its place within the Black Fort.'

'Tis a pity we were delayed here for so long, my King. The northern warriors refused to pass out of fear of the demons and spirits that lurk within the Roman defences.'

Drest, King of the Epidii shrugged his shoulders and let out a sigh. 'Tis hard to see what made them so afeart. The walls and ditches are so broken and overgrown that any man can see that only sheep and goats dwell here. Talorc did well to have his Drui speak some words and burn some herbs to drive the spirits away.'

Cinloch gave no answer out of a reluctance to praise the priest but instead feigned interest in something at the rear of the column.

'How is your wife?' Drest enquired, careful to avoid Cinloch's eyes. 'I feared she would tire you out.'

'She does!' Cinloch snapped back. 'I was as glad to leave her as she was to see the back of me. You have saddled me with a woman so bitter she can curdle milk with only a passing glance.'

'Mael will be unhappy for a while, good Mormaer.' Drest replied without bothering to hide his amusement at the older man's discomfort. 'But she is like a young and spirited mare. The harder and more often you ride her, the more compliant she will become. You must persist and do so knowing I am grateful for the service you have done for me. I will neither forget it nor fail to reward you for it.'

'I do not know if you will ever be able to adequately reward me for this. She is so full of poison and bile she wears me down with her complaints.'

'Hark!' Drest exclaimed, pointing to the south. 'A scout rides in and he comes on hard! He must have urgent news for us!'

Talorc came to join them just as the scout pulled his stallion to a stop. The horse was wild-eyed and strained against its bit as sweat foamed across its flanks.

'Their army awaits us in the glen beyond these hills!' The young man gasped, his dusty face marked with rivulets of sweat running down from his forehead. 'Their shield wall stretches across the valley floor with their cavalry placed behind it. I saw spearmen hiding themselves in the forests at either side before they chased me off!'

'They mean to draw us in so they can ambush us.' Cinloch concluded when the scout had finished. 'We should march around and outflank them. It would be madness to attack when they have had so long to prepare the ground.'

'That is what they will expect us to do.' Drest opined thoughtfully. 'Perhaps we should not so oblige them.'

'Let us turn the tables on them.' Talorc suggested from the depths of his hood. 'We should send the Smertae through the forest to outflank the Alt Clut warriors hidden in the trees. They are skilled in the art of moving silently and will be able to circle behind them and stay hidden until the trap is sprung.'

'Then they will cut them down from the rear just as they are set to attack our warriors in the shield wall!' Drest exclaimed happily. 'Their ranks will break in panic the moment they realise they are the prey and no longer the hunters.'

'Their shield wall will decide this!' King Manath of the Maeatae interrupted as he reined in beside them. 'The Romans taught them how to fight and they learned their lessons well. My father fought against them and always said that their lines could not be broken. You may throw all of your horse warriors and all of your spearmen at them but you will not break them. The horses will charge in only to shy away at the last moment and foul the infantry as they run in behind. It would be a slaughter.'

'It would be if we sent only the horses of the Caledones and the Carnonacae against them.' Drest countered forcefully. 'Your father never saw horses of the Epidii in the charge. They are trained from birth to go wherever their riders bid them. They will not shy away. They will smash those shields aside and tear great holes in their ranks with their flailing hooves. Our warriors and cavalry will then pour through those holes and make such a slaughter that the rest will turn and run.'

'Very well!' Manath replied, his eyes searching Drest's face for any hint of doubt or false confidence. 'Make sure your horsemen keep their discipline and do not go racing across the plain in their excitement. I will want my foot warriors close enough behind to reach those gaps before the Alt Clut have the chance to rally and fill the breaches.'

Drest acknowledged Manath with a slight bow of his head and turned to Talorc. 'Send the Smertae on. They must be in place before we come in sight of the Alt Clut dogs.'

'I sent them before I came to you!' Talorc replied with a smirk. 'They will be halfway there already.'

'You are ever impertinent, Talorc. I just thank the gods that you are my friend and not my enemy.' Drest laughed before leading them off.

They came in sight of the Alt Clut army in the middle of the afternoon. Four thousand men stood under their banners of the black, double-headed battle-axe. Their shield wall filled the glen from one side to the other, just as the scout had reported it. Drest brought the cavalry to a halt and set Talorc and his Drui to their rituals while the foot soldiers tramped into place behind them.

Cinloch stayed silent as he and Drest studied the enemy formation and peered into the thick forest for any sign of movement to indicate that

174

the Smertae were in place. He was still smarting from the praise heaped on Talorc and he kept his lips pressed tightly together for fear of revealing his petty jealousy.

'Tis good that you are cautious, Cinloch.' Drest said without lifting his gaze from the ground ahead. 'A king who surrounds himself with only hawks and wolves risks losing all to his impetuous nature. It is a wise king who chooses to also listen to the songs of doves.'

Cinloch nodded but found he could make no reply to a statement that was a rebuke wrapped up in a tissue of praise.

'Be in no doubt that your long service to my father is greatly appreciated.' Drest continued. 'But I will not risk you in the charge. I do not doubt your courage but it is no place for old men. You will remain at the rear and oversee the baggage at my command.'

'Your command?' The Mormaer raged as something snapped inside him and robbed him of all restraint. 'It is more than twenty years since I last stood in battle at the side of a King of the Epidii! It was I who helped your father carry your grandfather's body away after the slaughter under Maben's Rock. It was the proudest moment of my life to be at your father's left hand as he roared us on and up at the walls of the Black Fort when the air around us was thick with the spears of the Manau dogs! From that day to this, I dreamed only of seeing your father returned to his throne so I might fight at his side once again! After all those long years of struggle, you would dare to deny me the right to fight at the side of my King? I think not, Drest, son of Erp, beloved of Epona and King of the Epidii. Neither Tal nor all the wolves of Bladd could keep me from the charge! If you unjustly command me to go, know that I will not obey you and that I will take the consequences, whatever they might be!'

Drest stared back at him, his eyes wide in shock at the Mormaer's outburst and at the tears that now stained his cheeks.

'Very well!' He replied when he had gathered himself. 'I will not so dishonour you. We will strike at the Alt Clut together and I will not deny you your place at my left hand.'

18

'Why do they wait?' Mormaer Cluim demanded of King Ceretic of the Alt Clut, his eyes fixed on the distant ranks of horsemen.

'They stop to allow those on foot to catch up with them.' Ceretic replied as he waved his hand around his face in a vain attempt to swat the clouds of flies that swarmed around them. 'They will come when they have formed up and their filthy priests are finished with their dancing and their chanting. When they believe that their foul gods have been sufficiently invoked, they will charge forward like unthinking beasts and fall into our trap.'

'I do not like it!' Cluim persisted without taking care to disguise his sour temper. 'Not one of my scouts has returned since the sun reached its highest point and I fear they mean to distract us with the prancing of their dirty sorcerers. We should ride out now and scatter them before their foot warriors come up with them.'

'You forget yourself, Mormaer!' King Ceretic snapped back in anger. 'I have commanded you to stand so we might put an end to them this day. I will not have them dispersed only for them to regather and invade my lands again. I have had my fill of your sullen face and your uninvited criticisms! It has been a year since I took a small portion of your lands so it could be granted to my youngest son but still you sulk and moan like a spoiled child. It cannot be helped that the gods have blessed me with such potent seed or that I must find lands for every child that grows in the belly of my wife. If you cannot accept my decisions with good grace, then take yourself from my presence!'

'Then I will go and take my place in the line, my lord. My place is with my men. I will go and do your bidding there and, once again, spill the blood of your enemies so you might prosper still.'

Cluim dismounted without waiting for King Ceretic to give his permission and strode forwards through the ranks of warriors. They parted before him out of respect for his rank and out of fear of his knitted brows and glowering countenance. His fragile and fearsome temper was well known and no man wanted to give him reason to have them flogged or beaten to a pulp by their comrades. They had stood witness to his harsh and cruel discipline many times in the past and had no desire to be subjected to his brutality. Cluim gritted his rotten teeth, clenched his fists in frustration and muttered under his breath as he advanced.

'Move!' He ordered the warrior at the centre of the wall as he pulled him roughly from his place and put his own shoulder to the shield.

His nose wrinkled in distaste as his nostrils detected a foul stench in the air. It reeked so badly it overpowered the unwashed odour of the mass of men around him. He was about to demand to know which fool carried spoiled meat with him when a great shout went up and men began to rattle their spears against their shields. The thunder of it was so deafening it almost drowned out the rumble of the enemy horses as they reached the gallop and closed in on the Alt Clut formation.

'Brace hard!' He shouted as he steeled himself for the impact.

His words were lost in the din but the men were well-drilled and disciplined and had no need of his command. Those behind him immediately put their shoulders to his back to support him and keep him upright when the enemy came crashing in. He felt the earth shudder beneath his feet and held his breath in anticipation of hearing the sounds of enemy horses being thrown into chaos on being confronted by the solid barrier in their path. He did not see the great Epidii stallion as it battered through the shield wall. It threw men backwards with enough violence to crush their comrades' skulls and shatter their bones when they collided with them. Neither did he see the warrior next to him being trampled underfoot or know it was a flying fragment of this man's shield that cracked into his head and sent him crashing to the ground. He was oblivious to the flashing hooves above him and to the slaughter unfolding around him as his house warriors dragged him backwards through the already disintegrating Alt Clut lines. He remembered only the high-pitched keening that had filled his ears and left him wondering what poor animals were being tortured as the battle raged.

Cinloch nodded his thanks as he took the horn of ale from Uurad's hand. The Brude's makeshift tent might stink of mildew and rot but there was no denying that he could brew an ale sweeter and stronger than any other available in the shadow of the Alt Clut stronghold.

'Tis intolerable.' The Mormaer complained as he wiped the foam from his beard. 'He commands me to keep order during the siege and to make sure of our supplies but then gives leave to any man who asks to go charging off in search of loot.'

'Is it really so bad?' The Brude asked as he sucked ale from his moustache with a loud smacking of his lips. 'It's not as if the Alt Clut can threaten us now they have bottled themselves up in the Fort of the Heights. Their only way down is the ridge between the paps and it is so narrow that forty men could hold them there for a month.'

'That is what Drest says whenever I bring it up with him.' Cinloch grunted in disgust. 'He forgets how many warriors were lost in the opening battle and refuses to listen when I try to give him the count of how many were killed and wounded as the Alt Clut made their fighting retreat all the way here.'

'Aye! You must give King Ceretic credit for that. I was certain they would all be slaughtered when they ran from the field. If he had not used his cavalry to screen them as they fled, we would have run them down like dogs.'

'Instead, they fought a running battle all the way to their fort, turning on us at every ford and pass and forcing us to engage our horse warriors twenty times or more!' Cinloch blustered. 'Causing us casualties and delaying us until the first days of autumn. Now they will sit behind their walls and wait until the winter frosts drive us home. We should have every man, woman and child out gathering oats and barley to sustain us but Drest stands by while they all ride out to fill their purses and take slaves. Talorc has taken his Drui and the Smertae north in search of some magic that will bring the siege to an end. King Manath and his warriors scour the lands to the east of us and the Vacomagi, Manau, Phocali and Carnonacae Kings have all ridden south and fight one another for whatever spoils are left there. To make it worse, I hear rumours of two Alt Clut mormaers who have ridden to the far south-east to raise warriors there.'

'Then it is your duty to make King Drest listen to you.' Uurad told him. 'You must pull him from between Queen Stroma's fair thighs if you have to.'

Cinloch nodded and held out his horn. 'I will, good Brude. But only when I have fortified myself with more of your brew.'

Cinloch groaned as he came in sight of the shelter constructed for the Epidii King and his young wife. The area around it was as busy as a summer market. A long line of dewy-eyed supplicants and grim-faced petitioners stood patiently awaiting their turn to worship their warrior king or to seek his judgement in some petty dispute they deemed to be of high

181

importance. Drest and Stroma lay on the grass at the centre of the throng and basked in the early autumn sun. Drest groaned at Cinloch's approach and made a show of waving him away.

'Do not tell me you have been at your counting again, old man. I do not think I could bear it.'

Stroma pushed herself up on her elbows and shaded her eyes with her hand to see who her husband addressed. Cinloch felt his heart melt as she graced him with a smile of such sweetness it freed him from all of his feelings of frustration and irritation. She possessed a rare beauty and the mere sight of her raised his spirits more than anything else he had encountered in all the years the gods had granted him.

'You must not treat Mormaer Cinloch with such discourtesy!' She scolded her husband. 'Did I not tell you of how bravely he fought in the battle at the Glen of Tears?'

'You did not!' Drest retorted without bothering to look up. 'But I fear you are about to.'

'I saw him there just after leading my warriors through the broken shield wall. He sat upon his stallion as it reared up on its hind legs and thrashed its hooves at the skulls of the Alt Clut warriors. Even as he clung onto his reins, he slashed down at the spearmen with his sword and cut down so many of them his forearm was bathed in blood up to the elbow. The sight was quite magnificent and the courage he showed is deserving of our respect.'

Cinloch felt his cheeks flush hot at her compliments and at recalling the moment he had caught her eye in the chaos of the melee. The sight of her was burned into his memory. She, like all of her tribe, fought naked and with a ferocity that was breathtaking to behold. He had thought her to be a goddess incarnate as she hacked at the Alt Clut with rivers of dark blood running down her breasts.

'I do not doubt his courage.' Drest grunted as he pushed himself up. 'My father used to tell the story of the taking of the Black Fort. He would tell of how he started at the foot of the slope with a boy called Cinloch carrying his spears behind him. When he stopped at the top of those hard-won walls, he turned to find that the pale-faced boy had been transformed into a warrior who cut down at the Manau hordes in a frenzy. He said that his face was so soaked in blood that only the white of his eyes and teeth could be seen through the mask of gore. So, you may be sure that I know him to be a worthy warrior. It is only his nagging I object to. I know he means to vex me by berating me for allowing our allies to ride out in search of silver.'

'It is not that alone, my King.' Cinloch replied in the hope of gaining Stroma's support for his argument. 'I am eager to have us gather here in strength for my scouts report that Ceretic sent out two of his mormaers to raise warriors in the south. It is this intelligence that has forced me here to advise you that we must prepare to repel whatever force they might raise against us.'

'You should relax and take the time to rest your weary bones, Cinloch.' Drest replied with a dismissive shrug of his shoulders before lying back down and closing his eyes. 'I am already aware of what Mormaer Cluim and Thane Hen are about. Talorc told me of it before he left and has assured me he has it all in hand.'

'How does he have it all in hand?' The Mormaer demanded with a flash of anger. 'He has taken the Smertae and his Drui north on some fool's errand and has left us here to besiege a fort capable of holding out until long after cold and hunger have driven us away.'

'You know well that he is no fool.' Drest drawled as he opened one eye and fixed his gaze on the older man. 'The Smertae are bound for the coast and will return with prisoners from a village there that suffers with the plague. Talorc rides for the lands of the Venicones with coin enough to bring thirty of their best bowmen here. He will have them dip their arrows in the blood of the diseased villagers and send them flying over the walls of the Alt Clut stronghold. The Drui will then make sacrifices to the gods and the defenders will soon sicken and die. Talorc has promised it.'

'And what of the armies in the south? Will he magic them away with some dark sorcery? Has he promised you that?'

'Of course not, good Cinloch. He has sent Mamm Ru south to turn one against the other. They will destroy themselves and leave us to scale the Heights of the Clut and take possession of the fort.'

'You would trust our fortune to that foul hag? Tis madness to consider it. She teeters ever on the edge of insanity and cares for nothing other than the spilling of blood and the corruption of flesh. Did you not see what she did at the Glen of Tears? She had her Smertae creatures decapitate a thousand fallen Alt Clut warriors and nail their rotten heads to the branches of the trees. You would put your faith in such a depraved and twisted witch?'

'It's not that witch you should be worrying about.' Drest retorted calmly before yawning hard enough to crack his jaw. 'I hear that your wife makes her way here now. I would counsel you to take your warriors and go in search of silver for yourself. Something tells me you will need a great deal of it if you are to keep her from gnawing at your ears as fiercely as you now chew at mine.'

Cinloch looked at Stroma in the hope of receiving confirmation that he was being teased. Her sweet smile made him groan audibly for it told him that his suffering was about to increase significantly.

Cinloch pulled his cloak more tightly around his body but the morning air was frigid and he could not keep himself from shivering. He glared up at the walls of the Fort of the Heights but they stood in stubborn defiance of his efforts to will them to collapse.

'You should be warming yourself at your fireside, good Mormaer.' A familiar voice trilled cheerfully to his rear. 'A man of your years could easily sicken if the cruel wind was to chill him to the bone.'

'And whose fault would that be?' He retorted with more petulance than he had intended. 'We have suffered below those damned walls all through the hard winter months while your bowmen fire their shafts into the air. There has been no sign of the garrison sickening and it seems likely that all you are doing is providing them with kindling for their fires. Our warriors grow hollow-cheeked and fight amongst themselves while enemy armies hide themselves away and wait for us to weaken to the point where we are unable to repel them. It is high time you admitted your failure and allowed us to withdraw from this accursed place.'

Talorc placed his arm around the Mormaer's shoulders as if to comfort him. 'Come, Cinloch. Do not take your ill-temper out on me. I know what ails you. My Drui tell me that the fair Mael spends her days demanding silver you do not have and her nights demanding that you fill her belly with children you do not want. It would be enough to test the patience of the mildest of men.'

'Do not dare to presume to know what ails me!' Cinloch snapped, shrugging the priest's arm away from him. 'The source of my frustration is the absence of any sign of your stratagem bearing fruit. Surely, if the Alt Clut were afflicted by the plague, they would have started to tip the diseased corpses from their walls. All men know that evil spirits feed on the corrupted flesh.'

'King Ceretic is too clever for that. He knows such an act would reveal his weakness and encourage us to persist with our blockade. He conceals the pestilence behind his thick stone walls and prays for us to lose heart and take ourselves away. Even as we speak, the pile of corpses in his courtyard grows ever higher and each new day brings an eruption of boils on flesh that was clear and healthy only the previous day. Can't you smell it, Cinloch? Breathe deeply through your nostrils and you will detect the sweet and putrid stench of decay.'

'Tis difficult to tell.' The Mormaer sulked. 'We have been here for so long the ground beneath our camp is soaked in pish and is now more shit than earth. None of this will matter if we are attacked in our present condition.'

Talorc pulled his hood back and exposed his disfigured face. 'I know how much you distrust me but I give you my oath that you will not have to suffer here much longer. The wheels of fate are turning and Tal will deliver us before the earth and shit beneath our feet have thawed in the first light of spring.'

Cinloch turned to face the priest for the first time in the conversation and met his gaze. Talorc's ruined eye discomfited him, as it always did, for it felt as if it stared deep into his soul. The Mormaer shivered, though not from cold, before lifting his eyes back to the walls of the fort.

'We shall see!' He replied after a long pause, unaware that he was already alone.

19

The wheels of fate made one full turn and brought the Alt Clut army onto the horizon three days after Cinloch and Talorc's conversation beneath the heights of the fort. Three horn blasts transformed the camp from sleepy indolence to panicked disorder in an instant. Warriors ran in all directions in search of their weapons and their horses and called out instructions that were lost in the din. Mormaers and thanes bellowed and threatened until neat ranks were formed in spite of discipline grown rusty from lack of use.

'How many?' Drest demanded as he snatched his sword from his servant's hands after forgetting it in his hurry to pull himself into his saddle.

'Near eight hundred.' Cinloch replied smartly, his penchant for counting enabling him to make the estimate quickly.

'Seven hundred warriors!' Talorc corrected him with a sly glance at the Mormaer to take in his annoyance. 'Those at the back are camp followers, mainly old men, boys and cripples. They carry spears to give the illusion of strength. We so outnumber them that they cannot intend to fight.'

'The maimed priest is right!' King Forcus of the Phocali exclaimed from his saddle. 'They advance with their spears pointed downwards. They come to talk.'

'Look!' Prince Donal of the Caledones called out in his eagerness to impress Drest of the Epidii or, more likely, his comely wife. 'A single rider comes forward to parley. I doubt that we will see battle this day.'

Cinloch narrowed his eyes against the low winter sun but did not recognise the warrior who now rode towards them through the clouds of frozen breath coming from the nostrils of his horse. He came on slowly in his arrogance to show he had no fear of the mass of warriors before him. The Mormaer saw that his forearms bore a vaguely familiar criss-cross pattern of scars, both old and new, but could not quite recall where he had seen it before. The warrior's face was so swollen and bruised from battle it gave no clue to his identity. Cinloch only knew who he was when he opened his mouth to speak. Those same brown and blackened stumps had been bared at him at the gates of the Black Fort when King Ceretic came to demand his tribute.

'I have done what the hag demanded of me.' Mormaer Cluim of the Alt Clut declared as he reined in before them. 'Now you must keep your part of the bargain.'

'Where is Mamm Ru?' Talorc asked. 'I expected her to return here with you.'

'I neither know nor care.' Cluim replied with a shrug. 'When the battle was done and I had defeated your enemies for you, she asked for the head of Thane Hen. The last time I saw her, she was peeling the flesh from his skull and cackling as if she was demented. I left her there and came to collect what is owed to me.'

'How do we know you have done what was asked?' Cinloch interrupted him. 'Without the Smertae crone here to confirm it, we cannot be sure that warriors loyal to King Ceretic do not still skulk in the hills awaiting the call to come down and attack us.'

'You would question my word?' Cluim growled, his face twisting into a snarl as his hand reached for the sword at his belt. 'My servants have only just finished scouring my blade but I will happily soil it again if you would so insult me.'

'Do not think to threaten him!' Drest barked at him. 'I will tolerate no assault on any of my warriors, so would counsel you against it. Curb your temper and give answer to what was asked of you!'

'The only warriors left in Alt Clut.' He began, his decaying stumps clenched together in fury. 'Are those who stand behind me, those still trapped in yonder fort and those who followed Thane Hen and now lie rotting on a hill two days ride from here. Go! Ride to them if you will not take my word! But be quick about it! Your vile Smertae witch will have scraped the flesh from the bones of every last one of them if you delay for too long.'

'Very well.' Drest replied with a slight nod of his head. 'I will send men to confirm the truth of it but will take your word for now and will honour my promise. You understand the terms I have offered?'

'Aye!' Cluim acknowledged sullenly. 'You will set me upon the Alt Clut throne and, in return, I will provide a thousand warriors to march at your command. I will pay tribute in silver, grain and cattle and will offer up my wife and sons as hostages. I will also accept a bodyguard of your warriors to watch over me.'

'But first you will call all of your warriors here to watch as you kneel at my feet and swear loyalty to me as your superior and your king. Summon them now! I will hear your oath and accept them into my service.'

'I cannot give you a thousand warriors now!' He protested. 'I lost many men in the fighting and will be left with too few to garrison the Fort of the Heights when it falls. You must give me time to raise new warriors!'

'Then you will have to defend your walls with old men and boys, Mormaer. I will have what was promised to me and I will have it the moment you have kneeled to me.'

The siege of the Fort of the Heights came to an end just as the frosts of winter gave way to the weak sunshine and the first rains of spring. King Ceretic had remained stubbornly defiant in the face of plague and starvation but was brought low by base treachery. Men loyal to Mormaer Cluim within the fort's walls threw the gates open at his signal. They allowed his warriors to pour in unopposed and slaughter those defending the king

191

who had dared to strip him of his lands. The garrison, weakened and thinned by disease, was quickly overcome. Ceretic and his sons were overpowered and dragged from their hall to be thrown at the feet of the Epidii King.

'Here!' Cluim growled as he rammed the Roman standard Ceretic had extorted from Drest's father into the soft earth before him. 'I have done all that was asked of me.'

'Bastard dog!' Ceretic seethed at him, his face bloody and swollen and his clothes sodden and dirty from being forced to kneel in the filth of the camp. 'You will suffer for your treachery! All men will curse you for turning against your king! You are a fool if you think this flea-ridden pretender will honour his word when you have shown him how faithless and rotten you are!'

'It is you who is rotten, my King.' Cluim mocked him. 'I was ever loyal and true until you betrayed me by seizing my lands for your whelps. Lands that were ruled by my forefathers long before the Romans came to conquer them! All men know that no loyalty is owed to a king who breaks his oath to protect those who have spilled their own blood to keep him on his throne.' Cluim then sent a gobbet of phlegm flying into Ceretic's battered face. He turned to Drest of the Epidii. 'Do what you please with this wretch. I go to secure my stronghold.'

Ceretic showed no fear and met Drest's gaze steadily. The light rain had washed enough of the blood from his face to reveal how severely he had been beaten when he was dragged from the fort.

One ear had been torn away from his skull and the bones in his left cheek were broken badly enough to leave his face horribly misshapen.

'I will not beg for my life.' He declared. 'But will call upon whatever honour is left in you to spare my sons. Royal blood courses through their veins and it will add strength to the blood of your tribe. I have told them to submit themselves to you and they will do as I have commanded them. I also ask that you give me a death befitting a king. Drown me in the waters of the Clut so I might go to join my ancestors in the Underworld. Grant me this so the gods will smile down on you when you yourself are overthrown and are at the mercy of some other king.'

'I cannot!' Drest replied in a voice that was flat and devoid of feeling. 'You insulted my father and stood in defiance of my armies. I must make an example of you so others will understand the consequences of rebellion and treachery. I will behead you in the shadow of your own fortress and before the eyes of all who once kneeled to you. Your sons will not be held responsible for your false and perfidious nature. I will show mercy and give them good deaths by weighing them down with stones before casting them into the waters of the Clut.'

'Then I will curse you with my last breath and call upon the gods to rain pestilence and betrayal down upon you.' Ceretic raged at him, his face twisted in hatred. 'May you be the last of the Epidii and the one who leads your worthless people to oblivion!'

Drest unsheathed his father's sword as Ceretic raved and swung it down at his neck with sufficient force to part his head from his body and bring his ranting to an end. His sons wailed and wept at the sight of their father's head lying in the mud until Drest ordered Talorc to take them to the Clut so their bawling would no longer assault his ears.

The taking of the Heights of the Clut was a time of joy and great celebration but Cinloch found he could take little pleasure in the drinking and feasting that followed it. He could not complain about the share of the loot Drest granted him. The King was generous with all of his men and made the Mormaer of Arder twice as rich as he had been after the fall of Red Cloak's stronghold at Giudi. What troubled him was the manner in which the Alt Clut treasury was dealt with. He understood Drest's reluctance to send his own men into a fort so recently infected with plague but felt insulted when Talorc and his Drui were entrusted with the task of removing and administering its treasures. He tried to bite down on his jealousy but could not keep himself from accusing the priest of taking the greatest treasures for himself. Drest snapped at him in anger and berated him for his pettiness. The rebuke stung him so badly he absented himself from all of the festivities.

He was still sulking when Caledone scouts rode in to report that Dal Riata raiders had swept in from the west and were burning the settlement at Pert and laying siege to the Black Fort. His hopes of an early return to favour proved to be sadly short-lived when King Drest left him to command the baggage and the march of the foot warriors. He watched in misery as Drest, Talorc and the northern kings led the cavalry off to go to the aid of the garrison of the Black Fort. He suffered greatly on the slow advance north as Mael stayed stubbornly at his side and set about driving him to distraction.

'He thinks you to be too old and too cautious.' His wife told him as they plodded through the mist and rain. 'That is why he favours his priest. You counselled him to abandon the siege while Talorc encouraged him to persist with it. Does it not vex you to have him ignore your advice in favour of his?'

'Not at all.' He replied with as much lightness as he could muster. 'A wise king listens to many advisors. A wise and trusted counsellor does not lose confidence because of a single snub. Just a few weeks ago, he praised my performance in the battle and spoke of how his father had long held me in the highest regard.'

'It was not he who praised you.' Mael retorted with some vehemence. 'Twas his dark-haired bitch who sought to soothe you with compliments. She lulls you while casting her jealous eyes over the lands granted to you by Erp. I do not doubt that she whispers sweet words into her husband's ears and asks him to find lands for her brothers. Why should they be denied rich estates when a childless old man rules over more territory than any other

195

Epidii mormaer? If not them, then Talorc, the closest thing he has to a brother.'

'There is no truth to it.' Cinloch insisted as his head began to ache. The memory of Drest's attempt to send him to the baggage before the battle in the Glen of Tears gnawed at him even as he tried to banish the thought from his mind. 'I rode at his left hand as we charged at the Alt Clut, did I not?'

'Aye!' Mael shot back, the force of her loathing turning her beauty to ugliness. 'But for how long can you hope to occupy that position? He knows you promised his father you would scatter his ashes in the waves of the Short Sea. Once your vow has been honoured, what use will he have for you?'

Cinloch tried to dismiss her words as nothing more than the poison of a spurned and bitter woman but he continued to dwell on them even as the Black Fort came into view through the swirling fog. It did not help his spirits when he entered the hall of the fort to find Drest surrounded by Talorc and his allies as they celebrated the slaughter of the hated Dal Riata invaders. He accepted a horn of ale and listened sourly as Prince Donal of the Caledones and Typaun, the vassal King of the Manau, told of how Drest had ridden out of the shifting mists ahead of his cavalry and cut a bloody swathe through the enemy ranks before they even knew they were under attack. No place was offered to him in the inner circle and he felt the exclusion keenly as Drest basked in the adulation of the kings, priests, mormaers and thanes who had fought at his side in a battle Cinloch had played no part in.

He kept silent as Drest declared that they would now disperse and allow warriors to make their way home to plant their crops before returning in the summer to make war in the west against the dogs of Dal Riata.

'I will go to the homeland that was lost to us!' He roared as he thrust his silver goblet into the air above his head. 'But we will not go to conquer. We will go to destroy! We will scour the land of the vermin who came from across the sea and of those weak remnants of the Epidii who deserted my father and grandfather and chose to bend their knees to those vile slaughterers. I swear to you that I will take not a single coin in spoil but will give you leave to keep whatever you rip from the hands of my enemies in reward for your loyalty!'

Cinloch offered no counsel as none was requested of him. He stole away as the cheering and the drinking continued without him and went in search of his horse. He set off in the darkness, determined to enjoy his vast holdings for as long as he had them.

20

Cinloch dozed in the shade on the bank of the great pond to the south of the Arder. He had taken to fishing there each afternoon in order to escape Mael's constant complaints and to avoid the many requests and petitions put to him each day by his vassals, stewards and his household staff. Four fat trout lay on the grass at his feet and he sighed with contentment. His house warriors were close by, so he was not unduly alarmed when he became aware of the approaching riders. He screwed his eyes up against the sun and watched them as they drew nearer. A smile crossed his face when he was finally able to discern the outstretched crow's wings on the banner carried by the lead horseman. Queen Stroma of the Epidii commanded her escort to halt a short distance from him and came forward alone. She smiled as she dismounted and Cinloch thought it to be the most beautiful thing he had seen since he last set his eyes upon her.

'Good day, good Mormaer!' She called out as she came near to him. 'I hope I have not disturbed you.'

Cinloch pushed himself stiffly to his feet and kneeled before her as he took her hand to kiss it.

'This is an unexpected honour, Queen Stroma. Though it gladdens my heart to see you. Come! Sit in the shade!'

'Thank you, good Cinloch.' She replied with a smile sweet enough to bring a blush to his cheeks. 'Though I must insist that you address me as Stroma. There is no need for such formality when there are no servants to hear us.'

'As you wish.' Cinloch agreed with a bow of his head. 'I assume you have come to tell me that our campaign against the Dal Riata will soon be launched. I will be glad if I am right, for my warriors grow fat and lazy from lack of work. We took so many slaves from the kingdoms of the Manau and the Alt Clut that they have nothing better to do than spend their hard-won silver on ale and fight amongst themselves.'

Stroma laughed so prettily that Cinloch could not help but feel a pang of jealousy. Her spirit was so light and pure it served to enhance her beauty, whilst Mael's dark and sour soul made her far less fair than she appeared to be when her mouth was closed.

'I came because we miss you, Cinloch. Drest would have come himself but sought to spare himself from your wife's sullen scowling. Your long absence has weighed down upon my husband's shoulders. He is eager to have you at his side when he leads his armies into the ancestral lands of the Epidii. You were at his grandfather's side when he was overtaken by disaster and Drest would have you at his when the Epidii return there to take revenge for the wrongs they suffered.'

'I would not miss it for anything.' Cinloch replied. 'I was a boy when last I stood on Epidii soil and now I am an old man with more white than brown in my beard. I thank the gods that I will have the chance to return to stand in the lands of my ancestors. Just tell me when and where and I will bring my warriors there. You may rely upon it.'

'I never doubted it. Our allies will gather on the slopes beneath the Black Fort one week from now. Your warriors are to have a place of honour beneath our walls. Drest would have our northern friends see the full strength of the Epidii when they march in. Now, that is enough of business. I have gossip and am eager to share it with you.'

'Very well, but I must warn you that I am not completely ignorant of all that has happened in the Black Fort during my absence. Brude Uurad knows all and needs only a little ale to induce him to share it.'

'Then you will know it all already.' Stroma teased with feigned offence. 'I need not tell you of the great army encamped beside the Tae.'

'What great army?' The Mormaer demanded, his eyes growing wide in shock.

''Tis the army of King Uuid of the Venicones!' Queen Stroma gushed as she revelled in the joy of imparting news of great import. 'He came in force to retrieve his son from Talorc's care. It was such a sight to see! His warriors came with helmets adorned with antlers and wore heavy bronze armlets that flashed in the light of the sun. Brude Uurad told me they wear them to make their arms strong for the throwing of spears. You will see it for yourself as they will march with us into the land of the slaughterers and make common cause with us.'

'And how is the boy?' Cinloch asked, his mind spinning at her intelligence. 'When last I saw him he was in a lamentable condition and cried out in agony.'

'His legs are badly scarred but they are now straight and strong. Prince Uurd walked to his father and kneeled before him. I swear I saw a tear in King Uuid's eye. He sacrificed so many deer to show his gratitude to the gods that the Tae was turned red with their blood.'

'I can scarcely believe it.' Cinloch muttered. 'I thought it foolish when Talorc promised to make him whole and was certain the boy would die when he broke his bones and caused him such agony he begged for his throat to be cut.'

'I know!' Stroma exclaimed, seemingly oblivious to the disapproval in his tone. 'You would expect the boy to hate him for putting him through such an ordeal but the opposite is true. He worships him and has hobbled around after him like a puppy these last few months. Talorc has won us allies in both king and heir! We will march into Dal Riata with an army ten thousand strong!'

No man had seen anything to match the ravaging of Dal Riata. The brudes said that no greater force had been assembled since the High King Calgacus united the tribes to blunt the advance of the plundering Roman legions under the great chief Agricola. Drest's vast army advanced in an arc with the Venicones going ahead to provide a screen and stalk the retreating Dal Riata armies. The skills honed in the hunting of deer enabled them to shadow the enemy so closely that no movement went unobserved before being relayed back to Drest by mounted messengers. Every attempt to outflank their pursuers was thwarted by superior force and they were pushed steadily back towards the coast.

The progress of the invaders was marked by great columns of smoke rising into the windless summer sky from one horizon to the other. The destruction was so complete it sometimes appeared that all of the world was ablaze. Warriors grew rich on the months of unfettered pillaging. They disobeyed the order forbidding the taking of slaves and kept them just to carry their silver for them. The Smertae took to the slaughter with such frenzy they needed carts to carry the bones of their enemies with them. They nailed so many heads to the trees there was barely a branch left unbowed by the weight of skulls and rotting flesh.

King Drest called a halt when he finally came in sight of the coast and summoned his allies and his placemen to him.

'We will hold here.' He announced to them all. 'I will send the Smertae and the Venicones into the mountains to root out those who have taken refuge there. They intend to dart out and attack us before retreating back into the heights. The King of Dal Riata thinks he can wear us down in this way but I will not give him the opportunity. He has swamped his coastal strongholds with his warriors and we will leave them there to deplete their stores. We will harvest every last grain of wheat from their fields and leave them with nothing while we store enough to sustain us when we return for the final campaign in the spring. We will find them sorely weakened by the harsh winter months and will prise their starving warriors from their forts and empty their treasuries.'

The ensuing debate was hotly contested. King Forcus of the Phocali and King Birst of the Carnonacae were consumed by greed and argued for the campaign to be continued. They pointed at the Dal Riata forts in the distance and spoke longingly of the treasures hidden within them. Prince Donal of the Caledones and King Typaun of the Manau made common cause with their northern allies but were driven by a desire to prove themselves in battle rather than by an insatiable urge to further fill their purses. The Caereni, the Smertae and the Cornavi looked to Talorc for direction and, much to Cinloch's displeasure, so did King Uuid of the Venicones. It was Queen Stroma who called for silence and demanded that the opinion of Mormaer Cinloch be heard.

'Tis not a question of what is right and what is wrong.' He began hesitantly, suddenly aware that every eye was upon him and every ear awaiting his verdict. 'Tis a question of whether it is better to risk all against an enemy who is still strong or to wait until the spring when he is weakened by hunger and the ravages of winter and victory is more certain.'

He braced himself for the anger of those who opposed his view but none came. A hush fell over the gathering as warriors looked around the circle to gauge the reaction of their fellows. It was Mamm Ru who broke the silence from her seat upon the ground.

'The Mormaer is right.' The Smertae crone slurred. 'We have reaped enough to last us through to Beltain. Let us take what we have harvested and offer it in thanks to Tal so he may guide us to our destiny.'

Talorc met her eye and nodded his head in reluctant acknowledgement.

'I would be a fool to ignore the counsel of a man as wise and as courageous as the Mormaer. He has steered the Kings of the Epidii safely through the darkest of times and has brought them to within sight of a triumph none of us dared to imagine. Let us go so we might return to smash the Dal Riata slaughterers back into the sea.'

Cinloch blinked in astonishment at this turn of events and found himself struck dumb when the kings and mormaers spoke in turn to confirm their acceptance of what he had advised. He did not think anything could increase his satisfaction further until he became aware of Queen Stroma's gaze. She smiled when he caught her eye and gave him a wink of such coyness it caused his cheeks to burn.

A third of the army was sent away to oversee the harvest. A third remained in place to keep the Dal Riata pinned against the coast. The rest were ordered to sweep through the mountains and the barren, boggy lands of the interior to flush out those warriors who had hidden there to harass and harry the invaders. The Smertae and the Venicones proved to be relentless in the pursuit. Each day brought fresh reports of the capture and execution of warriors who had thought themselves to be hunters only to find that they were prey. King Uuid was taken at his word when he said he would no longer set his hounds to tracking the enemy for there were none left to find. The army turned to the east and carried its loot homewards just as the first flakes of snow began to fall and the first winds of winter started to bite at their extremities.

21

Those winter months were the busiest and most exhausting Cinloch had ever experienced. He rarely spent more than a single night in one place before being forced out into the elements to attend to the next important matter. The stewardship of his own lands alone was more than enough to occupy all of his waking hours. He was now also required to oversee the completion of vast new cellars at the Ern Fort and the Fort of Keld to store the huge quantities of oats, barley and wheat required to sustain their warriors through the spring campaign. Messengers from all of the northern kings pursued him relentlessly through the countryside with queries and complaints about how much grain and how many cattle they were expected to provide. He worked tirelessly to assemble an army of carpenters on the banks of the river Ern and set them to building enough carts to carry all of their supplies. They seemed to consume silver faster than they cut through trees for the timber they required.

Just when he thought he might have the opportunity for some rest, a messenger rode in from the Black Fort to inform him that King Drest had summoned him to his side. He could barely keep his eyes open as Drest and his allies pushed wooden markers around a rough map scratched into the hall's floor and argued interminably about the strategy to be adopted. The Phocali and Carnonacae Kings advocated most passionately in favour of dividing the army in three so all three of the most important Dal Riata strongholds could be besieged simultaneously.

'If we do not blockade them all.' King Forcus reasoned. 'What is to stop them from carrying their treasures away?'

'Tis true!' King Birst agreed. 'They will load their ships up and spirit it all away the moment they hear that the other forts have fallen.'

The sour-faced King Cluim of the Alt Clut was the most vociferous of those who formed the opposing faction.

'Only a fool divides his forces unnecessarily!' He snapped. 'Have you forgotten the fate suffered by my predecessor? If he had not sent some of us away, you would still be rotting in the mud beneath his walls.'

Cinloch groaned inwardly as the debate raged on, for it seemed to circle around endlessly with no conclusion in sight. His only consolation was seeing Talorc suffer as much as he was. King Drest had charged him with the responsibility of procuring sufficient weapons for the campaign ahead and it was clear that the weight of the task was taking its toll on him. The paleness of his skin and the darkness of the rings around his eyes spoke of long days of frustration and short nights of uneasy sleep.

'If you think carpenters are difficult.' The priest confided to him after one particularly long and fruitless discussion. 'Then I would happily trade them for blacksmiths. They demand silver and ore in impossible quantities and then complain that neither is of the quality they wished for.'

They soon found themselves united in more than just their misery. When they were pressed for their opinions, they overcame their personal dislike of Cluim of the Alt Clut and urged Drest to keep the army together. Like him, they were dismayed when Drest sided with the most avaricious of his allies just as his army was about to march.

'You said it yourself.' The King responded when Cinloch repeated his objections. 'They will have been weakened by the winter. I could march a tenth of my strength into their midst and they could not stand against it.'

'I pray that we will not live to regret it.' The Mormaer muttered to Talorc as they left the hall to finalise their preparations for the advance into Dal Riata.

The first days of the campaign were filled with wonder and excitement. Warriors marched across the foothills and the flatlands in an arc stretching from one horizon to the other. Cinloch and Manath of the Maeatae paused on the crest of a hill to oversee the advance and found themselves revelling in the spectacle.

'I never thought to see such a host as this!' Manath exclaimed in awe. 'I doubt that so many banners have ever marched together in all of history. No tribe can stand against us when faced by warriors of the spears, the axe, the crow, the sickle, the stag, the ram, the serpent and the stallion.'

'Aye!' Cinloch agreed. 'It is hard to believe how greatly our fortunes have been transformed. It was not so long ago that our two peoples were clinging to the earth by our fingernails with Red Cloak and Ceretic snapping at our heels. Now they are naught but dust and bones and we lead an army against those who drove my people from their lands.'

'We should give thanks to the gods for so favouring us, Cinloch. They will not hesitate to render us destitute and dispossessed again if they think us to be ungrateful.'

'I am grateful.' The Mormaer laughed. 'I am grateful for the lack of rain and thankful that the tracks have not been turned to mud. Look there! My carts make good progress and our warriors will not go hungry when they halt for the night. I give thanks to the gods for that. My life would be a misery if they lagged far behind. The kings, mormaers and thanes would line up to berate me for my failure!'

'You will be free of most of them two days from now.' King Manath replied. 'The army will divide itself when we reach the mountains of the Stallion's Back. Prince Donal of the Caledones and King Guram of the Vacomagi will lead their warriors north to besiege the heights of the Sea Fort and the Stone Fort. King Uuid of the Venicones, Typaun of the Manau, Birst of the

Carnonacae and Forcus of the Phocali will head south to blockade Brude's Rock, the Oval Fort and the Fort of the Fisher Folk.'

'That will leave only King Drest, King Cluim, Mamm Ru, Talorc and yourself to vex me as we advance towards the Crag Fort.' Cinloch retorted with a roll of his eyes.

'I am glad you did not mention my daughter.' Manath replied with a grin. 'I do not doubt that she also chews at your ears.'

Cinloch sighed. 'I will not deny that Mael is unhappy. She thinks I am too soft with King Drest and allow him to ask too much of me. It is like being trapped between two crows. When one stops pecking at my skull, the other starts rapping at me with its beak.'

'Then I will pray to the gods for the campaign to be short and smooth, good Mormaer. No man is more deserving of respite than you.'

Cinloch was grateful for his father-in-law's prayers and the gods saw fit to grant him peace for a full three days after the great army divided itself.

'Did I not warn you?' Cluim snapped as Drest and Manath of the Maeatae reined in beside him. 'Our path is blocked by the King of Dal Riata and all his warriors. He has too little strength to stand against our full force but outnumbers us here because you saw fit to cut our army in three. Now we must withdraw and hand all advantage to him!'

'How have they surprised us here, Talorc?' Drest seethed, his cheeks reddening in the face of the Alt Clut King's barbs. 'Tell me how your Drui crows missed such a horde!'

'King Loarn must be accompanied by a brude of remarkable power, my King. Only sorcery could conceal their presence from the Drui.' Talorc replied with a shrug. 'It matters not. We should give battle and finish them here. It will leave them with fewer warriors to defend their walls against us.'

'Give battle?' Drest barked in annoyance. 'Does your eye fail you? They have three warriors to every one of mine and they stand upon the high ground across the pass before us. Only a madman would charge in and waste his strength here. I must withdraw in disgrace and punish those who brought me to this.'

'I see more clearly than you, my King.' The priest retorted with barely concealed irritation. 'We need only outflank them to bring them to defeat. They are so confident in the strength of their position they will break when we attack them from both front and rear.'

'And how will we achieve it? Will you fly our warriors over their heads, my one-eyed priest?' Cluim snorted in derision. 'They will alter their position the moment they see our advance. We will have to withdraw and you will have to take your stripes as punishment for this failure.'

'But they will not see us, my black-toothed friend.' Talorc retorted sourly. 'For I will bring down such a fog that all sight will be denied to them. The Smertae will then lead King Manath and his Maeatae and King Drest and the Epidii around behind them. When the east wind blows to thin the fog, they will see you and the warriors of the Alt Clut here and will believe that our whole army still stands before them.'

'The sky is clear, Talorc.' Cinloch observed. 'The sun has already burned off what was left of the morning mist.'

'Then I must be about my work.' Talorc replied before signalling to the Drui priests and kicking his horse towards them.

'You know that he clutches at straws?' Cluim demanded of the Epidii King. 'You will not have us stand here while he prays and chants in the hope of delaying his punishment?'

'What does it matter?' Drest sulked as he waved his hand in the direction of the Dal Riata ranks. 'They will not move from a position of such superiority. It will cost us nothing to linger here awhile. I am in no hurry to embrace the disgrace of running from the fight.'

Cinloch remained silent for fear of rousing King Drest to greater anger. He kept his eyes upon the distant warriors who blocked the pass with a wall of shields decorated with the symbol of a running dog. He understood Drest's reluctance to turn to flight but knew that Cluim's assessment was sadly correct. There were too few of them to break the Dal Riata wall and any assault would surely result in their slaughter. The air remained stubbornly clear as the sun rose slowly to its highest point and the Drui chanted on and soaked the earth with the blood of dozens of animals.

'Will you stop your damned pacing!' King Loarn of the Dal Riata ordered his brother. 'You will unsettle the men.'

'I do not like it, brother!' Ferchar insisted, careful to keep his voice low so the men in the shield wall to their rear would not overhear him. 'This fog descended upon us unnaturally quick. Look! It is now so thick our rear ranks are lost in its whiteness. We should withdraw and find a new place to stand when it clears.'

'You jump at shadows!' Loarn shot back dismissively. 'You know well that fog comes in quickly off the sea at this time of year. If we are blinded by it, then so are these Pictish rats. I fear only that they will use its cover to allow them to crawl away from our swords.'

'They neither crawl nor flee!' The King's priestess proclaimed as she flexed her hands in the thick, moist air before licking at her fingertips as though she tasted them. 'Men still stand at the foot of this slope. They lack the courage to risk the rocky ground behind them when Lugh has stolen their sight from them.'

'What of the foul stench that wafts over us, Fedelma?' Ferchar demanded. 'It reeks of rot and decay. Would you dismiss such an omen?'

'Tis no omen, fair Ferchar.' She purred soothingly. 'Tis just the stench of the Picts. They are not like us. They are savage and filthy creatures who think nothing of lying in their own mess. Do not bend to your fears! Can you not feel the air quickening? A wind comes to disperse the fog and reveal our enemies to us!'

Ferchar bit his tongue for he did not share his brother's faith in Fedelma's powers. He thought her a fraud but had learned long ago to keep his doubts to himself. His servants had confirmed that Loarn often lay between her thighs but he could not understand why he would favour such a plain and loathsome bitch when he had the pick of all the women in his territories. The strengthening wind eased his tension a little and he sighed in relief when he caught a fleeting glimpse of the Pictish spearmen on the slope below through the shifting and thinning banks of mist.

'Stand ready!' King Loarn roared at his men. He smiled at the din of shields thudding together as they were overlapped all the way along the line to form an unbroken and impenetrable wall. 'Did I not tell you it would be so?' He asked his brother with a grin. 'See! They come at us! We will finish them today though the light is already fading.'

'Thanks be to Lugh!' Ferchar murmured to himself as the enemy spearmen emerged from the mist and began their march towards them.

'Praise him!' King Loarn declared happily as he took his place in the line. 'There are even fewer of them than I thought. Bang your shields, warriors of Dal Riata!' He bellowed at the top of his voice. 'Deafen them with our thunder as they charge at our wall!'

Ferchar crouched down behind his shield as the warriors of Alt Clut sent their heavy throwing spears high into the air. There was a moment of eerie silence as they arced up into the sky and seemed to hang in the air above him. Ferchar frowned in puzzlement when his ears detected a shrill and high-pitched screeching that caused his skin to crawl. He dwelled on it for no more than a single beat of his heart before the Alt Clut spears crashed down and snatched men from the middle and rearmost ranks. He ignored the cries of agony behind him and put his shoulder to his shield to brace himself against the enemy charge. He grimaced at the force of the impact but knew the battle was all but won when the Picts did not manage to knock his warriors a single pace backwards. He set himself to the grim task ahead and rammed his spear through the notch cut in his shield. He grunted in satisfaction when he felt it tear through cloth, flesh and sinew before crunching into bone. He twisted it viciously to inflict the greatest possible injury before pulling it back and thrusting it out again in search of a fresh victim to impale.

Ferchar's world was reduced to the area occupied by his shield and the spaces that opened up momentarily on either side of it. He dodged the sword blades that snaked through even the slightest of openings and was fortunate to suffer only glancing blows that tore the flesh of his forearm and his thigh. Those of his fellows who were grievously wounded, crippled or killed by such opportunistic blows were quickly replaced by men from the second rank so the integrity of the shield wall was maintained. He rammed his spear out time and time again until sweat ran into his eyes and his arm muscles ached and burned. He lost count of the number of times he hit flesh rather than enemy shields or empty air. He pushed himself on through his fatigue and extreme discomfort and was so intent on his task he was oblivious to the changes in the din of battle. It was only when another warrior took his place to allow him to attend to his wounds that he turned and froze in horror at the unfolding disaster.

The rearmost rank had turned to face a great horde of warriors charging out of the mist. They were led by ragged, blood-smeared creatures who ran without shields and brandished great sickles above their heads. They were followed by a greater number of men and women with painted bodies who charged in with spears and swords and carried shields marked with spears, horses, rams' heads and flying crows. Ferchar watched in despair as the lesser of the Dal Riata warriors struggled desperately to form a wall. The dark and bloody warriors darted between their spears and hooked their sickles over their shields before ripping them downwards and out of the defenders' hands.

The wall to the front still held but Ferchar knew it would begin to buckle and break as soon as men became aware that their army was assailed from behind. He found his brother and dragged him away from the fight. Loarn was bloody and still dizzy with the frenzy of battle and struggled to break away from his brother's grip.

'We must flee!' Ferchar hissed at him. 'The battle is lost. They crawled when the fog came in but not to escape us. They crawled over the rocky ground to outflank us. We must make away into

216

the mist and the fading light if we are to live long enough to defend your kingdom.'

'Fedelma!' Loarn stuttered, his eyes wide in shock at the sight of his army being put to slaughter. 'Where is Fedelma?'

'Your priestess is already away!' Ferchar spat. 'Much good she has done us!'

22

'You must not be disheartened, Loarn.' Fedelma chided him gently as he stared out to sea from the ramparts of the Crag Fort. 'These vagrant tribes and their Epidii King will not dare to assault our walls. You have held them here from spring to autumn and will hold them still until the winds of winter have driven them from your door.'

She reached up to stroke his cheek and offer him comfort. The wind buffeted his soft curls and made her think of him as a boy.

'My cellars are almost empty and no ships from Ireland will come to supply us now that the whole of the Carnonacae and Caereni fleets patrol our waters. Our other strongholds have fallen and the heads of the poor mormaers and thanes who held them now rot on spikes before my gates. My brother has been gone for almost three months without sight of a single Ulaid ship bringing warriors to aid us. If he could not buy us friends in Ireland with the weight of silver he carried away, then we are lost.'

'Do not dwell on our misfortunes.' She urged him. 'But think of what strength we still have. Our walls are still whole and are guarded by five hundred warriors. An army ten times the size of that camped below us could not shift us if you have the fortitude to persevere. We will prevail if only we can endure more suffering than those beasts who seek to unseat you. Think of your son and the throne he is to inherit.'

'You are right, of course!' King Loarn replied as he pulled himself to his full height and tried to shake off the feelings of lethargy and melancholy that weighed down upon him. 'I am tired, that is all. I scarcely sleep because my stomach is empty and aches from hunger and, when I do fall into fitful unconsciousness, I am plagued by dreams of my elder brother.'

'Tis only your mind playing tricks on you. Riagill was too weak to sit upon the throne. If you had shown mercy and let him live, the kingdom would have fractured into a thousand pieces as every mormaer and thane rushed to seize what he was incapable of holding. You should not torture yourself with guilt!'

'Tis not guilt, Fedelma. I loved my brother but he was too gentle for this world. If I had suffered him to live and ascend to my father's throne, the kingdom would have been lost and my family put to death. I had to spill his blood. There was no other way.'

'What plagues you then, if it is not guilt?' The priestess demanded. 'What causes you to toss and turn and suffer in your exhaustion?'

'It is fear. The dreams are so clear it seems as if I am back in his chamber with the knife still in my hand. His throat is already cut but he remains upon his feet and glares at me most horribly. One eye is the same blue that it always was but the other is as white as milk. He then points at me with blackened fingernails and mocks me with the last words I spoke to him before I took his life.'

'What words did you speak to him?' Fedelma demanded, though she was dismayed to see him become dejected once more.

'Don't run, my brother! Tis better this way!' A tear ran down Loarn's cheek as he spoke and his shoulders grew stooped again under the weight of the burden he bore.

'Come!' The priestess coaxed him. 'I have something to make you sleep and I will have meat for you when you awake. A full belly and some rest will restore your spirits!'

'You are like a beaten dog!' Mael snarled at her husband. 'You go crawling to Drest and Talorc when they summon you but you cannot see that they treat you with utter contempt. You have more warriors and lands than all of the other mormaers and most of the kings here but they insult you by making you master of carts.'

'Your judgment is skewed by your bitterness!' Cinloch snapped back as he hurried to pull his boots on so he could escape her assault. 'There is no greater responsibility than that of provisioning the army during the siege. Our men would starve without sufficient grain and cattle and we would be forced to retreat without securing victory. Drest values me, which is why he has entrusted me with this task.'

'If he values you so much, why were we allocated this pigsty while finer dwellings were given to those of lesser status? Why must we suffer the stench of pish and shit that clings to us even when we leave this hovel?'

'The servants have scrubbed and cleaned it a thousand times! We will not have to put up with it much longer.' The Mormaer grunted as he finally succeeded in pulling a boot onto his foot.

'They laugh at you behind your back and think you an old fool.' Mael scoffed, her face set hard in anger. 'I heard Drest joke about how you did not keep up with the charge as our warriors ran in at the Dal Riata rear. They all chuckled with glee at the thought of you hobbling in to arrive only when the fighting was already over.'

'That's not true!' Cinloch protested, his cheeks reddening at the accusation. 'My knee slows me down but I left the field with a sword as bloody as that of any other man.'

'He thinks you are too old!' She persisted with unnecessary cruelty. 'He will cast you aside when all this is done and he has no more need of your carts. He will award your lands to someone more able. You will see that I am right!'

Cinloch grabbed his cloak and ducked through the pigsty's low doorway. He strode away as quickly as he was able with one boot only halfway on. He gritted his teeth and resisted the urge to throw some rebuke back at his wife. Her words had stung him but he had no desire to rile her further and risk having her follow him out into the open to continue to castigate him. He spotted Drest and Talorc with a small group of nobles beneath the Crag Fort's heights. He quickened his pace and splashed his way across the muddy quagmire created by the early winter rains and the feet of five thousand warriors. Drest nodded to acknowledge him as he arrived before giving him a grin that suggested mischief was afoot.

'Come, good Cinloch.' He teased. 'Come and watch the Dal Riata priestess as she boils her cauldron on the walls and rains curses down upon us. It would be better for us if she was at my side as it seems my own priest has no more tricks for me. Perhaps she could work some magic and spare me from having to waste my warriors on those walls.'

Cinloch lifted his head and watched as the naked harridan danced behind the steaming cauldron and filled the air with shrill, discordant chanting. He felt his heartbeat quicken when she reached down and lifted a little infant high above her head. He saw it kick its little legs as she brandished it on high and winced when she plunged it down into the depths of the steaming cauldron. All the warriors around him held their breath as she pushed her arms and shoulders so far into the steam she was almost lost to sight. She did not move for long minutes before screeching at the top of her lungs and thrusting her left arm into the air. Only Talorc did not gasp in shock when they saw that the priestess held a tiny, white skull in her palm. Even Manath of the Maeatae and Cluim of the Alt Clut were pale and shaken by the sight of it.

'Tis a simple conjurer's trick.' Talorc drawled dismissively. 'The bairn was secreted behind the cauldron unharmed and an old skull hidden there for her to present to us. Tis merely a question of perspective, not sorcery. It is nothing but a show intended to strike fear into the hearts of the feeble-minded.'

'It is better than anything you have offered to perform for me.' Drest retorted as he hooked his thumb at the walls behind him. 'If you can call upon the power of the gods, I would bid you to do it now! Cinloch tells me that the cellars at Ern and Keld are almost empty. We will be finished here when there is nothing left to fill his carts.'

'You should not mock him, my King!' Cluim interrupted him. 'I saw him draw a fog from the clearest of skies. If I doubted his powers before, I do not doubt them now.'

'I have no need of my powers or of sorcery.' Talorc proclaimed with a shake of his head. 'When rats refuse to be drawn from their holes, we need only smoke them out. These rats will cower behind their walls though their bellies are empty but will throw their gates open and rush out if we deny them air to breath.'

'A bonfire?' King Manath exploded in disbelief. 'It would take a week and a forest of trees to build one large enough to shroud those heights in smoke! Even then, after exhausting all of our men in the effort, a light breeze would be enough to keep those bastards from choking!'

'What do we have to lose?' Drest asked, though his frown indicated that he was far from convinced. 'I would try anything to avoid losing warriors in an assault and the work will keep them from boredom and from killing one another.'

'It is your one-eyed priest who will be in danger of being killed if his plan does not succeed.' Manath grunted with a scowl. 'I doubt if all the kings here could stop their warriors from murdering him if all their labour was for nothing.'

The pile of wood at the foot of the crag grew painfully slowly despite all the men and women of the army toiling hard from dawn to dusk. The more trees they felled, the greater the distance the trunks had to be dragged across. The list of injuries grew as the week wore on and the Drui were kept busy tending to crushed limbs and axe wounds caused by the inattention of exhausted warriors. The Dal Riata jeered down at the workers and were vigilant and accurate enough to kill a dozen men with well-thrown spears as they struggled to heave new trunks into position. Talorc seemed oblivious to all of the dark looks and malevolent mutterings cast in his direction. Whenever the fatalities at the base of the wall were mentioned to him, he dismissed them with a wave of his hand and pointed out that every spear thrown was one less that could be borne against them. He remained composed when the wood was too wet to be lit on the seventh day and ignored Drest's complaints when the wind changed direction on the eighth and engulfed the camp in thick clouds of smoke from the smouldering trees.

'Have faith, my King!' He scolded him. 'I will make offerings to Tal and he will deliver us.'

'I thought you didn't need to call on the power of the gods for this!' Drest muttered as he stamped off in disgust, his eyes streaming from the sting of the smoke.

Cinloch crept out of the door of the pigsty on the morning of the ninth day and closed it behind him with sufficient care to avoid rousing his wife. He swore to himself and smiled at the wonderful sight before him. The thick column of smoke rose slowly into a windless sky and enveloped the Crag Fort in a shroud of grey and black. He mouthed a silent prayer of thanks to the Mother, for he was sure it was she, and not Tal, who had delivered them. He then ran in search of the King.

'It is time, my King.' Fedelma urged him. 'The Ulaid ships have attacked the Carnonacae fleet and have sent boats to carry us off. We must go! They will not be able to hold them at bay for much longer.'

'I should be grateful that my brother has come.' King Loarn coughed, the sodden rag at his face failing to keep the smoke from his lungs. 'I just wish he had not left it so late.'

'Hurry! Our warriors will pour out of our gates and charge at the Epidii pigs. Your bodyguard will screen us so we can get to the boats.'

'It will be a slaughter!' Loarn moaned as his priestess took his arm and guided him towards the courtyard. 'The way is so narrow that my warriors will be cut down before a wall can be formed. I should stand with them while you steal my son away. They should not be asked to fight when their king abandons them.'

'Do you forget what I said?' Fedelma hissed as she squeezed his arm hard enough to bring new tears to his eyes. 'It is only a defeat if you die here. A great victory will be won if you evade their grasp. We will buy new friends in Ireland and return to take what is ours. Your warriors will give their lives so you might escape. Do not betray them now!'

'You are right.' Loarn replied as he wiped at his eyes. 'Give the order! I will cut a path to the sea if I have to.'

Cinloch kicked at the sand with his boot and tried to conceal his feelings of humiliation and betrayal from his warriors. Mael's words haunted him and he could find no way to explain the insult away. To be denied a place before the gates was bad enough, but to be positioned on this miserable spit of sand was intolerable. No other mormaer had been kept so far from where the fighting would take place. He had been ordered to prevent the Ulaid boats from landing but none of them seemed to have any intention of making the attempt. They floated offshore out of range of his spears and their occupants seemed content to shout insults in their rough and savage tongue.

He watched on miserably as the gates were thrown open and the Dal Riata warriors charged out through the pillar of smoke and crashed their shields against those of his comrades. The steep slope gave the attack enough weight to send Drest's warriors reeling several paces backwards but Cinloch was not concerned. The line held and, even at some little distance, he could see that the fort's defenders were in a woeful condition. Their smoke-blackened faces were gaunt and thin from hunger and many of them coughed as their lungs burned from the effort of heaving against their enemy. He was so immersed in his misery he did not see the movement at first. A word from his most senior house-warrior was enough to draw his attention to the second wave now pouring from the gates of the fort. Half ran to support their comrades but the others turned hard to their right and began to scramble across the rocks towards the beach.

'The smoke is thicker on that side!' His steward exclaimed. 'King Drest will not see that they mean to escape.'

Cinloch turned to see the Ulaid warriors no longer bobbing on the water shouting insults and curses. They now heaved hard at their oars and sent their boats towards the beach at speed.

'At them! At them!' He roared and set the warriors of the Arder Fort charging across the wet sand.

He ignored the pain in his knees and the burning in his lungs to match the pace of those he commanded in his determination to avoid any accusation that he had arrived late to the fighting. The centre and the right wing crashed into the fleeing Dal Riata while the left wing turned towards the sea and cut down the first of the Ulaid as they splashed through the shallows. The half-starved garrison met their attack with a frenzy born of fear and desperation. Cinloch parried three blows aimed at his torso by a pock-marked animal who growled and cursed at him as he sought to cut him in two. Cinloch stepped backwards when he swung at him wildly, then buried his sword in his guts when the force of his intended blow left him momentarily unbalanced. A second snarling and black-faced beast immediately took his place and stabbed his sword so hard into Cinloch's thigh that its point crunched into the bone and lodged there. The pain it caused him was excruciating. It provoked such a fury in him he dropped his own weapon and punched his fist repeatedly into his attacker's face. He kept at it with such force he reduced his features to an unrecognisable pulp of gore and splintered bone.

When he paused to wrench the blade from his thigh, he saw that many of the fleeing garrison had reached the Ulaid boats and were now pulling themselves aboard. The sailors on the nearest craft were crying out in alarm as the weight of men and women clinging to its bows was causing their vessel to list precariously. Cinloch gripped hard on the Dal Riata sword blade and allowed himself a wry grin as the boat capsized and sent its thrashing cargo spilling into the waves. He pulled hard at the blade and gasped as a bolt of agony shot through him as it ground against the bone on its way out. He was still panting on the wet sand when he saw Talorc striding past him with three Drui on either side of him.

The priests carried no weapons and made no attempt to engage with the enemy. Cinloch pushed himself to his feet and limped after them. They passed through the mass of warriors locked in their struggle for life and death as if they were not there. No eyes turned towards them and no weapons were raised against them. Cinloch followed in their wake with his sword held ready but the enemy combatants seemed to gaze right through him and thrust neither sword nor spear in his direction.

'Hold there!' Talorc thundered at a small group making their way across the rocks.

The man at their head halted and seemed to freeze in shock. The woman behind him turned pale at the sight of the one-eyed priest and pushed at his shoulder to urge him on. When he did not respond, she turned to the warriors who escorted them.

'Get the boy away!' She ordered them. 'His uncle will shower you in silver if you deliver his nephew to him. Go now! I will stand with the King!'

Cinloch now recognised her as the priestess who had danced above them on the walls of the fort. She advanced on Talorc with her right hand held out before her and tried to bring him to a stop. The priest did nothing more than gently waft his left hand towards her but she reacted as if she had been struck with brutal force. Her back arched as her feet were lifted from the ground and she crashed down onto the rocks hard enough to knock the breath from her lungs.

'You!' The Dal Riata King hissed at Talorc, his eyes wide in fright.

'Do not run, brother!' The priest ordered him in a voice that was not his own. 'Tis better this way!'

Talorc reached out as he closed on the terrified Loarn and pressed the point of his blackened fingernail into the centre of his forehead. The touch was too gentle to break his skin but it caused him to collapse to the ground as if his spine had been severed. Cinloch gazed down at his dead and sightless eyes in stupefaction.

'But how?' He stammered in confusion. 'You barely laid a finger upon him!'

'The how of it matters little, good Cinloch.' The priest replied as he gestured at the Drui to lift Loarn's corpse. 'What matters is the fact that the Dal Riata King is dead. Our fight is done. Drest is now the most powerful king to have ruled these lands. It is his destiny.'

'And what of you, Talorc? What is your destiny?' The Mormaer demanded, raising his voice enough to be heard over the din of the slaughter. 'Mamm Ru said that you would slaughter three kings before ascending to a throne of your own. I watched as you took the lives of King Garthnac of the Vacomagi, Red Cloak of the Manau and now Loarn of the Dal Riata. I cannot help but wonder what kingdom is the focus of your own ambition.'

'You worry too much, Cinloch.' The priest replied in amusement. 'Are there not kingdoms enough for all of us?'

23

The Crag Fort's hall was crowded with warriors and Cinloch had to push his way through the gathered kings, mormaers and thanes as he hobbled towards the front. He found Drest sitting upon the elaborately carved wooden throne so recently vacated by Loarn of the Dal Riata.

'It will not do!' Brude Uurad fussed with a shake of his head that caused his long, snow-white locks to fall across his face. 'The Epidii King should not sit upon a throne decorated with the likeness of the Hound of Lugh. I will have our carpenters rub the wood down and replace it with a carving of Epona or the Great Stallion.'

'Leave it!' Drest ordered him. 'It will remind those who sit here in the years to come of the danger posed by the slaughterers from across the Short Sea. Perhaps it will serve as a warning of the cost of neglecting the threat and of placing undue trust in those who would unseat us.'

'Of course, my King' Uurad replied with a bow of his head. 'In any case, there are more important matters to be decided. The division of spoils, the fate of the prisoners and what is to be done with the Dal Riata priestess. These must all be resolved before our army breaks up and our warriors turn for home for the winter.'

'Then it will not take us long, good Brude.' Drest replied. 'I will take one third of the spoil and the rest will be divided amongst the kings and mormaers. Talorc will choose what treasures are to be retained on my behalf and will see to distributing the rest fairly. The prisoners are to be executed. I will not suffer a single one of them to live and remain in the lands they stole from my father. Talorc will see to it all.'

'I will give them to the Smertae.' The priest declared. 'I have no doubt they will despatch them most efficiently. I will spare only those craftsmen who will be useful to us. The Dal Riata boast some highly skilled carpenters, blacksmiths, fletchers and silversmiths. I will take them from the lands of the Epidii and press them into our service at the Black Fort.'

'Very well.' Drest agreed, though the way his nose wrinkled in distaste indicated that he was not wholly pleased with the suggestion. 'What of the priestess, Talorc? Did you examine her cauldron to see how the trick with the infant was done?'

'I did, my King, though it was the damnedest thing. When I ran my fingers through the cloudy water at its bottom, I found the bones and the boiled flesh of a baby. It seems it was no trick at all.'

'If that is the case, then perhaps I should take her into my service and harness her powers for myself.'

'Perhaps you should, my King.' He retorted. 'Though you should also consider the fate of her previous master. I hope she will serve you better than he.'

Drest grinned from the pleasure of eliciting such a peevish response from the normally unflappable priest.

'Do what you will with her. I leave her fate entirely in your hands. Now come! Brude Uurad insists that I allow him to conduct some ancient ritual.'

Cinloch followed the royal party as they left the hall and made their way down from the upper enclosure. He winced at the pain that shot through his leg with each step and fought to rise above the sting of rejection that threatened to overcome him. He groaned when Mael fell in at his side and gripped his arm in a show of offering support to her wounded husband.

'Did I not tell you so?' She whispered close to his ear as he limped along in his misery. 'He gives all responsibility to his priest and leaves you with nothing but your empty carts. You will be lucky to still hold your lands by the time winter is done.'

He made no attempt to refute her argument for he feared she was right. He was even grateful for her arm and the little comfort her touch provided. He hardly listened as Uurad explained the ritual he was about to perform. He knew of the footprint left in the rock below the fort by the first Epidii King, Eochaid, when he stamped his foot down to assert his authority. He also knew that every subsequent king, apart from Erp and Drest, had been anointed in oil as they placed their right foot in that same sacred indentation as part of their coronation rites. It should have filled him with satisfaction to see the ritual completed in the Epidii capital but he found he was unable to take any pleasure in it. Brude Uurad's singing of the Song of the Epidii brought him no joy even though the ending was now one of triumph and glory rather than the one filled with the woe of wandering and submission that had been sung for most of his life. He clapped along with the rest when the performance was done but did not cheer or even muster a smile. He thought only of reaching the sanctuary of his own hall when he turned to take his leave. A hand closed on his forearm from behind and brought him to an abrupt halt.

'Stay, good Cinloch.' Talorc instructed him quietly, his lips so close to his ear that he felt his breath against it. 'I would not have you miss this.'

The crowd parted as two Drui helped Mamm Ru shuffle forward until she stood at Drest's feet. She had grown more stooped and feeble since Cinloch last saw her but her eyes shone with an intensity that captured the attention of all the gathered nobles. They fell into an uneasy and expectant silence. Cinloch felt an overwhelming sense of dread wash over him.

'What foul business is this?' He hissed at Talorc. 'I know well that the Smertae crone does your bidding.'

'The wheel of fate has turned one full circle, good Mormaer.' The priest replied with a wink. 'We are the spokes and Mamm Ru the axle. Watch on as she spins us once again.'

'Behold!' The shrunken hag cried out in a voice of surprising strength and clarity for one so emaciated and so frail. 'The Wolf-Torn King of prophecy has delivered us from our enemies. Drest, Blood King of the Epidii, King of kings, great slaughterer and master of all the lands from the Dead Grey Sea to the Wall of Shame! All hail, King Drest, who will lead us all to glory! All hail, King Drest, who led the northern tribes and soaked the earth in blood from sea to sea and from the islands to great Caesar's walls! All hail, the Wolf-Torn King, who will lead us all to greater glory! Rejoice! The Wolf-Torn King has come and Tal will drink his fill of blood! All hail, the High King of All the Tribes! Who here will refuse to kneel before the High King and pledge themselves to him? Who here would deny him his right to stand upon the mound of the ancient kings at Sken and there be declared as sovereign and paramount? Who here would deny his power and dare to stand in opposition?'

King Manath of the Maeatae stepped forward to face the crowd. His face was set hard in determination and his hand was on his sword to show his willingness to fight anyone who opposed him.

'I will gladly kneel at Drest's feet and recognise him as High King of All the Tribes. He has freed my people from the tyranny of the Manau and the Alt Clut and has filled my treasury with silver. No other has earned the right to demand superiority' Manath then paused and looked into the faces of each of the other kings.

'Any man who stands against him will find me in his path! Any who dare to take arms against him will find me ever at his side! Any who would deny him will find themselves cursed and will be cast out!'

Cinloch felt his heart sink as one king after another stepped forward to make the same pledge. The boy king of the Caereni blushed red and dripped with sweat as he spoke the words Talorc had undoubtedly instructed him to recite. Stroma of the Acotti was passionate in support of her husband and urged all others there to recognise the legitimacy of his claim. Birst of the Carnonacae and Forcus of the Phocali talked of prosperity and full treasuries and of their hope that both would continue for many a year to come. Those who owed their thrones to Drest fell into line, though Guram of the Vacomagi and Typaun of the Manau showed greater enthusiasm than Cluim of the Alt Clut who frowned as he mumbled his oath. King Uuid of the Venicones spoke of loyalty won through courage and strength but qualified his vow by saying that such loyalty was owed only when it was deserved. Prince Donal of the Caledones was the most hesitant of all and could only promise to make haste for the north to persuade his father to agree to commit his people to Drest as High King. It pained Cinloch to realise this was no spontaneous outpouring of love and loyalty but was something that had been planned and rehearsed without his knowledge.

'It is agreed then!' Talorc proclaimed in a roar loud enough to be heard above the cheering, clapping and the stamping of feet. 'We shall gather together again at the mound of Sken to celebrate the spring festival of Imbolc and to raise Drest as High King in the sight of the gods!' The priest paused to let the nobles roar out their approval. 'Then let us drink and feast before we part! There are casks of ale in the great hall and the firepits are already lit to roast beef, pork and goat for us to gorge upon!'

Cinloch waited until the crowd had thinned before pulling Brude Uurad to one side.

'Is it not the most wonderful thing?' Uurad asked him joyfully. 'I thought I had clung to life this long just so I could return here to our historical capital before I died. Now I will participate in the raising of the High King! I am quite dizzy at the thought of it!'

'You knew of this?' The Mormaer demanded without bothering to hide his temper. 'How can you justify excluding the king's counsel from a matter of such great import?'

'I thought you knew.' The old man stuttered. 'I assumed Talorc was keeping you informed.'

'He told me nothing!' Cinloch seethed. 'I am ignorant as to what King Drest intends for me. It would seem that I am to be frozen out after all these long years of loyal service.'

'Ah! That would explain it.' Uurad muttered before stopping himself.

'Explain what?' Cinloch demanded. 'What did you mean by that?'

'Please ignore me, Mormaer.' The Brude stammered. 'I have misspoken. I should not speak of things I have overheard.'

Cinloch glared at Uurad and felt his stomach curdle as the Brude's cheeks turned dark red and beads of sweat gathered on his forehead.

'Twas probably nothing.' He began as he looked around to ensure no one was close enough to hear him. 'Drest and Talorc were deep in conversation and were oblivious to my approach. Talorc asked the King if he would miss you. Drest replied that he would and said that, with you at so great a distance from him, he would have to lean more heavily on Talorc for his advice.'

'It is as I feared.' The Mormaer gasped, his shoulders sagging and his legs trembling under the weight of his disappointment. 'I am to be sent away so Talorc can inherit my lands and my position. I was warned that this would come to pass but I refused to believe it.'

'It cannot be!' Uurad protested. 'He would not cast you aside. I must have misheard their conversation.'

'Do not try to comfort me, good Brude. The ties binding those two together go back to when they each pulled the other from the jaws of death. The bonds tying me to King Drest are delicate in comparison. I cannot hope to compete if Talorc is determined to usurp me. I will set off for the Arder Fort and see out my last winter within its walls.' He paused and took a breath to steady himself. 'Come! I will ask you to say a few words as I cast

Erp's ashes upon the waves of the Short Sea. It was his last wish and I will see to it before I leave.'

The light was already fading when Cinloch and Mael rode out through the Crag Fort's gates. It would have been wiser to wait until dawn to begin the journey home but neither of them could bear to linger for a moment longer. The sound of drums beating, pipes playing and feet dancing in celebration served to reduce their spirits further. They did not look back when the air was pierced by a high-pitched screaming loud enough to make them wince.

'What is that, do you think?' Mael enquired of her grim-faced husband.

'Tis the Dal Riata priestess.' Cinloch replied in a tone of complete disinterest. 'Talorc has decreed that she be boiled alive in her own cauldron.'

24

The winter months did not seem to drag on for as long as they normally did. Cinloch spent his afternoons watching over his lands from his walls and felt his heart grow heavier as the snows began to melt away and the earth thawed and turned to mud. The weak spring sunshine did nothing to lighten his mood as the dark cloud of the Imbolc festival drew closer.

'No messenger then?' Mael asked as she joined him on the rampart the day before they were due to leave for Sken.

'No.' Cinloch replied as he scanned the darkening horizon. 'Nothing since Brude Uurad sent his man to tell us of all the preparations for the enthronement.'

'Then he means to humiliate you by stripping you of everything in front of the gathered nobles. Do you doubt his cruelty now?'

'How can I? He has had the whole winter to come to me and tell me face-to-face. He could have spared me the torment of these past months and the agony of being reduced so publicly. It must be Talorc who is behind this. He has never forgiven me for my part in sending him north.'

'Then you should spare yourself. Come with me to my father. He will grant us lands on the coast where we can live well. Why would you subject yourself to his abuse when you do not have to?'

'I will not deny that I am tempted to avoid the indignity that awaits me in Sken but I cannot run from it. I thank you for the offer but cannot accept it for fear of being branded a coward or a deserter. I will take my stripes with my head held high. Only then can I think of slinking away to the coast to lick my wounds and see out my days in exile.'

'Then I will stand at your side and suffer along with you.' Mael reached for his hand and stroked it with a rare degree of tenderness. 'I swear to you that he will live to regret spurning us both.'

Cinloch and Mael declined Talorc's offer of a chamber in the Black Fort the night before the ceremony and instead rode on to spend the night at the Mormaer of Keld's stronghold. They were able to conceal their dark moods from their host and to make a show of enjoying his hospitality. The only trace of their bitterness came when Mormaer Curetan saw fit to praise Talorc for his skill in organising the ceremony.

'I cannot fault him.' The Mormaer gushed without noticing that his guests did not share his enthusiasm. 'He has spared neither expense nor effort. He had soil brought from the courtyards of each and every king and has spread it upon the mound of the ancient kings. Two hundred trees were felled, stripped of bark, fashioned into benches by carpenters and engraved with the insignia of every tribe before being placed in semi-circles around the mound. Every king, mormaer and thane will be there to see my nephew made High King and to kneel at his feet. It will be a spectacle beyond any seen by any living man or woman. The Black Fort was besieged by merchants all through the winter and I can't bear to think of the amount of silver he must have spent on cloth, jewellery and ornaments. He has stripped my lands of cattle and sheep for the feast and the streets of Pert have been reduced to mud by the passage of so many carts bringing casks of ale and mead for the festivities. I dread to think what it has cost him to bring together so many minstrels, singers, tumblers and acrobats to entertain us.'

'And your nephew is happy to have his treasury emptied by the priest?' Mael asked with a bluntness that did nothing to dent Curetan's joy.

'Oh, yes. Drest trusts him implicitly. The Drui took him north to the Dark Isles for purification almost a month ago. We will not see him until the ceremony itself.'

'Purification?' Cinloch asked, suddenly uneasy at the thought of Drest being at the mercy of the one-eyed priest's dark creatures. 'What does that entail?'

'A trial of some kind.' Curetan replied with a wave of his hand to indicate that he knew little of the detail. 'His soul must be cleansed if he is to be made High King in sight of the gods. Tis something of that sort.'

They made their excuses and retired to their chamber soon after. Mael clung to her husband under the blankets and furs and murmured words intended to soothe him. He feigned sleep to please her but spent most of the night awake as he wrestled with his growing sense of hopelessness and dismay.

They arrived at the mound of the ancient kings just as the sun began to burn through the morning mist. Long poles had been driven into the ground in a circle around the knoll to display the banners of every king and major mormaer. Sickles, axes, spears, serpents, bulls, boars, stallions, eagles and crows all fluttered side-by-side in the light morning breeze. The kings of all the tribes strutted as they paraded around the place in all of their finery. Forcus of the Phocali wore a headdress fashioned from a walrus skull with tusks so long they stretched down towards his bulging stomach and put him in danger of being impaled whenever he nodded his head. The beardless Caereni King attempted to make up for his lack of height by bearing a crown formed from the skulls and horns of three goats. Mael chuckled at the sight of him and wondered aloud how his skinny neck could support the weight of them. Manath of the Maeatae wore a cloak of eagle feathers that was so regal and beautiful it made the Mormaer feel quite shabby in comparison.

Cinloch forced a smile onto his lips as comrades old and new came to greet him and to chatter in their excitement about the day ahead. He was relieved when Uurad's apprentices came to guide them to their places. He made to follow Curetan and his wife as they filed along the second row of benches intended for the senior mormaers but was stopped by a smiling boy tugging at his sleeve.

'Not there, Mormaer Cinloch.' The boy instructed him as he bowed his head out of respect for his rank.

'Where then?' Cinloch muttered, exchanging a glance with Mael as he wondered what insult was about to be inflicted upon him. 'Am I to sit with the thanes and the placemen or stand at the back with the gawkers and the commoners?'

'Oh no, sir!' The boy replied happily. 'Brude Talorc has instructed us to ensure you are seated at the very centre of the first row.' He then leaned toward him and lowered his voice as if he was about to share a confidence. 'He said that he wants you close at hand so King Drest can deal with you the moment he is raised.'

'Grit your teeth, husband!' Mael muttered as she pushed him to follow the apprentice to their place. 'We will know what foulness the priest intends before too long. It will be over before we know it.'

Cinloch's suffering dragged on for more than an hour as Talorc let the anticipation build before the ceremony commenced. By the time the Carnonacae trumpeters lifted their horns and blew to herald Drest's arrival, his buttocks were sore from the hard bench and his nerves frayed from the excited chattering of the Caereni boy king who was seated beside him. Even in his distress, he could not help but gasp in awe as the procession emerged from the forest's edge and advanced slowly towards them. He saw immediately how the kingdom's silver had been spent and could not deny that the priest had a flair for pageantry. The cortege was flanked by a bodyguard of five hundred Smertae warriors dressed in robes of the finest and blackest material and carrying sickles that had been ground and polished so they shone and flashed silver in the rays of the morning sun. Their faces were not roughly smeared in blood as they were before battle but had been carefully painted so that the dark crimson stood out against the black of their cloaks. Two columns of hooded Drui marched at the centre, their black robes shimmering as the sunlight reflected off the flecks of silver and gold in the fabric.

They spread out as they approached and formed a half-circle around the mound of the ancient kings. Drest then emerged from their ranks and climbed to his place on the summit flanked by Brude Uurad and Talorc. The trumpets fell to silence as they stood there in robes and hoods of the finest and whitest fabric Cinloch had ever seen. The sun reflected off it with such intensity it caused him to blink. The gathered kings, mormaers, thanes and commoners seemed to hold their breath as the Drui began to chant and perform the ancient rituals of kingship. A glance to his left told him that even Mael was entranced by the majesty of it as her eyes were wide and her gaze fixed on the man who had once been her husband.

The crowd gasped involuntarily when Talorc and Uurad pulled daggers from their sleeves with a flourish. They gasped again when they turned to

Drest and sliced his robes and hood away from him. Cinloch was stunned by the change in him. He was leaner and more heavily-muscled than he had ever been and had been oiled so his skin glistened. His hair had been tied back from his face and the sides of his head shaved and tattooed with the insignia of all the tribes. The old markings on his face and torso had been redone so they shone out from his pale skin and his ribs had been marked with a broken spear for each of his victories in battle and broken arrows to denote the skirmishes he had won.

'He looks like a god!' Mael whispered from the side of her mouth and Cinloch could not disagree with her.

A basin of water was brought forward and Uurad and Talorc washed Drest from foot to neck. His face was last to be cleansed and Talorc did this with great ceremony. The four black lines drawn from forehead to chin in charcoal represented the legs of the Great Stallion and had been worn as the war-mask of the Epidii since the time of Eochaid. By allowing them to be wiped from his face, Drest was signifying that he was renouncing the Epidii throne and freeing himself from any ties to a single tribe. The rituals then turned to raising him to the status of High King of All the Tribes.

The sacrifices to the gods dragged on through most of the afternoon and soaked the earth at the foot of the mound with so much blood that pools of it started to form at Cinloch's feet. Each king had been invited to select the unfortunate beast to be slaughtered in the name of their tribe and to choose the god to whom it was to be dedicated. Sheep, goats, birds, horses, boar and deer were despatched easily enough but others proved more troublesome. The great, black bull of the Vacomagi had been fed with herbs to make him docile but he bled so prodigiously that Talorc's robes were turned from white to red. His great carcass was so heavy the team of oxen brought to pull him away struggled with the task. The Dal Riata warrior brought forward by the Smertae remained stubbornly upright after his throat was cut. He continued to sway unsteadily even when there could not have been more than a few drops of blood left in his veins. A collective sigh of relief came from the audience when he finally collapsed to the ground before any mutterings about ill-omens could take hold.

The last part of the ceremony was the most important, though it was mercifully short. Each king was called forward to give his oath of loyalty and his pledge of subservience to the newly raised High King of All the Tribes. They were first required to symbolically renounce their claim to kingship by surrendering their weapons to Drest. He then returned them along with their lands and authority as a gift from their superior. Most did so readily, but Cluim of the Alt Clut, Uuid of the Venicones and Onnus of the Caledones appeared visibly hesitant when Talorc commanded them to give up their weapons.

Cinloch observed these subtleties even as his stomach churned at the prospect of whatever fate awaited him when the ceremony was done. He was even able to summon some admiration for the one-eyed priest's craft. Each king was presented with a gift of great value and the Mormaer recognised most of them as the treasures Talorc had spirited away from the cellars of the forts they had taken. He felt a pang of regret for suspecting him of enriching himself when he was simply engaged in actions intended to strengthen his king. What pained him more was the realisation that Talorc boasted better instincts and a defter touch than he did himself. He watched the kings' faces as their gifts were unveiled and saw each of them transformed in delight. Even King Onnus of the Caledones broke into a wide grin when the cloth was pulled back to reveal a golden statue of a running boar that bore an uncanny resemblance to the symbol painted on the shields of his warriors. King Birst of the Carnonacae was even more enthusiastic about the coiled serpent presented to him, though it was likely he was pleased by the weight of the silver rather than the form of the sculpture.

The realisation that he was about to be usurped by a better man and a wiser counsellor brought Cinloch to new depths of misery. He tried to comfort himself by reasoning that things could not get much worse but was immediately proved wrong when Talorc commanded all there to kneel before the High King. He sighed as the half-congealed blood from the sacrifices soaked though his new trews. His only consolation was the hope of avoiding humiliation now that the ceremony and the rituals were over. He froze in fright at the sound of Drest's voice ringing out from the mound.

'I have renounced the throne of my fathers so I might rule over all the tribes with justice and impartiality. I have given an oath to favour no king over any other and so must seek new balance in the counsel given to me. To this end, I call upon each of you who has sworn himself to me to send your most trusted brude to the Black Fort to give me guidance. I swear to you that they will have my ear so your voices will be heard no matter how great a distance lies between us. Those who counselled me before will counsel me no longer. I will now put my faith in those most trusted by each of you.'

'Brace yourself, husband!' Mael whispered in warning as she reached out to squeeze his hand. 'Take your blows. It will be over soon enough.'

'No matter how much it might pain me, I must cast aside all vestiges of my former throne if I am to have your confidence.' Drest continued. 'I must therefore call upon Cinloch, Mormaer of Arder, to come before me and surrender his blade.'

Cinloch pushed himself to his feet and walked forward on legs that trembled so badly he was certain they would not bear his weight. He unsheathed his sword as he went and held it out to the High King as he sank back to his knees. Drest bent slightly to take it and immediately handed it to a Drui who took it away. That simple gesture told Cinloch there would be no reprieve. When the kings had given up their weapons, Drest had held them for only a few moments before returning them. The removal of his sword signalled the irretrievable loss of his position as counsellor.

'I know I have been too cautious in my counsel, my King.' He pleaded, his voice reduced to a whisper so others would not witness his disgrace. 'But did I not serve your father well? I bled with him on the Black Fort's walls and remained always at his side during the long years of want and suffering. Did I not also fight at your side against your enemies? I do not deserve to be so humiliated.' Cinloch felt his eyes fill with tears and became aware of Talorc stepping in close to them and gazing down at his abject display. 'Dismiss me from your counsel but leave me my lands and title at least!'

Drest stared down at him, his expression aghast and confused. His face then softened and his eyes filled with tears.

'You have mistaken me, good Cinloch. I would not dismiss you for your counsel. I have ever valued it. Your wisdom has always persuaded me away from reckless and impulsive acts. I know that I would not now stand upon this sacred mound if you had not been there to guide me. Your caution does not vex me!' He whispered as a tear ran down his cheek. 'When you scold me and warn me away from foolishness, it is my father's voice that I hear. I value it so highly it pains me to know I have failed to make that clear to you. Rise to your feet so I might make amends.'

Cinloch stood and frowned in confusion. 'But you have said that you must distance yourself from past advisors?'

'That I must do.' Drest replied before turning to snap at the Drui. 'Give me the blade!'

The Mormaer recognised the sword the moment Drest closed his hands upon it. It was as familiar to him as his own weapon for it had hung at Erp's waist throughout all the years he had served him. He had scoured its blade and overseen its sharpening countless times when he was a boy and had stood at Erp's side as he bathed it in Manau blood atop the Black Fort's walls. Drest unsheathed it and held it high above his head.

'All here have kneeled to me and recognised me as High King of All the Tribes.' Drest roared. 'All thrones are mine to give and mine to take away! Two now stand empty and it is my right to fill them as I see fit. Mormaer Cinloch is known to all of you. No man or woman would doubt his courage, wisdom or loyalty. He has guided my family and my people through the darkest of times and has devoted himself to the restoration of their fortunes. All thrones are won through blood, conquest or merit. I would trust no other man with the leadership of my people'

'All hail Cinloch, King of the Epidii!' Brude Uurad proclaimed as Drest pressed his father's sword into Cinloch's hands.

Cinloch took the weapon and stared at Drest's smiling face with his mouth agape. The High King reached out and pulled gently at his shoulder to turn him toward the gathered nobles. He blinked in astonishment as they took up Uurad's chanting of his name. The sea of faces was like something from a dream. Mael stood with her hand pressed to her mouth in shock as the Caereni King bounced up and down at her side and clapped her on the back in congratulation. Drest's mother, Brin, smiled at him and winked when he caught her eye. The significance of her approval was not lost on him, even in his current state of shock. Any potential successor to the Epidii throne would require her blessing in order to succeed. Both of Drest's uncles joined in with the acclaim, though Curetan did so with more enthusiasm than Elpin, the Mormaer of Ern. Cinloch raised his hand in acknowledgement and set the gathered nobles to cheering.

Brude Uurad ushered him back to his place among the others kings and he slumped down onto the bench at Mael's side. People reached out to offer their congratulations and to thump him on the back. His head spun as if he was drunk and he struggled to take it all in. He was so dizzied by it all he scarcely took notice as the High King began to speak again. It was only when Talorc kneeled before King Drest and reached out to take a polished sickle from his hand that he realised the priest was also being set upon a throne.

'All hail Talorc, the Drui King!' Brude Uurad cried out, his voice cracking from a long day of performing the rituals. 'All hail the new-made king!'

The lavish celebrations went on long into the night and Cinloch took the opportunity to fill his belly with roasted beef and pork washed down with sweet honey mead. He was wrapped in his furs against the chill of the night air and watching

252

a troupe of jugglers throw flaming torches high above their heads when he became aware of Talorc's presence at his side. The Drui King swayed unsteadily as he drank from a silver goblet.

'Did I not say that there were kingdoms enough for all of us?' The priest slurred happily.

25

'What would you give to have King Erp here with us this night?' Brude Uurad asked from his place by the roaring fire in the Crag Fort's hall.

Cinloch chuckled and drank another mouthful from his goblet of ale. The years since the fall of the Dal Riata had been the happiest and most productive of his life. His skills of stewardship and the wealth won during the years of conflict had enabled him to rebuild his kingdom with remarkable speed. The tenants who followed him west had raised homesteads from blackened ruins and turned fallow lands into fertile soil that bore plentiful crops and pastures that were now filled with horses, cattle and goats. The thanes he had raised to mormaers commanded their forts and their estates so efficiently they were now able to send him warriors and ships to patrol the coast, silver to replenish his coffers and enough grain and livestock to keep the kingdom fed during the hard winter months.

The stability brought by the uniting of the tribes under the High King had allowed his traders to thrive and the arrival of an heir to Drest's throne augured well for the continuation of this happy state. Even his relationship with his wife had flourished and the tenderness between them had endured in spite of the great sadness they suffered when their union produced only three stillborn children.

'I would gladly empty my treasury just to have Erp here with us for a single night.' Cinloch replied with a smile of both grief and joy. 'He would scarcely believe the tales I would tell him.'

'He would likely demand to know how your hair and beard have grown almost as white as my own.' The Brude laughed. 'And he would surely want to know how you came to possess both his kingdom and his beloved sword.'

'If only he had lived long enough to return to this place and be called king in the hall of his father. I would give anything to have witnessed that.'

'Aye!' The Brude responded as he stared into the fire with a wistful expression on his face. 'I felt his presence beside me as his son was raised as High King on the mound of the ancients at Sken. I do not doubt that his smile would have lit up the Underworld like a beacon.'

The two men sat in companionable silence and enjoyed the warmth of the flames and the effects of the sour Epidii ale. Cinloch shook his head in disbelief as he reflected on the path his life had taken. If any seer had foretold that such things would come to pass, sane men would have ridiculed him for daring to give voice to such nonsense. His mind wandered, as it often did, to the role Talorc had played in how their story had unfolded. It did not sit well with him to know that things would likely have turned out very differently if they had not sent him north as a beardless youth and then encountered him and the Smertae crone on that distant, frozen mountain. It pained him to conclude that such happenstance could only be the work of the gods and he frowned at the thought.

'What of the one-eyed priest?' Uurad enquired, once again demonstrating his uncanny ability to read Cinloch's thoughts. 'Will he accompany the High King when he comes?'

'I think not.' The Epidii King replied. 'The last I heard, he had gone off wandering to the south with his Drui. He will not vex us now.'

'What of King Drest? Will he bring trouble or is the visit routine?'

'I am not anxious about it, good Brude. He now spends his life travelling from the court of one king to the court of the next to collect his tribute, exert his authority and keep them close to him. It is merely our turn to be so honoured.'

King Cinloch of the Epidii climbed the stone steps to the wall above the gate the moment the scouts rode in to report their first sighting of the High King's party. He took his place at Mael's side and glanced along the ramparts to check all was in order. His tallest and most handsome warriors lined the walls so the fort seemed to bristle with spears. Uurad had spent weeks overseeing the craftsmen as they repainted every shield with the image of the Great Stallion so Drest would be welcomed by a show of Epidii force more powerful than any seen since the time of his grandfather. He would also be greeted by the sight of a banner above the gate bearing his own wolf's head emblem. Half of the fort's inhabitants had devoted themselves to its creation for the past few months. Cinloch allowed himself a smile at the thought of Drest's reaction upon seeing it. He then began to brush specks of dust from his new cloak.

'Calm yourself, husband.' Mael chided him. 'He will see that you have spared neither effort nor expense. Once he has had his warm welcome, his silver and his show of loyalty, he will ride away and leave us in peace.'

'By the gods!' Brude Uurad wheezed at his side, still breathless from climbing the steps. 'He has brought half of the kingdom with him.'

Cinloch cursed under his breath when he saw the truth of the squinting brude's words. The High King's retinue stretched far into the distance. Fifty Venicone horsemen formed a screen in front of the column and a bodyguard of two hundred Smertae flanked it on either side. King Drest and Queen Stroma rode at the head of their bannermen on black stallions that had been washed and brushed so their coats seemed to shine as if they had been polished. They were followed by a horde of brudes, servants, Carnonacae trumpeters and all of the hostages who made up the royal household.

'Tell the kitchens to add more water to the broth and the stew!' Cinloch ordered his steward. 'And have another dozen cattle slaughtered for the table! I will not leave my guests hungry.'

'Ignore him!' Mael instructed the servant. 'The tables already sag under the weight of the food heaped upon them. We could fill their bellies three times over and still have enough left to fatten every pig in the kingdom.'

The trumpeters blew on their horns to herald the High King's approach and Cinloch gave the signal for his warriors to beat their spears against their shields to give a thunderous welcome to their royal guests. Drest was grinning from ear to ear as he approached the gate and Cinloch was delighted to see the beautiful Stroma point up at the wolf's head banner and nod her head in approval. Brude Uurad nudged at him with his bony elbow to indicate that it was time for the ritual of welcome. The warriors fell to silence at his signal and he spoke the words Eochaid had first spoken a thousand years before the first Romans had sailed across the sea in search of new lands to conquer.

'What warrior dares to approach the gates of the royal stronghold of the Epidii? State your purpose under the eye of Epona or begone from my sight!'

'I am the High King of All the Tribes and come here with no ill-intent!' Drest replied. 'I beg only the hospitality of the Epidii King. Pray give me shelter and honour me with the protection of your walls.'

'Come, friend!' Cinloch replied with a smile. 'I will gladly give welcome to the High King and feed him from my own table. Come! Enter my gates!'

Drest and his wife rode through the archway and dismounted as every man, woman and child in the fort kneeled before them.

'Rise, Cinloch, King of the Epidii.' Drest commanded him. 'It is good to see you again.'

'It is good to have you here, my King. Come! Let me escort you into my hall. We have laid on such a feast, we will surely eat until we burst!'

The royal retinue attacked the heaped tables like ravenous dogs and drank so greedily Cinloch feared they would leave him with no ale or mead. Drest sat at the table of the Epidii King and consumed only a little of what was placed before him. He responded to Cinloch's enquiries pleasantly enough but his answers were short to the point of being terse.

'Are you well, my King?' Cinloch asked, his concern clearly visible on his face. 'If there is some other dish you would prefer, I will have my servants bring it to you.'

'I would be as fat as a pig if I ate every feast that was served to me.' Drest replied with a laugh as he patted his belly. 'But it is not food that sickens me.' He then glanced about him and lowered his voice. 'Come! I would have you take me to the place where you scattered my father's ashes.'

The Smertae warriors carried flaming torches to light the way to the beach and then fanned out around the two kings to give them privacy as well as security. Drest walked to the water's edge and breathed deeply of the cold sea air.

'How fares the kingdom, my King?' Cinloch asked when the silence had stretched on for longer than he was comfortable with. 'I sense that something troubles you.'

'The kingdom is at peace and prospers. It is the nature of my throne that torments me. I am ever surrounded by men who seek some advantage for themselves or for their masters. The brudes who offer me counsel spend all of their days engaged in bickering amongst themselves or in plotting and intrigue driven by the pettiest of motives and ambitions. They chatter away in my ears from dawn until dusk and will give me no peace. They shower me in praise for the simplest of acts and think I do not see that they seek only to ingratiate themselves so I will support whatever cause is dear to their hearts at that moment in time.' He shook his head and paused before continuing.

'Then I must constantly exert myself in order to keep all the kings happy. Forcus and Birst complain constantly if a river of silver does not run into their treasuries. Onnus of the Caledones and Guram of the Vacomagi seem to be always teetering on the edge of war over one piece of territory or another. Just as one dispute is resolved, another jumps up to take its place. It is exhausting. If it was not for you and Talorc, I would be driven to distraction. The Caereni, the Smertae, the Cornavi and the Drui do as he commands. Even the Venicones trouble me less now that King Uuid grows feeble and gives more authority to his son. Uurd is so grateful to Talorc for mending his crippled legs he will do anything he asks him to. Then there is you, good Cinloch. You have transformed this kingdom without complaint and without asking for a single coin from my treasury.'

260

'You did me great honour when you raised me up. How could I ask for anything more?'

'If only the rest were as faithful and as honest as you. That is why I was so eager to speak with you away from those who listen at my door and hide in the shadows in the hope of hearing some morsel they can feed to their masters. I have a plan to revive both my fortunes and my spirits and I would share it with the only man I know will speak truth to me.'

'Then tell me, my King.' Cinloch replied, keeping his voice even in spite of a feeling of dread that caused his stomach to clench. 'I will hear it, then offer counsel that comes from my heart.'

'Good! Good!' Drest rubbed at his chin as he spoke and his eyes flashed with excitement. 'I yearn for the days when I was not suffocated by the tedium of my court. I dream of the days when we rode across the land and drove our enemies before us. I was not mithered by petty disputes when I rode at the head of my army and put the Alt Clut and the Dal Riata to slaughter! We must raise the tribes once again, Cinloch! Nothing unites us more than our enemies and the prospect of taking their silver! I yearn for the glory of battle and mean to conquer all of the land between the walls of the Romans. The Votadini territory is there for the taking! They could not stand against us and such a victory would blow all these frivolous and foolish feuds away like cobwebs in a winter storm! Talorc has already ventured south to watch them and assess their strength. What say you, good Cinloch? Would you ride at my side once again?'

Cinloch took a long breath to steady himself and calm his racing heart. He saw desperation in the eyes of the High King and also a shadow of the fearless and reckless boy he had once been. It pained him to be the one to drive a dagger into the heart of his fervour but he knew that he must if their hard-won peace and prosperity was to be preserved.

'I know something of the burdens of kingship, my King.' He began. 'I spend long days stifling my yawns as my thanes and mormaers argue over some trifle that barely warrants a moment of my attention. Then I must suffer their whining when my judgement falls short of what they had hoped for. It is tedious and irksome but serves the purpose of keeping the peace. It is the glue that keeps us together and allows us to prosper. You cannot abandon your duty and risk all you have won for one last day of glory. The more important battle is that of holding the kingdom together so you might pass it onto your son! That is a battle worth fighting and you will find me ever at your side for the duration of that campaign.'

'I knew you would counsel me so!' Drest snapped in anger, though his shoulders slumped in defeat. 'Stroma said the same and urged me to consult with you. You would both damn me to a life of dreary banality!'

'I spoke true, just as you commanded me to. I am sorry if I have disappointed you, my King.'

'You might cause me frustration, Cinloch, but you never disappoint. I once told you that I hear my father's voice when you urge me to caution. It comforts me and fills the void left by his passing. I thank you and will heed your counsel. All other men seek favour or fortune and sing only songs they think will please me. I am grateful to you for your honesty in choosing a different ballad, though some notes were discordant and offended my ears.'

Cinloch nodded but kept silent. Long experience had taught him that acceptance of unpalatable counsel often came with a sting in the tail.

'It is good that you want to ease my burden.' The High King declared with a grin that bordered on malice. 'The other kings believe you to be a trustworthy and honourable man. They would accept your decisions if I appointed you to be the arbiter of all land disputes. If nothing else, the prospect of riding all the way here might persuade some of them to settle their own disagreements to spare themselves the journey. I will also send my son to you. I know you will teach him well and it will be good to have him far from the schemers in my own court.'

'Ii would be an honour to have Prince Nechtan in my care.' Cinloch replied, pointedly ignoring the poisoned chalice the High King had proffered.

'Good! He is as feisty and strong-willed as I was when I was a boy but I suspect that his tantrums and sulks will torment you less than those of the others who will soon be winding towards your door.' Drest patted his shoulder and gestured to his bodyguards to escort him back to the fort.

Cinloch stayed on the sand and stared out to sea as the sound of Drest's laughter faded into the night.

26

'It will be nothing, husband.' Mael insisted, though her tone lacked conviction.

Cinloch did not answer her but continued to gaze out across the wintry landscape from the rampart above the fort's gate. He did not pull his furs around him to protect himself from the bitter wind and seemed impervious to the chill that set his wife to shivering. He had been weighed down by a dark foreboding for the last few weeks. It now seemed to be too great a burden for him to bear and caused his back to bend and his shoulders to stoop.

It was almost three years since the High King had entrusted Prince Nechtan to his care and each of those years had brought him more pleasure than the last. The kingdom had continued to blossom, the treasury was richer than it had ever been, his army was strong, disciplined and well-equipped and his reputation for wisdom and fairness had grown through his deft handling of the multitude of disputes that had arisen between the kings, mormaers and thanes of the greater realm. The presence of Drest's son in their household had been a source of joy for them both. He shared his father's passion for both saddle and sword but was as quick and as keen at his learning as his grandfather had been. There was great satisfaction to be had from grooming such a promising lad for kingship. It was strange for Cinloch to be overtaken by such a sense of dread when the gods had seen fit to bless him with such good fortune.

'It is foolish to attribute such importance to dreams.' Mael scolded him. 'Brude Uurad might tell you that they foretell the future but you know well that most are nonsense. I used to dream that I was attacked by a sea-monster but nothing has yet leapt from the waves to devour me.'

'See!' King Cinloch exclaimed, jabbing his forefinger out into the snowy wastes. 'A horseman comes!'

'It signifies nothing!' Mael replied as she squinted at the distant rider. 'It will just be some ragged Caledone thane who comes to bend your ear about some miserable pett of land that was once owned by his grandfather's uncle's sister and has now fallen into the hands of some distant and undeserving cousin.'

Cinloch refrained from arguing with her and continued to peer out into the gloom as the figure drew closer. He breathed a heavy sigh when his worst fears were realised. The heavyset warrior came on at speed, gripping his reins in his right hand and a stout pole bearing the High King's wolf's head banner in his left.

'It is no petitioner.' He informed the shivering Mael with a weariness that dismayed her. 'They always come in pairs. One to make his claim and the other to refute it. This man has been sent from the Black Fort to summon me there. It seems that

I will be braving the worst of the winter just as I dreamt it.'

The journey east was more arduous than any he could remember. None of those he had made during the winter before the invasion of the Dal Riata lands came close, even though he had spent months in the saddle riding from one place to another to secure provisions for the campaign. The blizzards blew in so hard he was blinded and could not tell east from west and was forced to trust his horse to find the way. The snow was so deep that he had crossed the frozen Tae before he was even aware he had reached it. He would have struggled to find the Black Fort itself if it had not been for the great mass of warriors encamped below its heights. Their tents and makeshift shelters were weighed down with enough snow to hide them from sight but their campfires were built high to give them warmth and served as beacons to guide him to his destination. He cursed at the sight of so many gathered there, for it told him he was far from being the only king or mormaer summoned to Drest's hall.

He saw he was right the moment he entered the hall and paused to dust the snow from his shoulders and to scrape at the ice and slush that clung to his boots. King Forcus of the Phocali, King Manath of the Maeatae and King Birst of the Carnonacae were ensconced by the fire with horns of ale and plates of meat in their hands. King Onnus of the Caledones sat alone at the far side of the hearth, his face sickly and so thin that Cinloch did not recognise him at first. His great furrowed brows now sat above a face that was gaunt and drawn rather than the full and rounded cheeks Cinloch remembered. The rest were at the centre of the room gathered around the High King himself. Prince Donal of the Caledones, King Guram of the Vacomagi, King Typaun of the Manau and the boy king of the Caereni, now more a man than a boy, seemed to hang on his every word. King Uuid of the Venicones and Cluim of the Alt Clut were grim and looked as if they were awaiting their chance to interrupt to give voice to some complaint. Cinloch's observations were interrupted when Manath caught sight of him and called him over to the fire.

'By Bodor's breath, you are frozen!' He exclaimed with a welcoming smile. 'Come! Warm yourself by the fire! I will have the servants bring you ale and roast venison.'

'What is afoot?' Cinloch asked when he had both food and drink in his possession. 'Only dire news could bring us together at this accursed time of year. What have you learned?'

'I have learned little.' Manath responded in a cautious whisper. 'But what I know will not please you. The one-eyed priest is to join us tomorrow. I do not doubt that he will be the bearer of ill tidings. The High King will give no hint of his purpose until the Drui King is at his side. We are commanded to feast tonight and to show patience, for all will be revealed in the morning.'

Cinloch opened his mouth to reply but was brought to a halt by the High King calling to him.

'Come, Cinloch! Join me at the table and save me from these slavering dogs. Each one of them has a dozen complaints and you are the cause of them all! Come and shield me from their attacks! Fend them off so I might enjoy a bite or two at my own table!'

The feasting and drinking went on deep into the night but the Epidii King had little opportunity to enjoy the festivities. He soon grew tired of being called upon to explain his past judgements and became increasingly irritated as the kings consumed more ale and lost their inhibitions. The good-humoured banter of the early part of the evening had descended into acrimony by the time he was able to make his escape and close the door of his chamber against them.

Cinloch broke his fast with bread and ale in his chamber before crossing the frozen courtyard and entering the hall. Half of the company was already seated around the feasting table and he took the opportunity to greet some of those who had waylaid him the previous night. He was relieved to find that most of them seemed to bear him no ill will and the rest were so hungover they had no wish to revive their drunken arguments. He was exchanging news with Uuid of the Venicones when the chattering around them fell to a hush. He turned to see Drest entering the hall deep in conversation with Talorc, the Drui King. It seemed that he had just reached the fort after his months of wandering for he was in a lamentable condition. His cloak was ragged and filthy, his face was smeared with the dirt of the road and his boots were in such poor repair he had taken to binding them with strips of cloth to hold them together.

'The gods have returned our brother to us!' Drest announced to the room. 'He has news to impart that concerns every one of us. I will give him the floor so you may hear it from his own lips.'

Talorc nodded his acknowledgement to the High King and stepped forward. He cast his gaze around the chamber and licked at his lips as if he was unsure how he should begin. Cinloch was not fooled by the gesture. He knew the one-eyed priest too well to be taken in by the pretence. His every instinct told him that the coming speech had been carefully honed and rehearsed to ensure it would achieve the desired effect. He was also certain that Drest had already heard every word of it.

'I come before you, not as a king, but as a humble scout who has spent these past months wandering the lands of our enemies. I have learned much and have much I must share with you.'

Cinloch listened with only half an ear as Talorc spoke of the Votadini for he already knew much about them. He had once ridden to their capital at Din Eidyn at Erp's side and had gaped along with him at their great fort perched upon a steep and impregnable rock outcrop. The peasants they encountered told them of their king, the Votad, of their invincible army and of the carts laden with silver sent northwards by the Romans to pay them to defend the territory between the walls. They also spoke of their veneration of Father Sky, the river god Bodor, Maben, the god of youth, the Mother, the Maiden and the Crone and a host of the false gods worshipped by their foreign masters. Erp had been astonished that a people could believe themselves to be strong when they had allowed themselves to be made vassals. Cinloch snapped out of this fond remembrance when the priest seemed to have finished with the generalities of his report and moved onto the specifics.

'We have heard little of the Votadini since they were abandoned by their Roman overlords.' Talorc announced. 'This is because they have been embroiled in a long and vicious war with their southern neighbours, the Brigantes of Bryneich. They have also been forced to defend their coastline against persistent raiders from across the sea. I have learned that Votad Liff met with King Uurtigrm of the Brigantes in the autumn and took his silver in exchange for a promise of peace between their kingdoms. He now spends that silver on men and arms so he might satisfy his territorial ambitions in the north. I have seen his army at close quarters and it is a greater threat than any enemy we have faced before. Their warriors are drilled to fight in formations just as their Roman masters did. Every one of them carries five spears, a sword, a dagger and a heavy shield to hide behind. These shields are as tall as a man and are constructed from layers of wood curved for strength. They are covered with thick leather, reinforced with strips of iron and centred with a heavy iron boss. They fight just as our forefathers said the Romans did. The outside ranks overlap their shields to form a wall while those at the centre hold theirs above their heads so they can raise a fort on any battlefield. No spears, arrows or stones can penetrate it and no horse, not even the best Epidii warhorse, can be induced to crash into such a tight and solid formation.' The priest then paused for effect and took the time to look each of the gathered kings directly in the eye. 'The Votadini mean to make war with us! We must take the fight to them if we are to stop them in their tracks!'

Cinloch blew his cheeks out in exasperation. Talorc had succeeded in outmanoeuvring him and he had no argument compelling enough to refute his case. The priest and the High King exchanged a sly and meaningful glance and this served to confirm Cinloch's suspicions of collusion and so dissuaded him from urging them to caution. King Guram of the Vacomagi leapt to his feet to solemnly commit himself to the struggle ahead and was immediately joined by King Forcus, King Birst and the Caereni King. Manath of the Maeatae, Typaun of the Manau and Uuid of the Venicones rose to their feet more reluctantly before giving voice to their support. Cinloch was about to follow suit when King Onnus stood and cleared the phlegm from his throat. His voice was strong and clear and projected an authority that belied his frail and skeletal frame.

'Only a fool would be eager to rush into war on only the word of this foul necromancer!' He seethed as he glared at Drest with his yellowed, bloodshot and rheumy eyes. 'Would you trust this Drui with your kingdom in spite of his devotion to the blood rites of the filthy Smertae gods? Do as you see fit, but I will not sacrifice my lands and my people so he and his adherents can continue to worship at their rancid altar of vileness and obscenity. March south if you will, but you will march without the might of the Caledones!'

'Then march we will!' Drest retorted with such coldness it caused Cinloch to shiver. 'All men here are sworn to me and all men here will bring warriors to me when they are commanded to do so. Do not oppose me in this! It would not go well for you if you were to break your oath.'

'A High King cannot rule by threats alone, Drest of the Epidii.' Onnus growled. 'I never vowed to follow you as you hurtle towards a conflict driven by the bloodlust of your acolytes. You swore an oath to protect the kingdom and its people but now you race towards strife with unseemly haste without even attempting to treat with our neighbours. I will have no choice but to break with you if you persist with this reckless and misbegotten strategy!'

King Onnus then turned from the table and made off without giving Drest the chance to reply. The gesture would have had more drama and impact if he had been able to shuffle away more quickly and if he had not needed to lean so heavily on his staff. The High King moved swiftly to dispel the disquiet caused by the Caledone leader's outburst. He issued orders to his placemen on how many warriors they should bring and when. Cinloch kept his thoughts to himself and waited until the conference ended before taking the priest aside.

'This is a bad business, Talorc.' He muttered, taking care to keep his voice low. 'The Caledones account for a third of our strength and neither the Vacomagi nor the Venicones will be content to march their warriors away and leave their lands vulnerable and open to attack from their Caledone neighbours. Our plans and the kingdom itself will unravel if this cannot be resolved. Surely, we must now consider negotiating with the Votadini. I would be willing to act as an intermediary to discover what agreement might be reached with them.'

'Do not trouble yourself, good Cinloch.' The Drui King reassured him with a smile that only served to make his mutilated face appear more sinister. 'The Caledones will fall into line soon enough. Did you not see how thin Onnus has grown when the years of plenty have made all other men fat? He is gravely ill and already reeks of death. I doubt he will last the month and then his son will succeed him. Donal counts Drest as his closest friend and will do whatever he commands him to do. There is no need for you to fret over negotiations and such. We will ride to war before winter is done.'

'You intend to murder him!' Cinloch spat in disgust. 'How many kings have now perished at your hand and how many more will suffer that fate so you might achieve your ambitions?'

'None who are worthy of the name, my friend.' The one-eyed priest replied with infuriating pleasantness. 'Fear not, good Cinloch, for you are safe. I know that no man is more loyal to the High King than you, though you are a more cautious counsellor than I would like. I will not come to you in the darkness of your chamber with my face blackened and a Smertae sickle in my hand!'

Cinloch felt himself tremble at these words for they described the very dream that had tormented him and denied him sleep for the last few weeks. He did his utmost to mask his fear but knew the priest was not fooled by his pretence.

'Ride hard for the Crag Fort, King Cinloch.' Talorc mocked him. 'Raise your warriors, raid your treasury and rid yourself of doubt. The High King rides again and we will ride at his side!'

27

The might of the High King's army seemed to be reduced to insignificance by the sheer scale of the heights of Din Eidyn. Drest had to lean back in his saddle and crane his neck painfully to gaze up at the Votadini stronghold perched at the top of the cliffs.

'By the gods!' He cursed as the blustery and bitterly cold, wind whipped at his furs. 'I could throw every last one of my warriors at those walls without a single one of them breaching the ramparts!'

'Then be thankful you will not have to!' Talorc announced as he rode in to join them. 'The Votadini army is arrayed on the plain to the south of us. It seems they left only a small garrison here and expect us to give battle on ground they have chosen and prepared for that purpose.'

'How many?' Drest demanded with some trepidation. 'Is their strength as great as we feared?'

'Much, much worse, my King!' Talorc replied with a nonchalant shrug of his shoulders. 'They outnumber us by two to one and have drawn up in three divisions of five thousand men each with the centre positioned further back than the two flanks. They have two cavalry divisions of a thousand men each at their rear and have dug ditches around each division and a larger one to encircle and protect their whole army.' The priest laughed before continuing. 'My scouts watched as they went through their drills and told me it was an impressive and intimidating sight. They described the shield wall as unbreakable and positively bristling with spears.'

The truth of the report was confirmed after a short ride south to bring the Votadini army into view. Drest cursed at the sight of it.

'Our warriors will shit themselves when they see this! We will lose half of them to desertion before darkness falls. I would rather assault a fortress than charge across this plain at their ditches and spears!'

'When your father spoke of the Romans, he always said that the strength of their formations was also their weakness.' Cinloch offered as he cleared his throat.

'What help is that to me now?' Drest snapped, his face dark with anger. 'This is not the time for fond tales of your discussions with my father!'

'Their ability to construct a fort of shields upon the field of battle gives them all advantage when they are attacked.' The Epidii King persisted, though his cheeks had reddened in the face of the rebuke. 'It gives them none if their opponents refuse to engage and instead put them under siege. Then they must either stay behind their shields and starve or venture out and risk breaking formation as they go.'

'That is very clever, Cinloch.' Talorc admitted with reluctant admiration. 'Their walls will falter as they cross the ditches they have dug around themselves. If we surround them and wait in readiness, they must either come at us in disarray or starve behind their shields.'

'Their first instinct will be to stay in position and try to goad us into battle.' Drest declared, his voice now filled with more hope than anger. 'Every hour they wait will cause them to weaken from cold and want of supplies and will give us time to think of how their walls might be breached.'

'I may have the answer to that!' Guram of the Vacomagi announced from his saddle to the rear of them.

'Then let's hear it.' Drest commanded him. 'I will drown you in the riches of the Votadini if your suggestion works. I swear it now before the gods.'

Guram laid his plan out and gave an answer to every objection and criticism. When Talorc and Cinloch nodded to indicate they had been persuaded, Drest gave Guram his approval and ordered him to set the scheme in motion. King Guram asked for seven days to make the necessary arrangements but was given three and all of the resources at the High King's disposal. He turned his horse and rode immediately for the coast to board the ship of the Venicone King and lead the fleet northwards.

'Do you really believe it can be done?' King Donal of the Caledones enquired, his tone doubtful.

'If the winds stay fair and Guram can load his cargo as he has promised us, then we will have half a chance.' The High King replied. 'Whether or not the Votadini will oblige us by staying behind their ditches is another matter altogether. Let us pray that King Talorc can induce his Drui priests to dance prettily enough to please the gods.'

The Great Votad groaned as he pulled himself up and into his saddle. He stretched in a bid to relieve his aching joints after enduring a few hours of fitful sleep on ground still hard from the winter's frosts. His stomach grumbled in protest at being empty as he gazed out into the murk of the early dawn. He frowned at the sight of the campfires flickering in the darkness all around them and burned with envy at the thought of his enemies enjoying the heat of the flames while his own warriors shivered with cold as they awaited the call to rise from the frigid earth and take their turn in the shield wall. The sound of muttering reached his ears and, while he could not make out what was said, the tone of it told him that his men were moaning and complaining about the hardships of being besieged and trapped on the plain. There had been no firewood to be had after the first day and the last of the food had been consumed on the third. Even his cavalry had given up harassing the savages because their every move was shadowed and countered by the horse warriors who rode under the banners of the wolf, the boar, the stallion and the stag.

'Will they come at us today?' He asked Brecc, his most senior commander.

'I doubt it, Votad Liff.' The seasoned warrior replied with characteristic bluntness. 'Why would they risk all against our shields when they have us trapped behind our ditches? It costs them little to let us starve. We must sally out and engage them before our men weaken.'

Liff's nose wrinkled in irritation. He knew Brecc was right but was reluctant to admit it when he had insisted on waiting for the unwashed barbarians to break themselves on his shields. He had been certain that the uncivilised beasts lacked the discipline to restrain themselves in their eagerness to tear at their enemy. Instead, they had formed up out of range of Votadini spears and stayed in place while their naked priests chanted and danced and mocked his warriors by ducking and swerving to avoid the few spears thrown at them. The older man's silent disapproval served to sting him more than open insolence. When he told him that the integrity of the wall could not be risked by crossing the ditches, Brecc remained stubbornly silent and continued to stare vacantly into the distance. Liff promised himself he would have the bastard whipped and stripped of his lands when the battle was won. The thought cheered him enough to allow him to bow to the inevitable.

'I have waited long enough!' He announced as he summoned all of his royal authority and raised his voice so the men nearest to him would hear his pronouncement. 'Ready the men! If these cowards have not gathered the courage to come at us by the time the sun reaches its highest point, then we will take the fight to them!'

Brecc kept his expression impassive but cast a sly glance in the Votad's direction. The preening little shit had his nose in the air like a petty and petulant boy. The Votadini commander could not help but think he was not fit to lick his father's shoes. Votad Bubon would have led his men over their ditches before the Pictish dogs had the chance to organise themselves. He bowed his head as he took his leave and went to give orders to the men. His captains joined him as he went and fell into step beside him.

'Has he found his balls at last?' Canno asked with a sardonic grin.

'I was starting to think he had none.' Brecc retorted with a short and bitter laugh. 'It turns out they were just too small for him to find. We are called to readiness at last, so go and rouse your men. Distribute the last of the bread and ale to those who will stand in the first rank. I do not want them to be distracted by the rumbling of their bellies when we order them forward and across the ditches.' He paused and jabbed his thumb over his shoulder in the direction of the Votad. 'Make sure you are out of the sight of that worthless turd when you distribute the last of our supplies! He has done nothing but whine about his empty guts since our first night here. Let him go without until the battle is won. It will do him good to experience some of the suffering he has inflicted on the rest of us.'

281

The captains went about their business with a discipline and efficiency honed during long days of drilling their warriors in their formations. Men pushed themselves stiffly to their feet at their command and stretched their aching limbs before lifting their shields and shuffling into line. Brecc barked commands and snapped at those he found wanting even though he was happy with what he saw. A few stooped backs and bent shoulders were of no great concern after days of inactivity and sleepless nights spent shivering on the ground. The sun had barely risen above the horizon when three short horn blasts sent him running back to the Votad's side.

'They come!' Liff shouted in triumph. 'Did I not say they would, Brecc? Did I not tell you they would come to die upon our shields if only we had the wisdom and patience to wait them out! Was I not right to ignore your counsel?'

Brecc pulled himself into his saddle and looked out across the great mass of shields. He squinted against the sunlight shining directly into his eyes and strained to make out the detail of the shadowed throng advancing towards them. He could see nothing of the banners fluttering above their heads but saw enough to know they had organised themselves into three divisions and were now advancing on foot. He frowned to see that the first four ranks carried no spears, for it made no sense for them to attack his spearmen with only swords and axes. He looked for their cavalry and cursed in bewilderment when he caught sight of them following up the rear. He had expected them to send their horses crashing against the wall in an attempt to break it. His mind reeled as he struggled to understand why they would keep their most powerful warriors to the back while sending their weakest on ahead.

'Will you not admit you were wrong, Brecc?' Liff cajoled him in his childish desperation for approval. 'I would have your apologies now.'

'There is something amiss.' Brecc muttered as he flicked his gaze from one side of the field to the other. 'This is not right.'

'What is not right is your refusal to admit that my strategy was the better one.' Votad Liff persisted with a smug smile on his face.

It was then that Brecc realised what the Picts intended. Their front ranks were filled with their tallest warriors but even their height was not enough to fully conceal the great, black bulls they led forward. Brecc counted at least five of the beasts in the midst of each of their divisions and felt his heart flutter in his chest. A long horn blast set the enemy army to running and the front rank parted to allow the bulls through. Warriors with their faces painted red charged forward at the sides and rear of the beasts and jabbed at their flanks with sickles with enough cruelty to cause them to bellow in pain and to turn their backs red with their own blood. The Great Votad's eyes widened in shock and he clutched at his chest.

'The ditches will stop them!' He cried out, though his voice was so shaky it was clear he hardly believed it.

'Hold!' Brecc roared out but his voice was lost in the thunder of hooves and feet thumping into the hard ground.

He held his breath when the first bull disappeared from sight as it hit the outer ditch. It immediately reappeared on the near bank and charged wildly along the line of shields. For one horrible, sickening moment, it seemed that the beasts might baulk at the wall of shields and cause the attack to fail. That desperate hope was shattered when the air was filled with the din of great masses of horn, muscle and bone crashing into wood, iron and flesh. Splintered shields flew into the air all along the line, men screamed in agony and the whole army seemed to ripple as men threw their shields down from above their heads and began to fight for their lives. Brecc winced as a high-pitched keening assaulted his ears and was momentarily entranced by the rise and fall of the bloody sickles as they tore through the holes in the shield wall and cut their way into his ranks.

'Sound the retreat!' He ordered his herald when he realised the army was about to break. 'We will reform with the river at our back and make our stand there!'

'The Votadini do not retreat!' Liff screamed at him in rage. 'Would you dare to give such a command? I will not begin my rule in defeat! I will stand here with my men!'

'Die here if you must, you miserable shit!' Brecc growled. 'But I will not leave a single man to share your fate!' He then turned to the herald.

'Blow your damned trumpet! We teeter on the edge of collapse!'

Some men obeyed the signal and raised their shields to make an orderly, fighting retreat but others turned in panic and ran for the rear. It made little difference in the end. Both those who scrambled across the ditches and those who fought their way there at the side of their comrades were met by the horse warriors of the Epidii, Vacomagi, Venicone and Manau Kings. The Votadini cavalry resisted strongly at first but suffered badly under a hail of spears launched by the Maeatae warriors under King Manath's command. When they finally broke and galloped away, such a slaughter was made of their unmounted comrades their blood soaked the earth and turned it to mud.

Cinloch tried to push himself up from the ground but abandoned the attempt when the wooziness threatened to overcome him. He turned his head to spit a great gobbet of congealed blood onto the earth and breathed deeply in a bid to steady himself. The left side of his face was swollen badly enough to close one eye completely and blood ran into the other so he had to blink to clear it. These injuries blurred his view of the carnage around him but they could not conceal it entirely. The field was strewn with the corpses of warriors and horses and the air filled with the sobbing and groaning of the wounded. An Epidii warrior whimpered pitifully just out of his reach and clutched at her guts to stop them from spilling out through her fingers and onto the earth. He called to her but she was so lost in her agony she did not hear him. He began to crawl towards her but cursed and grimaced in pain when his left hand pressed against the ground. He blinked in disbelief at his mangled hand and the bloody stumps of two of his fingers.

He bit down on the panic now swelling in his chest and set about checking himself for injuries. He ran the fingers of his trembling right hand over his torso and belly. His tunic was soaked in blood and he was therefore both surprised and relieved to find that no holes had been torn in his flesh. His skull seemed to be similarly intact though his face was badly swollen and one ear had been reduced to a mess of gristle and pulp. He flexed his legs and grunted in satisfaction when the movement caused him no pain apart from the grinding of his left knee that was a relic of an old injury. He squeezed his eyes shut against waves of dizziness and nausea and waited for them to recede.

He let long moments pass until the sound of men muttering and shuffling close by caused him to stiffen and become fully alert. He blinked to clear his vision and saw two figures bending over a fallen warrior. He thought they were tending to a comrade or retrieving a corpse for burial until one of them unsheathed a knife and began to saw and hack at the dead man's fingers. It seemed that Votadini peasants had beaten the crows to the battlefield and were stripping the dead of their valuables before the first bird had arrived to feast on the eyes of the fallen. Cinloch scrambled unsteadily to his feet spurred on by both fear and disgust. He knew that these foul scavengers would not hesitate to cut his throat and steal his purse as he lay wounded. They were startled by his sudden appearance but did not scurry away in fright. The smaller of the two licked at his lips and seemed to be assessing his chances against a well-dressed warrior who was old, gravely wounded and unarmed. Cinloch read his intentions and cast his eyes over the ground in search of a weapon. He snarled when he spotted Erp's sword no more than an arm's length away and hobbled forward to snatch it up. It was dripping in gore from tip to hilt and he wiped at the grip with his sleeve before brandishing it above his head and roaring in fury at the loathsome corpse robbers. They hurried away like the cowards they were and only resumed their work when they had put some distance between them.

Cinloch's exertions caused his head to spin wildly and he had to push his sword into the earth and lean on it to hold himself upright. It was as he wobbled there precariously that a voice called out to him.

'Thank the gods, Cinloch! I thought you were lost to us. Your steward told us your horse was impaled on a Votadini spear and that a half-crazed warrior battered your skull into the ground with his shield as you struggled to regain your feet!'

Cinloch turned to see Drest dismount and begin to approach him with half the kings of the kingdom following in his wake. The High King smiled from ear to ear and was clearly drunk with the joy of his victory.

'We have routed them, Cinloch!' He exclaimed as he raised his arms in celebration. 'The great Vacomagi bulls tore holes in their walls and our warriors poured through the gaps and cut them to ribbons. There was such a slaughter that even the Smertae gave up in exhaustion and left us with more than a thousand prisoners to enslave! Is it not wonderful, my friend? Nothing intoxicates like the fury of battle and the glory of victory! Come! Embrace me, good Cinloch! I can see you are as giddy as I!'

'It is true, my King!' The Epidii King slurred with ill grace. 'I am giddy from the loss of my best stallion, two fingers, three teeth and an ear and from having my skull crushed by the boss of a Votadini shield. I doubt if I have ever been happier!'

Drest missed the acid in Cinloch's tone and roared with laughter as he came to embrace him.

'I would have excused you from battle on account of your age but I knew nothing would keep you from the fight. It did my heart good to see you charge at their cavalry and wet my father's blade in the blood of our enemies.' He then looked down and cried out in delight. 'See! You have not lost your finger! It is there! Tangled in your cloak!'

'Much good it will do me now!' Cinloch retorted sourly.

He glared at Drest as he broke into hysterical laughter and encouraged the gathered kings to join in with him. He cast his eyes down to see that his best cloak had been torn to rags and felt hot bile rise in his throat at the sight of his severed ring finger caught in the threads.

'I will help you find its partner!' Drest's eyes twinkled with merriment as he made a show of searching the ground for the missing digit.

'May the gods curse you and cause your balls to rot in their sack!' Cinloch spat through gritted teeth.

The insult was meant but did not puncture the High King's elation. He took the barb in good humour and laughed until tears came into his eyes.

'How I have missed your dark wit!' He declared with genuine fondness. 'Now I will return the favour and make your spirits soar yet higher, my friend! It will cheer you to know that the blood of the Votadini King still drips from my sword. He was caught crossing the river to the south of here as he ran from us like a coward. He sobbed like a child and begged for his life so cravenly even his own commander cursed him as a disgrace. The sight of it sickened me so much I took his head there and then. I have freed my warriors to pillage at will and have promised to claim no part of what they take. The kings are happy to have the freedom to so enrich themselves and have granted me whatever treasures are held in the Fort of Din Eidyn. You are to ride there to join the Caereni in besieging the garrison while the rest of us go south so we might plunder and gaze upon the stone wall the Romans built from one sea to the other.'

'As you wish, my King.' Cinloch mumbled as he fought against his pain, light-headedness and nausea.

'Do not fret, my friend!' Drest reassured him with a chuckle of delight. 'I will see to it that you don't lose out. We shall share whatever treasures the Votad has squirrelled away in his cellars.'

28

Cinloch's patience died after three days of misery below the walls of Din Eidyn. His dizziness was replaced by a crippling headache that thumped painfully with each beat of his heart and could not be dulled by ale, Brude Uurad's foul concoctions or short nights of fitful sleep. The holes torn in his gums when his teeth were smashed out by the Votadini shield made the eating of anything tougher than bread softened in warm water an unbearable torture. He was forced to refuse meat even when his stomach growled with hunger at the mere thought of it. The stumps of his fingers gave him little discomfort, though it troubled him that he could often feel them as if they had not been cut away. Uurad nodded when he told him this and recounted a tale of a warrior who lost his left leg but continued to torment his wife by ordering her to scratch his missing foot to relieve an itch that drove him to distraction.

The foul weather added to his gloom. The rain had begun to fall just as he took his leave of the High King on the edge of the battlefield. He was soaked by the time he came in sight of Din Eidyn and there had been no break in the downpour since then. Great clouds of steam rose from his cloak whenever he was able to sit close enough to a fire to dry himself. His temper broke when his boots became rotten and the soles loosened, leaving his feet permanently wet.

He called for his horse and rode unescorted to the gates of the fort. Once there, he ignored the spears pointed down at him from the ramparts and demanded parley. Long minutes passed with him muttering to himself in anger in the pouring rain before a young, pale-faced girl appeared at the top of the wall.

'What do you want?' She snapped. 'You have no business at this gate! My father has ridden out with his army and will return at any moment. He will sweep you peasants from his path and spike your miserable heads on these walls. Begone or you will be sorry!'

Cinloch shook his head in disbelief at the madness of being forced to negotiate with a child.

'Your father is dead and his army slaughtered. I come to accept the surrender of this fort. I promise you safe passage south if you comply. If you resist, every last one of you will die!'

The little head disappeared from sight and Cinloch sighed in frustration as a whispered conversation took place high above him.

'You lie!' The girl spat petulantly when her head popped back into view. 'You will not trick me so easily! Begone if you do not want my warriors to bring you down with their spears.'

'I speak true!' Cinloch replied. 'I can bring you his head and carts filled with the corpses of his men if you demand proof.'

The girl ducked out of sight again and stayed hidden for so long Cinloch was on the verge of giving up in disgust.

'Who are you to offer us safe passage?' She demanded, her eyes narrowed in suspicion.

'I am Cinloch, King of the Epidii, and I speak with the full authority of Drest, High King of All the Tribes. I give you my word that every person within your walls will be allowed to leave here unharmed.'

'You are no king!' She sneered. 'You are dirty and are dressed in filthy rags. I am Derice of the Votadini and will not be taken in by your lies.'

Cinloch blew his cheeks out in exasperation but the prospect of long months of rotting below the walls of the fort persuaded him to persist.

'Then I will call my men to me so they can confirm my identity. I will send carts out to the plain so they can be loaded with the corpses of your warriors and I will lay them out here so you will have your proof.'

Brude Uurad rocked with mirth when Cinloch told him of the exchange.

'I am glad you had no one there to witness it!' He chortled. 'The High King would make sport of it for the rest of your days. Cinloch of the Epidii bested by a slip of a girl!'

'She did not best me!' Cinloch protested, though he did it in good humour. 'I am certain she will change her mind when she awakens tomorrow and sees her father's head and a hundred of his warriors laid out before the gate. It seems harsh to inflict such a thing upon a child but

I can see no way around it. I have no appetite for a siege.'

A Caereni sentry shook Cinloch awake just after dawn to inform him that the Votadini had opened their gates. He shook his fist in triumph and rushed to pull his boots on and make his way to the fort. He almost sang with joy as he went at the thought of how surprised Drest would be when he arrived to find the siege already lifted and the fort occupied. The sight that greeted him on entering the fort caused his smile to fade. The fort's occupants were mainly women, old men and children. The women put him in mind of slaves. None were armed, most kept their eyes fixed upon the ground in subservience and it seemed to him that their lives were spent in daily chores and the rearing of their children. He thought it strange for a people to deny their women the joy of battle and foolish for them to deprive their armies of half the warriors available to them. Only fifty warriors had been left to hold the walls and many of them were weaklings or old soldiers with missing limbs or legs that were all but crippled. All the same, there were enough of them to have held the walls for months. He turned as Derice marched up to him with her chin held out in defiance.

'You promised us safe passage.' She declared, her voice less confident and steady than it had been when the height of the wall had separated them. 'Will you keep your word?'

'Aye!' Cinloch replied. 'I will keep my word. Lead your people off! They will not be accosted. But you must leave your valuables here for they are the spoils of war and the spoils fall to the victor.' He pointed at the wooden trunks carried by her servants.

'I have taken nothing but my blankets, my furs and my clothes. Search my baggage if you must! You will find no silver there.'

Cinloch gestured to the servants to open the boxes so he could inspect their contents. The first clattered so heavily against the ground he knew it contained something heavier than cloth or furs. When the lid was pulled back, it revealed a dolly made from straw with a scrap of cloth sewn around it to make a dress. The sight of it nestled amongst the blankets caused him such a pang of pity for the fatherless and destitute girl that he searched no further and waved them on. The girl turned and eyed him suspiciously as if trying to read his intentions.

'You know that the gods will punish you for this? The Votads are raised to their throne by Maben himself. He will have his revenge for my father's death. I doubt he will spare even as ragged a king as you.'

'The gods will judge each of us, Derice. We can only await their verdict. Go now! I will pray to Maben to keep you safe.'

He watched until the last of them had filed out through the gate and then set his warriors to searching for the Votadini treasure. He intended to have it all piled in the hall so Drest would marvel at the display laid out for him. Walls were broken, wells plumbed and floors dug up in every chamber but not one silver coin was unearthed by the time the sun set. Cinloch called for torches and urged the workers on as they continued the search long into the night. He called a halt only when his dirt-encrusted warriors began to slump to the ground in exhaustion. Long hours of toil had achieved nothing apart from littering the fort with piles of earth, broken timbers and scattered thatch. Cinloch gritted his teeth in frustration as he gazed around at the fruitless devastation. Only Uurad with a skin of ale and the promise of a dry bed beside a roaring fire was enough to persuade him to leave it until the morning.

The rising sun brought no joy along with it. The place looked much worse in the full light of day. Cinloch's spirits sank when the first scouts rode in to report that the High King had already crossed the southern river and would surely arrive at Din Eidyn in the early afternoon. He ordered his steward to set men to clearing away the mess made the day before and others to resuming the search. Everyone else was sent to light the fire pits, bring animals in for slaughter and help in preparing a feast for the fast-approaching kings and their retinues. When Cinloch was satisfied that all was in hand, he climbed to the battlements to watch for the High King's approach. The heights offered a commanding view and he caught sight of Drest's column even though it was still a long way off. He saw the cavalry galloping ahead, leaving a great body of spearmen to escort a long line of carts, prisoners and slaves. He shook his head and laughed bitterly at the prospect of the

High King's disappointment when he discovered he had given the wealth of the Votadini lands to his placemen and kept only an empty fort for himself. He thought it somehow fitting that Drest would enjoy no reward from a war he had entered into with such haste and reckless abandon. He hoped he might learn from it but long experience made him fear otherwise.

'Hail, good Cinloch!' The High King called in greeting as he passed through the gate and leapt down from his saddle. 'You should have come south with us! You would not believe the wall of the Romans! Such a weight of rock and stone was used in its construction, I cannot think how they accomplished it. To raise such a barrier from one sea to the other seems like a feat only the gods could achieve! Talorc, Typaun and Taran rode with me from one end to the other while the others burned and pillaged the Votadini lands. What a weight of silver and a great multitude of slaves they have taken! Even Birst and Forcus are satisfied and complain only of a lack of carts to carry it away.'

Cinloch forced a smile onto his lips though his stomach was twisted in dread. He let Drest babble away in his enthusiasm and waited for the moment when he would be forced to dampen his ardour.

'I have divided the conquered territories between Manath and Typaun and Taran will govern it for them. They have agreed to pay more tribute than I currently receive from either your Epidii kingdom or that of the Caledones. We will have more silver than we know what to do with and that is without considering the riches of the Votad himself. Come, Cinloch! You have broken the siege more quickly than I dared to hope and I can see you have searched the place most thoroughly. Tease me no further! Show me what you have unearthed!'

The smile melted from Drest's face as Cinloch told him of the long hours of digging and fruitless searching and tried to placate him by detailing the efforts still underway.

'You let the garrison march away without torturing a single one of them to give up the location of the Votadini hoard?' Drest growled with unconcealed fury. 'I did not expect such stupidity from you!'

'Calm yourself, good King.' Talorc cautioned him with an air of nonchalance. 'The treasure is here! I can taste it!'

Cinloch and Drest watched as the Drui priest began to pace around the muddy courtyard sniffing the air and flexing his fingers as if he detected the presence of something invisible to the eyes of all others. The Epidii King knew Talorc was putting on a display but could not read his intentions. He decided to remain silent as he was not eager to feel the heat of the High King's wrath again. The Drui pranced and paced for a few moments longer before stiffening and pointing a sharpened fingernail at a pigsty set hard against the wall.

'Here!' He declared in a tone of absolute certainty. 'Bring your diggers here!'

A rough stone step emerged from the dirt after only a few moments of scraping. Cinloch experienced intense feelings of relief at being spared Drest's anger and annoyance at being bested by the priest. Relief won out in the end and he was glad to be able to accompany Drest into the hall and eat bread with him while everyone else feasted on roasted meat. His belly was swollen with softened dough and bitter ale by the time Talorc strode up to the table with his robes caked in mud.

'Come!' He ordered them, his torn face lit up in delight. 'You must see this!'

Dirty, sweat-smeared men leaned on the shafts of their picks and shovels amongst the scattered earth and mounds of stony soil and watched the kings approach. Talorc gestured them onwards until they reached the top of eight stone steps and looked down to see a thick wooden door hanging off its hinges at the bottom.

'Go on!' Talorc cajoled them. 'I have had torches lit so you might gaze upon all the riches of the Votadini.'

The cellar walls and floor were of beaten earth with thick timber supports and cross-beams to support the roof above them. The dusty air was the same as that of the souterians used to store oats and barley beneath the Black Fort and the Crag Fort. The light of the flickering torches revealed that it had been many years since stale grains had filled this vault. Cinloch gasped at the sight of a stone statue of some Roman god or warrior carved with such precision he half expected it to leap at him. Every hair on his head, every rib, every fold in his cloak and even the veins in his wrist had been chiselled into the stone in exquisite detail. Sacks of coins were stacked high against every wall. Some of them were so full they had split under the weight of the silver sending their contents spilling onto the floor. Rough wooden boxes held richly decorated plates, goblets and bowls of both silver and gold. Others were filled with heavy golden rings, necklaces and bracelets of a quality no merchant had ever laid before a northern king.

'By the gods!' Drest exclaimed, his eyes wide in wonder and disbelief. 'What a kingdom I could build with this! There is enough here to choke the greed of even the Phocali and Carnonacae Kings. I could buy the loyalty of every one of my vassals and rule for a hundred years!'

'But how will we transport it north?' Cinloch asked, still stunned by the extent of the hoard. 'We will need a hundred wagons for this and there is not a single one to be had.'

Drest clapped him hard on the shoulder and laughed.

'I will leave that to you, good Cinloch. Now that my treasury overflows, I will need a man of honour and ability to administer it on my behalf. Take your third away to the Crag Fort and transport the rest to the cellars beneath my own stronghold. Pick whatever treasures you think will sweeten your wife, for you will be so busy I doubt she will see much of you.'

Cinloch took a breath to steady himself. He had not expected such a generous share and the prospect of such wealth caused his heart to thump in his chest. His joy was only partly tempered by his sudden appointment as treasurer, though he knew he had a long and arduous task ahead of him. What happiness was left to him was ripped cruelly away when Drest began to shout for his priest.

'Talorc! Come to me! My priest, my seer, my wizard! Come to me now so I might weigh you down in silver and gold! If it was not for your wisdom and talents, these riches would have stayed buried for some black-toothed peasant to stumble upon a hundred years from now. Come! Tell me what you would have and I will give it to you!'

The Epidii King chided himself for the petty jealousy he felt at seeing his rival rewarded and praised. He tried to bite down on his envy but could not stop himself from glowering at the dark priest as he picked out the richest of the treasures for himself.

He sought solace in the company of Brude Uurad later that night and the old man indulged him by listening to all of his complaints.

'How in the name of the gods did he know where to look?' He raged over his fourth goblet of ale. 'I searched every inch of the courtyard and saw no sign of the cellar! Drest thinks the gods give him powers but I know it is nothing more than foul trickery.'

'I fear you are right, my King' Uurad began hesitantly.

The use of his royal title when they were alone was enough to catch Cinloch's attention and bring his ranting to a halt.

'You know something, Brude Uurad!' He snapped. 'Tell me what you have learned.'

'I can prove no connection.' He stuttered as his face turned pale and he subconsciously rubbed his hands over his thighs to ease his anxiety. 'But I came upon the Smertae encampment when I went in search of mosses and roots to make a poultice for your hand. It was then that I saw her amongst their prisoners.'

'Saw who?' Cinloch demanded, though the sickening feeling in his stomach told him he already knew the answer.

'The Votadini girl.' Uurad replied in a faltering tone. 'She was tied to a post with the other women. The garrison must have crossed paths with the Smertae on their way south. They will have slaughtered the men and boys and taken only the women and girls as slaves. She told me they tortured her until she betrayed the location of her father's treasure.'

'I promised them all safe passage!' Cinloch exploded as he leapt to his feet and reached out for his sword belt. 'That filthy bastard has made a liar of me! I will tear his guts out and spread them across the floor!'

Uurad grabbed at his wrist and held it with remarkable strength as he peered into his eyes with great intensity.

'You must calm yourself, my friend! Talorc rode with the High King and will deny any knowledge of this. The King will not hold him responsible for the sins of the Smertae. Who do you think Drest will choose if you force him to decide between you and the priest? Are you confident he would favour you over him? He will think you to be a fool who is consumed with jealousy. Do not act in anger, I beg of you!'

Cinloch snatched his arm away and paced the floor in frustration.

'I know you are right but I would sacrifice all to bring that dark-hearted bastard down. He makes a sport of tormenting me and wins all favour through trickery while I bear the burden of the toil and tedium Drest presses upon me. He rips away the joy of every victory and leaves me bitter and seething. Now he has caused me to break an oath made to an innocent child. It tears my heart to think of the horrors that poor girl will suffer at the hands of the Smertae and their filthy crone.'

'Then that is one hurt I can ease, good Cinloch.' Uurad murmured softly. 'I was able to persuade the Smertae to part with the girl in exchange for my purse, my grandfather's staff and my good wool cloak. She sleeps with my apprentices now. I thought to take her back to the Crag Fort with us. Your wife might some comfort in her while you are away.'

'You are a good friend, Uurad.' Cinloch told him as he reached out to accept a goblet of ale. 'I know how much it must have pained you to give up your grandfather's staff. I cannot recall ever seeing you without it clutched in your hand. I will miss you when I am called away to administer Drest's treasury.'

'Then take me with you.' The old man implored him with a chuckle. 'I would jump at the chance to study the artefacts in the Votadini hoard and I don't see why I should stay to be vexed by your wife when you have made good your escape.'

29

The role of treasurer to the High King proved to be a more of a blessing and less of a curse than Cinloch had feared. Drest and Stroma spent much of their time travelling between the forts of the vassal kings to collect tribute, settle disputes and distribute favours and so left Cinloch to his own devices in the Black Fort. Brude Uurad passed his days in the cellars examining the Votadini treasures. He had to be coaxed out to eat and to spare his old eyes from the strain of peering at objects in the dim and flickering torchlight. When he grew too blind and feeble to negotiate the worn steps safely, Cinloch had servants bring new items up from the depths so the Brude could inspect them in the full light of day. The Epidii King shared his fascination for all things Roman and took joy in each of his discoveries and in his wide-eyed wonder at how mere men could carve, cast and sculpt such delicate, intricate and beautiful things. They would often marvel at the multitude of gods worshipped by the foreign invaders and argue over whether any of those captured in gold, bronze or stone were the same as those they themselves venerated.

They also took pleasure in selecting the most appropriate gifts for the High King to present to his vassals to delight them and strengthen their ties to him. The Phocali and Carnonacae Kings were the easiest to please as they valued Drest's offerings simply by the weight of gold and silver they contained. Uurad and Cinloch took care to choose only the ugliest and crudest of items for them as they knew they would be melted down or chopped into hacksilver within days of being received. Statues, cups and bowls bearing images of wolves were reserved for the Smertae, who took them as representations of the wolf-god, Bladd. The Caledone, Vacomagi and Venicone Kings could be delighted by anything depicting a boar, a bull or a stag. Those who had an emblem not replicated anywhere in the hoard were placated with great sackloads of the finest of the coins or with inferior goods rendered in silver by the craftsmen Cinloch had gathered in Perth.

Prince Nechtan was a further source of pleasure for the Epidii King. He brought him from the Crag Fort to continue his instruction and never had any cause to regret his decision. The boy had an insatiable thirst for knowledge and immersed himself in the work of the smiths, the farmers, the hunters and the carpenters. He was always plaguing Cinloch and Uurad with questions about their work with the hoard and about the business of the kingdom. When scolded for troubling them, he did not sulk but went off quite happily to hunt, ride or to practice with spear and sword. They both agreed that he would make a fine king if the gods smiled upon him and let him live long enough to ascend to the throne.

Even his home life flourished in the years after the fall of the Votadini. When he was able to return to the Epidii lands, he found Mael quite contented as she fussed and fawned over the Votadini princess. Derice had settled in quite nicely and gradually grew less troubled by the nightmares of Smertae blades tearing at her flesh. The ragged scars on her back and legs would never heal completely but Cinloch could not help but smile when he saw they had faded already.

His only sadness came at the end of the third summer after the fall of Din Eidyn. He found Brude Uurad in his chair in the courtyard and thought he was dozing in the warmth of the afternoon sun. It was only when he touched him to shake him from his sleep that he felt his cold skin and knew he had gone to the gods. It gave him some comfort to know he had passed peacefully for his dead face was a picture of serenity and contentment. He should have been happy that Uurad had spent his last years in tranquillity and fulfilment but he still sobbed in grief as he touched his old face and said goodbye to his most enduring and truest friend.

He carried him back to the Crag Fort and called on every king and brude in the kingdom to come to stand at his pyre. It was a tribute to the old man's wisdom and good character that so many of the great and the good of the kingdom took to saddle or ship to speed their way to the Epidii capital. It would have both pleased and amused the old Brude to know that his funeral was attended by more kings and priests than those of any of the Epidii kings he had served. Even Talorc and his Drui tore themselves away from whatever foul business they were engaged in and rode hard for the Fort of the Crag. Cinloch feared that Talorc would demand the right to conduct the funeral rituals and was surprised when he was humble and asked only to participate along with the rest of Uurad's apprentices.

'He was like a father to me and took me under his wing after the wolf tore the flesh from my face.' He declared solemnly. 'I bear him no ill will for his part in sending me north to my death. I would honour him as my teacher and play my small part in speeding him on to the gods.'

Drest nodded his approval and agreed it was fitting that the rites be performed by those who had learned them at Uurad's feet. He then surprised both Talorc and Cinloch by announcing his intention to perform the Song of the Epidii in the light of Uurad's flaming pyre.

'I have heard him sing the song of our people so many times I now know it by heart. I will honour his wisdom, loyalty and friendship by performing it just as he did. The gods will see that he had the love of the High King of All the Tribes and will surely find him a seat at their table in the Underworld.'

Uurad's pyre was built higher than any ever seen before and burned with such heat it melted the very sand it sparked and blazed upon. Drest sang the song of his people and so closely mimicked Brude Uurad in his movements and facial expressions it caused tears to run down

Cinloch's cheeks. It was as if the old Brude had been made young again and capered on the sands as his earthly remains were consumed by the flames. The Epidii King kept vigil until long into the night and watched as the great pyre was reduced to a pile of glowing ash. Brin, Erp's widow, stood at his side and took his arm to comfort him. The wind that had blown the fire into an inferno now blew great clouds of ash, embers and sparks into the air and carried them out across the waves.

'Look, Cinloch.' Brin murmured. 'The gods are so impatient to have Uurad among them they do not wait for us to scatter his ashes onto the sea. They have sent a wind to hurry him on his way.'

'Tis a nice thought.' Cinloch replied with a smile still strained by his grief. 'Though I can't help but think his passing leaves us all poorer. He has been a constant in all of our lives like an anchor holding a ship steady in both fair and foul weather. I pray it is not a sign we are about to be cast adrift.'

'Tis much worse than that.' Brin whispered. 'His passing has left you and I as the last of the old ones. It is a sign that our time is almost past. Soon, they will stand at our pyres and watch the flames reduce us to ash.'

Cinloch hushed her and told her not to be foolish but still shivered at the thought.

Brin was carried off by the first frosts of the winter and Cinloch remembered her words as he stood in the light of her pyre on the banks of the Tae. He brooded on them as he rode west to scatter her ashes on the same waters that had received those of her husband and Brude Uurad. He tried to focus on past victories and triumphs and a long life well-lived but found he could not cast his sadness aside. It was if a black cloud was hanging over his head and he could not shake off a sense of foreboding and a fear of ill times ahead. Even the news that Queen Stroma was again with child did not cheer him but instead made him dwell on the likelihood of him not living long enough to see the child reach adulthood. His spirits did not improve when he returned to the Black Fort and resumed his work with the treasury. The pleasure he had taken in the Votadini hoard was absent now Uurad was gone and he did what was required of him with joyless efficiency. He plumbed new depths of despondency when Drest returned home full of complaints, bitterness and discontent.

'What is the state of my treasury, good Cinloch?' He demanded from his throne two days after his return from the court of the Venicone King. His scowl betrayed his irritation as he stroked absently at the fur of the bearskin he had won hunting with King Uuid and his warriors.

'It is much depleted, my King.' Cinloch replied without any hint of apology. 'Which is not surprising since we still pay out far more than we take in. The bribes you pay out to your vassals account for almost half of what is taken in tribute. The weapons you buy, the labour for the improvements to the Black Fort's defences and the exorbitant prices demanded by the merchants

310

who follow your retinue across the kingdom account for most of the deficit. We will be paupers in two years if we carry on as we are, or four if we tighten our belts.'

'What can I do?' The High King snapped, his face twisted in frustration. 'I am bored with these sub-kings with their constant demands and petty squabbles. I make gifts to them so they know they have the love of the High King but, even as they receive them from my hands, they fill my ears with complaints about one or more of their neighbours. The Caledones and the Vacomagi are never without some miserable spit of land to argue about. The Carnonacae and the Caereni cannot help but seize one another's ships even though there is trade enough for both of them. The Manau and the Maeatae constantly raid cattle from one another and then deny it to my face and demand that I take their side against their neighbour. It is intolerable. They are more like children than kings!'

'The High King is father to all of his people.' Cinloch replied without any trace of sympathy. 'The burden of resolving such disputes rests upon your shoulders.'

Drest glared down at him and scratched at his beard. A smile crept onto his face as some thought occurred to him.

'Did I ever tell you about the southern priest Talorc and I encountered as we rode along the Roman wall? Talorc was fascinated by him and invited him to make camp with us and share our food. His name was Finian and he told us he worshipped a god from across the sea. His name was Christ and he allowed himself to be tortured and killed so his death might be used to fill his followers with such guilt they would obey his every command. We thought him a fool to worship such a weak and devious god but he said one thing that has stayed with me. He said that evil gods make work for idle hands. It makes me wonder if my vassal kings have been idle for too long and if it is the dark gods who feed on their boredom and cause them to bicker and fight. Perhaps it is time to give them something to better occupy themselves with and to let them find silver of their own instead of constantly picking my pocket. Perhaps it is time to venture into the lands to the south of the wall and seize the wealth of the Brigantes.'

'War?' Cinloch demanded as he felt his guts turn to water at the thought. 'Have you not had battles enough? Do you not have lands enough and more vassals than you can endure? You rule all the lands from sea to sea and from the Dark Isles to the Romans' stone wall! Why risk all that for some adventure when you do not know what sleeping beast you might awaken with your invasion?'

'I knew you would counsel me so.' Drest replied with a shrug. 'It is exactly what my father would have said. It was only a thought. I just thought to test it on you. We shall have peace and I will continue to suffer these petty disputes.'

The peace lasted until the spring when King Donal of the Caledones came to the Black Fort to report that the Smertae and the Caereni were at war.

'The Smertae suffered badly over the winter and took to raiding the Caereni sheep.' He informed Drest and Cinloch before he had even had the chance to remove his cloak and take refreshment. 'When they saw how badly their flocks were depleted, the Caereni went in force to demand recompense and were routed by Smertae warriors. It is said they spilled so much blood on the snow that the stain could be seen from miles away. Talorc has gone to Mamm Ru to bring an end to the fighting but even he may not be able to keep them apart.'

'Curse that vile Smertae crone and her foul people!' Drest raged. 'If they must have blood, then let them drain it from the veins of our enemies! I will not have them slaughter my own armies just to satisfy their thirst! Send out the call! We will ride beyond the far wall this summer and raid the lands of the Brigantes!'

Cinloch opened his mouth to protest but was interrupted by the High King before he could form an argument to persuade him to reconsider his decision.

'Hold your tongue, Cinloch! I know you do not support me in this and so will excuse you from accompanying me on the grounds of your age and infirmity. You will remain here and rule as High King in my stead.'

30

The summer was one blessed with unusually warm, dry weather and Cinloch passed his time at the Black Fort quite pleasantly. Even Mael's complaints did not trouble him. Her taunts about him being cast aside and abandoned seemed ridiculous when he controlled the keys to the treasury and had the authority to wield all the powers of the High King. He spared himself from the frustration of dealing with the trickle of petitioners who arrived at his gates by making his judgements quickly and answering those who challenged his decisions by pointing his finger to the south and inviting them to go and appeal to the High King himself. Precious few of them accepted the challenge and Cinloch laughed at those embittered enough to do so as their chances of finding the army were slim and their odds of a successful appeal if they found Drest were even more slender. He took to spending his afternoons drinking ale and fishing from the banks of the Tae and was often joined there by the Mormaer of Keld.

'Does it not bother you to be so far from the fighting, Cinloch?' Curetan enquired during the course of one idyllic afternoon. 'These battles will be the first where you have not taken your place in the line beside my brother or my nephew.'

'No.' Cinloch replied, surprised to find that the thought of it caused him no pang of regret. 'I suppose it must be because I opposed the campaign. In the past, I would have ranted and raged and demanded my place. I thought this adventure to be an unnecessary risk but my counsel was ignored. I just pray that my caution will be proven to have been misplaced.'

The first of the carts and the packhorses arrived at the Tae just a few days later and stood as testament to the success of the raids on the Brigantes. Cinloch had to sacrifice his afternoons of tranquillity and relaxation and instead throw himself into the tedious work of inspecting and supervising the columns of horses and wagons that wound their way north. He set guards on the roads to ensure that no spoils were spirited away before he could claim the third due to the High King. Even this share proved to be so vast the Black Fort's cellars were soon filled and he was forced to arrange for silver, grain, oats and barley to be transported to other forts for storage. The slopes around Pert became so crowded with cattle, sheep, goats and pigs he had to press his own servants into service to herd them to pastures not already stripped bare. The great hall was piled high with cloth, clay jugs, goblets and silver plate. The courtyard was filled with anvils, picks, spades, ploughs, hammers, tongs, shields, spears and swords. The lack of space even forced Cinloch into requisitioning the royal stables and tethering the High King's beloved stallions outside the walls.

Drest's triumphant return home in the autumn marked the beginning of the last years of plenty. The feasting lasted for days and the slim, bronzed and ecstatic High King basked in the adoration of his placemen and his subjects. It seemed that no greater warrior king had ever set foot in the kingdom of the tribes. His vassals would stamp their feet and howl in approval when he told of how he had chased the Brigante warlords from their strongholds and then pillaged their lands at will while they skulked away and watched on from the forests. It was to his great credit that he chose not to scold Cinloch for his caution but to honour him instead.

'I have filled the treasury so it creaks at the seams, Cinloch.' He told him when they were able to steal a moment together away from the conquering kings and their mormaers and thanes. 'I would trust no other man to administer it for me. Will you return to the Crag Fort and manage my riches from there?'

'I will, my King.' Cinloch replied in relief at not being upbraided for his erroneous counsel. 'I will do it gladly.'

'Good! Good!' Drest grinned at him. 'I will place all that is precious to me in your steady hands, my friend. Once my new son is born and has been weaned from the teat, I will send him to you so he may enjoy the same instruction Prince Nechtan has received. I see the benefit of your wisdom in him.'

316

Cinloch saw little of the High King over the following five years. Messengers arrived from the Black Fort every few days so all treasury business could be transacted efficiently and without any misunderstandings arising. The Epidii King rose with the first light of dawn so all administrative matters could be dealt with during the course of the morning. This left him free to pass his afternoons with Princes Nechtan and Clunie and Princess Derice. He had set them the task of scratching the emblems of each of the tribes into the earth of the courtyard when Queen Mael came up beside him and took his arm.

'I think you were a brude in some past life.' She murmured as she laid her head against his shoulder. 'You are never happier than when you are teaching them about the gods, the stars or which crops should be sown in soil that is dark or that which is heavy with clay. Our brudes watch on with sullen faces as you teach them the words of the Song of the Epidii and the movements of the Dance of the Epidii. They think you usurp their position.'

Cinloch laughed in delight. 'I care not, good wife. It gives me such joy I will not surrender the task to any of them. Only Brude Uurad would have taught them better. I will take them to the sands at dusk to light a fire in his memory. Will you accompany us? It would please me to have you there.'

'I would like nothing better but must regretfully decline,' She replied with a grimace. 'I have promised Derice I will sew with her.' She then leaned closer and dropped her voice to a whisper. 'She has set her heart on making a dress fine enough to steal the heart of Prince Nechtan.'

Cinloch raised his eyebrows in a show of surprise although he knew well enough that Mael and Derice were as thick as thieves in their plotting. Such a match would please him greatly, though it would not be his decision to make.

The Epidii King watched as Nechtan and Clunie ran around collecting driftwood for Uurad's fire. He found himself envying their boundless enthusiasm and their tireless limbs. It seemed like an age since he had been free of the aches and pains that came with the passing of the years and longer since he had been able to run without limping. When he deemed the pile to be sufficiently high, he passed his flint to Nechtan and instructed him to set it alight. The boy chewed at his lip in concentration as he scraped furiously and sent a shower of sparks onto the tinder. His mind wandered back to the days when Uurad had entrusted him with his own flint and taught him how to make fire. It made him smile to see the Brude's learning being passed onto yet another generation and happier still to think of Nechtan teaching it to his sons and grandsons long after he had gone to the gods. He was snatched from this pleasant reverie by Clunie calling out in boyish delight.

'Look Cinloch!' He cried. 'Look at all the pretty ships!'

Cinloch squinted into the fading light but saw nothing but the foaming tips of the white-capped waves. He was about to scold the boy for his stories when he caught sight of the first of the sails. His breath seemed to catch in his throat and his heart stop in his chest. He blinked furiously to clear his vision and leaned on his staff to steady himself. The nearest sail bore the Dal Riata emblem of the running dog and those behind it carried the triple-wave insignia of the Ulaid. Cinloch had stood on the walls of the Crag Fort with his father and watched those same sails fill the horizon as the ships beneath them carried the Irish slaughterers across the Short Sea to conquer the lands of the Epidii. He cursed and called the boys to him just as the horns were blown from his walls to sound the alarm.

'How many?' He demanded when his steward met him at the gate.

'I counted thirty before the darkness swallowed them, my King. I fear they have come in strength.'

'They will not risk their ships by landing in the darkness, so we have some time to prepare. Bring all the townsfolk inside the walls and tell them to bring all food and valuables with them unless they want to provide sustenance to the slaughterers. Send messengers to all of our forts to command my mormaers and thanes to close their gates against the invaders. Prepare my bodyguard to ride to the Black Fort with the Princes.'

'You would send your whole bodyguard with them?' The steward demanded in shock. 'That will weaken our garrison here.'

'Do you think the High King will thank us if his sons are lost to these bastards?' Cinloch spat in rage. 'I would rather oppose them with only a handful of men than face Drest's wrath if his boys were taken or killed! Send them now and command them to tell the High King that the Dal Riata and the Ulaid no longer make war and tear each other to ribbons! They have joined forces and now come to conquer the land of his fathers!'

Cinloch stood on his walls and gazed out to sea in the weak light of the early dawn. He had counted a hundred ships and more came into sight as the sea mist was thinned by the light morning breeze.

'What emblem is that?' Mael asked from her place at his side. 'I have never seen it before.'

'It is the cross of the foreign god Drest spoke of.' Cinloch replied. 'It seems that the Ulaid now worship a god so feeble he allowed mere mortals to kill him. If the gods smile down upon us, the slaughterers will be infected by his weakness.'

'Will you ride out to give battle when they come ashore?'

'No.' Cinloch replied with a shake of his head. 'They will not land in one place but will spread themselves out along the coast to deny us the chance to defeat them in the shallows. Then they will join together to besiege us. We will hold out behind our walls until Drest raises his army and marches west to relieve us. Only then will we ride out to assail them from the rear as they turn to face the High King's assault.'

'It could be months before he comes to our aid. Do we have supplies enough for such a siege when you have filled our cellars with the High King's silver?'

Cinloch chose not to reply to his wife's question for the answer was already known to them both. If Drest was slow to raise his forces, they would starve.

'You should have sent Derice away with the boys!' Mael snapped. 'She is not safe here.'

Cinloch nodded but said nothing. He knew Mael was right and he cursed himself for not thinking of it at the time. He fixed his eyes on a distant Carnonacae trading ship and groaned as it was overtaken by the faster Irish vessels and then boarded. More friendly trading ships would suffer the same fate before word of the invasion spread.

'They come!' Cinloch's steward cried out as he pointed out to sea.

The distant sails billowed in the wind and then carried their ships towards the shore at great speed.

'Everyone to the walls!' Cinloch roared. 'Let them see our ramparts filled with spears! Let them know it will cost them dear if they attempt to assault our stronghold!'

'You will not mask our lack of warriors by filling their places with girls and old men.' Mael sneered with a bitterness that was now rare for her. 'Do not encourage them to attack by laying our weakness out before them.'

'A spear thrown from these heights by an old man will kill just as surely as one thrown by a warrior in the prime of his years!' Cinloch replied, though his defiance was tempered by doubt.

The Dal Riata returned to the Crag Fort at dawn the following day. Their progress through the Epidii countryside was marked by columns of smoke rising up from the homesteads they destroyed as they advanced. More than a thousand of them had gathered below the walls by the time the sun reached its highest point and their leaders came forward to stand beneath the gate. Cinloch glared down at them as they babbled away in their foul and uncouth tongue.

'The one with the broken and twisted nose says he is Loegaire, King of the Ulaid, and the yellow-toothed man beside him is King Reuda of the Dal Riata.' Cinloch's brude translated for him. 'The younger man says he has come to reclaim the fort of his father. He offers to slaughter only our men and to mercifully take our women and children as slaves if we will surrender ourselves to him. He also seems eager to reassure us that our women are too ugly for him to rape, though I might be mistaken as it is hard to understand him.'

Cinloch could see no resemblance between the ragged dog below him and the boy the Dal Riata witch had sent to the boats as Talorc and his Drui closed on her and King Loarn. It felt as if a hundred lifetimes had passed since he had stood upon those sands and watched the invaders put to slaughter.

'What response shall I give, my King?' The brude asked. 'They demand our answer.'

'Say nothing!' Cinloch instructed him. 'I will waste no words on these beasts. They will have their answer when the High King rides in to soak the earth in their blood.'

The invaders did not tarry beneath the gates for long. They threw curses up at the ramparts and spat on the ground before turning back towards their encampment. The garrison watched on helplessly as they rode out to destroy and burn all that had been built in the years of Cinloch's rule. Long weeks passed with an endless procession of carts rumbling their way to the coast to unload the wealth of the Epidii into the holds of their ships. They took a great number of slaves and Cinloch soon lost count of those marched past his walls. His misery was deepened by hunger as the garrison and the peasants sheltering with them tore through his meagre food supplies with disheartening speed. After two full cycles of the moon had passed and the first chills of winter were felt on the wind, he stopped lifting his eyes to the eastern horizon in the vain hope of catching sight of the approach of the High King's army. Mael scolded him for wallowing in his despair but he could not keep himself from climbing the ramparts to spend his days witnessing the slow and steady devastation of his realm.

He was standing above the gate taking in the scene of desolation below him when he caught sight of a dark figure making his way through the encampment. The distinctive black hood and robes marked him out from the Irish warriors scurrying around him. None of them paid any heed to his passing and no head turned in his direction as he strode forward. Cinloch held his breath and waited for someone to cry out in alarm but Talorc, King of the Drui, went unmolested until he disappeared from sight below the walls of the fort.

Cinloch blinked and shook his head in disbelief. He looked to his steward and his brude but neither of them gave any sign of having seen anything untoward. He wondered if the lack of food was causing him to lose his mind and suffer from hallucinations. He had almost accepted that his mind was playing tricks on him when the warriors on the sea wall began to cry out and point towards the shore in great agitation. His nostrils told him what was happening long before he had hobbled over to join them.

The invaders had drawn their warships up onto the beach for safety and they now ran around the long line of ships in panic. Every third vessel was already ablaze and their crackling timbers spat out such showers of hot embers and sparks that they caused their neighbours to smoulder. Cinloch threw his head back and roared with laughter at their vain attempts to save what was left of their fleet. One crew managed to drag their craft back into the sea but, even as its keel was pulled from the sand, it was already in flames. He searched the beach for some sight of Talorc but could see little through the thick smoke and the crowds of Irishmen who now rushed in from their encampment in time to see the disaster unfold.

'Come!' His steward hissed at him as he pulled at his sleeve. 'Come quietly to the far wall so you do not alert those who now crowd around to gawp at the burning ships! Come quietly so we do not give warning to our enemies!'

Cinloch followed him to the far wall and demanded to know what was urgent enough to justify denying him the pleasure of witnessing the misfortune of the accursed invaders. The steward pointed to the eastern horizon and grinned in delight when Cinloch's mouth fell open in surprise. He did not need to see the distant banners to know who commanded the fast-approaching mass of cavalry. There were so many horse warriors they could only represent the combined might of the Caledone, Venicone, Maeatae and Manau cavalry. The steward then tugged at his sleeve again and pointed to the north. Cinloch saw nothing at first but then became aware of brief flashes of red in the woods beyond the settlement. He squinted his eyes as hard as he could and then gasped in astonishment.

'Is it?' He demanded as he reached out and took hold of the steward's forearm.

'Aye, my King. Tis the Smertae gathering at the edge of the forest. They will attack from the north and outflank these stinking bastards as they turn to face the High King's charge.'

'By the gods, we are saved!' Cinloch exclaimed with such joy and relief it made him light-headed. 'And we will attack from the rear! Command our warriors to muster at the gate! We will rush out just as the cavalry hits them!'

With no ships to run to, the Dal Riata and the Ulaid were forced to turn and face the full force of the charging cavalry. Much of their ragged line was broken by that first assault and what little was left disintegrated entirely under Smertae sickles and the swords of the garrison. No warrior was spared, with near two thousand of them massacred on the sands around the smouldering remains of their ships. Those few fortunate enough to escape into the surrounding countryside were hunted down remorselessly by the Smertae and the Venicone hounds. Cinloch ordered his men to search through the mangled corpses for the Ulaid and Dal Riata Kings but they could not be found.

'I cannot even offer you a feast as thanks for our salvation, my King' Cinloch apologised when Drest found him in the courtyard. 'I have barely a grain of wheat left in my cellars.'

'It matters not, good Cinloch!' Drest beamed, his face smeared in blood and dirt from the battle. 'The slaughterers from across the sea have learned that Epidii lands are not so easily won!' He paused and clapped the Epidii King's shoulder. 'In any case, I have brought beef and venison enough for all of us. I thought you would be in need of a good feed. I also have wagons filled with ale which should arrive in time to moisten your throat. Come! Let us celebrate now and tomorrow we will ride out to put an end to those who besiege your other forts!'

31

It took a full week to clear the invaders from Epidii lands. Word of the flight of their kings reached the ears of those besieging the Stone Fort and the Fort of Spears and they took to their ships rather than face the might of the High King's army. Those further inland were caught by surprise and paid a heavy price for their insolence. The few remaining stragglers were hunted by the Smertae and the Venicone dogs. When they were captured, their heads were torn from their bodies and spiked on the branches of trees.

Cinloch played host to Drest, Talorc, Donal of the Caledones, Typaun of the Manau, Manath of the Maeatae and Uuid of the Venicones. He was surprised to find he had missed their company and he took great pleasure in drinking with them and reliving past battles, skirmishes and other near misses. If nothing else, it distracted him from Mael's foul mood and her sharp tongue. She was furious because Derice had been afflicted by the pox during the siege. She scowled hard whenever she saw him and berated him for failing to send her away and spare her the sores that now disfigured her face. Even Manath shook his head in disapproval of his daughter's behaviour and scolded her for not giving her husband the respect he was due.

Drest was reinvigorated by the defeat of the slaughterers and was so elated he lifted the spirits of all in his company. His lust for adventure was satisfied so fully he spoke only of his plans for the future and of his hopes for a period of long and lasting peace. Cinloch began to dread the day of their departure and thought that life would be much duller once they were gone. He was not to discover if his fears were well-founded, for the sudden arrival of a dirty, bedraggled and bloody rider threw all into disarray. The poor man was dishevelled and filthy and Cinloch did not recognise him as he was helped into the hall. It was only when King Manath leapt up in horror that he realised it was Taran of the Maeatae who now limped in and dripped blood on his floor.

'What has befallen you, my boy?' Manath demanded as he kneeled before him and ran his hands over his blood-soaked tunic. 'Call for the brudes to see to his wounds! My nephew has been grievously wounded!'

'It is not so bad, Uncle.' Taran wheezed, the paleness of his face giving lie to his words. 'Our southern army has been routed in the Votadini lands!'

'Routed?' Manath exclaimed, his own face turning white at the news. 'How so? How many of our warriors were lost?'

'Only a handful of us were able to escape them. They attacked us on the march and were intent on leaving no warrior alive.'

'Who was it, Taran?' Drest demanded. 'Was it the Brigantes? Did they cross the wall to have their revenge?'

'No, my King.' Taran coughed weakly. 'They did not come from south of the wall. They came across the Eastern Sea in their great ships. Their shields were painted with the likeness of an eight-legged horse.'

'The Anglii!' Typaun of the Manau interjected. 'My father spoke of them. They are mercenaries who worship Sleipnir, the horse of Woden, the king of the gods. They are fearsome warriors who will fight for anyone with enough silver to buy their loyalty.'

'Then we will march south to avenge those who fell at their hands.' Drest announced in a growl. 'An attack on one tribe is an attack on us all! We will drive these dogs back into the sea and then turn on their paymasters! They will rue the day they dared to show me their teeth!'

Cinloch urged his brudes to hurry to attend to Taran's wounds and sighed at having experienced what was surely the briefest peace in all of history.

Hengist stamped his feet in a bid to bring some feeling back into his toes but had no success as the leather of his boots was as frozen as the ground he stood upon. He blew a great cloud of frozen breath into the frigid air as he waited for his son to gallop across the open plain between them. The ranks of Anglii warriors at his back stood in silence with their shields gripped in one hand and their spears in the other. He allowed himself a smile of fatherly pride at how quickly Wulf forced his mount on. The boy threw himself from the saddle as he hauled at the reins to bring the beast to a halt.

'None of our scouts have returned from the north, lord.' Wulf reported, the soft down on his chin white with the frost of his frozen breath. 'I went as far as the Great Fort on the Heights and had no sight of them.'

'We have no need of scouts now, my son.' Hengist observed with a grimace. 'See there! The High King of the Painted Ones rushes towards his death!'

Wulf nodded to confirm he had seen the enemy reach the crest of a low hill to their west. He was not fazed by the sight of such a large body of cavalry. He remembered how quickly the horse warriors with the shields decorated with three spears had fallen when faced with Anglii steel. He smiled at the thought of the glory to be won in reducing that distant horde to torn flesh and splintered bone. Woden would smile down upon them if they won such a famous victory.

'Where is my brother?' Lord Hengist demanded. 'Have we had sight of his sails?'

'No, lord.' Ulric answered from his place behind him. 'The winds do not blow in his favour.'

'Then we will have to win this battle without him. What of the Brigante dogs? Have we had sight of them?'

'No, lord. The last of their messengers said they would be here before the day was half done but we have heard nothing from them since dusk yesterday. They must be close by.'

Hengist cleared his throat noisily and spat a great gobbet of phlegm onto the frozen earth.

'I doubt if they will march quickly when they can leave us to do their dirty work for them.' The Anglii leader drawled. 'No matter! We will finish them here and go in search of King Uurtigrm for our payment.' He then pulled a purse from his belt and turned to the ranks with a roar. 'A purse of silver and all of the land from here to the wall for the man who brings me the head of the Pictish King!'

The Anglii warriors roared their approval and thundered their spears against their shields.

Drest cocked his head as the breeze brought the sound of the distant drumming to the top of the hill. He nodded to himself in satisfaction and exchanged a smile with Cinloch.

'The mercenary dogs are calling to us.' He observed with a shake of his head. 'It always gladdens my heart when an enemy is eager to embrace his own death.'

'They match us in numbers.' Cinloch informed him when he had finished his rough count of the Anglii ranks. 'Although most are on foot. We should sweep them aside even if they fight as fiercely as Taran described.'

'They will greatly outnumber us when their friends reach the plain.' Talorc interrupted him.

Cinloch followed the priest's outstretched arm and squinted into the distance. He saw nothing but a slight ripple in the land on the far horizon. He thought it might be nothing more than a herd of cattle being driven north by their drovers until a break in the clouds caused the sunlight to glint off so much polished metal the column seemed to sparkle.

'So, the Brigantes march furiously towards us!' Drest spat with his face twisted in derision. 'Ha! Their weak king ran from me while I ravaged and burned his kingdom from one coast to the other! It seems he has found his courage at last and has come to have his revenge! Let him come at me so I can heap defeat upon all of the other humiliations I have inflicted on him!'

Cinloch did nothing more than glance in the High King's direction but the gesture was enough to earn him a stinging rebuke.

'Do not speak, Cinloch! Say not a single word! Your eyes burn with disapproval but I would rather you did not give voice to your thoughts. You scolded me for raiding the lands of the Brigantes and warned me it might provoke just such a reaction. I remember you telling me that a wise man does not kick out at a wasps' nest if he does not want to be stung. Tis done now and I will pay the price for it!' He then turned to Talorc. 'Any word from Cluim?'

'No, my King.' Talorc replied. 'I sent riders to the Heights of the Clut before dawn but none have returned yet.'

'No matter!' Drest replied with a shrug of his shoulders. 'I will finish them here with or without the warriors of Alt Clut. The Brigantes and their mad dogs will regret ever crossing the wall.'

'We should withdraw and wait for all of our allies to join us!' Cinloch urged him.

'Cinloch is right.' King Manath interjected. 'The Anglii and the Brigantes will outnumber us by three warriors to two of our own. It makes no sense to make battle when they have the advantage of strength.'

'I do not mean to give them the time to join their forces.' Drest growled. 'I will route the Anglii before the sun reaches its apex and then turn to face the Brigante King.'

'No army can fight two battles in a single day!' The Epidii King protested. 'Our warriors will be exhausted and in no state to fight!'

'Neither will the Brigantes!' The High King countered. 'Look at how they hurry towards us. They will barely be able to stand by the time they reach the plain.'

'The choice is no longer ours to make.' Talorc exclaimed. 'See! The filthy mercenaries already advance in their eagerness to soak the earth with their own blood!'

'Good! Then let us go out to meet them!' Drest ordered them. 'Cinloch! Lead the Epidii horse to the ridge on their flank! It will unnerve them and force them to weaken their line by concentrating more men on that side. Ride in when you see them break! We'll take neither slaves nor hostages here!'

Cinloch watched as the Caledone and Venicone cavalry thundered towards the Anglii ranks. He was certain their lines would collapse under such a great weight of horseflesh and could not see how they hoped to stand with only their small, round shields to protect them. They launched their spears with deadly precision and brought down more than fifty horses with their first volley. It disrupted the charge and caused men to fall out of line but the great mass of cavalry rumbled on unaffected. He tensed himself in anticipation of the crash of the impact and was left dumbfounded when none came. The Anglii did not stand but broke formation at the very last moment. They used their shields to deflect the points of the Caledone spears and then spun, ducked and dived so the horses galloped past them leaving their riders vulnerable to both sword and spear.

Cinloch winced at the carnage below him and at the sounds of screaming men and horses as the Anglii set about inflicting heavy losses with ruthless efficiency. The first wave of Caledone foot warriors fared little better. The mercenaries fought in small groups with each man defending the flanks of his neighbours. The Caledones attacked with their characteristic ferocity but seemed to struggle badly against their foreign adversaries. Cinloch reckoned that the Anglii cut down three warriors for every one they lost and saw some their men continue to fight on even after suffering two or three blows.

Only the arrival of the Smertae saved the High King from suffering his first defeat. They seemed to climb over their Caledone brothers in their eagerness to tear at the enemy. They screamed their death song as they went and used their sickles to tear the Anglii shields aside so their comrades could slice throats and pierce skulls. Cinloch did not wait for the Anglii to break for they retained their discipline under the onslaught and stayed in their groups to fight their way to an ordered retreat. They turned and ran only when they came in sight of the river and the Epidii horsemen rode after them to cut them down from behind. Cinloch slashed down at their heads with Erp's sword and found that the pains and infirmities of age were lost in the red mist of the battle rage. The Epidii King called a halt at the riverbank and watched as many of the Anglii were swept away by the currents. Only a handful made it to the far bank to cough and splutter in the shallows.

He dismounted and went to examine a mercenary who lay on the frozen earth with his guts puddled around him. The man groaned as Cinloch poked at him with the point of his sword. He peered closer to confirm his suspicions and shook his head in disbelief when he saw the hundreds of tiny iron rings sewn into the cloth of his tunic. It explained why so many of the Anglii had been able to fight on after being struck by sword blades. The little rings would provide little protection from a spearpoint or a hammer blow but were enough to stop a blade from slicing through flesh. He turned at the sound of Drest's battle horns and saw the Caledones, Venicones,

Maeatae and Manau already forming up to face the approaching Brigantes.

He found the High King resting on the ground at the front of the army and felt his stomach churn at the sight of him. His hair was plastered to his skull with sweat, his cloak was dirty and torn, his left eye was swollen and bruised and fresh blood seeped from an open wound on his torso. He was not shocked by the injuries themselves but was badly discomfited by the fact it was Drest who had suffered them. He could not remember him being anything more than grazed or scratched in all the years he had known him. The wounds were minor but were enough to dent the air of invincibility responsible for drawing all of the tribes to him.

Drest waved Talorc and Stroma away from him and told them not to fuss.

'The Brigante King will think his mercenaries have weakened us.' Drest told his commanders. 'That is why he has abandoned all caution and drives his warriors on so hard. Let us use his haste against him! We will form up on the bank of yonder stream. No sane man would attack us in so strong a position but perhaps his thirst for revenge will spur him to recklessness. Let us position our warriors while Talorc prays to the gods for their blessings.'

The Brigante King did not even allow his warriors to stop to catch their breath. His commanders ordered the cavalry into their ranks and sent them into the charge while the foot warriors came on behind carrying their great rectangular shields decorated with his ram's head insignia. The Brigante horsemen were defeated before they reached the High King's line. Their horses slowed and hesitated on the stream's far bank and were slaughtered as Venicone spearmen launched volley after volley into the flesh of both men and beasts. The Brigante foot fared little better. Their shield wall grew ragged and broken as they climbed over the corpses of their comrades and crossed the uneven banks of the stream. The unblooded Manau reserves threw themselves at the spaces between the Brigante shields and hacked down with their swords in such a frenzy that droplets of blood formed a mist in the air above them. By the time they began to falter, the dead were piled so high in the stream the weary Smertae were able to cross it without wetting their feet.

There was no rearguard action to cover the Brigante retreat. The moment they saw their king ride away with his bannermen, the warriors broke and ran for their lives. Cinloch led his Epidii cavalry in the pursuit and kept at it until the light began to fade. His arm ached from cutting down so many of them and only a few stragglers were left when he finally called his warriors back.

The firepits were already ablaze by the time he reached the camp and the aroma of roasting beef caused his empty stomach to gurgle noisily. He found Drest holding court with his commanders.

'No king has ever defeated two armies in a single day!' He boasted as he allowed his goblet to be refilled. 'Did you see how the Brigante King fled? Did I not tell you he is a coward? I destroyed his filthy army and sent him away to skulk in his forests!'

Cinloch saw through this bravado and knew that every other king there did so too. They might clap and roar their approval but they could not ignore the loss of more than half the army. Talorc seemed to detect this unwelcome undercurrent and sought to raise their spirits by telling them he had dreamed of a wolf slaughtering a lamb. He held a Brigante shield on his arm and thumped at its ram's head emblem with his fist as he told his tale. His skills as a bard and the strength of the Maeatae ale proved to be a powerful combination and he succeeded in enticing even the grim-faced King Manath into joining the celebrations.

The mood did not last long. The Venicone scout came to King Uuid and whispered into his ear with some urgency. Cinloch knew the tidings were bad from the expression on Uuid's face.

'The Brigante King did not run far.' The Venicone King announced solemnly. 'My scouts tracked him as he went south and found another Brigante army awaiting him less than a day's march from here.'

The process was repeated less than an hour later when the Manau scouts arrived back from the coast. King Typaun did not share Uuid's gift for discretion and he questioned them harshly within the hearing of all of the kings.

'How many ships?' He demanded as he bombarded them with queries. 'You are certain it was the Anglii insignia on the sails? More than two thousand warriors? Are you certain? Did you count them? Did you count them again?'

Even the High King's shoulders seemed to sag under the weight of ill tidings.

'We will go north to await the arrival of our reinforcements!' He announced in a tone severe enough to discourage any disagreement. 'When we have joined forces with the King of Alt Clut, we will be ready to defeat them again!'

32

Cinloch was filled with foreboding the moment the Fort of the Heights came into view. A low mist hung over the waters of the River Clut but it was so thin even a blind man could see the spearmen filling the walls above the fastened gates. King Cluim of the Alt Clut stood on the rampart above the fort's entrance and glared down at them as they drew near.

'Do you not see my banners?' The High King demanded. 'Do you deny your king entry to your fort?'

'You are no king of mine!' Cluim growled in a vicious and bitter tone. 'I have felt sick to the very pit of my stomach every time I have been forced to kneel before you and give you that name. The gods have raged to see one of true royal blood debase himself before a vagrant tyrant such as you! Did you think I had forgotten how you slaughtered my kinsmen? Did you think I had forgotten the insult of being forced to hail you as my superior when you perched on that dung heap at Sken? I forget nothing! You will find no sanctuary here! I will watch on as your enemies devour you and then ride out to dance on your bones!'

'You have forgotten much, you black-toothed traitor!' Drest raged up at him. 'You have forgotten you are king only because I made you so after you turned on your own overlord. You would be nothing without me! Do you forget that I hold your own sons as hostages? Do you think I will hesitate to gut them from crotch to throat if you defy me?'

'I have other sons.' Cluim retorted with a dismissive wave of his hand. 'Do what you want with them. Nothing will induce me to crawl at your feet!'

'You will not live to see the spring!' Drest bellowed at him with barely suppressed fury. 'I swear to it! By the time this is done, I will have wiped your seed from this earth and brought an end to your line!'

'We should withdraw, my King.' Cinloch implored him as he cast a wary eye over the grim-faced warriors above them. He knew they could cut them down in an instant if Cluim was to give the order. 'The Alt Clut outnumber us and the Anglii and the Brigantes are in close pursuit.'

Drest spat on the ground beneath the gates and pulled at his reins with such force his horse squealed in protest as he wheeled it around and kicked it away from the fort. Talorc took the brunt of the High King's fury as they went and he ranted at the priest in white-lipped rage as they rode to rejoin what was left of their army.

'You are to blame for this, Talorc! You and your all-seeing Drui have failed me! What use are your crows, your dreams and your portents if they give me no warning of such monstrous treachery? I was a fool to have placed my trust in you and to have made you the King of the Drui! My enemies close in on me so quickly that I must turn and fight even though there is no prospect of victory. Go! Take yourself from my sight! I cannot stand to look at you!'

Talorc turned deathly pale and was brought close to tears by this torrent of abuse. Cinloch was surprised to find himself beginning to feel some small amount of pity for him. The priest's lip quivered just as it had after he was savaged by the wolf all those long years before.

'I will take myself away, just as you have commanded me to do!' He wheezed in dejection. 'But I will never forsake you! I will pray to the gods and bid them to bring down a storm to halt your enemies in their tracks and allow you to escape to the north. I swear this before Tal and offer my soul to him!'

Drest kicked his horse into a trot without acknowledging his words.

'He does not mean it.' Cinloch offered in a bid to comfort him. 'He speaks harshly through fear and frustration. He will call you back to his side when he has recovered his temper.'

'Urge him northwards, good Cinloch.' Talorc replied as he began to turn his horse. 'Do not allow him to stand! I will bring a great blizzard to steal the sight of our enemies. Then I will go to deal with he who has betrayed us.'

'Cluim?' The Epidii King demanded in disbelief. 'He is surrounded by two thousand warriors. Do you mean to fight them all by yourself?'

342

Talorc leaned down and tapped his fingers against the ram's head on the Brigante shield strapped to his saddle.

'There is more than one way to defeat an enemy, good Cinloch. You, of all men, should know that.'

Cinloch watched him go and shook his head in astonishment. He was not convinced by the priest's defiance and thought it to be little more than the sulking and posturing of a petulant boy. He urged his horse into the gallop and raced to catch up with Drest and what remained of their army. He searched the land as he went in the hope of spotting ground that might offer them some advantage when they were forced to turn and face the pursuing Brigante and Anglii armies. He stopped several times to examine the more promising spots but quickly rejected them all. None offered enough of an edge to make up for being outnumbered by more than four to one. The first fat flakes of snow began to fall from the sky just as he came in sight of the High King's bodyguard. They fell so thick and fast the world was soon lost in a blanket of white and his field of vision reduced to no more than a dozen paces.

'That'll slow the bastards!' Drest crowed in delight when he finally managed to find him in the murk. 'Our cavalry will screen us as our foot warriors march themselves north to join with our reinforcements.'

The blizzard blew for more than a day and the High King's spirits rose higher with each passing hour. When the wind began to drop and the snow became lighter, Drest led his retinue to the crest of a hill to see what progress their enemies had made while the world was shrouded in white. Cinloch had not yet reached the brow of the hill when familiar and distant sounds caused him to cock his head and crease his face in puzzlement. He held his breath and dared to hope his ears were not deceiving him. He drew in a sharp breath when his horse reached the summit and he was presented with a clear view across the frozen plain. He was at too great a distance to identify the two armies but it was clear they were locked in battle.

'By the gods!' Drest exclaimed in wide-eyed wonder. 'My enemies tear at one another and turn the snow red with their blood! What sorcery has caused this to pass?'

'Perhaps your wizard will have the answer to that.' King Uuid of the Venicones suggested as he pointed to the east. 'He gallops in so hard I have no doubt he is eager to tell us of the part he has played in this.'

Talorc slowed his black charger as he neared them and made them wait for their answers. He asked for ale to moisten his throat and only spoke when Drest was close to bursting with curiosity.

'It seems that some bastard scaled the walls of the heights and cut the throats of King Cluim's wife, his young sons and that of his infant daughter.' The priest informed them in a tone of feigned indifference. 'The vile assassin was disturbed in the act and had to jump from the walls to make good his escape. In his haste, he left his shield on the ramparts. King Cluim was so overcome with grief and rage he took one look at the ram's head on the Brigante shield before leading his warriors out through his gates to take revenge on the foul Brigante invaders.'

'And where is the Brigante shield that hung from your saddle not two days ago?' Cinloch enquired, fully aware he was playing a supporting role in the Drui King's performance. 'Were you forced to abandon it in order to escape our enemies?'

Talorc said nothing but bowed his head in false modesty and favoured those who praised him with the most enigmatic of smiles. Drest embraced him and slapped him on the back with both force and enthusiasm.

'I should never have doubted you, my brother. Forgive me for speaking to you so harshly! You have bought me time enough to save my kingdom. Reinforcements now gather at Pert from all corners of the land. By the time the invaders have recovered themselves, they will face an army greater than any they have seen before. Together, we will scour them from the earth and toss their blackened bones into the sea!'

Cinloch braved the mud and the constant spring rain and rode the land between Pert, the Black Fort and the Tae to do what he did best. He counted. He counted the horned Venicone warriors as they practised hard with their spears and the Caereni swordsmen as they clashed their blades against those of their comrades. He counted the Caledone and Venicone horse warriors as they were drilled in their battle formations. He took a tally of the men and women of the Manau, the Cornavi and the Maeatae as they gathered at their campfires and estimated the number of sickles the foul Smertae could muster against the enemies of the High King. The higher he counted, the calmer he felt and the less his stomach cramped and clenched in anxiety. The force assembled on the banks of the Tae was at least as great as the horde brought together years before to drive the Dal Riata back into the sea. He counted between ten and twelve thousand warriors. He could be no more precise as they swarmed around like ants, leaving him uncertain as to how many were missed and how many were counted more than once. Young warriors had been called to take the place of those lost on the plain but there were enough scarred and battle-hardened veterans to provide the steel needed to harden their ranks.

Messengers rode in almost every day carrying tidings that lifted Cinloch's spirits still higher. It cheered him to hear of King Uurtigrm limping back over the wall at the head of the weakened Brigante army and of his mercenaries turning for the coast and boarding their ships. He clenched his fist in triumph when he was told of the grievous wounds suffered by King Cluim as his rage drove him to cut a swathe through the Brigante ranks in his determination to strike down King Uurtigrm in the midst of his bodyguard. Some said he would die from his injuries while others thought he would eventually recover if only the gods willed it. Cinloch did not care which version was correct.

It was enough to know that the turncoat suffered. He drank in celebration with the other kings when a merchant came to the Black Fort with a tale of the Anglii fleet being scattered by a terrible storm. He then joined with them in pissing on a collection of their small, round shields found on a beach after two of their ships were broken on the rocks.

Cinloch's head still thumped from the great volume of ale he had consumed when his servant came to shake him from sleep to announce that his wife was approaching the Black Fort. He belched when he bent down to pull his boots onto his feet and grimaced as bitter bile rose to his throat. He knew the tidings were bad the moment he set his eyes upon her. Her face was as stern and as sour as he had ever seen it. Both Mael and Derice were filthy with the dirt of the road and their horses were so caked in mud he knew they had ridden to him in great haste.

'The Irish dogs have crossed the sea in greater strength than before!' She snapped without bothering to exchange greetings. 'We awakened to the sight of their ships filling the horizon as far as the eye could see. Their sails bore the symbols of the Dal Riata, the Ulaid and the Ui Neill. They came ashore so quickly we were lucky to get away. They now besiege our forts and fill the air with smoke as they burn their way across our lands!'

Cinloch attempted to comfort her but could do nothing to ease her temper. Both she and the pock-marked Derice glared at him in reproach and disdain as he tried to reassure them that their lands would soon be retaken and cleared of the verminous slaughterers.

'Perhaps it would be better if you spent less time drinking and more time fulfilling your royal duties!' She scolded him before sweeping past to leave him gawping in front of all who had witnessed the exchange.

Drest succeeded where he had failed. He listened to Mael carefully and then acted without hesitation.

'We will march west immediately. They have heard of our troubles in the south and think to take advantage of our weakness. We will sweep them back into the sea before they have the chance to realise their mistake. King Uuid of the Venicones and King Typaun of the Manau will go to defend our southern border and discourage the Alt Clut, the Brigantes and the Anglii from making any advances during the summer months. We march today and will forage as we go!'

The advance was painfully slow as the Irish raiders did all they could to avoid a pitched battle. They dispersed at the first sight of cavalry and took to skulking in the hills and the forests, emerging only to engage in hit and run attacks before disappearing again. Rooting them out was painstaking work and would have been done more quickly and more efficiently if the Venicone hounds had been with them.

Cinloch suffered greatly during those long weeks in the saddle. His clothes were saturated from the constant rain and they rubbed against his saddle so hard that little skin was left on his thighs and buttocks by the time the Crag Fort came into view. He was also troubled by the high number of casualties inflicted on them during the advance. Less than half were incurred during enemy ambushes or small-scale attacks, with the rest being caused by accidents as horses and warriors lost their footing on slippery rocks or in mud. The Caledone King complained that the scouring of the Epidii lands had cost him more warriors than had been lost in the battles on the southern plain.

The joy he felt on reaching the coast proved to be short-lived. He groaned when he saw that the invaders intended to make their stand beneath the heights of the besieged Crag Fort. They had made good use of the time won through their delaying tactics. Ramparts had been raised and trenches dug in the sodden earth and the multitude of sharpened stakes driven into the ground was enough to cause even the bravest of warriors to hesitate at the thought of launching an assault.

'Let them rot!' Drest growled when he saw it. 'We will bury them in their own trenches when we are done with them.'

There was substance to his defiance but there was also an element of bravado. He left them to moulder behind their sodden ramparts for two full weeks but constantly cast his eyes to the east and to the south in search of messengers bringing news of the enemies who lurked there. When his patience and his nerves were stretched to breaking point, he ordered that every spear be collected and carried to the top of the Crag Fort's walls.

'Why would I waste my warriors on their spikes when I have spears enough to slaughter them all?' He demanded of his placemen. 'Order your best spearmen to the top of the wall so they can send their shafts plummeting down upon them!'

The first few shafts were thrown directly downwards and thumped uselessly into the piled earth of the invaders' rear rampart. The next warrior to throw launched his spear high into the sky and Cinloch watched from the ground as it arced upwards before descending at an incredible speed. The warriors around him burst into cheers of delight when it smashed into a Dal Riata shield with a splintering crack and brought a squeal of pain from the miserable fool who huddled beneath it. He watched on as spears rained down on the enemy for the rest of the afternoon. The spectacle was both horrific and fascinating and he found he could not tear his eyes away from it. There was no shield strong enough to withstand the impact of a spear thrown from such a great height and the injuries they caused were the most dreadful he had ever seen. King Manath grabbed at his arm and pointed at an Irish warrior who had been skewered from his right shoulder to his left hip.

'By the gods!' The Maeatae King declared in morbid excitement. 'The spear has passed clean through him and buried itself in the ground so it holds him upright! I have never seen such a thing or heard a warrior scream so horribly!'

Cinloch nodded, though the shrill, agonised screeching caused him to wince and tore at his nerves. He breathed a sigh of relief when one of the poor bastard's comrades finally put him out of his misery by slashing his throat.

'How many?' Talorc demanded when he came to his side just as the sun was beginning to set.

'Not enough!' Cinloch admitted. 'Less than a quarter of them have fallen.'

'But now they have no shortage of spears.' The priest observed with typical bluntness. 'We should leave them to rot amongst their own corpses but Drest will not have the patience for that. He is itching to return to the east lest our enemies in the south come against us.'

'Aye.' The Epidii King replied with his shoulders sagging in weariness. 'He will order the assault though it will cost us dear. I have tried to persuade him to leave enough warriors to besiege their positions but he is set on marching in strength.'

The battle horns blew with the first light of the rain-soaked dawn and the High King's warriors charged in at the invaders on all four sides of their square. The water-filled ditches and the ramparts of mud brought the advance to such a crawl the Irishmen picked off their attackers at will with the spears gifted to them the previous day. Sheer weight of numbers told in the end but the trapped warriors could neither run nor surrender and so fought on with a savage and desperate fury.

Cinloch did not see the Maeatae King struck down but watched as his bodyguard carried his lifeless corpse away from the battlefield. He mouthed a silent prayer to the Crone to speed his old friend's way to the Underworld. He then forced his legs on through the thick, cloying mud so he could wet his blade and free more Irish souls to accompany his old ally on his last journey. Such a slaughter was made of the last of the encircled Ulaid dogs that more than one of the High King's warriors suffered wounds at the hands of their own frenzied comrades.

Men cried out in triumph when the last of them fell but the celebrations were muted by the foulness of the weather and the grief caused by the loss of so many friends. A barn was demolished to provide enough dry wood for King Manath's pyre but it did little more than smoulder in the hard, pouring rain. Only when straw was brought from the fort's stables did it blaze hot enough to turn him to ash.

If Prince Taran had not died from the wounds he received at the hands of the Anglii, it was he who would have been declared King of the Maeatae. With both uncle and nephew gone to the gods, it was Mael the Maeatae mormaers raised to the throne.

'Now your wife is more powerful than you.' Drest teased Cinloch when he had proclaimed Mael as Queen.

'Then that is something that you both have in common!' Stroma shot back with ill-concealed glee. 'Even if my husband is loath to admit it.'

33

The last vestiges of tenderness left between Cinloch and Mael were lost on the death of her father. She snarled in his ear constantly on the long and miserable trek from the Crag Fort to Pert. He cursed her as they struggled through the flooded roads that had been churned to a morass by the passing of so many warriors. What little bile was not reserved for him was directed at Drest. She called him a fool and berated him for the loss of so many good men and women. When Cinloch stayed silent, she used his talent for counting to taunt him.

'Count them now!' She demanded, her cheeks flushed with anger. 'He lost half of his army on the plains and has now lost half of that which replaced it! If he continues this way, there will be no army left by the first snows of winter. Where are your balls? Look for them now! You must stop him before it is too late! Before he risks the whole kingdom!'

'I will try!' Cinloch snapped back at her, though his words sounded weak even to him.

He knew there was little chance of the High King paying any heed to his counsel for only Talorc and Stroma now had his ear and he had never heard either of them oppose a single one of his decisions. His worst fears were realised when scouts came to the Black Fort to bring word of Anglii and Brigante armies crossing the wall. They also reported sightings of messengers riding freely between their armies and the Alt Clut stronghold.

'Let them come on!' Cinloch implored him. 'Their lines of supply will be so long our cavalry will easily disrupt them. Let us not give battle when we are so weakened. Let them starve outside our gates while we recover our strength!'

'You would have me sit here while they destroy and defile my lands?' Drest demanded as he clenched his teeth in frustration. 'We cannot see out a siege when the last months of summer and all of the autumn and winter stretch out before us. We must strike out at our enemies and put them under siege before they can so imprison us. We will march for the Alt Clut stronghold at dawn!'

Cinloch cast his eyes around at the gathered kings in search of some word of support. He knew that most of them shared his concerns but they all stared at the floor and gave no voice to their misgivings. Even Queen Mael did nothing but shake her head in disapproval of his faltering attempt to urge the High King to caution. He gave a bitter laugh and threw his hands up in exasperation.

The Alt Clut showed no such inclination to bend to the will of the High King. They shared his reluctance to be subjected to a siege and so arrayed their warriors on the broken ground beneath the Fort of the Heights. Cinloch groaned when he caught sight of them there and his shoulders slumped at the prospect of another costly battle.

Drest surveyed the serried ranks and rubbed at his beard in contemplation. Talorc had thrown off his robes and was making his horse prance up and down just within the range of their spears. The dark sickle, crow and cauldron tattoos on his pale torso marked him out as a Drui. The symbols caused many of the nervous enemy warriors to make the sign of the Mother to ward off any of the spells he might cast. He rained curses down on them and mocked them as he easily ducked and dodged the few shafts they launched in his direction. Cinloch could not help but smile at the display.

'Cluim must be dead.' Drest declared with no little satisfaction. 'He would never set his shield wall on such uneven ground. See how ragged the line is at the centre? No warriors can withstand a charge on such poor terrain. Whoever commands these men now is not fit for the task.'

They watched as Talorc wheeled his horse around and galloped towards them. He grinned as he came and could scarcely contain his glee.

'The clash with the Brigantes has weakened them greatly!' He exclaimed breathlessly as he reined his horse in. 'I counted less than two thousand of them and their line is filled with fresh-faced girls and beardless boys. We need only charge in and they will fold!'

'Good! We will break them here!' Drest proclaimed before telling Talorc to order the warriors to their places. 'You do not have to take your place at my side, good Cinloch.' He informed him when the priest had ridden away to do as he was bidden. 'I know you think I have brought this misfortune upon myself by raiding over the wall in defiance of your counsel. I will not heap one insult upon the other by commanding you to come to remedy my error. Go where you will and do so with my blessing.'

'Where would I fight but at the side of my king?' Cinloch replied as he drew his sword from its scabbard. 'I have no place other than that at your side.'

Drest grinned at him with such happiness the Epidii King felt his spirits soar. All fears and reservations were forgotten as the battle rage began to take a grip on them both.

'Then let us put an end to these treacherous dogs!' Drest roared with fury. 'Let us cut them into so many pieces the crows will not have to work for their feast!'

The High King kicked his horse into the gallop, leaving Cinloch and the rest of his cavalry furiously spurring their mounts onwards in his wake. The Epidii King leaned forward in his saddle and lifted his sword high in readiness for his first strike. The thundering mass of Epidii, Caledone and Maeatae cavalry struck fear into the hearts of the cowering Alt Clut and their line seemed to tremble as nervous warriors adjusted their grips on their shields. Only a handful of them gave in to their terror and ran as the charge came in but it was more than enough. Drest steered his stallion at a space between the shields at the centre and Cinloch aimed for another to the left. The slaughter began the moment the shield wall was breached. Cinloch slashed his blade down at their heads while his stallion kicked out viciously, his heavy hooves breaking bones and shattering skulls. The hardened Alt Clut warriors stood their ground and offered determined resistance but the battle was lost the moment the horsemen were among them. Cinloch cut down until his sword was thick with blood and offal and stopped only when he was too breathless to continue. He reined his horse in and watched as the foot warriors came in to finish the job.

The slaughter continued all the way to the gates of the fort and left a trail of corpses lying along the path it had followed. The fleeing warriors hammered at the wooden barrier with their fists and begged the garrison to admit them. Their pleas were ignored to spare the fortress from capture and they were left to their fate. With no place to run to and no hope of escape, the Alt Clut turned to make their last stand. They filled the ravine before the gates with their shields and used their axes to inflict as many casualties as they were able before they fell. They fought with the viciousness and determination of cornered wolves and refused to surrender themselves. Drest ordered one assault after another until his dead lay so thickly their corpses formed a barrier for the Alt Clut to fight behind.

'We must disengage, my King!' Cinloch roared when Drest came back from his place in the line for the third time. 'Let the spearmen finish them from distance! The battle is already won and we are losing men here when it is not necessary.'

Drest panted as he leaned on his sword in exhaustion. His face was dirty, bloody and dripping with sweat as he glared at Cinloch.

'It would be a shame to finish a famous victory in such a cowardly fashion.' He groaned. 'I would rather end the dynasty of the Alt Clut in battle so the bards will sing of it for a thousand years.'

'And what will the bards sing of when we have too few warriors left to stand against our other enemies?' Cinloch snapped. 'The Brigantes and the Anglii still march against us and we will need all of our warriors to oppose them. Do not waste any more of them here! You will have other opportunities to sacrifice them to bring glory to your name!'

Drest stared at Cinloch in silence long enough to make him fear he had spoken too harshly. The High King had the power of life and death over all of his subjects and his eyes now burned in fury at Cinloch's insolence. The Epidii King held Drest's gaze despite his discomfort as he was certain that breaking it would be taken as weakness. He released a silent sigh of relief when the High King finally dropped his eyes to the ground.

'Very well!' He muttered with evident reluctance. 'But you will command the slaughter. Let it be known that it was the Epidii King who ordered our warriors to withdraw and sent his own

358

spearmen to cut them down like animals. Let's see how you like it when the bards sing of that.'

The Epidii spearmen made short work of the tightly packed Alt Clut warriors. The sun had not yet set by the time their numbers were reduced sufficiently to persuade Cinloch it was time to send his foot warriors in to cut down the last of them. Those who had complained that the work was not fitting for warriors of their status were soon silenced when they were set loose to loot the dead of their valuables. Fires were lit amongst the strewn corpses and the air was filled with the sounds of drinking and celebrating as the sun slid beneath the horizon.

The revelry was more muted around Drest's campfire as the cost of the victory began to sink in. One enemy had been defeated but two were left and the army had been seriously weakened by the loss of hundreds of warriors in the fighting at the base of the Heights of the Clut.

'There will be more than enough of us to face the Anglii and the Brigantes when the Venicone and Manau Kings reach us with their armies.' Drest proclaimed in a bid to reassure the gathered kings.

They nodded their agreement but Cinloch studied them as the High King spoke and saw doubt in their eyes. Even those who adored him and counted him as their friend did not seem entirely convinced by his words. King Donal of the Caledones kept his gaze fixed upon the fire as Drest spoke and only opened his mouth to complain about the number of warriors he had lost here, in the Epidii lands and out on the plain. Drest seemed to miss the bitterness and criticism in his tone and responded by promising him revenge on his enemies.

Cinloch was unable to sleep when he lay down on the earth and huddled beneath his blanket. His sense of unease was so great and his mind raced so hard he was still awake when the first of the stragglers came in. The Manau warrior was caked in dry blood from a deep wound to his scalp, he had neither spear nor sword in his possession and was filthy from head to foot.

'They're all gone!' He stammered as Cinloch called for ale to be brought for him to calm his hysteria. 'All slaughtered! They left no one alive!'

Cinloch coaxed the story from him piece by piece and felt himself grow light-headed as the full extent of the disaster was revealed. The trembling warrior told him of King Uuid and his Venicones engaging with the Brigante army while Typaun of the Manau marched south to outflank them. He described how the first of the Anglii armies had suddenly appeared on a crest of a hill to the east of them just as Typaun turned to attack the Brigantes from the rear. The mercenaries had not hesitated but charged down at the Manau while they were still in disarray.

'They tore into us before our shield wall was formed!' The filthy straggler whimpered with tears running down his cheeks. 'We broke under the onslaught and turned to flee but were met by another army coming in from the west! They let no warrior escape! I was struck down and awakened to find myself covered in blood and surrounded by the corpses of my kinsmen!'

'What of King Typaun?' Talorc demanded from his place in the crowd gathered around the young warrior. 'Did he escape them?'

'I searched the field for him.' He whimpered. 'I found him among the dead heaped at the centre. They had hacked him to pieces.'

'What of the Venicones?' Drest growled at him, his face dark with anger.

'I know not, my King. They were still fighting when I took myself away. They were assailed from all sides. I doubt that any survived.'

'You ran!' Talorc spat at him in fury. 'You left them to die, vile coward!'

The priest darted forward with such speed Cinloch was unable to stop him. He saw only a flash of his dagger in the firelight and then the warrior was clutching at his throat in a vain bid to stop his blood from spraying out into the air.

'Idiot!' He raged at Talorc. 'Now we will not learn of the fate of King Uuid! Your temper and your lust for blood have cost us dear!'

'The fool could tell us nothing more.' Talorc retorted. 'He ran for the hills before the battle was done. I doubt if we will have to wait long for news of the Venicone King.'

Cinloch seethed with fury but said nothing more. He was certain Talorc had acted to stem the flow of bad tidings so the sub-kings would not be brought to panic. The attempt had only limited success and was to prove to be entirely futile when

361

the first light of dawn saw King Uuid and the ragged remnants of his army limp into camp.

The old king rode with only four of a bodyguard that had once numbered in the hundreds. He led a horse behind him bearing the corpse of his once-crippled son. Even Talorc seemed stunned by the sight of Uurd's lifeless and mutilated body tied across his saddle. Cinloch counted only eighty foot warriors, most of whom were wounded.

'Come, King Uuid!' Drest urged him. 'I will have food and ale brought for you and your warriors. I would have you tell of what has befallen you.'

'There is nothing to tell.' Uuid replied with such melancholy and despair it caused the hairs to stand up on the back of Cinloch's neck. 'My army is lost, my only heir is dead and my people are finished. Our southern enemies are too strong for us and will inherit the lands we once held. I go north to bury my son and will then take to the forest so at least a few of my people might live through the tempest to come.'

'I am your High King, Uuid of the Venicones.' Drest replied in a tone intended to assert his authority. 'You must stand with me now just as you have for all these years past. Both you and your people will have my protection.'

Uuid then laughed a laugh that was empty and desolate. He pointed a gnarled and twisted finger at Drest and wagged it like a brude scolding a dull-witted apprentice.

'You cannot even protect yourself, Drest of the Epidii. You do not realise it yet but your reign is already over. Flee while you can or stay here and perish!'

Cinloch watched the old man ride off to the north with a growing sense of foreboding. The destruction of such a once-powerful ally was a grave threat to the unity of the kingdom. He joined with Drest and Talorc in trying to steady the nerves of the sub-kings. Drest made a great show of sending messengers to all corners of the kingdom to demand fresh reinforcements. Talorc ordered the Drui to make sacrifices to the gods and drew their attention to all of the portents and signs that promised a great victory in the days ahead. Cinloch, for his part, went from one king to another to persuade them that their survival was dependent upon unity. He made no promises or outlandish claims but used numbers to convince them of the wisdom of standing together against the Brigantes and the Anglii.

Their failure was laid bare by the rising sun. They found the Carnonacae, Phocali and Vacomagi encampments empty and stripped of all that could be carried away. Drest kicked at the smouldering ashes of their campfires in fury at their treachery.

'Cowards! Ungrateful dogs! Vile bastards! Birst and Forcus are weak, old men who care for nothing but keeping their silver! Guram is king only because I made him so! How can they abandon me now? How were they able to creep away in the darkness without us knowing about it?'

'The manner of their leaving does not matter now!' Cinloch interjected. 'We must consider only what is left to us. Without the Venicones, the Manau, the Phocali, the Carnonacae and the Vacomagi, we do not have the strength to stand against the invaders. We are left with only the depleted armies of the Epidii, the Caledones, the Smertae, the Cornavi, the Caereni and the Maeatae. I doubt if we could muster more than three thousand warriors and our enemies can field more than two times that number. We must withdraw to the Black Fort and hold out there until the winter storms cause our enemies to freeze and starve.'

'I am High King of All the Tribes and will not hide away from these pigs like a frightened child!' Drest raged, his face set in anger and grim determination. 'We will withdraw to Pert and make our stand there. I will raise my banners and send out the call for every able-bodied person to join us there. Neither age nor sex will be spared! I will raise an army of such greatness my enemies will tremble in fear and my faithless allies will curse themselves for their weakness and lack of manhood! Once the Anglii and Brigantes have been vanquished, I will turn north and punish those who broke the oaths made to me at Sken. Disloyalty will be repaid with death and the destruction of their heirs! I swear this before all the gods!'

34

'We advance too slowly!' Hengist complained immediately on entering the Brigante King's tent. 'My scouts report that the painted dogs are gathering a great army on the banks of the Tae! We should have pursued them after we defeated the deer people on the plain. If you had listened to me then, they would not have had the chance to gather their strength!'

King Uurtigrm leaned back in his chair and waved his hand dismissively. He thought of the Anglii leaders as wild dogs whose ferocity had to be reined in until the moment came to unleash them upon his enemies.

'Patience, Hengist. Patience!' He drawled in a tone intended to soothe their wild impulses. 'It is just as I explained it. We burn their forts as we go so we do not leave their garrisons free to rush out and nip at our heels. We force their miserable peasants to harvest their crops for us so we will have grain and oats enough to sustain us through the winter. We go slowly so our victory will be absolute. I have no wish to act in haste and then be forced back here in the spring to finish the job.'

Hengist exchanged a look with his brother that told him Horsa shared his frustration. They found Uurtigrm's condescension infuriating and they had to grit their teeth to hide their rage.

'Their army grows larger the longer we delay.' Horsa protested. 'We should fly at them now! I do not understand why you would want to let them grow in strength.'

'Dear boy!' Uurtigrm began with a smugness deliberately employed to cause them the greatest possible irritation. 'Do not make the mistake of taking me for a fool. My strategy is based on intelligence that is far beyond your means. My spies tell me that the Painted King has been abandoned by his friends. He rebuilds his army with children and crippled old warriors who should be sat at their fires reliving their glory days with those few comrades fortunate enough to have survived this long. If the prospect of facing these weaklings fills you with fear, then I will provide you with comfort. I have sent emissaries across the sea to offer my hand in friendship to those who would lay claim to the lands in the west.'

'Not the Irishmen?' Hengist snorted, his lip curling in disgust. 'They are animals. I will share no spoils with them!'

'Your spoils are safe, my boy.' The Brigante King reassured him. 'You will have all I have promised you. You will have your lands and the hand of my daughter. The Irish want no part of it. The Dal Riata and the Ulaid ask only for the lands to the west. I will gladly give them the barren mountains and stinking bogs and let them waste their warriors against Drest's shields. I do not see why you would object to it.'

'Very well!' Horsa conceded, though his expression reflected his reluctance. 'We will continue to burn and pillage but we will not slow our pace. My warriors have no desire to winter in this miserable place.'

Cinloch grimaced as he climbed the steps to the top of the Black Fort's walls. His back and knees were stiff and sore after a long day of drilling his warriors on the flat ground on the banks of the Tae. He scanned the horizon and sighed at the sight of columns of smoke rising into the darkening sky in every direction. Those to the southwest caused him the greatest despair. He knew they came from the destruction of the Arder Fort and the surrounding farmsteads. It pained him to know that all he had built during his long years of toil would soon be nothing but ash.

The ravaging of the lands of the Votadini, the Epidii, the Manau and the Maeatae was marked not just by the towers of smoke but also by the constant stream of ragged and wretched peasants who ran ahead of the invaders' advance. It gave him no comfort to know that these miserable creatures were immediately armed and pressed into service. They might swell the ranks depleted in recent engagements but they could not make up for the hundreds of hardened veterans who now lay rotting in the mountains and out on the plain.

He turned at the sound of approaching footsteps and felt himself tense when he saw the High King climbing the steps towards him. He flicked his eyes back to the far horizon and steeled himself for the confrontation he had been dreading for days.

'I used to laugh at my father.' Drest began as he came to Cinloch's side. 'I thought he was foolish to spend so much silver on improving these defences. Now, when I gaze out from these walls, I see the sense in it. Our enemies would lose hundreds of men on those ramparts, ditches and spikes if they were reckless enough to make an assault. We have so many spears stored here no army on earth could overcome us.'

'You must put a stop to this madness!' Cinloch croaked, his mouth and throat suddenly dry. 'It is insanity to make our stand here. I have spent these last days drilling children, cripples and toothless, old crones to stand in the line. Some of them lack the strength to lift their shields from the ground and the skill to wield either spear or sword. They will be slaughtered like lambs by the wolves who now come at us! We should not be preparing for battle. We must flee or bring them inside our walls to prepare for a siege. You must know there is no hope of victory.'

'There is always hope, Cinloch.' Drest replied, his enthusiasm undented by the Epidii King's weary pessimism. 'Do you not remember when we were threatened by the might of Red Cloak of the Manau and King Ceretic of the Alt Clut? We rode north together in search of allies when everyone told us it was hopeless. We despaired when Onnus of the Caledones offered us no help but we did not give up. We limped into the frozen mountain wastes with only a handful of men and rode out at the head of an army of Smertae. Within a few short weeks, we had brought the Vacomagi

King to defeat. Think of all we have achieved in the days since then! You kept faith with me in the darkest of times and you must do so now!'

The Epidii King shook his head and turned to look Drest directly in the eye.

'There is no hope here. We have five thousand warriors with only half that number capable of surviving for more than a moment on the field. The Brigantes come with five thousand warriors and the Anglii with four thousand more. The Dal Riata and the Ulaid will bring a further five thousand to our door. All sense dictates that we should flee! Do not sacrifice your people for the sake of your pride! Let us withdraw so at least some of them might live! I beg you!'

'I will neither run nor hide.' Drest insisted. 'If my people perish here, it will be the will of the gods. They will have proven themselves to be weak and unworthy of their High King. If we are defeated, the future will rightly belong to the stronger southern tribes.'

'It will be a massacre!' Cinloch gasped as he clutched at the rampart to steady his trembling legs. 'All those poor children!'

'Gather your courage!' The High King commanded him. 'Do not be so ready to bow down in defeat! How many times have we pulled victory from the jaws of despair? We have tricks enough to do so again. Talorc and his Drui have damned a stream on the plain. The Anglii and the Brigantes will have to wade through a bog to reach our shield wall. You will command our foot warriors and hold them there. I will lead our cavalry out to the west and scatter the Irish slaughterers before the morning is done. We will then wheel around and attack the southern raiders from the rear. The victory will be hard-won but it will be all the sweeter for it.'

Cinloch chewed at his lip as he assessed the strategy. The numbers would be less daunting if the Irish could be kept from the fray but it would still require a miracle to prevent them from being overwhelmed.

'What if we cannot hold them?' He demanded in his desperation to find some faint glimmer of hope. 'What if the children and the grandfathers are unable to stand?'

'Keep the Smertae in reserve! How many times have we seen them turn a battle through the ferocity of their charge? Send them in wherever the line buckles or bends. If the situation is truly hopeless, then make a fighting retreat to the Black Fort and use the defences to hold them there. I will ride to your aid and finish them in the shadow of our walls!'

Cinloch stayed on the rampart when the High King took his leave of him. His stomach churned as his mind raced and veered from optimism to hopelessness and then back again. His head favoured caution but his heart enticed him towards putting his faith in the man who had led him to levels of glory and riches deemed impossible by all men until they were achieved. His eyes searched the dark horizon as he wrestled with his thoughts. His gaze lingered on the hundreds of pinpricks of light in the blackness.

Each one of them was made by a campfire set to warm the hands of his enemies.

When the night air had chilled him enough to make him shiver, he made for the hall in search of ale and a fire to warm him. He immediately wished he had retired to his chamber instead as his spirits plummeted the moment he entered the room. The chamber reeked of the stench of the Smertae warriors who guarded the doors and lined the far wall. Mael, King Donal of the Caledones, the Caereni King and all of their mormaers sat on one side of the fire with expressions of gloom and despondency etched on their faces. Drest, Stroma, Mamm Ru and Talorc stood before them in a state of agitation. Drest paced up and down with manic fervour as he tried to persuade them of the inevitability of victory. Whenever his energy waned or he paused to draw breath, one of the others would pick up where he left off.

He accepted a horn of ale from a servant and took a seat on a bench at Mael's side.

'They have sent the Smertae to guard us.' She whispered as Talorc told them of some dream of wolves and lambs the gods had visited upon him the previous night. 'They fear that we will steal away in the night. Two of them accompany me even when I go to empty my bowels.'

'I think you are mistaken.' He told her, though he knew it was unusual for them to be inside the hall. 'None have been sent to guard me.'

'That is because they know you will not run.' She laughed with genuine amusement. 'They know you will stand by him even in his madness.'

Cinloch drank heavily as the High King and his acolytes continued to harangue them. The bitter brew was undeniably strong but it had no good effect on him as the night dragged on.

Uurtigrm of the Brigantes watched as the enemy cavalry charged out of the fort and thundered down the steep slope before turning to the west.

'The Painted King is less stupid than I believed him to be.' He informed the mounted mormaer at his side. 'He means to keep the Irishmen from joining the battle.'

'It will make little difference, my King.' Mormaer Bada replied. 'We outnumber them by two to one. We will have broken them long before the Irish arrive.'

'Perhaps it would be better to send the Anglii in first. It would make for a more even contest.'

'Is that wise?' Bada asked, careful to maintain a respectful tone in spite of his disquiet. 'I doubt they will be happy with such an order.'

'Their happiness is the least of my concerns. In any case, I have agreed to pay a purse to every warrior still standing when the battle is won. They will empty my treasury if the victory is too easily achieved. Let them earn their reward and thin their ranks in the process!'

'It will be no easy victory, my King. The Painted Ones have flooded the field in front of their line. See how the water glints in the sun? The sodden earth will slow the Anglii charge!'

'Then let them advance with wet feet! It is a small price to pay for what I have promised them.'

Cinloch watched with bated breath as the Anglii formed their line and began to advance. He flicked his eyes between them and the distant mass of Brigante warriors.

'They come on alone!' King Donal gasped in disbelief. 'Certain victory was in their grasp and they have spurned it!'

'They send their mercenaries to weaken us.' Cinloch cautioned the younger man. 'They will then come to finish us.'

What little confidence the High King had instilled in him the previous night had dwindled to nothing when he went to inspect the ranks in the first light of dawn. Too many shields were held in young fingers or in hands twisted with age for him to harbour any real prospect of prevailing. The enemy decision to split their forces now caused a small, desperate glimmer of hope to blossom in his heart. He rode along the line and called the spearmen and the little children with their slingshots to the front.

'The bastards will slow when they come to the flooded ground. They will raise their shields above their heads when the first spears are thrown. That is when you slingers must fill the air with your stones. Some of them will drop their shields when they are struck and will fall prey to our spears. Do not stop to rest your arms! Force yourselves on until no stones are left. The children should then run for the forest! The shield wall is no place for the young!'

'I am glad you did that.' King Donal told him when he was finished. 'I told the High King it was madness to sacrifice our bairns but he was adamant that none should be spared. It will steady our warriors to know their children are safe.'

'Aye!' Cinloch agreed with a weary shrug. 'It will free them to worry about the fate of their grandmothers, their beardless boys and their daughters not yet in the first flush of womanhood. Let us pray to the gods and beg them to let at least some of them survive the day.'

Donal was about to make some reply when the three hundred Smertae of the reserve began to screech their discordant and repulsive battle song. He turned to gaze at them and gave a shudder at the sight of their dark eyes staring back at him from blood-smeared faces.

'I feel the need to wash myself whenever I have been in the presence of those foul creatures.' He informed Cinloch in disgust. 'But I would rather have them at my back than be forced to face their flying sickles in the heat of battle.'

'If we had ten times their number, no enemy warriors would live long enough to see the sun set on this day.'

'Then use those you have wisely, good Cinloch. My warriors will hold the centre. Look to the left wing where the Caereni King has barely enough hardened warriors to fill his front rank. If we are to collapse, it will begin there. Watch carefully and send the Smertae in the moment the line begins to falter.'

The thunder of Anglii spears being beaten against their shields marked the end of their conversation. Donal rode off to take his place in the line, leaving Cinloch with only his mormaers and thanes around him. The Epidii King waited until the Anglii advance was slowed by the sodden earth before commanding his spearmen and his young slingers to begin their bombardment. The first volley of shafts did little damage but the flying stones caused men to lower their shields and Cinloch smiled as warriors began to cry out in pain and fall from the line. His heart began to thump in his chest as spaces opened up between the round Anglii shields. He dared to hope that the slaughter might be averted even as the ragged advance closed on them. He roared at the spearmen and slingers to stay hard at their work until the enemy ranks were only four spear lengths away. He ordered them back and away when the Anglii cried out in fury and went into the charge.

The clash of one wall of shields against the other was like a thunderclap. Some of his warriors were pushed back by the force of it but the second and thirds ranks put their shoulders to their backs and held them in place. Cinloch sent a silent prayer of thanks to the Mother when he saw the line was holding, though it was bugling horribly in several places. He rode along the rear rank and shouted encouragement to those who heaved at their shields to hold the enemy back while their comrades stabbed their spears and their swords between the shields in the hope of tearing into enemy flesh. The air was filled with the sounds of warriors grunting and cursing under the strain and with the terrible screaming of those whose flesh and sinew was torn by the blades of their opponents. Those who fell were immediately replaced by the warriors behind them and the grass was soon covered with the dead and the wounded.

He ordered fifty of the Smertae to go to the aid of the Caereni as the left wing was being pushed backwards and looked set to wheel around on itself and expose the army's flank to the enemy. He did not watch them as they charged in but knew from the change in the tone of the battle that their impact was both great and immediate. He did not understand the rough Anglii tongue but there was no mistaking the panic in their voices as they cried out under the Smertae onslaught.

The battle was now reduced to a grinding and vicious struggle between the warriors on either side of the wall. Cinloch was aware that the stamina of those engaged in the melee would decide whether the day was won or lost. It was a miracle that his depleted army had held their ground for so long but he knew in his heart it could not be sustained. A great number of his veteran fighters had fallen and untested youths and half-crippled old warriors were now taking their places in the front rank. They did not stay there for long. They fell so quickly he expected the line to be breached in more than a dozen places at any moment. He ordered the Smertae to him and was about to lead them forward when the Caereni on the left wing began to shout and fill the air with their cheering.

His mouth fell open in shock when he saw what had caused them to call out in jubilation. Talorc rode out of the sun at the head of more than a hundred mounted Drui. His hood was drawn back, his head had been shorn of its hair and his face painted with blood. The Drui at his heels held their sickles high above their heads and raced towards the Anglii ranks with their black robes billowing out behind them.

'The Drui King means to join the battle!' The Mormaer of Keld gasped. 'He must have emptied the Isle of the Priests to bring every last one of them here!'

Cinloch was too stunned to speak and just gaped as the priests tore into the Anglii and scattered them with the force of their attack. Their right wing collapsed under the onslaught and the triumphant Caereni and Smertae warriors wheeled around to attack their centre from behind. The Epidii King held his breath as he knew battles were won and lost in such moments.

Any hope of avoiding a disastrous defeat was dashed when he caught sight of the Brigante advance. The running foot warriors had yet to reach the marshy ground but their cavalry was already closing in on the backs of the Drui, the Smertae and the Caereni at the centre. Cinloch cried out to give them warning but his voice was lost in the din of battle. He saw Talorc turn in his saddle and bury the point of his sickle in the skull of the leading attacker but he was quickly overcome and disappeared from sight in the midst of the melee.

The battle was lost in that moment. The Smertae still held in reserve ignored Cinloch's order to hold and instead streamed across the field towards the place where Talorc had fallen. They tore a bloody hole in the ranks of the attacking cavalry but were quickly enveloped by the charge of the Brigante foot warriors. Their sickles could still be seen rising and falling above the heads of the skirmishing warriors but they were so outnumbered they had no hope of prevailing.

Cinloch drew his sword and turned to his mormaers and his bodyguard with a heart so heavy he feared it would burst in his chest.

'We have sacrificed our children and our grandparents in vain, my friends. I have no more warriors to deploy and no more tricks to play. All that is left for us is to join the fray and go to the gods with whatever honour we can win from our enemies!'

He did not turn to see if they followed him but kicked his horse into the gallop and aimed it at a break in the shield wall and the Brigante warriors who now poured through it. He roared as he went and gave himself to the exhilaration of the battle rage. He was not restrained by any desire to preserve his own life and so fought with abandon and did not bother to count the number of warriors who fell at his hand or had their skulls caved in by his stallion's flailing hooves. He saw nothing of the axe that shattered his horse's foreleg and was thrown to the ground with such force he slammed into the earth before he could even reach out to break his fall. The darkness took him far from the din of the battle and away from the agony and the suffering of the last of his people.

35

Cinloch knew he had not reached the Underworld when his eyes flickered open to reveal a sky still bright with afternoon sun. He immediately closed them again in an attempt to drive away the dizziness that made him feel as if the earth was sliding away beneath him. When he drifted back into consciousness for a second time, he realised he was being dragged backwards across rough ground by the collar of his tunic.

'Did we prevail?' He asked, though he was still too groggy and confused to understand what was happening.

A face appeared in the centre of his vision and he had to squint in order to bring it into focus. Donal of the Caledones was so bloody, battered and bruised that Cinloch did not recognise him until he heard his voice.

'Would I be dragging your carcass from the field if we had prevailed?' He slurred through mashed and swollen lips. 'We were routed and the victors now slaughter our wounded and loot the corpses of our dead for their silver. Only a handful of my warriors still live. They have gone in search of horses to carry us north. You must accompany me. There is nothing here for any of us now!'

Cinloch groaned as he was racked with pain from every part of his body. His left arm had been rendered useless by the fall and his nose had been broken badly enough to cause shards of bone to pierce his skin.

'I cannot, King Donal. What of the High King and Talorc? What of my wife? I cannot flee until their fates are known.'

'The High King is lost. No warriors returned from the west but I saw twenty or more of their horses run across the plain with their saddles empty. It would seem that the Irish slaughterers were not so easily scattered. Talorc fell on the field. I saw him fighting with his priests and the Smertae until they were all swept away by the Brigantes.' Donal held his jaw as he spoke but it was badly broken and he could not stop it from clicking horribly with each word. 'As for your wife, the last I saw of her was her back as she ran at the head of those few Maeatae warriors still left to her. There is nothing left for you here.'

'What of the Princes? I will not abandon them. Help me to the Black Fort so I might take them away. Give me your hand! I am so sore I cannot get myself up.'

He was not even halfway to his feet when the dizziness overwhelmed him and the darkness returned to reclaim him.

The distant voice was so sweet he fancied that the Maiden herself was singing to welcome him to the Underworld. He smiled with happiness when he finally found the courage to open his eyes as he did not believe he had ever seen such a beautiful face.

'Ah, good Cinloch.' Stroma soothed him. 'We feared you were lost to us. I give thanks that you, at least, were spared.'

He cast his gaze around him and sighed when he recognised the familiar stonework of the walls of his chamber in the Black Fort. His arm had been bound, his wounds tended to and the blood and filth washed from his skin. He saw that Stroma had also been ministered to by the brudes. Her wound was evidently a serious one as blood still seeped through the layers of bandages wrapped tightly around her abdomen.

'What of your husband, my Queen?' He asked on noticing her eyes were red from the shedding of tears. 'King Donal told me he was lost.'

'Not he, thank the gods!' Stroma replied as her eyes filled with tears. 'We tore through the ranks of the slaughterers and soaked the earth with their blood but we were so outnumbered we could not break them. We fought on until our numbers were so diminished we knew victory was beyond us. Drest gave the order to turn back for the Black Fort just as Nechtan was knocked from his horse.' She paused as a sob escaped from her lips but quickly gathered herself enough to continue. 'My husband hacked his way to his side but could not save him. He was unhorsed by the horde as he cut his way out and would have perished along with our son if it had not been for his uncle. Elpin charged in with such fury the Irishmen leapt from his path and cowered away from him as he pulled Drest onto his saddle.'

Cinloch grasped her hand in his and drew in great breaths to keep himself from weeping. He had raised Nechtan from the time he could walk and was so filled with grief for his loss he could not trust himself to speak.

'What of the rest?' He asked when he had regained his composure.

'Any who still live have abandoned us. They ran like the cowards they are and have left us to be besieged by the Anglii, the Brigantes, the Dal Riata and the Ulaid. King Donal took himself north after carrying you here. The Cornavi took flight before the battle was done. The Caereni King was cut down on the field and his bodyguard carried his corpse away before it was cold. Your wife and her Maeatae warriors have hidden themselves away in the hills to the west.' Stroma's lips curled into a snarl of bitterness as she spoke these words. 'All we are left with are the thirty Smertae who lived through the battle, a handful of Epidii and Manau warriors and a few hundred of those warriors too badly injured or too slow to run for the north. There are too many mouths for a long siege and not enough warriors to defend our walls against a prolonged assault.'

'All gone!' Cinloch exclaimed as he tried to take it all in. 'Even Talorc! Even the dark priest who started it all! I have seen him stride through enemy ranks without a single blade being swung in his direction. I never thought I would live to see him fall in battle!'

'You will not live so long!' A hoarse voice croaked from the far side of the room.

Cinloch turned his head and could not hide his astonishment on seeing Talorc laid out on a bed of straw with Mamm Ru dabbing some foul ointment onto his naked torso. There was not one square of his flesh that was not torn, horribly swollen or darkened by black and purple bruises. His already mutilated face was now so bloody and mangled he could only be identified by his dead, white eye. He was so pale Cinloch thought him to be closer to death than to life.

'The Smertae cut their way to him through the ranks of the Anglii and the Brigantes and carried him away as the battle was lost.' Stroma informed him. 'I thought him dead when I first set my eyes upon him. I do not know how Mamm Ru was able to keep him from the gods.'

'The Smertae will always protect him.' Cinloch declared as he caught sight of two of the dark warriors guarding the chamber door. 'See how they now stand over him?'

'They are not here to protect me, good Cinloch.' Talorc wheezed through his bloody and swollen mouth. 'They stay only so they can carry my corpse away with them when I finally die. They will add my bones to those of their ancestors and derive powerful magic from the remains of a Drui King. They are my keepers, not my saviours! It would have been better if they had left me upon the field.'

'Then it was all for nothing!' Cinloch spat in despair. 'All that we won has been lost! Our people and our lands thrown away needlessly! Even you, who has ever encouraged the High

King in his recklessness, must now see that we have wasted all that we gained!'

'Even you must be able to see it was not all for nothing, Cinloch.' Talorc retorted. 'The gods give us life and then torment us with want, hunger, disease and all manner of grief. Think of all we achieved in spite of all that stood in our way! No men before us have ever won so much. Would you curse the gods for all of our victories and the honour, glory and riches they brought us? We ruled a kingdom so vast it was beyond the dreams of even the greatest of kings. Would you rather have lived out a miserable life filled with mediocrity, only to die in your bed? Why waste a life when it can be filled with triumphs? I would do nothing differently if I had my time over again! All men die but I regret nothing now that my time draws near. We must hold our courage so we can go to the gods as warrior kings and not as miserable, snivelling dogs. They will salute us for the glory we won and bid us to join them at their feasting table.'

'They will curse us for the fools that we are, Talorc! They will ask us why we could not hold onto what was already within our grasp. They will damn us for bringing our own people to slaughter! It is just your insanity that makes you too blind to see it!'

'You should go to my husband.' Stroma urged him as she pulled gently at his arm. 'He will not leave the walls but has asked to see you before our enemies begin their assault. Go quickly! They already mass for the attack!'

It seemed as if the whole fort had been infected by the priest's madness as Cinloch limped out into the courtyard and made his way towards the gates. He shook his head in disgust at the warriors who drank greedily from skins of ale looted from the cellars and at those who sprawled on the ground in their drunkenness. He hobbled on and could not even bring himself to look at those inebriated fools who sang and danced and the others who copulated openly without caring who might see them. He gritted his teeth against the pain from his injuries and began the long climb to the top of the wall.

He paused at the top of the steps to catch his breath and glanced at the warriors who stood on the ramparts. He saw the same haunted and hopeless expression on every one of their faces. Some were clearly drunk and swayed on their feet and almost all of them were wounded, filthy and exhausted. Drest stood alone at their centre and looked to be in a similarly miserable condition. His face was cut and grey with exhaustion and he seemed to have aged ten years in the course of a single day. He smiled as Cinloch came to his side but the gesture contained neither warmth nor humour.

'I cannot believe how many of them are still standing.' He declared as he swept his hand out towards the thousands of warriors gathering at the foot of the slope. 'And more of the bastards arrive with each passing hour. We will have to fight hard to hold them until our allies arrive to relieve us.

We should have the Drui make sacrifices to speed them here!'

Cinloch could not tell if he shivered from the cold, from his wounds or from the fear instilled in him by the sight of the enemy warriors arrayed below him. Their banners fluttered in the late afternoon breeze and displayed the emblems of the Anglii, the Brigante King, the Dal Riata and the Ulaid. There were even a small number of flags decorated with the black axe of the Alt Clut. It was clear that they did not intend to starve the garrison into submission. Warriors were already being herded into their ranks and tree trunks were being carried forward to be used to batter at the gates of the fort. He began to count them out of habit but then stopped himself. An accurate tally would be of no use when it was obvious they had more than enough warriors to overwhelm the beleaguered garrison three times over.

'There are no Drui left, my King.' He declared in a voice so devoid of emotion it sounded strange to his own ears. 'Neither are there any allies who now ride hard to our rescue. The Phocali and the Carnonacae abandoned us and went north to hide with their silver. Guram of the Vacomagi has shut his army away behind the walls of the Bull Fort. The Venicones, Maeatae, Manau and Caledones have so few warriors left they can offer us no help. The armies you yearn for are made up of ghosts who can do no harm to our enemies. We have no tricks or strategies that can save us. There is nothing left for us but to make our last stand here! All is lost! Our long journey is almost over.'

Drest blinked at him as if he could not comprehend the meaning of his words. The High King looked so utterly lost in that moment that Cinloch felt an urge to offer him some comfort. Only the thought of poor Prince Nechtan lying dead on the ground prevented him from speaking.

'You should not scold me, Cinloch.' Drest growled with his lips twisted into a sneer. 'If the gods pour spite down upon us, it is only because our kings were too petty and cowardly to be worthy of the High King sent to rule them! If it was not for their weakness and disloyalty, our kingdom would have stretched far below the wall of the Romans. Their greed and faithlessness proved their inferiority and now the future will belong to the tribes of the south or to the raiders from across the sea. They will endure and go on to fight for ultimate supremacy while we are forgotten!'

'It is you who has brought us to ruin, my King, not the weakness of our friends. Your ambition and recklessness have led us here! If you had heeded my counsel, our armies would not have been slaughtered, your son would still walk among us and we would still hold lands enough for a hundred kings!'

Drest glared at him with such hatred in his eyes Cinloch feared he would strike him down.

'What would you have me do, Cinloch?' He snarled through clenched teeth. 'Would you have me plead for forgiveness and then go to my enemies on bended knee?'

The High King's eyes filled with tears as he spoke and the façade of his fury slipped just long enough to reveal the depths of his misery. Cinloch felt his heart clench in his chest and the desire to berate him fell away to nothing.

'You know well I would never ask that of you. I would forfeit my own life before I would see you on your knees.'

'Then fight at my side this one last time, my friend! Let us send so many souls to the Underworld the gods will believe that the world has ended!'

Cinloch accepted the High King's embrace and held him until the horns were blown to herald the enemy advance.

The fighting continued until long after the sun had set. Torches were lit on both sides of the wall so the butchery could continue in spite of the gathering gloom Wave after wave of attackers threw themselves at the walls only to be cut down by spears thrown from above. The dead were piled so high at the gates it seemed that their comrades would soon be able to use the corpses as steps to take them to the top of the wall. The real struggle began when the last of the spears was thrown. With no threat from above, the enemy were able to scramble their way to the ramparts and to batter at the gates with their tree trunks. Cinloch lost count of the number of skulls he split open and the number of hands he severed as desperate warriors attempted heave themselves over the wall. So many of them came, it was inevitable they would eventually overwhelm the defenders as they tired and their numbers were thinned.

Cinloch knew the end was near when Erp's sword shattered as he brought it down on the iron rim of an Anglii shield. He stared at the broken blade in disbelief until Drest shook him and commanded him to gather himself.

'Our defences will soon be breached, good Cinloch.' He exclaimed breathlessly. 'And I must ask one last thing of you!'

'Anything, my King! Name it and it shall be done!'

'We will make our last stand in the courtyard but we will not be able to hold them there for long. Go now to my wife and my son! I will not have them left to the mercy of these savages. You know what you must do!'

Cinloch stared at the Phocali dagger in Drest's hand and recognised it as the one his mother had carried with her all of her life.

'No!' He croaked. 'Do not ask this of me! It is too much!'

'You must!' Drest insisted. 'You know they will rape and torture them both before tearing them to pieces. Ask Talorc for a potion for little Clunie so he will fall asleep before you cut him. You must tell him that his father loves him just as you slide the blade across his throat. I would have him leave this world with those words still in his ears. Stroma will understand why you do it. Just ask her to close her eyes and then strike quickly. There is no other I would entrust this to.'

Cinloch accepted the blade but continued to shake his head in horror.

'Send Talorc to me!' The High King ordered him as he turned back to the wall. 'We once pulled one another from the jaws of death. I would have him at my side when they close on me again! Tell him we will slaughter so many of these bastards we will be carried to the Underworld on a wave of their souls!'

Cinloch's path across the dark courtyard was lit by flaming torches arcing through the air from the far side of the wall. Smoke poured from the roof of the hall as the damp thatch began to catch flame. He bit down against the pain that jarred him with every step and hurried towards his chamber. Stroma looked up as he came through the door and favoured him with a smile of such beauty it caused his heart to break. It faded when she caught sight of his grave expression and turned to horror when she saw the dagger in his hand and read his intention.

'No, Cinloch!' She pleaded as leapt up to put herself between him and the bed little Clunie now slept upon. 'Not that!'

'I must! Do not make this harder for me, I beg you! I would rather die than see any harm done to a single hair on his head! I will do it quickly to spare him from the brutality of our enemies. He will die soon enough and will go more gently at my hand. Stand aside before I lose my courage! Let me be done with it so I can go back to my place on the wall and let some bestial warrior bring an end to my suffering!'

'That is not his fate!' Mamm Ru hissed from where she crouched on the floor. 'And this is not where your journey ends, Cinloch of the Epidii.'

'But the High King has commanded it!' Cinloch protested in his misery.

'Have you not disobeyed your King before?' Talorc demanded as two Smertae warriors pulled him to his feet and supported him as he wobbled on legs too weak to hold him upright. 'Now you must commit that same sin again! Even I, who has been more loyal and steadfast than any other, will not obey when Drest orders the destruction of his own line. The blood of the Epidii Kings must live on in defiance of his command. Fate has chosen you as the one who must carry the burden of preserving Eochaid's royal legacy. You must carry the boy away to safety.'

'Have you lost your mind?' Cinloch spluttered in frustration. 'Have your wounds festered and driven you to insanity? We are besieged! There is no safe route away from here! We will all be dead with a few short moments! The only question yet to be answered is what manner of death we will suffer! Give me a potion to stop the boy from waking and I will send him to the gods while he is surrounded by love and not by snarling hounds set on tearing his flesh from his bones!'

Talorc smiled in spite of the agony of his wounds and raised a trembling hand to point in the direction of the rear wall.

'You are the architect of your own salvation, my friend. You remember the cellars you dug to store all of the grain needed for our campaign to free our lands from the Dal Riata? The ones where Brude Uurad spent so many days in your company examining the Votadini treasures? You extended them so far beyond our walls they will now provide you with your path away from here. I set the Smertae to digging before you first awakened. They will break the surface the moment you command it and send you on your way. Go now, good Cinloch! Go before it is too late!'

'Your mind is clouded by desperation, Talorc! The cellars do not stretch far enough to take us beyond the enemy line. We would emerge in the midst of their ranks and I would rather spare the boy the horror of being cut to pieces by their blades.'

'Do you not remember how I strode through the ranks of the Vacomagi and those of the Dal Riata before I took the lives of their kings? That is how you will pass through the snarling hordes of Anglii and Brigante warriors. If you hold tightly to the boy's hand and keep your courage, you will make clean way! Hold this in your right fist and squeeze it as if you mean to break it.'

The one-eyed priest extended a shaky hand and placed a small round stone with a hole in its centre in Cinloch's open palm.

'The Drui called it the Eye of Tal and were in awe of its power. Use it well, Cinloch! Get Clunie away so our people might live on!'

'Take him to my mother's people!' Stroma commanded him before leaning down to wake the boy with a kiss. 'They will give him shelter from his enemies and from those allies who turned against us!'

'Come, my Queen!' Talorc urged her as Mamm Ru placed his sickle into his hand. 'The fort burns and the battle quickens.'

'Will you not come with us, Stroma?' Cinloch pleaded. 'There is no need for you to perish along with the rest!'

Stroma reached out to stroke the old man's face as tears filled her eyes.

'I must go to my husband, good Cinloch. I would not have him fall without his Queen by his side. I will tell him you have carried his son away. It will comfort him to know that Clunie lives on and has your wisdom and strength to protect him. Go with the gods and go with the love of your Queen.'

Talorc lurched to his side and reached out to lay his hand on his shoulder.

'I will take your place at the High King's side for this last struggle. We cheated the wolf-god all those long years ago and must now go to his jaws together. The gods will settle for nothing less! Do not think that you abandon your King! This battle is not yours to fight. Your trial will begin when you are beyond these walls. Go quickly and with all my blessings! I will pray for you both with my dying breath!'

Epilogue

The Smertae did not speak when Cinloch approached with the boy but immediately started to hack at the cellar roof with their sickles. The air grew heavy with smoke as soil and stones fell to the floor in a shower. Cinloch knew they had broken through the surface when lumps of moss and grass fell along with the earth and the din of the battle was suddenly clear and no longer muffled and distant. They heaved him upwards and held him there as he struggled to pull himself through the ragged opening. He flinched at the sight of a Brigante warrior lying on the grass only a few paces away. He was wounded and grunted in pain as he tried to stem the blood that flowed from his ruined shoulder but he did not cry out in alarm as Cinloch had feared. The old man clenched his fist more tightly around Talorc's stone before pushing himself upright.

The slope was littered with the dead and the wounded and was crowded with hundreds of enemy warriors awaiting their turn to assault the walls. The Black Fort now burned hard enough to bathe the whole hill in flickering light. Cinloch shook his head and shrugged his shoulders in sadness at seeing the old place destroyed. Roars of anger, shrieks of agony and the clash of metal on metal filled the air and told him that this last, desperate battle was nearing its climax. A lump came to his throat when his ears detected the faint but familiar tones of the Song of the Epidii. He would have sobbed at this last act of defiance by the doomed garrison if the Smertae had not thrust Clunie up through the hole in the ground.

'Do not look at them!' He ordered the boy as he led him through the ranks of Brigante warriors. 'They will not see us if we do not meet their eyes.'

That walk was the longest of Cinloch's life. He did not stop until they reached the forest's edge. He then turned to gaze upon the Black Fort for the last time. The fort was still in flames but was not burning as brightly as it had before. The roof of the great hall had collapsed in on itself and part of the east wall had come down with it. It pained him to see all of Erp's work destroyed. He had spent years of his life strengthening the defences only to witness them being brought to nothing in the space of a single day. He let his shoulders slump forward in despair. He was so sore and weary the arduous trek north seemed beyond him. He was too crippled to hunt, had too little silver to buy food or horses and knew he could trust none of his former friends to help him now that the High King had perished. He was prevented from sinking further into the depths of melancholy by Prince Clunie calling out in delight.

'Look! See the Smertae! They are running for the forest! Call them here, Cinloch! They are loyal to us and will offer us protection!'

Cinloch instinctively dropped to his knees and watched as the Smertae ran for the cover of the trees. There were eight warriors in total and they carried several burdens between them. At least three of them were bent under the weight of corpses and the sight of them caused Cinloch to shiver. He caught a brief glimpse of long, straggly white hair spilling from a bundle on the shoulders of the rearmost warrior. It gave him no pleasure to know that Mamm Ru had survived the carnage. He cursed the unfairness of the Smertae crone outliving so many others who were more pure of heart than her.

'Call out to them, Cinloch!' Clunie urged him. 'They will come if you order them to.'

Cinloch opened his hand and saw that Talorc's stone had disintegrated into dust and sand. He tilted his palm and let it trickle away.

'The spell binding them to us has been broken, Clunie. It would be better if we did not encounter them here. Come! We should put some distance between ourselves and our enemies.' He took the boy's hand and limped on into the forest. 'I will take you north to the island of your mother's people. You will find safety there, though I doubt they will have a place for me. I will stay with you until you are in their hands.'

'I will not let you leave, Cinloch.' The boy replied earnestly. 'My father and mother told me you were always to have a place at our side. I will not dishonour them by breaking their word.'

They trudged on and struggled through the thick undergrowth. They did not speak as they had to concentrate in order to avoid losing their footing in the darkness. They made faster progress when the moon grew full and they came across a drover's track. The boy sang as they went, his voice sweet and pure as he repeated the words learned at Cinloch's knee. He sang of Epona and Eochaid and of Erp and the years of wandering and hopelessness. He sang of Manau spears filling the air below the Black Fort's walls and of a Wolf-Torn King who ruled the land from sea to sea and from the Black Isles to great Caesar's walls.

'Why do you cry, good Cinloch?' The boy asked when he became aware of the old man's distress.

'I cry because I am an old, old man and old men are often foolish.' Cinloch replied with a smile tinged with both grief and hope.

Made in United States
North Haven, CT
10 June 2022

20084387R00243